"Why do you want to marry me, Eben?"

Isabel asked b
housekeeper?"

"Hell, no!"

"Don't swear

"I'll swear if
what does a ma...

"That depends on what he's trying to accomplish!" she replied tartly.

"I'm trying to get you to *love* me!"

Stung, Isabel felt her face turn scarlet. "And what does a woman have to do to get *you* to love *her*?"

He groaned, pulling her tightly against him. He slanted his mouth over hers, teasing with his tongue until she opened to him. When they were both breathless, Eben lifted his hand a fraction of an inch. "My God, who taught you to do that?"

"You did!" Isabel gasped. "Is it . . . terribly wicked?"

"Oh terribly." He sank backward on the blanket, carrying her with him . . .

PLAYING WITH FIRE

VICTORIA THOMPSON

AVON BOOKS ◆ NEW YORK

PLAYING WITH FIRE is an original publication of Avon Books. This work has never before appeared in book form. This work is a novel. Any similarity to actual persons or events is purely coincidental.

AVON BOOKS
A division of
The Hearst Corporation
1350 Avenue of the Americas
New York, New York 10019

Copyright © 1990 by Cornerstone Communications
Published by arrangement with the author
Library of Congress Catalog Card Number: 90-93159
ISBN: 0-380-75961-6

Special Printing: June 1993
First Avon Books Printing: November 1990

AVON TRADEMARK REG. U.S. PAT. OFF. AND IN OTHER COUNTRIES, MARCA REGISTRADA, HECHO EN U.S.A.

Printed in the U.S.A.

RA 10 9 8 7 6 5 4 3 2

To my sister, Dr. Sue Bredekamp,
in appreciation for all she has done
to make the world a better place
for children

Chapter 1

Quieting her grief with an inelegant sniff, Isabel Forester resolutely finished arranging the pastries on her mother's prized silver tray. Positioning the tarts and petit fours carefully to cover the worn spots in the silver plating, she irrelevantly recalled Hamlet's line, "The funeral baked meats did coldly furnish forth the marriage tables."

She winced at the irony of her thoughts. The way her dear father's parishioners were eating, she doubted there would be enough left from his funeral baked meats to furnish so much as a tea sandwich tomorrow. And, of course, no marriage table lurked in her family's future. Isabel's mother had long since gone to her eternal reward, so her father left no widow who could remarry with unseemly haste, and his only child certainly had no plans in that direction. At twenty-nine, Isabel was well-ensconced in spinsterhood.

Finished with her task, Isabel wiped her hands,

1

removed her apron, and smoothed the bodice of her black bombazine mourning gown. Satisfied she was presentable, she lifted the heavy tray and carried it to the door leading from the rectory kitchen into the foyer of the dining room. Carefully she turned and backed against the swinging door, opening it with her hip as she maneuvered the tray through the opening. The instant she emerged into the anteroom, she heard a woman's voice rising above the deferential murmurs of the other mourners.

"What do you suppose poor Isabel will do now?"

Poor Isabel froze in her tracks. The questioner was a Mrs. Hazard, one of the few people in her father's congregation who had ever shown her genuine kindness.

"Why, I imagine she'll go back to teaching in that boarding school, won't she?" another woman replied. Isabel couldn't remember her name. "I heard they promised to save her position when she had to come home to care for her father. What other choice does she have? An unmarried woman with no prospects should be grateful to have a situation like that waiting for her."

"I expect she will have to go back to teaching," Mrs. Hazard allowed. "It seems a sin to waste herself catering to all those spoiled, rich girls, though. A woman as accomplished as Isabel should be married with a family of her own."

"All the accomplishments in the world don't make up for a lack of beauty and charm, particularly where catching a husband is concerned."

Isabel felt the heat of humiliation rushing to her face. As if she even *wanted* a husband!

"But a good nature should count for something," Mrs. Hazard argued. "Isabel is the sweetest, most humble, most unassuming, most *dutiful* young woman I know!"

Dutiful! Isabel inwardly raged. Talk about being damned with faint praise! If only they knew what it had cost her to appear humble and unassuming all these years. For two cents she'd forget she was the minister's daughter and give both those women a piece of her mind. Suddenly the tray tilted in Isabel's trembling hands, and a cherry tart careened off, hitting the floor with a splat.

Isabel's startled "Oh!" drew everyone's attention, and in another moment someone had relieved her of the tray and someone else had gone for a rag with which to clean up the mess.

"Isabel, dear," Mrs. Hazard said, drawing her aside in an obvious effort to distract her from her grief. "Did you make these lovely tarts yourself?"

"Yes, I did," she replied, controlling her temper with some difficulty. Then she remembered her father's admonitions against pride and demurred at the compliment. "I only hope they taste as good as they look."

"I'm certain they do," Mrs. Hazard said. "You are an absolutely wonderful cook."

Before Isabel could mutter her thanks, the other woman snickered again. Mrs. Pursely, Isabel suddenly remembered. That was her name—and an appropriate one, too, she thought, noting the woman's pursed lips.

"Oh, yes," Mrs. Pursely drawled. "We all know of Isabel's accomplishments. She cooks, she sews, she gardens, she even sings. She is virtually the perfect *housewife*. Is there anything at which you don't excel, Isabel?"

"I'm not very skilled at keeping my temper," Isabel snapped, instantly wishing she hadn't when she saw the woman's shocked expression. Her father would be so upset to hear she'd spoken so disrespectfully to . . .

But wait a minute—she didn't need to worry about being the minister's daughter anymore! Dearly beloved Reverend Forester was well past knowing or caring how his only child conducted herself, and his

reputation was also well out of harm's way. Isabel
need never give another thought to how her behavior
might affect the congregation's opinion of him.

That meant she would never again have to cheerfully acquiesce when pressed to perform some onerous task. She would never again have to step aside
gracefully when someone else wished to claim the
glory for doing something she could do far better,
and she would never, ever have to feign humility
when others took the credit for what she had done.

She was free!

"Have you decided what you're going to do now?"
Mrs. Hazard prompted, as if sensing Isabel's dangerous mood. "We understand the school where you
taught wants you to come back."

"Yes, Miss Snodgrass is holding my position for
me, but perhaps I won't return," Isabel predicted
recklessly, feeling almost giddy at the prospect of her
newfound liberty.

Mrs. Pursely's eyes widened in disbelief. "You
can't possibly expect to stay here! This house belongs
to the church, and the new minister will—"

"I know perfectly well to whom the house belongs," Isabel informed her, taking great pleasure in
cutting her off. How often had she longed to be just
as rude to these people as they were to their impov-
erished minister and his family? "And you may rest
assured I have no intention of spending one night
longer in this house than I absolutely must."

"Then . . . then you have another position?" Mrs.
Hazard stammered, obviously uneasy with Isabel's
strange behavior.

Isabel's mind raced as she searched for a perfectly
shocking lie to make Mrs. Pursely gape. It came to
her instantly, so clearly she could almost see the advertisement as it appeared in the magazine she had
been reading to her father shortly before his death.
"Why, yes, I do. I'm going to Texas to teach school."

Mrs. Pursely did not disappoint her. The older

woman's mouth dropped open in a most unladylike manner.

"Texas!" Mrs. Hazard echoed in astonishment. "That's at the ends of the earth. You can't mean you'd leave New York State for that . . . that *wilderness!*"

"I'd leave New York gladly," Isabel replied, surprised to realize she was telling the truth. "And I go to the wilderness because I wish to live deliberately," she continued, paraphrasing Thoreau as she warmed to the subject. "To confront only the essential facts of life, and see if I cannot learn what it has to teach, and not, when I come to die, discover that I had not lived." With a start, Isabel realized she had finally voiced the fears she had been harboring for months now as she had nursed her dying father, the fear of dying herself without ever actually having experienced life.

"It's the strain she's been under," Mrs. Pursely whispered to Mrs. Hazard in alarm. "Should we fetch the doctor?"

But Mrs. Hazard only smiled. "You may have something there, Isabel," she said after a moment. "I've always thought your talents were being wasted, and it's a sin to waste one's talents. Your father always said so."

"Yes, he did, didn't he?" Isabel mused as the truth of Thoreau's words sank in. She was almost thirty years old, nearly halfway through her allotted three-score years and ten, and not once in all those years had she ever really *lived!* "So I'm going to Texas just as soon as the arrangements are complete," she heard herself say.

"Well, I never," Mrs. Pursely clucked, but Mrs. Hazard patted Isabel's arm.

"I only hope Texas is ready for you, my dear."

Turning up his collar against the wintery wind, Eben Walker crossed the dusty street in front of his blacksmith shop and strolled toward the schoolhouse, near the edge of the small town of Bittercreek, Texas. He felt no need to arrive on time for the school board meeting. The more of the meeting he missed, the less he would have to listen to Bertha Bartz's opinions, and that woman had an opinion about everything on God's green earth.

At least the meeting would shorten the time he had to spend with Amanda this evening, he thought, squinting into the setting sun. The girl would be irritated when he came in late for supper, but he wouldn't have to sit across the table from her while she stared at him accusingly with her mother's eyes and waited for him to do or say whatever it was she wanted him to do or say.

God in heaven, he couldn't figure out what had come over her lately. Folks said she was growing up, but it was more than that, a hell of a lot more. The happy little girl he'd raised single-handedly had become as sour-tempered as a herd of turpentined bears. Sometimes he even wondered if she'd found out, somehow, about her mother. . . .

But no, it couldn't be that, because he was the only one who knew, and he sure as hell hadn't told her. It had to be something else, but what, Eben had no idea. With a sigh, he mounted the steps to the schoolhouse and went inside. To his disappointment, he found the other board members patiently awaiting his arrival.

"You're late," Bertha Bartz informed him, rising from her chair at the head of the table that usually served as the teacher's desk. The table stood on a raised platform, and from this vantage point, she towered over his six feet. With her graying blond hair pulled tightly into a bun, her plain face twisted into a frown, and her hands folded primly beneath her enormous bosom, she looked like a disapproving schoolmarm preparing to discipline a recalcitrant child.

Why were women with big breasts always so over-bearing? Eben wondered idly as he dismissed her rebuke with a grunt and turned to greet the other members of the board.

Bertha's husband, Herald, sat on the far side of the table. He smiled weakly, tugged at his stiff collar, and nervously patted his thinning brown hair. Although he ran Bittercreek's only mercantile and was probably the richest man in town, Herald was not particularly prepossessing. He was a full four inches shorter than his wife, and she outweighed him by a good fifty pounds. Scrawny as a scratch farm bantam was what Eben's mother would have said about Herald Bartz, and Eben had often wondered how the little bantam had managed to breed five strapping youngsters out of the big sow grizzly he'd married.

"Evening, Herald, Paul," Eben said, nodding to the man seated opposite Herald. Paul Young ran the hardware shop in town. As a bachelor about Eben's own age, Paul made a good companion on the rare nights Eben sought the comforts of the local saloon.

The other men returned his greeting as Eben unbuttoned his coat and took the seat at the end of the table opposite Bertha, who still regarded him with a disapproving glare. Not for the first time, Eben decided Bertha was probably the moving force behind the financial success of Bartz's store.

When Eben was seated, Bertha banged the table with her gavel. The nitwit who had armed that woman with a hammer ought to be horsewhipped, Eben thought. Bertha smoothed the fur collar of the coat she still wore against the chill of the schoolhouse, cleared her throat importantly, and said, "This meeting will now come to order. Herald, please read the minutes of our last meeting."

With great ceremony, Herald reached into his pocket, pulled out a pair of pince-nez spectacles, and settled them across his nose. Then he picked up the single sheet of paper before him and read aloud.

" 'Minutes of the December fourth meeting of the Bittercreek School Board. Meeting was called to order by President Bertha Bartz. Minutes were read by Secretary Herald Bartz. Minutes were approved as read. President Bertha Bartz announced the resignation of our schoolteacher, Miss Alice Hargrove—"

"Ahhh, sweet little Alice," Paul murmured sadly. "I'll never forgive Steve for stealing her away from me."

Bertha rapped the table. "Order, please," she said sharply, glaring at Paul, who ignored her.

"Maybe I'll challenge him to a duel," Paul continued. "What do you think, Eb?"

Eben pretended to consider. "Steve's a pretty good shot. Do you think Alice is worth the risk?"

"Gentlemen," Bertha rebuked them, pounding furiously with her hammer. Paul, oblivious, contemplated Eben's question.

"I'm not sure. Maybe I'll wait until I see our new teacher before I decide."

"Mr. Young!" Bertha screeched. "This is unconscionable! You know perfectly well our most serious problem here in Bittercreek is our inability to keep a schoolteacher for our children because the bachelors in this town start proposing to her practically the instant she steps off the stage."

Paul snapped his fingers as if he'd just made a wonderful discovery. *"That's* what I'm doing wrong," he informed the other two men. "I've been waiting until she gets her bags unpacked, when I should have—"

Eben silenced him with a frantic gesture. Bertha was turning purple, a dangerous sign. "Let's get this over with," he suggested. "You got some applications for us to look at?" he asked the mottled president.

"I haven't finished reading the minutes," Herald reminded him.

"I move we approve the minutes as read," Eben said.

"But I didn't read them!" Herald protested.

"Second," Paul said.

"All in favor," Eben said.

"You're out of order!" Bertha objected furiously.

"Aye," all three men said.

"Now let's see those applications." Eben reached for the papers lying on the table in front of Bertha, but she snatched them out of his grasp and clutched them protectively to her bosom, where Eben knew they would be safe—at least from him.

"We have three applicants," Bertha announced breathlessly a few seconds later. She probably had her stays laced too tight, Eben thought.

"Did any of them send photographs?" Paul asked hopefully.

"No, because I specifically did not ask for photographs this time," Bertha informed him.

Paul's face fell in comic disappointment, and Eben had to cough to cover a laugh. "Who are the applicants?" he asked.

"As I said, there are three. The first is a young man who—"

"Nay!" Paul cried, lifting his hand to indicate he was voting. "We've already got enough young men around here. It's young women we need. Right, fellows?"

Herald chuckled, then caught himself as his wife shot him a murderous look.

"I don't believe you take your responsibilities on this board seriously, Paul," Bertha told him sternly.

"You've got that right, Miz Bartz," Paul agreed. "I don't even know how I got this job in the first place; do you, Eben?"

"We were elected," Eben reminded him, "although we never did find out how we got nominated in the first place."

"You were nominated by the people," Bertha snapped, beginning to look a little purplish again.

"But why?" Paul wanted to know. "At least Eb here

has a kid in the school. I don't have any kids at all. Or none that I know of, anyways."

Bertha gasped while Herald and Eben had a coughing fit. By the time the men had recovered themselves, Bertha's homely face had turned magenta, and her chin trembled ominously. Eben decided he'd better get the meeting back on track.

"Who are the other applicants?" he asked with a placating smile.

Bertha's bosom still quivered with indignation, but she managed to reply, "One is a sixteen-year-old girl whom we cannot possibly consider, and—"

"We could if you'd asked for a photograph," Paul protested. "She might be big for her age."

Eben kicked him under the table and managed to keep his face straight. "And the last one?"

"Is a maiden lady of twenty-nine from New York State. She has excellent credentials—"

"Good God, *twenty-nine!*" Paul exclaimed in dismay.

"She's still younger than you," Eben pointed out, unable to resist irritating Bertha.

"But she's an old maid! She probably has a face like a horse and—"

"Her appearance is of no concern to us!" Bertha interjected testily.

"It is to me," Paul insisted. "Miz Bartz, you know how scarce women are out here. It's the school board's bounden duty to keep the community supplied with young, marriageable females."

"It is the school board's duty to provide our children with an education," Bertha contradicted him. "We are extremely fortunate to have two candidates who seem quite likely to remain with us for what's left of the school term this year and possibly even to return for the fall term."

"Yeah, because nobody's likely to want to marry either the fellow or the spinster," Paul said in disgust.

"Can't we wait a few more weeks to see if we get a more likely candidate?"

"Mr. Young, it is already February. If we wait any longer, we may as well wait until fall."

"I doubt the kids would mind," Paul said, earning a frown from the president.

"We will now vote on the two candidates," Bertha announced, rapping the table with her gavel.

"I thought there were three," Herald said, drawing his wife's wrath.

"As I said, the girl is much too young," Bertha fumed. "All in favor of the gentleman, say 'aye.'"

Silence greeted her request.

"All in favor of—"

"Horse face," Paul muttered dejectedly.

"—of the other lady," Bertha continued doggedly.

"Aye," the three men replied without much enthusiasm.

"Thank you, gentlemen," Bertha said sarcastically. "Our new teacher's name is Miss Isabel Forester."

"At least she's a woman." Paul sighed. "Who knows, somebody might want her, horse face and all. Winters out here can get mighty cold when a man sleeps alone."

Bertha's hammer crashed onto the table. "Meeting adjourned," she growled, and gathering up her papers, headed for the door like a schooner at full sail. Herald scurried to collect his minutes, spectacles, and coat, but he paused a second before going after her.

"The reason you two got picked for the school board is because you both live in town and can get to the meetings easy," he whispered.

"Herald!" Bertha called sharply from the doorway.

"Coming, dear," Herald replied, hurrying after her.

When the door closed behind the oddly matched couple, both Paul and Eben sighed wearily and reached into their coats for tobacco. Paul rolled a cigarette while Eben filled the briar pipe he always carried with him.

"It's a hell of a thing," Paul said when they had smoked for a minute in silence. "The way things are going, I might never find myself a wife."

"Do what other men do," Eben suggested. "Go back East for a few months until you find one."

"If I wanted to live in the East, I'd still be there," Paul grumbled. "Only thing I can't understand is why you aren't as anxious as everybody else around here to get yourself a woman."

Eben stiffened, instinctively defensive, then reminded himself Paul spoke in innocence. Feigning nonchalance, Eben shrugged. "I've got Amanda to cook and keep house for me, and I don't have to ask her permission when I want to go out for the evening."

"But a daughter don't provide the same kind of comfort a wife does on a cold night," Paul pointed out with a comic leer. "Besides, Amanda won't be around forever. A few more years and you'll be as bad off as I am, with no woman to do for you at all."

Eben puffed on his pipe, and visions of the past rose up around him with the smoke. "Sometimes being married is more trouble than help," he mused aloud.

Paul's eyebrows rose in surprise, and Eben instantly regretted his revealing remark. "You talking from experience?" Paul asked. When Eben didn't reply, he said, "You never say much about your wife. Is that why? Because you weren't happy?"

But Eben had no intention of discussing his marriage, not even with his best friend. He managed a smile, pushed his chair back, and rose to his feet. "I'd better be on my way. Amanda'll have supper waiting."

Paul didn't press the issue. He rose, too, and followed Eben out.

"The way things are going, I may have to wait for Amanda to grow up so I can marry *her*. How old is she now, anyway?"

"Fourteen," Eben told him with asperity. "You'll have a long wait."

The wind had picked up, and the men hunched into their collars against it. "Well, maybe this Miss Forester won't be as bad as we think."

Eben smiled around his pipe stem. "At least if she has a face like a horse, you won't have to worry about anybody else stealing her away from you."

Chapter 2

Isabel closed her eyes and locked her jaw, determined not to throw up again. Pressing her handkerchief to her nose, she inhaled frantically, but even the lavender-scented cloth could not mask the horrendous odor emanating from the man sprawled on the seat beside her in the stagecoach, snoring loudly. The sound put Isabel in mind of a sawmill, and the smell . . . Well, the smell was like nothing in her experience.

The stage jolted violently, jarring the man awake, but he only blinked once and looked around before succumbing to sleep again. The sawing resumed immediately.

Tears burned Isabel's eyes, and she didn't even bother to dab them away since there was no one to see them. What on earth had ever possessed her to come to this godforsaken part of the world? For nearly a week she had endured the rigors of train travel, with its cinders and dirt and bad food and rude men and uncomfortable seats and less comfortable beds. She had thought her troubles were over when she reached the end of the line, but she had discovered train travel was luxurious compared with a journey by stagecoach.

All day yesterday she had been jounced unmercifully over boulder-strewn tracks that some wit had labeled "roads." Each time the stage stopped for fresh horses, the passengers were herded into a squalid shack and offered the foulest concoction of beans and grease Isabel had ever imagined. Unable to swallow even a single mouthful, she had survived on black coffee alone for two days.

Not that the idea of even good food appealed to her now. The swaying of the coach had made her desperately ill. Then, this morning, a new passenger had boarded, the odiferous creature beside her. The driver, sensing her distress, had offered to let her ride up top with him, but Isabel was too debilitated to consider such precarious seating, and the man had insisted on riding inside so he could sleep.

Fresh air was what she needed, but if they opened the coach's leather curtains so much as a crack, the coach instantly filled with clouds of dust that made breathing impossible.

Dirty, hungry, exhausted, and ill, Isabel wanted to scream out her misery, but she knew if she began, she would never stop. Perhaps when the stage next halted, she would instruct the driver to simply leave her behind so she could lie down on something that wasn't moving and die in peace.

To her intense relief, the stage began to slow, and the driver yelled, "Bittercreek ahead."

Her stop. Thank God! Her ordeal would soon be over. Automatically she lifted a trembling hand to her hair, which she knew must be coated with the dust that had been blowing relentlessly into the coach through every crack from the moment she had started this journey. Her clothes and her skin must also be coated, and even if she had the strength to do so, she had no means with which to freshen up. Bittercreek would have to take her as filthy and disheveled as she was. At least the person meeting her was a woman, a Mrs. Bertha Bartz. Surely Mrs. Bartz would understand Isabel's need for a hot bath and a soft bed, and would whisk her away before too many people saw her in her unfortunate condition.

As the stage rattled to a halt, her fellow passenger roused himself with a snort. "Are we here?" he asked of no one in particular. Isabel felt no need to reply, since before she could even collect her wits, he had thrown open the door and made his exit.

Isabel patted her hair and tested to see if her hat was still in place. Satisfied that it was, she brushed ineffectually at the traveling stains on her duster and resolutely swallowed a wave of nausea. Summoning her last reserves of strength, she gathered her purse, slid across the seat, and somehow managed to rise. As she did, a scrawny little man stuck his head inside and said, "Miss Forester?"

"Y-yes," Isabel replied uncertainly.

He smiled. "I'm Herald Bartz. Welcome to Bittercreek."

"I . . . Thank you," Isabel managed.

When he offered his hand, she took it gratefully and stepped unsteadily down into blazing sunlight. Momentarily blinded, Isabel at first thought the noise was a roaring in her head, but as her vision cleared, she realized she was surrounded by a crowd that must have included every man, woman, and child within a hundred miles. And all of them were cheering at the top of their voices.

Isabel's wavering gaze swept the crowd, picking out an individual here and there: a rather large, forbidding woman; a pretty young girl holding a bouquet of flowers; the nondescript Mr. Bartz; and a handsome man with dark eyes.

The handsome man with the dark eyes was frown-

ing at her, as if he didn't like a single thing about her.
But Isabel didn't care, because she was going to die,
right here and right now, in front of God and everybody. The man's image swam, then blurred just before everything went black.

Eben saw her sway and jumped forward to catch
her as she fell. The cheers quickly became a groan of
concern as the schoolteacher slumped into Eben
Walker's arms. He struggled a moment, not quite
certain what to do until Bertha said, "Pick her up,
you idiot."

It was highly improper, but nobody defied Bertha
Bartz when she spoke in that tone, so Eben scooped
the woman up against his chest.

"What happened, Pa?" Amanda asked, her blue
eyes wide with alarm.

"I reckon she fainted," Eben said, looking askance
at his burden. The woman wasn't any bigger than a
minute, and probably didn't weigh much more than
his biggest sledgehammer. She'd be a surprise to
Paul, though. She didn't look the least bit like a horse,
although at the moment she did look like she'd been
pulled through a knothole backward.

"Oh, dear," Bertha said, hovering over him. "This
was a terrible idea. I should have known the poor
thing would be worn out from the trip."

Eben found himself surrounded by women, each
of whom was offering conflicting advice.

"Chafe her wrists."

"Get her out of the sun."

"Throw water in her face."

Children crowded around them, jostling to get a
look at the schoolteacher from behind their mothers'
skirts. It was a hell of a mess.

"What should I do with her?" Eben shouted to
make himself heard.

"Take her to my house," Bertha shouted back, bar-
reling into the crowd to clear a path for Eben to follow.

"But what about my flowers?" Amanda wanted to know as she trotted at Eben's heels.

"From the looks of her, she might best use them on her grave," Eben snapped.

"Pa, what a terrible thing to say," Amanda chided, her cheeks pink with outrage.

Luckily the Bartz house was nearby, so Eben didn't have to endure his daughter's wrath for long. In a matter of minutes he had Miss Forester inside, away from prying eyes.

"Take her upstairs, the first door on the right," Bertha instructed, waving him on. She effectively blocked Amanda and the Bartz children, who would have followed him, and Eben made his way carefully up the stairs.

Isabel's senses returned to her slowly. With consciousness came the sensation of being carried. She knew she must be dreaming, of course. Why would someone be carrying her? Still, everything seemed so real. Strong arms held her, just as she remembered being held when she was a child, cradling her closely, making her feel secure. Her head rested against a solid shoulder. Gradually she became aware of an over-whelmingly masculine scent, pipe tobacco overlaying musky maleness. How odd. Her father had never smelled of pipe tobacco.

Her befuddled brain instantly cleared. She really was being carried, and the man carrying her was most certainly not her father! Who on earth . . . ? An image of the dark-eyed man who had glared at her in her last moment of rationality flickered before her mind's eye.

Surely not! But when she opened her eyes a slit, she saw the same chocolate-brown hair curling beneath the flat-crowned hat, and the same determined thrust of jaw. In profile, he looked as disapproving as she remembered, or maybe he just thought she was too heavy as he climbed the stairs.

Stairs? Good heavens, where was he taking her?

And *why*? A hundred lurid tales of kidnapping and white slavery streaked across her memory, and panic welled within her for just a moment before she remembered that white slavers were hardly likely to kidnap a skinny, aging spinster. Still, a lone man was taking her somewhere, and such a thing was highly improper under *any* circumstances, most especially when the woman in question was unconscious.

Before Isabel could decide whether she should protest, he reached the top of the stairs and angled her body so they could pass through a doorway. Catching a glimpse of a bed canopied in pink ruffles, Isabel experienced a renewed sense of panic. Deciding that discretion was the better part of valor, she slammed her eyes shut as he laid her on the soft mattress. At least if he tried to attack her, she would have the advantage of surprise when she offered her resistance.

Eben carefully laid his dusty burden on the spotless comforter of what he guessed must be Bertha's daughters' bed. The woman didn't move, didn't even groan, and Eben recalled his thoughtless words to Amanda. Could she possibly be . . . ? But then he noticed the rapid rise and fall of her gently rounded bosom beneath her gray duster, and the spots of color in her cheeks. She might be feverish, but she was alive.

She wasn't bad-looking, either, underneath the heavy layer of travel dirt. Not exactly a beauty, but then, Eben had learned to distrust physical beauty. Her face had strength and character, qualities he found far more attractive.

It had been a long time since Eben had been alone with a woman in a bedroom, and the novelty stirred feelings long dormant. Although her coat effectively hid most of her charms, his imagination had no trouble filling in the concealed details from the visible clues—her slender white neck, her graceful, long-fingered hands, and the well-turned ankles encased in high-buttoned boots—and, of course, what he'd learned about her from holding her in his arms. Some women might sew padding into their clothes to enhance their curves, but this woman's curves were real enough, soft and yielding, just as he remembered female flesh.

Somewhere along the way, she'd lost her hat, and her hair had sprung loose of its pins. The color of honey, it was long and thick and spread across the pillow in a flowing wave. Eben had an impulse to touch it, knowing instinctively how silky it would feel between his fingers.

In repose, her fine features appeared almost childlike. He could hardly believe her a woman of twenty-nine. Perhaps Bertha Bartz had made the first mistake of her entire life and sent for the sixteen-year-old girl instead.

Bertha caught him smiling at his thoughts. "I hardly see anything amusing in the situation," she informed him imperiously.

"I was just thinking she's a puny little thing," he improvised. "We'd better hope the Zink twins don't decide to come to school. They'll squash her like a bug."

Bertha humphed. "Get along with you, now. You know you shouldn't be in a lady's bedroom."

Eben didn't bother to remind her that he was there only at her behest; he made his escape gladly. Besides, he couldn't wait to ride Paul a little about his inaccurate predictions. Isabel Forester wasn't at all what they'd been expecting.

A puny little thing! Squash her like a bug! Isabel thought in outrage, not certain whether she was more insulted or dismayed by the man's opinion of her. So much for her fears of being ravished.

Feeling more than a little foolish, she waited until she heard the door click shut, then opened her eyes cautiously. The formidable-looking woman was just turning back to face her, and she didn't seem nearly as formidable now as she had at the stage. In fact, she looked distraught. "What a perfectly horrible man," Isabel said to let the woman know she wasn't really at death's door.

The woman's surprise was comic, and she laid a hand on her impressive bosom in the general region of her heart. "You're awake," she exclaimed.

"Yes," Isabel said, gingerly pushing herself up into a sitting position. "I'm terribly sorry to have given you such a fright. I don't know what came over me."

"I believe it's fairly obvious what came over you," she disagreed. "I've ridden that stage myself. You must be simply exhausted."

"And half-starved, too. I haven't been able to eat for days. Please believe me, nothing less could have caused me to faint. I'm not at all prone to such behavior, I assure you."

The woman dismissed such a notion with a wave of her hand. "Oh, dear, I'm afraid we haven't actually met. I'm Bertha Bartz."

Isabel took her offered hand, pleased at the firmness of the woman's grip. "I'm so happy to meet you, Mrs. Bartz. Your letters were most helpful."

"But, of course, I didn't tell you exactly how grueling the trip would be or you never would have come," Bertha told her with a twinkle in her eye. "And I must apologize for the scene at the stage. Everyone was so anxious to see you that I thought a little welcoming ceremony would not be amiss. Please forgive me for being so thoughtless."

Isabel smiled at her hostess. Behind Mrs. Bartz's forbidding exterior lay a kind woman. "I will gladly forgive you if you can arrange for me to have a bath *immediately* and . . . Oh, no! I'm afraid I've ruined this lovely spread," Isabel exclaimed, scrambling up from the bed as rapidly as her stiff limbs would allow.

"Nonsense," Bertha decreed. "The dust will shake right out. I'll have my husband bring your baggage up, and I already have the boiler full of hot water.

We'll have you cleaned up in no time. As I told you in my letters, you'll be staying here with us for the first week. After that you'll move on to someone else's house, since the families all take turns boarding the teacher. Are you hungry?"

Isabel winced at the thought of food. "Perhaps a cup of tea for now."

"Certainly," Mrs. Bartz said briskly, heading for the door.

Feeling slightly dizzy, Isabel resisted the urge to sink back down onto the bed again, but the sight of the dust-covered spread reminded her of the disturbing man who had brought her here. "Uh, Mrs. Bartz?"

She paused at the door and turned back expectantly. "Yes?"

"Who . . . who was the man who . . . who carried me here?" she asked, hating the heat she felt rising in her face at the memory of being held so intimately by a complete stranger.

"Eben Walker. He's a member of the school board." Mrs. Bartz smiled kindly. "And he really isn't as horrible as you might think from the way he was talking. He didn't know you could hear, and he's absolutely right about the Zink twins. It's a lucky thing I thought to make him a member of the welcoming committee. I doubt poor Herald could have carried even a little thing like you up all those stairs."

Mrs. Bartz left in a swish of skirts, and Isabel could no longer resist the temptation of the bed. Surrendering to the weakness in her knees, she lowered herself carefully until she sat on the very edge so as to do as little further damage as possible.

Eben Walker, she thought as she tried to control her spinning head. The spartan, masculine name suited the big man she had glimpsed so briefly. She recalled his imposing height and sun-darkened skin. It was still a shock to see leading citizens with brown faces. In the East, only laborers would be tanned, but she had rapidly learned that most Texans bore the mark of the sun, even the most prosperous of ranchers.

She also remembered Eben Walker's well-cut suit and the way its blackness mirrored the sheen of his longish hair. He was quite strong, too, she thought with a small smile, recalling how safe she had felt in his arms. And his scent, so disturbingly masculine ... Isabel felt a tremor of reaction, so slight that at first she hardly recognized the unfamiliar emotion for what it was: excitement.

Good heavens! What had come over her? First, she'd fainted for the one and only time in her life, then she'd been carried in the arms of a man she'd never met, and now she was entertaining romantic notions about him. What a silly, schoolgirlish thing to do. Isabel had long since given up dreaming about men who would never look at her twice, and she had no intention of starting up again at this late date.

No, she had come to Texas to make a new life for herself, and that life would not include a man. If she had any doubts on that score, she need only recall the expression of disapproval in Eben Walker's dark eyes the instant before she'd swooned into his arms. And she should most definitely remember his disparaging remark about her size. Men liked women who were plump and healthy-looking, women who appeared to be capable of bearing and raising a brood of children. Nobody wanted a skinny, dried-up old maid.

Besides, Mr. Walker probably already had a wife and brood of children. He would certainly have no interest in Isabel Forester. And Isabel Forester had no interest in him, either. She finally had a life of her own to live, and she couldn't wait to get started.

Chapter 3

"**D**o you think she'll be here?" Paul asked for what Eben guessed was the tenth time in as many minutes.

"The schoolteacher wouldn't dare miss church on her first Sunday in town," Eben said with some irritation at his friend's impatience. The man was making a fool of himself over a woman he'd barely even laid eyes on.

Paul was eagerly scanning the crowd gathered in the churchyard, and Eben caught himself looking around just as eagerly for a glimpse of Isabel Forester's honey-blond head.

What had come over him?

"You did say she was pretty, didn't you?" Paul inquired, also not for the first time.

"No, I didn't," Eben insisted, but Paul only smiled knowingly.

"You were mighty happy to tell me I was wrong about her looking like a horse," Paul reminded him.

25

"And I noticed you couldn't seem to talk about much else except her last night."

"Because that's all *you* wanted to talk about," Eben protested, although he knew Paul was right. Eben had been only too glad to answer Paul's questions about the new arrival.

And all that talking had probably triggered Eben's dream last night, the one in which a petite, honey-blond woman had joined him in his lonely bed, the dream that had jolted him awake in the middle of the night, damp with sweat and aching with need. Yes, Paul must've brought it on with his interminable questions about Miss Forester.

Or else it was the unfortunate fact that Isabel Forester was the first woman Eben had held in his arms in longer than he cared to recall. When he closed his eyes, he could still remember her softness against his chest; and the heady, womanly scent of her body. Her skin, as white as milk, would feel like satin, warming under his hands; her hair, a silky curtin drifting through his fingers. . . .

"There she is," Paul exclaimed, rudely interrupting Eben's fantasies. "Hell, she don't look twenty-nine at all."

"Watch your language," Eben chided. "Remember where you are."

Paul was too busy straightening his collar to pay him any mind. Eben found himself straightening his own collar.

What had come over him?

Of course, she did look mighty pretty in the morning sunlight, a whole sight better than she had the last time he'd seen her, even. Although he preferred her hair loose, he liked the way she'd pinned it up and frizzed it around her face. Her hat was ridiculous, like most women's hats were, but she'd tied it under her chin at a jaunty angle. He only wished she weren't wearing a cape. He would've liked to get a better look at her figure.

"You're going to introduce me, aren't you?" Paul asked.

"I haven't met her myself, if you'll remember," Eben said, irrationally irritated by his friend's interest in Miss Forester.

Paul snorted. "You practically put her to bed. That must count for something."

Eben glared, but Paul ignored him, too intent on Miss Isabel Forester's approach to care about Eben's disapproval.

Isabel couldn't believe how much better she felt after a good night's sleep in a real bed and several meals of truly wholesome food. She'd actually been surprised by the sight of her own reflection this morning. Indeed, she'd hardly recognized the flushed, bright-eyed creature staring back at her from the mirror. She was almost pretty!

Her new wardrobe had also bolstered her confidence. Having sold all her parents' meager possessions, save for a few keepsakes, Isabel had for the first time in her life been able to afford the stylish clothes she had never enjoyed as either a minister's daughter or a poor teacher. She had spent most of the six weeks since her father's death sewing in preparation for her new life.

Beneath her black wool cape, she wore her very best dress. Doomed to wear black for her year of mourning, Isabel had compromised by selecting a fabric in the newest of colors. At first glance it appeared to be black, but when the light caught the shiny material, it glowed with the interwoven green threads. Wearing it made her feel as if she knew a magical secret. Her ignominious arrival notwithstanding, today was the first day of her brand-new life, and Isabel was determined to enjoy it thoroughly.

With Bertha Bartz on her right and Herald Bartz on her left, she resolutely made her way into the crowd. If there was one thing at which a minister's daughter was adept, it was meeting morning worshipers. Ber-

tha made the introductions to the first group of matrons. Isabel smiled and shook hands all around, but
her smile was not returned. Instead the women studied her solemnly. She was just about to ask if her
petticoat might be showing when one of them said,
"Are you sickly? Ain't no use having a schoolmarm
if she's going to be sick all the time."

"Oh, no, I'm perfectly healthy," Isabel assured
them, realizing her faint had given them an incorrect
impression.

"Maybe that's why she had to come way out here,"
another woman said. "Maybe they wouldn't have her
back East because she took sick."

"But I—"

"You're not consumptive, are you?"

"Certainly not!"

"We don't have no use for weaklings out here,
missy," a third woman informed her sternly. "Nor
for women who get the vapors every time things get
a little rough."

"I never get the vapors!" Isabel insisted, then their
skeptical looks reminded her that she had fainted
practically into their laps the instant she arrived in
town. "I mean, I'm generally quite healthy. You
needn't worry," she tried in a more reasonable vein,
but no one seemed impressed.

She looked to Bertha for help, but the president of
the school board seemed as nonplussed as she. Looking beyond Bertha, Isabel saw a group of children
staring and pointing and *giggling*! Good heavens, had
she made herself a laughingstock?

"Miss Forester, Miss Forester!"

Grateful for the distraction, Isabel turned to see
Carrie Bartz, Bertha's oldest daughter, whom Isabel
had met that morning at breakfast, approaching with
another girl in tow. Carrie had, unfortunately, inherited her mother's prodigious height and lack of
beauty, and showed every indication of assuming her
titanic dimensions as well. The girl beside her was

her exact antithesis, pretty and petite with corn-flower-blue eyes and cornsilk-blond hair. She seemed vaguely familiar, perhaps because she possessed exactly the kind of perfect beauty Isabel had spent much of her youth coveting.

"Miss Forester, I'd like you to meet my best friend, Amanda Walker."

"I'm pleased to make your acquaintance," Isabel said, offering to take the girl's hand.

Slightly flustered, Amanda blushed as she tentatively accepted Isabel's gloved fingertips. "I'm pleased to make your acquaintance, too," she murmured shyly, dropping a slight curtsy.

Enchanted, Isabel smiled as Amanda suddenly remembered the flowers she was clutching in her other hand. "Oh, these are for you."

"Why, thank you," Isabel said. When Amanda held out the posy, Isabel suddenly remembered why she looked so familiar. "You were going to give me flowers yesterday!"

"Yes, I was," Amanda replied in amazement. "I can't believe you remember."

Isabel gave her a self-mocking grin as she took the flowers. "I didn't see very much, but I did see you standing there."

"And you must've seen my father, too. He was the one who . . . who caught you."

"Your father?" Isabel asked uneasily, guiltily remembering her reaction to the man. Oh, dear, this sweet girl was one of his "brood."

"Yes, Eben Walker," Bertha reminded her. "The, uh, gentleman who carried you to my house."

"Yes, I . . . I don't believe I ever had the opportunity to thank him," Isabel said weakly.

"I'll be glad to fetch him right now so you can," Amanda offered, and before Isabel could object, the girl disappeared into the crowd.

Bertha was already introducing her to an elderly couple whose names Isabel hadn't heard. She smiled

politely and tried to convince them she wasn't possessed of a weak constitution while her mind raced
with thoughts of Eben Walker. Why on earth should
she be so uneasy about meeting him face-to-face? He
would have no idea she'd briefly entertained those
silly thoughts about him. He'd introduce her to his
wife, and they would all become great friends. Perhaps they would even someday laugh about how he
had carried her from the stage and put her to bed.

"The weather is unseasonably warm, isn't it?" she
said to the elderly couple in an attempt to change the
subject from her dubious health.

"Oh, no, we usually get warm weather by the first
of March," the elderly gentleman informed her.
"Grass is greening up real nice, too. Be a good year
for cattle."

"For sheep, too," someone behind Isabel said.

She whirled in surprise and came face-to-face with
Eben Walker.

He was much taller than she remembered, and
broader, too, putting her in mind of an oak tree, solid
and unmovable. No wonder he thought her puny.

"*Sheep!*" the old man to whom she had been speaking cried. "Don't mention that word in God's front
yard!"

"God made the sheep, too," Eben Walker pointed
out reasonably. "Don't you remember Christ being
called the Good Shepherd?"

"Well, if he'd've lived in Texas, they'd've called him
the Good Rancher, because not even God Hisownself
would run sheep around here."

Walker opened his mouth to reply, but Amanda
tugged at his sleeve. "Pa, *please*," she begged, and he
reluctantly turned his attention to Isabel.

She'd remembered his eyes accurately. So brown,
they were almost black, at least they held no disapproval this time. Instead, he seemed wary, guarded.

Amanda cleared her throat importantly. "Miss Forester, this is my father, Eben Walker."

He touched his hat brim, and Isabel suddenly felt breathless.

"I believe I owe you a debt, Mr. Walker," she said, hoping her smile looked natural. She forced herself to glance over his shoulder and try to guess which one of the women in the yard was his wife. Surely the woman would appear in another second and rescue her from this uncomfortable situation.

"Think nothing of it, Miss Forester. I'm sure Mrs. Bartz would say it was part of my duty as a member of the school board to escort the new teacher to her home." His answering smile lit up his lean face, and Isabel saw that he was even more attractive than she'd remembered. She judged him to be in his midthirties, and in his smartly tailored broadcloth suit, he looked like the quintessential pillar of the community.

"You did a lot more than just 'escort' her," a second man said, grinning over Eben Walker's shoulder. "Eben here has already refused to introduce me, and I can't blame him one bit for wanting to keep you all to himself, so I reckon I have to do the honors myself. Paul Young at your service, ma'am."

He tipped his bowler hat, and Isabel, mortified at being reminded of her earlier encounter with Mr. Walker, nodded numbly in response. What on earth did he mean about Mr. Walker wanting to keep her all to himself? And why in heaven's name was Mr. Young grinning at her as if he found her the most fascinating woman he had ever seen? Men hardly ever looked at her at all, and certainly not as if they found her attractive. "Pleased to meet you," she murmured uncomfortably.

"I'm a member of the school board, too," Young added cheerfully.

"Then your children will be my students," Isabel said with some relief. She must have been mistaken. The man was married, so he couldn't possibly have been flirting with her.

"Oh, no, I don't have any children. I'm a bachelor,

just like Eben here." Isabel's surprise must have
shown, because he hastily added, "Course, Eben's a
widower, which is why he's got Amanda."

"I see," Isabel murmured, and she really was beginning to. Eben Walker wasn't married, so no wife
was going to rescue her. When she looked back up
at Walker, he was frowning at Mr. Young, who didn't
seem to care. Isabel was going to have to salvage the
situation herself. She smiled her best Sunday smile.
"In any case, I'm delighted to make your acquaintance
at last, Mr. Walker," she said, extending her gloved
hand.

Startled, Walker hesitated just a second before lifting his own hand to take hers, and when he did,
Isabel gasped. It was filthy: the nails stained; the callused palms gray with ground-in dirt. He had the
hands of a common laborer!

Seeing her shock, he dropped his hand instantly.
"It won't rub off, Miss Forester," he informed her
grimly.

"I . . . I'm sorry," she stammered in dismay, knowing she had offended him dreadfully. She certainly
had no objection to shaking his hand, no matter how
dirty it might have been. It was just that from his
demeanor she had somehow expected the smooth
hand of a shopkeeper.

"Pa's the town blacksmith," Amanda explained,
her anxious gaze going back and forth between Isabel
and her father. "He washes every day, but his hands
stay like that anyway."

"Oh, the blacksmith, of course," Isabel said, feeling
like a total idiot. How on earth could she ever make
amends? Before she could even consider the problem,
however, the church bell began to clang, summoning
the congregation to worship.

"Time to go, Amanda," Mr. Walker said stiffly.
"Nice to meet you, Miss Forester."

"But, Pa, I was going to ask Miss Forester to sit
with us," Amanda protested.

"I'm sure she has other plans," he said, taking the girl by the arm and leading her away.

Isabel watched them go in dismay.

"Perhaps you'll sit with me, then."

Isabel looked up at Paul Young, of whom she had barely taken notice before. He was a tall man, almost as tall as Eben Walker, and his pale blue eyes were kind. He had a nice smile, and he wasn't bad-looking, which made Isabel wonder why in the world he would want to sit with her. In Isabel's experience, two single people sitting together in church was tantamount to announcing their engagement, but perhaps customs were different here in Texas.

"I really don't—" she began, but Bertha came to her rescue.

"She most certainly will not sit with you her first day in town," Bertha decreed, taking Isabel by the arm and directing her toward the church door, much as Eben had done with his daughter a few moments earlier. "Try to remember what I said about keeping our teacher for the remainder of the term. It's your duty as a member of the school board."

"I was only trying to make her feel welcome," Mr. Young complained, following at their heels.

Bertha dismissed his explanation with a disgruntled "Humph."

Then they were inside the church, and Bertha conducted her to an empty pew near the front. The decor of the church was simple, from the plain wooden pews to the austere muslin curtains at the windows. For a moment Isabel indulged herself in bittersweet nostalgia. If her father had come to this church, his first instruction to her would have been to embroider a little color into the altar cloth and the curtains. Her father did so love bright colors.

Blinking at the sting of tears, she noticed the small pump organ beside the pulpit. Someone had gone to great trouble and expense to bring the instrument to this distant place. She forced herself to think about that and not about her loss, and, after a moment, she regained control of her emotions.

By the time Isabel had removed her cape and laid it on the bench beside Amanda's flowers, everyone had taken their seats, and the minister in his black robe climbed the steps up into the pulpit. His snow-white hair glinted in the morning sunlight, and for a moment Isabel thought of the many times she'd seen her father standing in his pulpit exactly the same way. Suddenly she began to feel at home.

"Please rise and sing with me hymn number one hundred seventy-eight, 'A Mighty Fortress Is Our God.'"

Isabel rose, watching the organ expectantly, but no one moved toward it as the parishioners shuffled pages in the silence.

"Who plays the organ?" Isabel whispered to Bertha.

"Mrs. Smiley, our minister's wife, used to play until the arthritis crippled her hands. No one else knows how to, I'm afraid," Bertha whispered back.

"I do," Isabel said without thinking, and instantly regretted it. Would they think her unladylike to put herself forward her first day in town?

"You do?" Bertha exclaimed loudly enough to turn curious heads. Before Isabel could respond, Bertha turned to the minister and called, "Pastor, Miss Forester can play the organ."

Reverend Smiley's wrinkled face brightened. "She can? Would you play for us, Miss Forester?" He laughed, "We haven't had music in a month of Sundays."

Isabel could not possibly have refused. Acutely aware that every eye was upon her, she quickly made her way up to the front of the church and took her place on the organ stool. The height was perfect, so she hastily adjusted the stops, then found the foot pedals and began to pump. Since she didn't need a hymnal to play the music to the familiar hymn, she simply began. The first notes were thin and reedy until the organ filled, then the sound swelled joyously. When Isabel finished the introduction, the congregation joined in, their voices rising above the sweet call of the organ.

"A mighty fortress is our God, a bulwark never failing," they sang, and Isabel joined them for the second line.

"Our helper he, amid the flood of mortal ills prevailing."

The joy of the music washed over her, carrying her with it. For the first time in her life, Isabel was truly free, and she closed her eyes and imagined she could sing loudly enough so even her parents could hear her, to let them know she was going to be all right.

"For still our ancient foe doth seek to work us woe. His craft and power are great . . ."

But something was wrong. What had happened to the rest of the congregation? Why did it seem she was the only one singing?

"And armed with cruel hate . . ."

Isabel opened her eyes and glanced over her shoulder.

She was right; they had all stopped singing, and everyone in the church was staring at her in wide-eyed astonishment.

Isabel's feet ceased their pumping, and the music died in a whining moan. She glanced up at the minister, who was staring at her with the very same astonishment as everyone else. For an endless moment the silence stretched.

At last, completely mortified, her face flaming, Isabel ventured, "Was I . . . playing too fast?"

Her question seemed to break the spell. The minister blinked and shook himself while the rest of the congregation shuffled and shifted in unison.

"Oh, no, Miss Forester, your playing was just fine," Reverend Smiley assured her.

Isabel frowned. People were still staring, although they were being more discreet about it now, except for Eben Walker, who scowled at her with the same stern disapproval he'd shown yesterday just before she'd fainted into his arms. A shiver of reaction danced up her spine, and she forced herself to look away from him. What on earth had she done to offend everyone?

"Perhaps you'd prefer to sing without accompaniment," she tried.

"No!" several people in the audience cried, and the others murmured their agreement.

Reverend Smiley cleared his throat. "I'm sorry we've been so rude to you, Miss Forester, but I believe I speak for everyone when I say we were simply overcome by the beauty of your voice."

"My voice?" Isabel echoed, appalled at the realization that she had probably been drowning out the whole congregation. She'd experienced the problem before. "I'm terribly sorry! I didn't mean to sing so loudly."

"But we're very glad you did," Reverend Smiley insisted. "God has given you a great gift."

Isabel knew all about her gift. She also knew about the jealousy it inspired in the hearts of doting mamas who wanted *their* daughters selected to sing the solos in the church choir. Although she recognized it was a sin to hide her light under a bushel, experience had taught her to keep it dim. How could she have forgotten herself on her first day in town?

But when she glanced over her shoulder at the congregation again, she was surprised to see a few tentative smiles.

"Why don't somebody tell her to sing some more?" a child asked in a piping voice.

His mother instantly hushed him, but when she looked back up at Isabel she said, "Would you, please?"

"Yes, would you?" Reverend Smiley said, nodding his encouragement.

Others in the congregation added their affirmation,

and slowly Isabel's embarrassment began to fade. They really did want her to sing!

"I'd be happy to," she said, but before she could do so, Bertha spoke up.

"The girl can't sing with her back to us. Turn that organ around, somebody. Eben Walker, moving an organ shouldn't be much trouble to a strapping fellow like you."

"I'll help," Paul Young offered, stepping eagerly into the aisle before Eben Walker could respond.

Hating the heat she felt rising in her face again, Isabel hastily rose from the stool and stepped out of the way, hardly daring to look at the men who came to move the organ lest she discover Eben Walker had refused the summons; not that she could blame him, of course, after the shameful way she had treated him out in the churchyard.

But when she hazarded a glance, she saw he had indeed come forward, although he certainly wasn't happy about it. His dark frown was a marked contrast to Paul Young's sunny smile. "How do you want it moved?" he asked grimly.

Isabel was tempted to say she didn't want it moved at all, but she managed to keep a civil tongue in her head. "I suppose at an angle, like this," she said, indicating the position with her hand.

The two men set to the task. Young kept grinning, until Isabel began to wonder if he was simpleminded. Walker's dour expression never changed, nor did he deign to glance in her direction. Isabel knew, because she couldn't seem to keep her eyes off him. Something about his broad-shouldered form and the way his muscles strained against the fabric of his suit as he wrestled with the organ drew her attention like a magnet.

A memory stirred, a poem she had taught her students at Miss Snodgrass's school: *The smith a mighty man is he, with large and sinewy hands; and the muscles of his brawny arms are strong as iron bands.* Isabel

couldn't help recalling she had been held in those
brawny arms, and the ease with which he moved the
heavy instrument left her feeling somewhat breathless.

"That all right?" he asked, startling her back to
reality.

"Oh, yes, fine," she replied, trying not to sound
as disturbed as she felt. Good heavens, the whole
congregation was watching. She only hoped they
couldn't read her thoughts. "Thank you, gentlemen,"
she added briskly.

"Our pleasure, Miss Forester," Paul Young said
with a dazzling smile. Eben Walker said nothing at
all, and Isabel busied herself with positioning the
stool so she wouldn't be tempted to moon over him
as he strode back down the aisle to his seat.

Until now the congregation had remained standing,
and they took this as the signal to sit down again.
Isabel seated herself on the stool and began working
the pedals. Only then did she consider what she
would sing, and almost of their own volition, her
fingers struck the opening notes of her father's fa-
vorite hymn, "There Is a Balm in Gilead."

A small pain flickered in her heart, but she knew
her father would chide her for mourning him. He was
in a far better place now, a place where he need never
sing a song like this again. The thought made her
smile, as she had been taught to do when she sang,
and she managed to swallow the lump in her throat
just in time to start the verse.

*"Sometimes I feel discouraged, and think my work's in
vain . . ."*

Usually when she sang, the faces in the crowd
blurred, but this time she kept them in focus, startled
to see the warm smiles and the glitter of approval in
the eyes staring back at her. Gone were the skeptical
frowns of those who feared she might be too frail to
do the job for which she'd been hired. Gone were the
children's smirks.

"There is a balm in Gilead to make the wounded whole . . ."

They listened, enraptured, as Isabel's strong contralto filled the building and reverberated back.

"If you can't preach like Peter, If you can't pray like Paul . . ."

She poured herself into the song, and the words flowed as sweetly as the balm of which she sang.

". . . There is a balm in Gilead to heal the sin-sick soul."

The last note died away into total silence, and Isabel sat completely still for several seconds, loath to break the spell. She was just about to rise from her stool and return to her seat when someone started clapping. Of course, people did not applaud in church. It was one of those things that simply wasn't done, and she expected the person to quickly recover himself and stop. Instead, the others joined in. Appalled, Isabel cast an apologetic look at Reverend Smiley only to discover he was clapping, too!

Isabel didn't know what to do. Bowing was certainly out of the question, as was hiding behind the organ, which was her inclination.

"Sing another one," someone called.

"Yes, please," Bertha's voice demanded.

Abashed, Isabel looked to Reverend Smiley, who nodded vigorously. Anxious to stop the embarrassing tribute, Isabel struck the first notes of "O for a Thousand Tongues to Sing."

Isabel held the audience enthralled as she sang that song of praise, then three more songs.

Eben listened in growing misery. How could God have blessed such an arrogant woman with such a beautiful voice? He supposed he wouldn't mind listening to it for the rest of his life, or watching her either, for that matter. When she sang, her face took on a glow that made her look like an angel, and Eben had to keep reminding himself how very human she was. He recalled vividly the way she'd recoiled at shaking the hand of a workingman. Well, Eben knew all about women like that, women who thought they were better than everybody else. He was lucky to have discovered she was one of them before he got too far along in being attracted to her.

Something poked at his arm, and when he looked down in annoyance, he found Amanda was trying to get his attention. "Pa," she whispered, "do you suppose we could invite Miss Forester for dinner after church?"

Eben frowned. Invite her to dinner? Invite Miss Isabel Forester to dine at Eben Walker's humble home? She'd probably laugh right in his face. His gaze sought her again, and to his surprise, she was looking right at him.

Isabel had been so caught up in singing, she had lost her hold on reality until she happened to catch sight of Eben Walker's sun-darkened face. He leaned down to hear something his lovely daughter was saying to him over the swell of the music. Amanda's entreating smile would have melted a stone, but Walker frowned and looked straight at Isabel.

For one startling second their eyes met, and Isabel knew beyond doubt that Amanda's remark to her father had concerned her. Walker's frown deepened, and he shook his head at the girl. Amanda's sweet smile instantly transformed into a heartbroken moue.

Obviously Eben Walker didn't appreciate Isabel's singing at all, and the knowledge took the joy right out of it for her. She let the last notes of the song die.

"Thank you," she said with a stiff smile, ignoring the protests as she rose from her stool. "I believe I'll give Reverend Smiley an opportunity to preach his sermon now."

Although Isabel's seat was near the front of the church, more than a few people stopped her on her short trip to shake her hand and tell her how much they had enjoyed her singing. The women who had complained about her health were wiping tears from their eyes as they murmured their gratitude. They enveloped Isabel with warmth, giving her the welcome they had withheld earlier. Apparently her singing had won everyone's heart.

Everyone except Eben Walker, she thought as she took her place beside Bertha again. One man's opinion should not matter, but still, his rejection stung, particularly when she remembered it was her own fault. If she hadn't behaved like a snob, they might at least have been friends. Isabel thought she might like having Eben Walker as a friend.

After Reverend Smiley got done thanking Isabel for her songs and expressing the gratitude of the entire congregation, he told them he didn't have much energy for anything else. He simply expounded a bit on unexpected blessings, then summoned Isabel to play for the closing hymn. She wisely did not sing along, so the service ended without incident. The moment Reverend Smiley dismissed them, virtually everyone swarmed to the front of the church to meet and greet Miss Isabel Forester, a woman they now felt was going to be a great asset to the community.

Everyone except Eben Walker.

His adorable daughter came, however. "I never heard anybody sing like that," she told Isabel, her bright eyes shining with admiration. "I didn't even know people *could* sing like that."

"Part of it is my training," Isabel demurred. "I was extremely fortunate to have studied with a singing master, a friend of my father who gave me the lessons for free because he thought I had a good voice."

"Could you teach me to sing like that?" Amanda asked, and Isabel recognized the longing in the girl's face. She had seen the emotion often enough reflected back from her own mirror, the desire for something most likely unattainable. Isabel couldn't have refused even if she'd wanted to.

"I would be happy to teach you and anyone else who wants to learn. If enough people are interested, perhaps Reverend Smiley would let us start a choir."

"A choir! Did you hear, Carrie? Miss Forester is going to start a choir!" Amanda ran off to tell her friend, and Isabel's heart followed her. What a charming child. Eben Walker was truly blessed to have her.

When Carrie came back in a few minutes to confirm the news, she informed Isabel she couldn't wait for school to start tomorrow. Isabel also looked forward to it with great anticipation. Once she started teaching, she would be far too busy to worry about broad-shouldered widowers with dark, brooding eyes.

Isabel and the Bartz family were the last to leave the building as Reverend Smiley and his wife locked up behind them. Isabel was thinking she had made the right decision in coming to Bittercreek when she glanced around and saw sweet little Amanda Walker standing in the street talking to a very handsome young man.

The fellow stood a head taller than she, and his clothes marked him as a cowboy. Isabel guessed him to be about twenty years old. A man that age should be far too worldly-wise to waste his time on a child like Amanda. Still he smiled down at the girl with the kind of unabashed pleasure Isabel had no trouble recognizing.

As a teacher, Isabel had often warned her charges at Miss Snodgrass's school about young men and their lustful intentions, but obviously no one had warned Amanda. The girl smiled up at him coyly, her cornflower eyes issuing an invitation she couldn't possibly mean. She was just a child! Where on earth was her father? What was he thinking to let a young girl flaunt herself like this?

"Who's that Amanda's talking with?" Isabel asked Bertha with what she hoped was nonchalance.

"Oh, dear," Bertha murmured when she noticed the couple in the street. "Carrie, go ask Amanda to come to dinner with us, will you?"

Carrie scooted away, and Bertha's gaze met Isabel's. "His name is Johnny Dent. He works at one of the local ranches."

"I didn't see him in church," Isabel ventured.

"And you won't," Bertha replied acerbically. "I wouldn't let any daughter of mine near a man like that."

Isabel was relieved to see Bertha understood the problem and was willing to rescue Amanda from the current situation. Of course, someone would have to explain the real problem to the girl before she innocently got herself in trouble, someone who could handle the situation delicately.

As if reading her mind, Bertha said, "Eben just lets that girl run wild. What she needs is a mother to look after her, but I don't suppose she'll ever have one."

"Why not?" Isabel asked before she could stop herself.

"Well, because if Eben Walker ever intended to marry again, don't you suppose he would've done so long before now? He's been a widower since Amanda was a baby, but to this day he's never even looked at another woman."

In her old life, Isabel would never have presumed to inquire into someone else's private affairs, but this was her new life. "Do you think he . . . ? He couldn't still be in love with his wife!"

Bertha shrugged. "He never speaks of her, not even to his daughter, or so Carrie tells me. I can only guess it's because he can't bear to. It's a pity, too. If nothing else, he owes it to the girl. She should have a woman to look after her."

The thought of Amanda's need stirred all sorts of images in Isabel's imagination. Once she had dreamed of having a husband and children, but she had long since accepted that she would never be anyone's mother. She would certainly never be Amanda Walker's mother.

"Perhaps she just needs a teacher," Isabel said.

Chapter 4

Isabel couldn't get used to having spring come so early. When she had left New York at the end of February, the trees were barren, the ground still frozen and snow-covered. A bare week later, she'd arrived in Texas to sunshine, warm breezes, wildflowers, and green grass.

Standing in the doorway of the one-room schoolhouse, she savored the beauty of the pink blossoms adorning the tree in the schoolyard. When Bertha had given her a tour of the school yesterday after church, she had informed Isabel the tree was a redbud.

The school itself was one long room made of logs. The "desks" were planks of wood set in rows, and the students sat on benches. In spite of the crude furnishings, however, Isabel found the school well stocked with books and maps and slates and all the other supplies she would need as a teacher.

The Bartz children had accompanied Isabel this morning and helped her open the school. Now they

45

played in the yard with the rest of the students who had begun to arrive. Some came on foot from various parts of town. Others came on horseback, which explained the fenced area behind the school. With practiced ease, the children unsaddled their mounts and turned them loose in the enclosure.

Soon the yard was full of children, and Isabel watched in alarm as the boys raced around in the dirt, yelling like banshees, heedless of their clothes and shoes. Good heavens, boys were much wilder than she had remembered. Would she be able to cope with them?

Bertha had told her to expect twenty-four students, and when Isabel counted twenty, she clanged the iron triangle hanging by the school door to summon them inside. Appointing Carrie Bartz and Amanda Walker as her helpers, Isabel soon had the children seated according to age. The morning passed quickly in a blur of new faces. Isabel thought up some games to help her learn their names, then challenged them to stump her by changing seats when her back was turned. By noon she knew all of those present and even the ones who hadn't come. Mercifully, the infamous Zink twins were among them.

"Barclay Plimpton ain't here," one of the boys informed her when she asked about the absentees. "And we don't care, neither. His father's a damn sheepherder."

"Roger!" Isabel scolded, shocked to her core to hear a child swear so casually.

"That's what my pa says," the boy defended himself. "That's what everybody says."

"Not *everybody*," Isabel corrected. "*No one* will swear in my classroom. Is that understood?"

"Well, nobody likes the Plimptons anyhow," Roger insisted. "They brung sheep in, and everybody knows sheep ruin the grass."

Isabel knew no such thing. Sheep had grazed for decades in New England, and for centuries in Europe, and the grass there had survived intact. Still, she felt reluctant to contradict the students until she understood the situation better. She recalled the old man who had reviled sheep yesterday in the churchyard, and the way Eben Walker had defended them. He seemed to be a reasonable man. She wished she could discuss the matter with him, but doubted he would talk to her at all.

Sighing at the thought, Isabel dismissed her class for lunch. When she followed the children outside, she found Carrie and Amanda had saved her a place beneath the redbud tree. The two girls sat on the grass with their colorful calico skirts spread modestly around them. Isabel noticed what a pretty picture they made, in spite of Carrie's unfortunate lack of beauty, and wondered if they hadn't planned the pose for effect, as girls their age were wont to do. If so, Isabel thought with amusement, they had wasted their time since none of the other students seemed to appreciate it.

The girls waved her over.

"Mama packed your lunch with mine," Carrie explained, indicating the lard pail that had been converted into a lunch pail. Inside, Isabel found a sandwich filled with a generous portion of cold chicken, and a piece of apple pie.

Although Isabel judged the piecrust to be a trifle tough, she enjoyed the meal almost as much as she enjoyed the animated chatter of the children around her. The girls at Miss Snodgrass's academy were never permitted to chatter.

"We were awful glad to hear that the new teacher was a lady," Amanda was saying. "Especially when we heard you were from New York. We're hoping you can tell us about the latest styles and all."

"I suppose I can," Isabel allowed, thinking a little guiltily of the time she had spent studying those styles before making her new wardrobe. Some would find the concern frivolous.

"Of course, Mama gets *Godey's Ladies' Book*," Carrie said, "so we know what the styles are, but we have trouble copying them."

"Well, I'm a fairly good seamstress, so perhaps I can help," Isabel said, trying to sound modest.

"Did you make that dress you had on in church yesterday?" Amanda asked. Isabel nodded. "That was the most beautiful dress I've ever seen," she exclaimed.

"We never saw material like that," Carrie added. "I told Amanda it was really green, but she wouldn't believe me at first. What kind of fabric is it?"

"Sateen, which is just a shiny cotton," Isabel explained, warming to their enthusiasm. "The color is called invisible green because you have to look so closely to see it."

"Maybe Mama can order some for the store," Carrie said. "I know everybody in town'll want a dress just like it now."

"It wouldn't be a good color for you girls, though," Isabel cautioned. "You're much too young to be wearing something so dark."

"What colors should we wear?" Amanda asked, leaning forward eagerly.

Isabel pretended to study them while she tried to think of a tactful way to tell Carrie Bartz that her brown dress made her look as if she'd been dead three days. "Of course, your mother probably likes darker colors for school because they don't show the dirt so easily, but both of you girls would look lovely in pastels. Pinks to bring out your natural coloring, and blues to accentuate your eyes. Amanda can wear lots of fussy ribbons because she's petite, but Carrie, you should choose more tailored styles because of your height."

"I hate being so tall," Carrie complained.

"But it's quite fashionable to be tall, and you can carry off a style much better than Amanda or I."

Carrie brightened instantly. "I can? How?"

"And what styles should I wear, Miss Forester?" Amanda asked, not wanting to be left out.

For a few minutes they discussed the various styles that Isabel thought would flatter each girl's figure, until Isabel felt the time was right to bring up a topic to which she had been giving considerable thought.

"Amanda, who was that young man I saw you talking to after church yesterday?" she asked with creditable nonchalance.

Amanda blushed scarlet, and Carrie giggled behind her hand.

"That's Johnny Dent," Carrie informed her when Amanda did not reply. "He's sweet on Amanda."

"He is not!" Amanda insisted, but not very convincingly.

"I notice he's not in school today," Isabel tried. "Is he one of the absentees?"

"He's too old for school," Amanda said, a little defiantly, Isabel thought.

"He's almost twenty," Carrie added, confirming Isabel's worst fears and earning a black look from Amanda. "He works out at the Rocking Horse Ranch."

"Is he a friend of your family?" Isabel tried, knowing she would be disappointed.

"Well, Pa knows him, I guess," Amanda said uneasily.

"And allows him to call on you?" Isabel prompted, already knowing the answer.

"Pa doesn't care," she replied, her defiance no longer in question.

"You mean he doesn't know," Carrie said slyly.

"Hush up, Carrie Bartz," Amanda snapped, hastily gathering her lunch things.

Isabel made an effort to salvage the situation before Amanda ran off. "Amanda, I'm sure your father would like to know if this young man is interested in you."

"No, he wouldn't," Amanda insisted. "He doesn't

want to know anything about me." When she would
have risen, Isabel grabbed her arm.

"Please don't be angry," Isabel said with what she
hoped was a placating smile. "I certainly didn't mean
to pry into your affairs. I was only interested because
...because Mr. Dent is such an attractive young
man," she improvised, "and because his feelings for
you are so obvious."

Isabel had Amanda's full attention now. "They
are?"

"Well, I can't say I've had much experience with
young men," Isabel said, using a tactic that had
worked well for her in the past in winning the confidence of young girls, "but he certainly seemed smit-
ten. Carrie agrees; don't you, Carrie?"

"I already said so, didn't I?" Carrie said huffily, still
annoyed by Amanda's order to hush up.

"I thought surely you must know," Isabel continued, watching Amanda's reactions carefully. "Of
course, he is quite a bit older than you, and you may
have misunderstood his attentions."

"I didn't misunderstand," Amanda said, then
blushed again. "I mean, he's already told me he likes
me."

"Then he has offered for you," Isabel said with false
enthusiasm.

"Not... not exactly," Amanda admitted.

"But you said you'd marry him," Carrie protested.

"Not to him!" Amanda cried, then quickly recovered her composure. "I mean, I know he's going
to ask me, and when he does, I'll say yes."

"How old are you, Amanda?" Isabel asked kindly.

Amanda hesitated. "Almost fifteen."

"You won't be fifteen until next December," Carrie
reminded her.

Isabel widened her eyes. "I'm surprised Mr. Dent
would want to marry a girl so young."

"He said he thinks I'm grown-up for my age,"

Amanda said defiantly, her azure eyes suspiciously moist.

"And so you are," Isabel agreed. "You must excuse me for being cautious. You see, I've known a few young men—and I'm sure Mr. Dent isn't like this at all—who pay their attentions to girls much younger than themselves because they believe those girls will be innocent and trusting and easier to . . . to fool."

"To fool how?" Carrie asked, fascinated, while Amanda frowned.

Isabel pretended to be reluctant to tell them. "You must know that some young men are perfectly willing to take advantage of a girl if given the opportunity."

"You mean *seduce* her?" Carrie asked in a horrified whisper.

"Exactly," Isabel confirmed.

"Johnny isn't like that!" Amanda snapped, obviously furious at the turn of the conversation.

"I'm sure he isn't," Isabel said, "which is what makes me wonder why he doesn't speak to your father about courting you. If Mr. Dent truly cares for you—"

"He does!"

"—then he will be most careful of your reputation. Your reputation is a fragile thing, Amanda, as I'm sure you know. Once lost, it can never be regained."

"And my mama always says a girl doesn't even have to really do anything bad," Carrie added. "People only have to think she did, and she'll be ruined."

Plainly, Amanda did not approve of the way this conversation was going. "Johnny would never do anything to hurt my reputation."

"Never intentionally, I'm sure," Isabel agreed, "but perhaps he doesn't realize how odd it looks for him to see you without your father's knowledge and approval."

"I told you, my father doesn't care what I do," Amanda insisted, her pretty face mottled with outrage.

"Then he should be happy to grant Mr. Dent permission to pay his addresses," Isabel concluded with perfect reason. To her relief, she saw that Amanda was at least now considering the possibility that her Johnny's intentions were not completely honorable.

Still, Isabel knew she had a lot of work ahead if she was to protect Amanda from her own innocence, and her best ally in the struggle would be Amanda's father. Unfortunately, Eben Walker was probably the last person who would willingly unite with Isabel Forester in a common quest, even if the beneficiary of that quest was his own daughter. Isabel could have groaned aloud at her stupidity.

"Well, girls, why don't we try to organize some games before the boys succeed in murdering one another," Isabel suggested with forced cheerfulness, rising from her seat beneath the redbud tree. "Amanda, does the school have a jump rope?"

Amanda's quick smile told Isabel she carried no grudge, probably because she had no inkling that Isabel was plotting to ruin her romance. Isabel only hoped she would succeed.

By the end of the day, Isabel finally understood the magnitude of the challenge she had accepted in taking this job: *boys*. Nothing in her previous experience had prepared her for these rambunctious bundles of energy who seemed incapable of sitting still for more than five minutes at a time. Although she never would have credited it, Isabel actually missed her former students at Miss Snodgrass's, spoiled and difficult as they were. At least she had never had to chasten them for bolting from their seats for no apparent reason or for swearing in class. She supposed she should just be grateful the Zink twins hadn't shown up.

"We'll walk you home, Miss Forester," Amanda told her as the other children streamed out the door after Isabel dismissed them. Carrie and the younger Bartz girl, Julie, waited while Isabel shrugged into her jacket, although the warm afternoon certainly didn't call for additional covering. Still, propriety demanded she not go about the town in her shirtwaist, and Isabel had taught young ladies the rules for so long, she couldn't bring herself to break them now.

Isabel fell in step with the girls as they walked slowly toward town. Then she noticed the children had all left the schoolhouse and made straight for one particular building in town instead of going their separate ways toward home.

"Where are the others going?" Isabel asked.

"To my father's shop," Amanda said without much enthusiasm. "They all like to watch him work."

"Your father?" Isabel couldn't quite imagine the dour blacksmith welcoming a hoard of unruly children into his place of business.

"Would you like to see the shop?" Carrie asked. "Mr. Walker does wonderful things in there."

"Of course," Isabel said, experiencing a small surge of anxiety over the prospect of seeing Eben Walker again. But if she was going to help Amanda, she would have to make peace with the girl's father. Pretending not to notice Amanda's reluctance, Isabel followed Carrie across the street.

As they approached the long, low building, Isabel recalled more of the poem about the village blacksmith: *Under a spreading chestnut-tree the village smithy stands.*

Of course, the trees here were live oak, and Isabel very sensibly supposed any tree would suffice to provide shade for what must be a sweltering occupation. She knew how hot cooking could be, and a smith's fire must be quite a bit hotter if it melted iron.

From inside the open double doors of the shop came the sound of children's laughter and the clang of a hammer on metal. Isabel pictured the brawny arm wielding the hammer, and something fluttered in her stomach, like a bird trying to escape.

She blamed the sensation on the apprehension she

felt at coming face-to-face with Eben Walker again. Knowing the man disliked her put her at a definite disadvantage, but then, she was only going to see if she couldn't undo the damage she had done yesterday, when she had recoiled at shaking hands with him.

If possible, she wanted to be friends with Eben Walker. Just friends. He wasn't really her sort of man anyway. A blacksmith was a laborer, after all, a man who worked at a trade. Isabel's tastes ran toward cultured professional men who appreciated art and beauty. Or at least she imagined her tastes would run that way if she'd ever been given an opportunity to exercise them.

Then she saw the weather vane on the roof of the shop. Almost a yard long, it trembled in the slight breeze, but not so much that Isabel couldn't clearly see the intricacy of its design. It depicted a very realistic-looking blacksmith standing at his anvil, one hand holding the tongs, and the other a raised hammer. Behind him was a horse with an "&" resting on its back like a tiny caricature of a rider. The horse stood on a large horseshoe inside of which were the letters "ER." Along the bottom of the weather vane ran the letters "E. Walker." Being a lover of puzzles, Isabel had no trouble at all interpreting the rebus: "E. Walker, blacksmith and horseshoer."

Someone had spent many hours on the sign, someone who possessed great skill, someone who had a definite love of art and beauty. The bird Isabel had imagined fluttering in her stomach started pecking.

"Oh, dear," she said aloud as Carrie dragged her through the open door. Amanda followed reluctantly.

"Keep away from the horse, Roger," Walker's voice called sternly. "You'll spook him, and I'll never get him shod."

Roger backed obediently away from the animal, and Isabel made a mental note of the tone Walker had used, hoping she might be able to exact the same obedience from Roger and the other boys if she could only duplicate it.

The boys and girls alike were gathered around the anvil, watching wide-eyed as Walker raised an enormous hammer and brought it crashing down on the rosy horseshoe resting on his anvil. Isabel jumped.

In his work clothes, Eben looked even more imposing than he had in his dress suit. Above his long leather apron, his shoulders were covered only by a thin shirt rolled up at the sleeves. Isabel could plainly see her imagination had failed to prepare her for the reality of Eben Walker.

Vaguely she remembered some other lines from the poem about the blacksmith:

> His hair is crisp, and black, and long,
> His face is like the tan;
> His brow is wet with honest sweat . . .

More than Walker's brow was wet. His shirt clung damply to his muscular back, leaving nothing to Isabel's inadequate imagination. He was made like a marble statue she had once seen in a museum, perfect and beautiful and totally male. Isabel's breath snagged on something sharp in her chest. Probably the beak of that darned bird, she thought in dismay. She'd have to get hold of herself if she was going to accomplish her purpose.

"I still have the ring you made me, Mr. Walker," one of the little girls said.

Isabel had never imagined a blacksmith made jewelry. Seeing her confusion, Carrie whispered, "He bends horseshoe nails into rings for the little girls." Amanda rolled her eyes and assumed a bored expression.

"I lost mine," another complained. "It fell off when I was walking to school, and I never found it."

"Must've made it too big," Walker said with a smile

that took Isabel's breath again. "When you come to-morrow, I'll make you another."

"Will you? Oh, thanks, Mr. Walker!"

Oh, dear, Isabel thought, how could he be kind, too? She never would have imagined him catering to the children in such a way, yet clearly he did, and they adored him for it. Eben Walker was rapidly shaping up to be an ideal man. Thank heaven Isabel was too sensible to start entertaining any romantic notions about him. Such a course could lead a woman to terrible heartache, and Isabel certainly didn't need any heartache in her new life, not any more than she needed a man, ideal or not.

"Roger, keep away from the horse, or I'll duck you in the slack tub," Walker warned. He watched the boy until he was well away from the animal again, then, as if sensing Isabel's gaze at last, he looked up and caught sight of her.

With regret she saw his dark eyes narrow and his expression harden from the open friendliness he had displayed with the children to wariness. She could easily imagine why Amanda might think him un-feeling. "Miss Forester," he said without a hint of welcome.

"The girls suggested I come in to see your shop," she said, managing a weak smile in the face of his coolness. "I must say, I'm impressed."

He glanced around at the clutter of tools and scrap metal as if trying to find some reason for her to be impressed. His skeptical frown told her he failed.

"I saw your weather vane outside," she hastily ex-plained. "It's quite a work of art. Did you make it yourself?"

"A long time ago," he admitted grudgingly.

"Pa made it when he first opened his shop. I was just a baby," Amanda explained with a sudden burst of enthusiasm. "Isn't that right, Pa?"

He ignored her question. "The kids like to come in after school and watch me work."

"So I see," Isabel said, straining to hold her smile in place and frantically trying to think of something to say that would drive the wariness from his eyes. Obviously flattery was not the ticket.

"Make the sparks fly, Mr. Walker, please?" wheedled the youngest Bartz boy.

Walker glanced down at the horseshoe he still held with his tongs. "I reckon I have to, since this shoe went cold while we've been talking."

He turned to the forge and shoved the shoe into the pile of smoldering coals. Reaching up, he grabbed the lever above his head and gave a mighty pull. The huge bellows hanging from the ceiling wheezed and whooshed. The coals blazed red, and sparks flew up the flue like a hundred fireflies racing to escape.

The children cried out in appreciation, and the smaller ones clapped their hands in glee. Isabel had to clench her hands to keep from clapping, too.

When the shoe glowed red again, he hastily turned and placed it on the anvil without so much as a glance in Isabel's direction. Picking up his hammer, he laid a few blows on the shoe, then strode to the waiting horse, which had been tied securely to the wall. The animal shied a bit, but Walker spoke softly and ran his hand soothingly down the horse's flank.

When the horse was calm, he picked up the hind foot and tried the shoe for fit. Apparently satisfied, he strode back to the forge and plunged the glowing shoe into a tub of water, where it hissed, then cooled to blackness in a cloud of steam. The children shouted their approval, as if the cloud had been created simply for their enjoyment, and Walker smiled again, that soul-wrenching smile which Isabel knew he would never smile for her.

"You'd better get along now," he warned. "Your folks'll have my hide if you're late getting home."

Isabel felt sorry for the children, who moaned their disappointment. She guessed he was dismissing them because he wanted to get rid of her. Not that she

blamed him, of course, but she also knew she couldn't
let things go on like this between them. If Isabel
wanted to help Amanda—and Amanda desperately
needed some help—she must have her father's approval.

Reluctantly the children started to drift away, calling their good-byes and their promises to see Mr.
Walker tomorrow. Carrie and Amanda turned to go,
too, then hesitated when Isabel did not move.

"Would you girls mind going on ahead? I'd like to
speak to Mr. Walker for a moment."

Amanda's blue eyes widened, and she glanced at
her father anxiously.

"I'm afraid I was rude to him in the churchyard
yesterday," Isabel explained softly. "I'd like to apologize."

Amanda's frown called her a liar, so Isabel added,
"If you want your father to know about Mr. Dent,
you will have to tell him yourself. I have no intention
of doing so."

The girl seemed relieved, but still she hesitated until
Carrie caught her arm and pulled her along with a
giggle. "They want to be alone, silly," Carrie whispered, making Isabel cringe with mortification.

Amanda's expression could have been simply in-
credulity at Carrie's romantic notion, but perhaps she
was jealous of her father, as any motherless daughter
might be. Isabel would have been the first to tell her
being jealous of an old-maid schoolteacher was simply ridiculous.

Suddenly Isabel was alone in the large room with
Eben Walker. He glanced up, obviously surprised to
see her still there. "You got a horse to be shod, Miss
Forester?" he asked with a trace of sarcasm.

Isabel swiftly thought of various ways to begin the
conversation, and discarded all of them as too defensive. Fighting the first stirrings of panic, she said the
first thing that sprang to her mind.

"Did you know Henry Wadsworth Longfellow wrote a poem about you?"

Isabel wanted to snatch the words back as soon as she'd said them, but then realized with some relief that she had inadvertently said something to put him off guard. He now looked confused instead of contemptuous. *"Who?"* he asked.

"Longfellow. He's a famous poet."

Plainly he was intrigued. He laid the cooled horseshoe and tongs down on the anvil. "How could somebody famous write a poem about me?"

"Well, it's not about you in particular. It's called 'The Village Blacksmith.'"

He thought this over. "How does it go?" he asked, crossing his arms over his leather apron in silent challenge.

Isabel ran through the lines in her mind, realizing she couldn't quote the parts about his muscles or his honest sweat, at least not without blushing. "Well, the verse that reminded me of you goes:

'And children coming home from school
Look in at the open door;
They love to see the flaming forge,
And hear the bellows roar,
And catch the burning sparks that fly
Like chaff from a threshing-floor.'"

Isabel waited, holding her breath for what seemed a long time as he scowled across the room at her. Then, slowly, so slowly she at first thought she was imagining it, he started to smile. His lips twitched slightly, as if he were resisting the impulse, but it was too powerful for him. As she watched in amazement, Eben Walker's well-formed mouth stretched into a grin.

Isabel blinked and her heart jolted in her chest. Could it have been only a few moments ago when she had predicted this would never happen?

Except he wasn't really smiling at her. He was smiling at Longfellow, she reminded herself sternly.

"I'll be," he muttered. "Why would somebody famous write a poem about a smith?"

Isabel improvised, knowing she didn't dare let the subject drop for fear of losing the little advantage she had gained. "Perhaps he saw the—" she groped for a word "—the nobility of your work."

The smile vanished instantly, and Isabel's stomach dropped. "I mean, you know how poets are," she explained hastily. "They find the beauty in the common things of life."

"I guess being a smith is pretty common," he remarked grimly, and Isabel could have bitten off her tongue.

"Mr. Walker," she pleaded. "Please, I didn't mean..."

His scowl was back, and her mind went blank in the face of it. Anything she said was likely to make things worse.

Finally he said, "What *did* you mean?"

Laying a hand over her churning stomach, she drew on the last reserves of her courage. "Mr. Walker, I...I believe I owe you an apology."

"Why?"

Well, he certainly wasn't going to make this easy, was he? she thought in dismay. "I'm afraid I...I offended you yesterday."

"Well, you didn't, so don't fret yourself about it." He picked up the shoe, pulled another hammer from an assortment hanging on a tool stand near the anvil, and strode over to the horse. Every jerky movement belied his calm denial. Isabel watched in frustration as he pulled the horse's hoof up between his legs, positioned the shoe, pulled a nail from his apron pocket, and began to pound it into place.

The animal sensed his fury, and Eben felt the horse shifting in resistance to his touch. He forced himself to remain calm. What in the hell did she think she was doing, coming in here like this and spouting all sorts of drivel about poems and the nobility of pounding iron? She'd already made it painfully clear she thought he was lower than the dirt under her pretty little feet. Why'd she have to come in here looking all clean and starched and perfect when he was dirty and sweaty and stinking of horse? Was it just to make him feel lower?

Of course, Eben already knew the answer to his questions. Experience had taught him just how cruel women could be and how much pleasure they took in turning the knife once they'd stuck it in a man. Why should Isabel Forester be any different?

One by one he pounded in the nails, never even glancing up, so he wouldn't have to see her pert little bustle swing as she left in a huff. When he had finished, he pulled the clinch cutter from his apron pocket and snipped off the tips of the nails protruding from the front of the hoof, then clinched them down. With an irritated sigh, he realized he'd left his rasp by the anvil. He lowered the hoof and straightened to go get it. To his surprise, Isabel Forester still stood exactly where he'd left her, a determined tilt to her cute little chin. He guessed she just wasn't finished with him yet, and braced himself for whatever further torture she had in mind.

"Mr. Walker," she began, and he had to admit she really looked sincere. In the dim light of the shop, her smooth white cheeks looked pink, and her eyes— what color were they, anyway?—glittered strangely, almost as if she were holding back tears. "I wish we might start over again. Both times we have met before, I'm afraid I haven't been at my best."

He had to agree with her there, at least about the first time. Passing out cold in the middle of the street wasn't likely to impress anyone, although Eben hadn't minded too much. With the world being the way it was, he would probably never again have the opportunity of holding Miss Isabel Forester's trim little body in his arms, at least not with her consent. It made a warm memory for a man who slept alone.

As for starting over, Eben knew only too well you couldn't go back and change things, no matter how much you might want to. Still, the idea intrigued him, and looking at Miss Isabel with her golden hair, and her pink lips, and her tiny waist was pleasant enough for him to want to prolong the moment, regardless of the consequences to his self-esteem. "If we could start over, what would you do different?" he asked at last.

Her astonishment amazed him, and he watched in wonder as her stiff shoulders sagged with what appeared to be relief. Then she smiled, a little shyly and more than a little uncertainly, as if she were afraid he might yet do something untoward.

"Well, first of all, I would say I'm very happy to meet you." Before he could guess what she was about, she stuck out her lily-white hand and closed the distance between them with several long, purposeful strides.

Stunned, he could only stare down at her hand as if he had no idea why it was there. In truth, he wasn't sure he did. He looked from her hand to her face. Her expression was hopeful, and she was still smiling. Her teeth were small and white, and he found himself wondering how she would taste if he swept the soft inner recesses of her mouth with his tongue.

Alarmed by the way his thoughts were going, he glanced down at her hand again. It was still there, small and expectant.

"I washed it, Mr. Walker," she said.

His gaze lifted to hers again, and he saw the mockery in her eyes. But it was self-mockery.

"I didn't wash mine," he warned, realizing he had unconsciously stuck his hands beneath his apron as if to hide them from her critical scrutiny.

"It really doesn't matter," she replied, and he saw she was telling the truth.

Slowly, still somewhat reluctant, he pulled his hand from beneath his apron and wiped it perfunctorily, if ineffectually, on his trouser leg. Painfully aware of the griminess of his palm, he cautiously touched it to hers, prepared to give her only a token handshake.

But once again Isabel Forester surprised him. She gripped his hand firmly, the way a man would have, although no one would ever mistake her delicate skin for a man's. At her touch, memories exploded in his head, the sensation of flesh against flesh, the ecstasy only a woman's velvet body could bring.

Blood roared to his head, and his body quickened, making him immensely glad his heavy leather apron hid this appalling reaction to her innocent gesture. "I'm..." He had to clear the hoarseness from his throat, and he tried for wryness. "I'm very glad to meet you, Miss Forester."

He'd intended the words as a joke, something to break the tension she had so unwittingly created, but he realized they really *were* meeting for the first time. He was a little surprised to find he thoroughly approved of Miss Isabel Forester.

Her smile wavered just a bit, as if she had also sustained a slight shock from the touch of their hands, but of course, that was just his imagination. "And I'm very glad to meet you, Mr. Walker."

Was her voice hoarse, too, or was it just the roaring in his ears?

For a long minute he pondered the question until he remembered he was still holding Miss Forester's hand. With great reluctance, and even greater regret, he released it.

She gave a nervous little laugh and laid her hand on her chest, right above her heart. He wouldn't mind putting his own hand there, where he could feel the life pumping through her, and the soft swell of her breasts. While he waited for her to think of something else to say, he spent a delicious moment imagining how it would feel to fill his hands with her yielding flesh.

"Amanda is really a lovely girl," she offered finally. "You must be very proud of her."

She'd said the one thing certain to distract him from his lecherous thoughts. "I wouldn't exactly say that," he hedged, thinking of the times lately when he'd been tempted to strangle the impudent little puss.

"Perhaps you're too humble to take credit for what you must feel is a gift from God," she went on, and listening to her, Eben realized her speaking voice was almost as lovely as her singing voice. A downright pleasure to listen to. "But I can see Amanda has been well brought up, and you must accept some responsibility for that."

Eben began to feel uneasy again. Miss Forester seemed intent on flattering him, and he couldn't imagine why she'd go to all the trouble. "I reckon you haven't seen her throw one of her fits," Eben remarked. "She's usually on her good behavior when she's at school."

To Eben's surprise, Miss Forester smiled knowingly. "Has she been making your life difficult?"

"I'm afraid so," he admitted ruefully, wishing the light were better in here so he could see the color of her eyes.

"I am, of course, interested in the welfare of all my students," she was saying, "and that extends to their family lives. If you're having problems with Amanda, I would be more than happy to help. I have quite a lot of experience with girls her age. Before I came here, I taught at a young ladies' finishing school, but you already know that since you are on the school board."

"Oh, yeah," he muttered, loath to admit he'd had no idea of her background when he'd voted to hire her. "Well, if you think you can do anything with her, go right ahead. She hardly ever talks to me anymore."

Plainly Miss Forester thought this a great tragedy, but Eben couldn't say he minded when the alternative was having sweet little Amanda throw one of her fits.

"Young girls often have a difficult time talking to their parents," she said, her lovely eyes awash with sympathy. "And it's probably more difficult for Amanda because she doesn't have a mother. She must miss her dreadfully."

"I doubt it. She never knew her mother," Eben said, wishing he could make the same claim.

Miss Forester's eyes widened, and Eben knew something of his attitude must have been evident to his visitor.

"Amanda was only a year old when her mother died," he hastily explained, deciding he'd better get off the subject of his departed wife before he let his true bitterness show and lost Miss Forester completely. "I really would be grateful for any help you can give me with Amanda. She . . . she needs a woman's hand," he added, surprised he'd thought of such a reasonable argument.

Miss Forester smiled up at him as if he'd given her a diamond or something. "Oh, thank you, Mr. Walker. I'll try to live up to your confidence in me. And I . . . I hope we can be friends," she added almost hesitantly.

"Well, sure," Eben replied, only too willing to make such a promise.

To his amazement, she blushed crimson. "I mean, we'll probably be working together since you're on the school board and everything. You're actually my employer."

The words were like a dash of cold water in his face, dousing all his stupid notions. Miss Isabel didn't want to be friends with Eben Walker. She wanted to be friends with her *boss*.

Suddenly this whole thing made sense, her determination to make up to him, her desire to mother his poor orphaned daughter. *She was worried about her job!*

The pain of realization was like a knife in his stomach. What an idiot he'd been to imagine she might be interested in him as a man!

When he didn't reply, she grew flustered. "Well, I . . . I guess I'd better let you get back to work," she said uncertainly.

"Yeah, that horse is getting tired of waiting," he said, surprised to hear how normal his voice sounded when fury boiled so violently inside him.

"I'm glad we had a chance to talk," she said tentatively, but he refused to respond, knowing he couldn't trust himself. "Well, I'll be seeing you."

"Yeah, sure."

"Good-bye."

"Good-bye."

Through narrowed eyes he watched her go. Hadn't he known what she was the minute she'd walked in here? Hadn't he told himself she was just like all the others? Just like dear departed Gisela, she was only interested in her own advantage, and she'd use Eben and anyone else who came along however it suited her. He supposed he should be grateful to Gisela for teaching him not to trust a female. The lesson was the only positive thing to have come from his disastrous marriage.

At least he'd found out about Miss Isabel Forester right up front, he told himself grimly, before he'd let himself have feelings for her. Now he'd be safe.

Chapter 5

All things considered, Isabel felt satisfied with her conversation with Mr. Walker. They were friends now. Mr. Walker had said so himself, and he had even sought her help in dealing with Amanda. Isabel's past experiences qualified her for nothing so much as handling the problems of young girls, so she felt more than equal to the task. And if in the course of her duties she occasionally had to consult with Mr. Walker, she would not find the association awkward.

Or would she? she wondered as she walked toward the Bartz house. When Isabel recalled the intensity of Eben Walker's dark eyes and the sensation of his callused palm against hers, she also recalled her shocking reaction to him.

It had been like hearing a particularly stirring piece of music, one that moved her soul and made her heart pound and brought tears to her eyes. Except Eben Walker didn't exactly make Isabel want to cry. Instead he stirred other, less familiar emotions, so unfamiliar, in fact, that Isabel couldn't even begin to understand what they were. A few times in his shop, she'd felt almost physically ill.

A quotation sprang to mind: "Love is a sickness full of woes, All remedies refusing."

Love? What on earth had brought that ridiculous thought to her mind? She certainly wasn't in love with Eben Walker. She hardly knew the man. And she had no intention of falling in love with anyone, now or ever. Useless emotions would waste her time and energy, and she had far more important things to do with her new life than spend it falling in love with a man. Which was, of course, just as well, since no man was likely to fall in love with her, either.

Bertha Bartz stood at her front door, frowning impatiently. "Did you get lost?" she asked with some concern.

"Didn't Carrie tell you? I stopped at the blacksmith's shop to speak with Mr. Walker," Isabel said as she mounted the porch steps.

Bertha's expression changed from worried to disapproving. "You're as bad as the kids, stopping off to watch him work."

"I . . . I wanted to let him know I'm available to help him with Amanda," Isabel explained, uncomfortable under Bertha's scrutiny.

Bertha's heavy eyebrows lifted. "That's real smart. I never figured you for a sly one."

"Sly? What are you talking about?" she asked as Bertha stepped aside so she could enter the house.

"Eben Walker, of course. He's probably the most eligible bachelor we've got in this town, and believe me, we've got a few. Nobody else ever noticed him before, though, and you've set your cap for him before you even got your clothes unpacked."

"Bertha!" Isabel exclaimed in genuine dismay. "I haven't set my cap for Mr. Walker."

Bertha gave her a skeptical look, turned on her heel, and headed down the hall toward the kitchen.

Isabel followed anxiously at her heels. When the kitchen door swung closed behind them, Isabel said, "Bertha, you can't think..." Her voice trailed off when she couldn't decide how to phrase her explanation.

"I can't think you came to Texas to find a husband?" Bertha finished for her, lifting a pot lid to examine the simmering contents. "I can, and I do. You picked a good place, too. You'll have plenty to choose from around here, so maybe you shouldn't settle on Eben just yet. He's probably the hardest one to snag, anyway; the way he's still pinin' for Amanda's mother."

Stunned, Isabel could only stare as Bertha gave the contents of the pot a cursory stir. Finally she asked the only thing that made any sense at all. "Is this some kind of joke?"

Bertha took a sip from the spoon. Satisfied, she replaced the pot lid and turned to Isabel with a frank smile. "Not unless you consider finding a husband a joke."

Isabel stared at her incredulously. "I can't believe you haven't noticed that I am well past the age when a woman considers such things."

"A woman only *stops* considering such things when she's six feet under the ground, Isabel, and I have a feeling you've got a lot of life left in you yet."

Isabel felt her cheeks burning with humiliation. "Well, I can't deny I've thought about it, but you're cruel to suggest any man might return my interest."

"Why shouldn't a man be interested in you?" Bertha asked in genuine surprise.

"Because..." Isabel hesitated, loath to list her shortcomings. Then she recalled her father's admonitions against pride. "Because I'm no longer young, I'm too skinny, and I'm not pretty."

"Pretty?" Bertha scoffed. "What good is pretty? It fades quick enough, and then what do you have left? I'll tell you what pretty gets you: the attention of a no-good saddle tramp like Johnny Dent, who's dead set on ruining poor Amanda Walker. No, a girl is better off to be plain. That way she'll only attract the good men."

"Or no men at all," Isabel said with more bitterness than she had intended.

"Pshaw!" Bertha exclaimed. "Look at me, plain as a post, and I've got a husband, and a rich one to boot."

"I could have had a husband, too, if I'd wanted one," Isabel blurted.

Bertha's wise eyes narrowed speculatively. "But you didn't want to marry a man you didn't love," she guessed.

"I didn't want to marry a man I didn't respect," she contradicted, recalling the two men who had offered for her so long ago. In those days she had still entertained girlish dreams of true love, so the thought of spending her life with a man she not only didn't love but didn't particularly like had seemed abhorrent. She was glad to realize the long, lonely years in between had not changed her attitude.

Bertha nodded sagely. "But you think you can respect Eben Walker."

"Eben Walker would never look at me twice!" Isabel exclaimed in frustration.

"You're probably right," Bertha said with humiliating frankness. "But not for the reasons you think. If Eben doesn't come around, it's because he's still grieving over his dead wife. But he's not the only man in these parts, and any one of them would be glad to have you. Hasn't anyone told you how difficult it is for us to keep a schoolteacher around here because the men are so desperate for wives?"

"No," Isabel admitted with a frown.

"Well, it is, but I want you to know we expect you to finish the term regardless of who proposes to you in the meantime," Bertha cautioned, wagging her finger in Isabel's face. "Maybe I should encourage you to flirt with Eben—that would guarantee you'd stay single longer."

"I'm sure you don't have to worry," Isabel replied stiffly. "You can't really believe anyone is going to propose to me ever."

Bertha sighed. "I'm very much afraid someone may propose to you on Saturday night."

"What's happening on Saturday night?"

"The dance. We're holding a dance in your honor to welcome you to town."

Isabel's heart sank. She had learned to hate all social events where men and women paired off in partners, because she always found herself on the bench with the aging matrons and the other "unclaimed blessings." Bertha's predictions of proposals notwithstanding, Isabel knew she would be extremely lucky if anyone even asked her to dance. She smiled wanly. "I promise to refuse any and all proposals I receive on Saturday night."

"I'm serious, Isabel," Bertha insisted. "I don't believe you understand the situation."

Isabel didn't think *Bertha* understood the situation, but she wasn't about to explain it any further. "Please, don't worry about me. I won't desert my students, whatever the temptation. Now," she continued, "what may I do to help with supper?"

"Oh, dear, you're not a good cook, too, are you?" Bertha said in dismay.

"What do you mean, 'too'?"

"I mean in addition to being able to sew your own clothes and sing like an angel."

"I've always enjoyed cooking," Isabel confessed, not certain why Bertha considered this bad news.

Bertha sighed again. "Oh, well, I suppose I should have guessed," she muttered. "You probably want to make some fancy dish for us."

"I could stir up a cake or a pie," Isabel offered, confused by her hostess's reluctance to accept the offer.

"The girls will want to help you," Bertha warned.

"I'd be glad for the company."

Bertha's massive bosom heaved, and she pointed to her pantry. "You should find everything you need in there. If not, send Carrie over to the store. I'll tell the girls."

Perplexed, Isabel watched her go. All in all, Isabel was certain this was the most confusing conversation she had ever had.

"Why do they call it pie if it's a cake?" Amanda asked as Isabel slid the round layers of Washington Pie into Bertha's oven. Carrie and her younger sister Julie watched in awe.

"I have no idea," Isabel replied with a smile. The girl had a smudge of flour on her adorable nose, which Isabel wiped off with a towel.

"Will you write the recipe down for me so I can make it myself?" Amanda asked.

"Certainly. I'll give it to you tomorrow in school."

Amanda smiled in obvious delight.

"Write it down for my mother, too," Carrie said, not to be left out.

"Perhaps you should all wait until you taste it before you decide whether you want the recipe or not," Isabel cautioned.

"I'll want it just because it's easy," Amanda informed her. Amanda had told her she did all the cooking for her father and herself, and kept house, too. The girl carried a heavy load, especially now that school was back in session.

"Shouldn't you be getting your own supper?" Carrie asked. "It's pretty late."

"I put some beans on this morning," Amanda said with a sigh. "I just wish I had some cake to serve with it."

"Why don't you come over after you eat so you can have some of this?" Carrie suggested.

"Yes, do," Isabel agreed, and Julie Bartz added her encouragement.

"Pa doesn't like me to go out in the evening," she hedged.

"Bring him along," Carrie said with a sly grin. "I know he'll want to sample Miss Forester's cake."

Isabel wanted to inform Carrie Bartz that she was wasting her time trying to play matchmaker with Isabel and the blacksmith, but she thought of Shakespeare's admonition, "The lady doth protest too much," and held her tongue. In any case, nothing would frustrate Carrie's matchmaking more quickly than to simply witness its abysmal failure. "Yes, bring your father, too," Isabel said guilelessly.

Amanda frowned, but she said, "I guess he can talk to Mr. Bartz or something."

By the time Amanda led her father into the Bartz's dining room a few hours later, Isabel was more than prepared to see him again. She smiled serenely when he nodded a stiff greeting, and no one would have guessed how hard her heart was pounding.

He looked freshly scrubbed. His mahogany hair lay smooth against his head, and his jaw appeared newly shaven. He wore work clothes, jeans and a shirt, but they were spotlessly clean. Although the shirt didn't cling to his body the way it had this afternoon, she could still clearly make out the outline of his broad shoulders beneath the fabric. Her stomach did a small flip.

"Amanda said she and the girls made some special dessert," he said to Bertha, who smiled benignly.

"Actually, Miss Forester made the cake. The girls only watched, but sit down and join us. We're all dying to taste it."

Herald pulled extra chairs to the table, putting Mr. Walker directly across from Isabel. Amanda sat at the other end, next to Carrie.

Bertha had gone back into the kitchen and now

returned, bearing Isabel's finished cake. The children "oooed" as she set it on the table.

"It's really nothing fancy," Isabel demurred. She glanced up, and caught Eben Walker's eye. To her surprise, he was frowning. Perhaps he didn't like sweets, she thought inanely.

Bertha began to slice the cake and pass the pieces around the table.

"What's in the middle?" Peter, the youngest Bartz boy, asked suspiciously.

"Applesauce," Isabel told him gently. "And sugar on the top."

Still looking suspicious, he pinched off a piece of cake and nibbled. "Mmmmm," he said, breaking into a smile.

"Use your fork," his mother cautioned. "And wait until everyone is served.

"Delicious, Miss Forester," Herald Bartz exclaimed. "It's a good thing you'll only be staying with us a week, or I'm afraid my waistline would suffer."

Isabel smiled politely, thinking Herald could use a little fattening up.

Bertha frowned in mock disapproval. "It's just as I feared, Herald," she told her husband down the length of the table. "In addition to her other talents, Miss Forester is an excellent cook. Don't you agree it's a tragedy, Eben?"

Eben Walker looked up in surprise. "What?"

He alone hadn't said a word about liking the cake, but Isabel noticed he'd already eaten half of it.

"I said it's a pity Miss Forester is also a good cook. I'm afraid once word gets out, some desperate bachelor will steal her from us, and we'll be without a teacher once more."

Walker looked down at his plate as if considering the truth of her statement, and Isabel held her breath, waiting for him to refute the claim. "I reckon it's a possibility, all right," he allowed after a moment.

"We must take every precaution to ensure that

doesn't happen," Bertha continued as if she didn't see the murderous glare Isabel was giving her. "Eben, I'm counting on you as a member of the school board to keep Miss Forester busy for as many dances as possible on Saturday night."

"Sure, I'll get Paul Young to help me," he agreed grimly.

"You most certainly will not. Paul Young is the most desperate bachelor we have." She bestowed another smile on Isabel, still ignoring her horrified expression. "I'm only trying to make it easier for you to keep your promise, my dear."

Walker's head snapped up. "What promise?" he asked suspiciously.

"Isabel promised to teach until the end of the term," Bertha informed him. "I'm counting on your help, Eben," she repeated.

Walker forked another hunk of cake, lifted it to his mouth, and chewed speculatively. After what seemed a long time, he said, "Well, I sure won't tell anybody how good this cake is."

Mercifully, Bertha turned the conversation in another direction, and Isabel allowed herself to breathe again. She even managed to choke down a few bites of cake, although in spite of the high praise it had received, it tasted like sawdust in her mouth. It was a wonder, she reflected, that no one had yet murdered Bertha Bartz.

When everyone had finished, Bertha said, "The girls will take care of the mess. Why don't we adults go into the parlor for a little visit. It's been a long time since you called on us, Eben."

Apparently only used on special occasions, the ornate parlor looked to Isabel more like a museum dedicated to displaying all the tasteless excesses of modern decor. Peacock feathers rested in an elephant's foot beside the tiled fireplace. On the mantel, an ebony winged Victory supported a clock on her head. On either side of her stood heavily prismed ruby glass candle holders, which matched the red velvet settee and chairs. Stuffed with horsehair and stylishly rigid in construction, the furniture offered little comfort. The red flocked wallpaper and heavily draped windows lent the room a funereal air that forbade cheerful conversation.

As the last person to enter the room, Isabel found the only seat left to her was on the settee beside Eben Walker. Since she knew this wasn't his choice either, she took her place gingerly, determined to make this as easy for him as possible. She only wished the settee had been longer, since Mr. Walker's large frame took up a great deal too much space and left her little room with which to create a discreet distance between them. Perching primly on the edge of the sofa, she feigned polite interest in the conversation and tried not to notice Eben Walker's masculine scent.

"Have you heard what Plimpton's up to?" Herald asked Walker.

"You aren't going to talk about those horrible sheep, are you?" Bertha interjected, but Isabel saw an opportunity to learn more about the subject.

"Oh, please do. My students mentioned the Plimpton boy today and said some awful things about his father. Why is everyone so upset?"

"Because he brought sheep into cattle country," Herald said, as if that explained everything.

"Can't the sheep survive here?" Isabel tried, hoping for a more thorough explanation.

"Oh, they can survive just fine," Herald assured her, "except they ruin the grass for the cattle."

"Only if they're allowed to overgraze," Walker contradicted him.

"But everybody knows their hooves tear up the ground, and they leave that god-awful smell behind, so cattle won't graze where they've been—"

"That smell goes away in a few hours," Walker informed him impatiently.

"You seem to know a lot about sheep, Mr. Walker,"

Isabel remarked. When he turned his dark gaze on her, she thought he looked wary again.

"I grew up in sheep country, Miss Forester."

"Back East?" she asked, wondering how he had acquired a Texas accent.

"No, right here in Texas. Although a lot of Texans don't like to admit it, we've had sheep here almost as long as we've had cattle."

"You're from Fredericksburg, aren't you?" Bertha asked. Isabel thought Walker stiffened, as if he were about to deny it, but Bertha didn't wait for an answer. "That's south of here, between Austin and San Antonio," she told Isabel.

"A lot of Germans settled in that area, and they aren't ashamed to raise sheep," Walker said.

"Well, they should be," Herald declared.

"You don't know a damn thing about it," Walker said in irritation, then seemed to remember where he was. "Excuse me, ladies, but I get a little tired of all this ignorance. Herald, I know it's not your fault. You're just repeating what you've been told by folks who know even less than you do."

"Eliminating ignorance is my job," Isabel said, "and I know the children are as guilty as anyone of spreading all these falsehoods about sheep. They spoke rather disparagingly of the Plimptons, too, and I'm afraid they might mistreat the Plimpton boy if he comes to school."

"If he's anything like his father, he won't give a . . . he won't care what the other kids say about him," Walker told her.

"But children can be terribly cruel. I can't imagine the Plimpton boy would be unaffected, and in any case, I don't see any reason why he should be subjected to prejudice unnecessarily. Perhaps if I could teach the children about sheep, I could eliminate some of the problem."

Walker's eyes narrowed, an expression she was beginning to recognize. "What do you care about the Plimpton kid? You've never even set eyes on him."

"Indeed, Isabel," Bertha said. "This really isn't your problem. You're only the schoolteacher."

"Exactly," Isabel told them. "Mr. Walker himself said the root of the whole problem is ignorance. Even an educated man like Mr. Bartz is misinformed on the subject."

Seeing Herald's preening response to her compliment, Isabel was glad for once that her father had trained her to be diplomatic.

"Miss Forester is right," Herald said, beaming at her. "All I know about sheep is what my customers tell me, and they're all cattlemen."

"But there must be some truth to their concerns," Bertha insisted.

"Like I said, if sheep aren't tended properly, they'll chew the grass right down to the roots and then tear up the bare ground with their hooves," Walker explained. "Plimpton's no fool, though. He's hired some Mexicans who really know what they're doing."

"Mr. Walker, do you have any books on sheepherding I could borrow?" Isabel asked, earning another dark look.

"No, I don't," he said sharply. "Sheepherders don't write books."

"I was only thinking that if I could educate myself on the subject, I would stand a far better chance of easing the Plimpton boy's entrance into school."

His eyes twinkled with what might have been amusement. "You really take this teaching business serious, don't you?"

Somewhat irritated by his condescension, Isabel lifted her chin. "Not all of us are fortunate enough to have a trade, Mr. Walker. Some of us must get by on our wits."

"You must do pretty well, then," he remarked, but before Isabel could decide what he meant, Bertha interrupted.

"You don't need a book, Isabel," she said with a triumphant smile. "Not when you have Eben right here. He can teach you everything you need to know."

Isabel felt the heat rising in her face. "I . . . I'm sure Mr. Walker doesn't have time for a project like that."

"He would if you boarded at his house next week," Bertha said.

Isabel stared at her in horror. She couldn't be serious. Isabel was afraid even to glance at Eben Walker for fear of what his reaction to the suggestion might be. Even worse was her fear that he might think she had put Bertha up to all this. "You . . . you can't expect me to board at the home of a single man," Isabel tried, wishing her voice sounded steadier.

"Oh, we worked that out a long time ago," Bertha assured her. "Each family has to board the teacher for a week, so when Eben has his turn, he stays at his shop. It's all very proper, even for a preacher's daughter. I'll just change the schedule so Eben has you next week."

Hearing no objection from Walker, Isabel hazarded a glance at him. To her surprise, he was smiling, a strange half smile that looked almost resigned.

"I reckon Amanda'll be real pleased to hear the news," Walker said, rising from his seat. "I'll wait until I get her home before I tell her, though," he added. "Thanks for the cake, Bertha. Miss Forester."

Before Bertha could object, he was through the parlor door and calling his daughter from the kitchen. Bertha and Herald hurried to see them out, while Isabel sat where she was, slightly stunned by the whole proceeding. How had her life gotten so completely out of her control?

Isabel had little time to brood over the upcoming trials of the Saturday night dance and her future stay at the Walker home. At school the next day she encountered two entirely new and more immediate concerns. The first arrived early in the morning in the most unusual conveyance Isabel had ever seen.

The vehicle looked like a buggy without the top, and was really nothing more than a boxy seat on large wheels. Painted bright green and striped with vermilion, it was pulled by a smart-looking horse. The three passengers, a man, a woman, and a boy, were all dressed as if they were attending an important social event.

The man and boy were built exactly alike, short and stout. On their identical plump bodies they wore identical black broadcloth suits, snow-white shirts, cravats with stick pins, and bowler hats. The woman, equally plump, wore a heliotrope gown of corded silk that had been styled by the hand of an expert, and a perfectly wonderful hat perched on her carefully pomaded hair. White lace frothed at her throat and cuffs, and she carried a matching parasol to shade her delicate complexion from the harsh Texas sun.

The man called, *"Hallo!"* as he reined the vehicle to a halt in the schoolyard. "I say, you must be the new teacher."

Isabel nodded, inspiring the round little man to bellow with delighted laughter. An Englishman, she thought, noting his accent and his pale complexion and rosy cheeks. The few children who had arrived for school gathered under the redbud tree to watch.

The man set the brake on the strange wagon and jumped down with surprising nimbleness. The boy followed while the man assisted the lady. As the three of them walked toward Isabel, smiles lifting their doughy faces, Isabel realized they reminded her of dumplings. The absurd thought made her want to laugh, but she managed to maintain her decorum.

"Oliver Plimpton here," the man said, removing his bowler to reveal hair as golden, if not as plentiful, as his wife's. He sketched a brief bow in Isabel's direction. "My wife, Rosemary, and my son, Barclay."

She should have known. "I'm pleased to meet

you," Isabel said, shaking hands all around. "I'm Isabel Forester. I was wondering why Barclay wasn't in school yesterday."

"Would have been except no one told us you'd arrived. Bit of an outcast, you know, what with the sheep and all. Dashed nuisance, but there you are."

"I'm so glad you're here, Barclay," Isabel said, welcoming him with a warm smile. "How old are you?"

"Thirteen," the boy said, pulling himself up to his full, if insignificant, height. He didn't smile back.

"How much formal schooling have you had?"

"Barclay always studied with a tutor until we came to America," Mrs. Plimpton said, lifting a fragile handkerchief to her eyes as if the thought of coming to America distressed her. "Of course, it's impossible to find a tutor in this godforsaken country."

"Now, Mrs. P.," Plimpton soothed. "Miss Forester seems just the thing. Not a tutor, of course, but jolly good all the same, eh, what?"

Mrs. Plimpton leaned closer to Isabel. "The other children don't like Barclay."

"Mother!" Barclay cried, aghast.

"Don't worry," Isabel told them both. "I've already heard all about the sheep, and I assure you I have no intention of letting my students display any prejudice toward your son."

Mrs. Plimpton frowned uncertainly, but Mr. Plimpton rubbed his hands together and gave a booming laugh. "What did I tell you, Mrs. P.? Just the thing."

"Mr. Plimpton, if you don't mind my asking," Isabel said, "why *did* you bring sheep to this country when the residents object so strenuously?"

He looked genuinely puzzled. "Free country, eh, what? Man can do whatever he wants with his own land. Wouldn't dream of telling these dashed ranchers what to do with theirs."

"I see," Isabel said, and she was beginning to think she did. Last night Eben Walker had told her Oliver Plimpton didn't care what other people thought, and he had been only too right. "Well, I'll do whatever I can to make sure Barclay enjoys my class."

Barclay frowned, but his parents seemed relieved and quickly took their leave. As she watched them mounting their eccentric conveyance, she asked, "What is that thing?"

"A dog cart," Barclay replied stiffly, as if that explained everything.

"Is it supposed to be pulled by dogs?" Isabel asked in amazement.

"Oh, no," Barclay assured her, and for the first time he looked as if he might smile. "It's used for hunting. The dogs ride in a box underneath the seat."

Isabel liked his accent. He obviously had taken great pains to adopt the characteristic Texas drawl, and the combination of British and Texan lent his speech a fascinating flavor. Before she could induce him to speak again, however, the children in the yard started barking.

Barking? Isabel looked over to find Roger Stevens and the three Bartz boys, Herald Jr., David, and Peter, yapping like a pack of dogs.

"What on earth . . . ?" she murmured aloud, and when she looked to Barclay for an explanation, she saw his face had turned scarlet.

"Bark, bark, bark-ly!" the boys howled. "Bark, bark, bark-ly has lost his sheep and doesn't know where to find them—"

"Herald! Roger! The rest of you, get over here at once," Isabel shouted, hoping her tone approximated the one she'd heard Eben Walker use to such effect yesterday.

They raced over, still grinning, apparently unaware of Isabel's fury. "What is the meaning of this?" she demanded when they had skidded to a halt in front of her.

"This is the sheepherder we told you about, Miss Forester," Roger said blithely.

"And does the fact that his father raises sheep give you the right to make fun of him?" Isabel asked.

The boys' smiles faded, and none of them replied.

"Perhaps Barclay should make fun of all of you because your fathers *don't* raise sheep," she suggested.

"That's silly," Roger protested.

"Why is it silly? Perhaps sheep are infinitely superior to cattle."

"They are," Barclay said, and Roger lunged for him. Isabel caught him.

"You'll be awfully sorry if you get into a fight," Isabel warned before turning him loose again. He stared up at her defiantly, but he made no further move toward Barclay.

"I'm not afraid of them, Miss Forester," Barclay said.

"Of course you aren't. Why would anyone be afraid of such ignoramuses?"

"Ignor-what?" Roger said, knowing instinctively he had been insulted.

"Ignoramus. It means a person who is ignorant."

"We're not stupid," Herald Bartz protested.

"I didn't say you were stupid. I said you were ignorant. Stupidity is an accident of nature, and you can't do anything about it. Ignorance is a temporary condition. It means you simply don't know something."

"We know a lot of things," Roger insisted.

"I'm sure you do, but you don't know a thing about sheep," Isabel said, acutely aware she was quoting Eben Walker.

"I know they stink and they ruin the grass."

"They do not!" Barclay cried.

"Since I know you boys have no desire to be ignorant, I'm going to give you the opportunity to improve yourselves. As punishment for your rude behavior to Barclay, I want you each to write a five-hundred-word essay on the ways in which sheep are superior to cattle."

"What!" they all shouted in outrage.

"They *ain't* superior to cattle," Roger informed her, "so how can we write that they are?"

"Are you so sure? Obviously Mr. Plimpton believes they are, or he wouldn't have braved his neighbors' disapproval to bring them here."

"Five hundred words!" David wailed.

"Yes, five hundred words, and I suggest you try to find some people who know a lot about sheep to give you some ideas."

"I won't do it," Roger said. "You can't make me."

"No, but I can inform your parents that you have defied me and failed to do an assignment. Will they be pleased?" The boys' frown told her she had struck a nerve.

"But who can we talk to?" Herald asked.

Isabel smiled tolerantly. "I'm sure if you give the matter some thought, you'll think of an answer. Now go back to your play, and remember, no more name-calling."

The three bigger boys drifted away, scuffing their feet and casting Isabel black looks over their shoulders, but young Peter Bartz didn't move.

"Miss Forester?" he said to draw her attention.

"Yes, Peter?"

"I don't even *know* five hundred words."

"Oh, yes, I'd forgotten, you're only six," she said, hiding her smile. "You may give your report orally, then."

"What's 'orally'?"

"Out loud, in a speech to the class."

His stricken look told her that was the worst punishment of all. "And I'll make all the others read theirs to the class, too," she added.

Somewhat placated, Peter followed the others out into the yard. Pleased with herself, Isabel turned to Barclay Plimpton, whose pale blue eyes had turned storm-cloud gray. "I don't think they'll be calling you names anymore," she said by way of comfort.

"Perhaps not," he replied coldly, "but they'll hate me worse than ever."

Isabel's second problem arrived during the lunch break. The children were engaged in a game of hide and seek. Isabel was sitting on the school steps, watching, when she noticed a boy lurking on the edge of the corral.

At first she thought he must be one of the hiders, then she realized she didn't recognize him. Curious, she rose from her place and walked closer. The boy stood half-hidden by one of the posts of the corral, and he peered warily at her. She guessed he must be eleven or twelve. His lanky legs stuck out several inches below his ragged pants. His equally ragged shirt hung loose on his slender frame, and his hands and face were almost as dirty as his bare feet.

"Hello," Isabel said, instinctively speaking softly, as if to a wild animal.

Still wary, the boy stared up at her, his gray eyes darting as if looking for sources of danger.

"What's your name?" she asked.

His wiry body stiffened, but he didn't reply.

"Aren't you supposed to be in school?"

"I don't go to school," the boy said, looking past her at the children at play. Isabel saw longing in those gray eyes.

"Why not?"

The small mouth tightened. "My pa . . . My pa says book learning is a waste of time."

"I see," Isabel said. "And who is your father?"

"His name's . . . Will Potts," the boy admitted reluctantly.

"What does your father do for a living?"

The boy's chin went up a notch. "He's the swamper over at the Dream."

Isabel blinked. Swamper? The Dream? Neither

word held any meaning for her. "What is the 'Dream'?"

"Dave's Dream, the saloon," he told her. "Don't you know nothin'?"

"Oh, and your father owns the saloon," she guessed, thinking that explained everything. Only a man depraved enough to sell spirits would allow his child to run ragged and forbid him to attend school.

"No, I told you, he's the swamper."

"Oh, yes, so you did," Isabel said, still confused. "Perhaps if I spoke with your father, he would—"

"No!" the boy cried in genuine alarm. "Don't you talk to him. Don't tell him I was here, or he'll have my hide!"

Before Isabel could protest, the boy was gone, running like a deer through the field behind the school until he disappeared into the undergrowth.

When she turned back to the yard, she saw the children had stopped their game to watch. She hurried over to them.

"Does anyone know who that boy was?"

"That's Larry Potts," Carrie Bartz informed her importantly. "His father's a drunk."

"Carrie, what an awful thing to say," Isabel scolded.

Carrie's homely face flushed with mortification, but she stood her ground. "He is. Ask anybody."

The rest of the children murmured their assent.

"He said . . . That is, does anyone know what a 'swamper' is?" Isabel asked after a moment.

"His pa cleans up the saloon every night," Roger Stevens offered. "At least he does when he's able to work."

"Does Larry have a mother?"

"No, she's dead," another child said.

"Where does he live?"

"They've got a dugout down by the creek," Roger said.

"But you mustn't think of going down there," Amanda warned with a worried frown.

"Oh, no," Carrie agreed.

"Course, if you do, you won't need no directions on how to find it," Roger reported happily. "You can *smell* it a mile away!"

This information sent the other children into gales of laughter, which Isabel was unable to suppress. She left them to return to their play. Tonight she would talk to Bertha and Herald and find out what they knew about the Pottses.

"Sounds mighty sweet," Paul Young remarked from the doorway of the blacksmith shop.

Eben looked up from the tool he was repairing. "Me pounding iron?" he guessed with a grin.

"Don't be an ass," Paul chided. "I mean the singing from over at the church."

In the silence they could both hear the children's voices raised in a hymn of praise, and the drone of the organ supporting them. They'd been practicing after school for three days now.

"Course, I prefer hearing Isabel sing alone," Paul said.

"She give you permission to call her by her Christian name?" Eben asked, more irritated than he cared to admit at hearing Paul refer to her so familiarly.

"Not yet," Paul replied confidently. "After the dance tomorrow night, I reckon she will, though."

"You got something planned I ought to hear about?"

"I can't imagine why you'd need to know," Paul said, striding to the anvil where Eben had been working.

"So I can get you out of town ahead of the lynch mob."

Paul gave a shout of laughter. "I merely intend to make Miss Forester aware of my admiration for her person."

"Seems like I remember you saying she looked like a horse," Eben said sourly.

"You know I only said that before I saw her. Fact is, she's a mighty handsome woman. *I* remember *you* saying so, too."

Eben wasn't about to admit it. "She's not bad . . . for her age."

Paul frowned, and for a moment Eben thought he'd inadvertently managed to put a damper on Paul's enthusiasm for the new schoolteacher. But only for a moment.

"I admit she's a little long in the tooth, but she sure don't look it. I suppose women don't dry up as fast back East. Anyway, if she cooks half as good as I've heard—"

"Where'd you hear about her cooking?" Eben asked sharply.

"Why, from Herald. He's been bragging to everybody how good he's been eating all week what with Miss Isabel in the kitchen."

Eben shook his head, wondering what Bertha would do to her poor husband if she found out about his treachery.

"I can't believe you haven't heard," Paul added.

"Oh, Herald didn't have to tell me a thing," Eben said maliciously. "I've eaten over there a time or two myself this week."

"What!" Paul exclaimed. "You sneaky, underhanded . . . Why didn't you tell me?"

"Bertha swore me to secrecy," Eben said with feigned innocence.

"And you figured if the rest of us didn't know, we wouldn't be so anxious to steal her away from you," Paul accused.

"She isn't mine to steal," Eben insisted, not bothering to analyze why the admission irritated him so. After all, she was a conniving little witch, wasn't she? If Paul wanted her, he could have her.

"Maybe she isn't yours yet, but a blind man can see you've got your eye on her."

"Are you crazy?" Eben demanded, and to his surprise, Paul grinned again, a smug, knowing grin.

"That's it, isn't it?" Paul murmured, as if to himself.

"What's it?" Eben asked uneasily.

"Little Miss Isabel's got to you, hasn't she?"

"What are you talking about?"

"Who would've thought a prim little old maid could get you all hot and bothered?"

"You're a jackass," Eben said in disgust, but Paul only laughed again.

"You're not blushing, are you?" Paul asked, pretending to peer more closely at Eben's face. "Or maybe your comb's just turning red, you randy old rooster."

"I never would've thought a 'prim little old maid' could get you all bothered, either," Eben said in self-defense.

"Oh, I'm not bothered exactly," Paul said smugly. "I've been thinking more about what a comfortable life a man would have with a woman like Miss Isabel to cook and clean for him. Although," he continued, teasing, "I've got to admit a warm bed's even more attractive than a hot meal. All that honey-colored hair spread across the pillow . . ."

"*Paul*," Eben said in warning, and Paul raised both hands in surrender.

"All right, but it does make a pretty picture."

Too pretty, for Eben's peace of mind. The image had already troubled his dreams more than once during the past few nights.

From outside they could hear the shouts of children as they emerged from the church.

"Choir practice must be over," Paul observed, wandering back to the open doorway to watch. "Good God, is that the Plimpton kid?"

Eben grinned in spite of himself. "Yeah, Amanda

said Miss Forester finally convinced his parents to let him wear jeans to school like the other boys."

"I hardly recognized him without his monkey suit. Hey, the kids are going for their horses," Paul said in surprise. "Don't they stop by here on their way home anymore?"

"Since she started choir practice the other day, they don't have time, although Roger Stevens and the Bartz boys came in the other day to find out what I knew about sheep."

"They came by my place, too. Course, I don't know a damn thing about sheep. What made them so all-fired curious about woollybacks, anyway?"

"Miss Forester," Eben informed him. "Seems she's making them do reports on the subject."

"On sheep?" he asked incredulously. "I'll be damned." His gaze drifted back out toward the street, and Eben guessed he was watching for Miss Isabel so he could intercept her.

"Was there some reason you stopped by this afternoon?" Eben asked with a trace of sarcasm.

"What? Oh, yeah, I wanted to tell you the horseshoes you ordered are in."

"Good, I'll get them first thing tomorrow."

"Fine," Paul said absently, his attention still on the street. Just as Isabel's small figure emerged from the church, he murmured his farewell and left. Eben noted with disgust that he was heading for the church.

With a sigh, Eben turned to his forge and caught the slightest movement from the corner of his eye. Glancing toward the back door, he saw the ragged figure of Larry Potts sidling inside.

"You got any work for me today?" the boy asked almost belligerently, but Eben wasn't fooled. He knew how desperate Larry was and guessed that the nickle he paid the boy for sweeping up would probably buy what supper he had tonight.

"Sure. I'll be done here in a minute. You can start

sweeping over there." Eben pointed to the far side of the shop and returned to work. Larry would likely bolt if Eben paid him too much attention.

Eben had just finished banking the fire in the forge when a sweetly familiar voice called his name. He turned to find Isabel Forester standing in the doorway, holding her schoolbooks to her chest. The sight of her trim figure outlined by the setting sun sent a swift jolt of pleasure through him, but he quickly reminded himself she hadn't come to be admired.

"Miss Forester," he replied, automatically brushing his hands on his pant legs. "Did your horse throw another shoe?"

She smiled a little at his jest. "You know perfectly well I don't have a horse, Mr. Walker." She came inside a few steps, looking around.

"None of your students are here, if that's what you're after," he said, feeling inordinately pleased that she'd given Paul Young such short shrift and that Paul would have seen her coming directly to him.

"I thought I saw Larry Potts," she said, peering into the shadows.

Calling himself a fool for feeling disappointed, Eben glanced around. The broom the boy had been using lay in the middle of the floor, but there was no sign of him. "He spooks easy," Eben explained, wishing he could get close enough to smell her.

"Does he come in here often?"

"A couple times a week," Eben said, wondering why a conniving witch would be so interested in Larry Potts's comings and goings. "He sweeps up, and I give him a nickle or two. He won't take charity," he added, seeing her frown.

"I don't suppose he will," she said. "Did you know his father won't allow him to attend school?"

Eben shrugged. "I'm not surprised. Will Potts is an ornery cuss."

"I thought perhaps I should try speaking to Mr. Potts and—"

"I wouldn't," Eben said in alarm, trying in vain to picture the neat Miss Forester and the wild and woolly Will Potts holding a civil conversation.

"Bertha advised against it, too," she said, still frowning.

Eben liked the tiny crease between her eyebrows. Paul was right; she hadn't dried up at all. In fact, her skin looked satin-smooth, but, of course, Eben would have to be satisfied with imagining how it might feel beneath his callused fingers. "You may've convinced Oliver Plimpton to let Barclay wear jeans, but you won't get Will Potts to send his son to school, Miss Forester. The boy's probably not worth your trouble, anyway."

"How can you say such a thing? Just because he's poor doesn't mean he won't amount to something. Abraham Lincoln was poor, and he grew up to be president of the United States."

Eben rolled his eyes. "I'd be a little careful of using Lincoln for an example around here," he advised. "Some folks still carry a grudge about the late unpleasantness, you know."

"Oh, dear," she said, her distress a delight to behold. "I'm terribly sorry. I hope I didn't offend—"

"You didn't offend me. I grew up with a lot of Yankee sympathizers, but like I said, some folks are still a little touchy."

She smiled her gratitude, and Eben's breath snagged in his chest. She came pretty close to beautiful when she smiled, and Eben found it increasingly difficult to remember why he hadn't liked her before.

"Thank you for the advice," she said. Her expression grew thoughtful, and Eben felt a slight sense of foreboding.

"I don't suppose you know Mr. Potts well enough to—"

"No, I don't," Eben assured her. "In any case, I wouldn't try to tell another man how to raise his son. Why should it matter to you whether Larry comes to school or not? Seems like you've already got plenty of other kids to worry about."

She fiddled with the books she held, then met his gaze squarely. "Every child deserves an education, Mr. Walker. If he then chooses to make a failure of his life, that is his decision, but he should at least have a choice in the matter."

Eben could only stare, stirred as he was by his own memories of a man who had taken an interest in a ragged orphan boy and taught him blacksmithing. Oddly enough, Isabel Forester reminded him of Gunther Pfeister, with her determination to salvage poor little Larry Potts. Maybe Eben had misjudged her when he'd decided she was only interested in herself.

The silence stretched between them, and Eben sensed her reluctance to leave even though they'd apparently finished their conversation. "Was that the only thing you wanted?"

She looked a little embarrassed. "I suppose it was." She started to turn toward the door.

Eben could have cursed his brusqueness. He hadn't meant to send her on her way. He said the first thing that popped into his head. "I was starting to think you're like all the other girls who come in here wanting me to make them a ring."

As he'd hoped, she smiled again. "How did you guess? And you're very sweet to offer, because I was too shy to ask you outright."

Eben thought she was teasing him. He couldn't believe she really wanted a piece of junk like that.

"It's just a horseshoe nail," he reminded her.

"Could I order one?"

"No," he said, and instantly regretted it when he saw her disappointment. "I mean, you don't need to order it because it only takes a minute to make one."

"Could you do it now?"

He glanced at his forge. The coals were still hot.

He could have them roaring again in a few seconds. "Sure."

She smiled again, and Eben knew he'd have agreed to hammer out a coach and four horses if she'd asked him to. Maybe she really was a witch. Still, if he was going to do something for her, he might as well get something in return.

"I'll have to measure your finger," he lied. He'd made so many of these, he could pretty much guess how big to make it.

"Oh, certainly," she agreed, coming forward.

"You can put your books on the anvil," he suggested, and was gratified to see she didn't hesitate. He'd half expected her to want it wiped off first, but apparently she wasn't as fastidious as he'd thought.

Her books disposed of, she faced him with an expectant smile. She stood no more than an arm's length away. Eben could smell the fresh, floral scent of her hair and see the fine, smooth texture of her skin. He had a sudden and wholly unexpected urge to take her in his arms.

"Is something wrong?" she asked, apparently sensing his appalled reaction to his desire.

"Oh, no," he assured her hastily. What had he gotten himself into? "I need your hand."

"Oh, yes, of course." She held it out.

This was what he'd wanted, to touch her again, but when he reached for her hand, he saw once more the contrast between his own blackened fingers and her immaculate ones. How could she bear for him to touch her?

When he took her fingers, though, she didn't flinch. Her skin was even softer than he remembered, her hand fragile and delicate, the hand of a lady. She was everything that he was not, educated and cultured, genteel, and most of all, innocent. He had no right to touch her with hands that bore the stains of worse things than the labor he did, no right at all.

She released her breath in a trembling sigh, and

when he glanced up, he saw her cheeks were flushed, her pink lips slightly parted, as if in invitation. Desire surged in him like a molten tide, and for an instant he could almost feel her body pressed against his, her soft, sweet mouth yielding to his own.

"Don't you need to measure my finger?" she asked, startling him. For a minute he couldn't think what she was talking about, then he remembered.

"Uh, no," he said, dropping her hand instantly, guiltily. Could she see what he'd been thinking? Was that why she was blushing? He turned away so she couldn't see any more and reached for a pair of tongs. "I just needed to see it closer."

Digging into the pocket of his apron, he pulled out a handful of nails and took great pains to select the best one.

Isabel laid the hand he had been holding against her midriff and covered it with her other hand, as if she could somehow retain the sensation of his flesh against hers. It had been so startling, so much more exciting than the last time when they had shaken hands, that she hadn't wanted it to end. Even now, her hand felt tingly, alive.

She watched, fascinated, as he inserted the nail in the tongs and carried it to the forge. He did something to the fire and pumped the bellows, his muscles rippling as he made the sparks fly. In a minute or two, he withdrew the nail, and she saw it was red-hot. For some reason, she felt awfully warm, too.

He moved gracefully for such a large man, and she couldn't seem to take her eyes off his hands as he twisted the tiny nail skillfully around the end of a small metal cone to form a ring. She remembered the way those hands had felt, rough yet gentle, against her bare skin. And when he'd held her hand, she'd been unable to breathe. Suddenly she realized she wasn't breathing now, and forced herself to inhale the rarified air. With it came his scent, musky and male, so different from anything in her experience, and she recalled the first time she had noticed it, the day he'd carried her from the stage and laid her on Carrie Bartz's bed. Her knees went weak at the memory.

He examined the ring, holding it up with the tongs, and, apparently satisfied, plunged it into the slack tub. The hiss of the steam startled her, and she realized she wasn't breathing again.

When he turned back to her, he was drying the ring with an old rag. His smile looked strained. "See, I told you it would only take a minute." He tossed the rag aside, held the ring up to show her it was finished, then held it out for her.

She should have just taken it and been satisfied that their fingertips might have brushed once more. Instead, she responded to some mysterious instinct and held her hand out, palm down, fingers splayed, in silent invitation for him to slip it on himself.

Eben blinked in surprise. She couldn't mean for him to . . . ? But when he looked into her eyes, he saw the mischievous glint, the silent challenge. She was a witch, he was sure of it now, and she was bent on torturing him. But it was such sweet torture. He took her hand, savoring the feel of her silken palm against his, and slipped the crude ring onto her finger. It fit perfectly.

"Well," she said. She sounded breathless, but perhaps she was only surprised. Her eyes glittered in the dim light, and he wanted to pull her closer so he could look down into them and watch them darken with desire just before he kissed her.

"Thank you," she whispered, breaking the spell.

He released her hand at once. "No trouble," he said, his voice slightly hoarse. He cleared his throat.

She held her hand up and admired the ring as if it had been a diamond. "You do very nice work, Mr. Walker."

"Better not wear it too long," he warned gruffly. "It'll turn your finger black."

"I don't mind," she replied, and he could almost believe she didn't.

Once again they stared at each other in silence, aware that she no longer had a reason for lingering.

"I guess I'd better be going," she said after a moment.

"I was just getting ready to close up."

She nodded and reached for her books. When she had them settled against her side, she glanced around again and apparently caught sight of Larry's broom still lying in the middle of the floor. "You won't forget to tell Larry I was asking about him, will you?"

Eben shook his head. "I'll tell him, but I still think you're wasting your time with him," he finally said. "Larry's not the type of kid to sit still long enough to learn anything."

She smiled again, and Eben felt a strange sensation in the general area of his heart. "I would at least like the opportunity to try. Can I count on you to give him a word of encouragement?"

"I guess so," Eben allowed, more than a little surprised at his own willingness. "That is, if you haven't scared him off for good."

"Thank you, Mr. Walker. You really are a very kind man."

"Not likely," Eben muttered. If she knew the things he'd done, she'd probably never speak to him again. But then, she didn't ever need to find that out, did she?

"What was that, Mr. Walker?"

"I said, you'll save me the first dance tomorrow night, won't you?" he heard himself saying.

Chapter 6

"Pa, aren't you ready yet?" Amanda called impatiently from the front room.

"Just about," Eben replied, checking his appearance one last time in his shaving mirror. He supposed he looked as good as he ever would. He'd slicked back his hair so it would remain neat throughout the evening. Not that he expected to do a lot of dancing, but a man couldn't be too careful.

He checked the place on his chin where he'd nicked himself shaving. At least it had finally stopped bleeding. Of course, a short woman would be looking right at it when he danced with her, and Eben hadn't forgotten he'd claimed Isabel Forester for the first dance.

His chin wasn't his only concern, either. He'd scrubbed his hands with lye soap until they were raw, but he'd still been unable to get them truly clean. Then he'd rubbed them with a mixture of butter, oil of organum, and iodine to soften them, but they'd still feel rough to a lady.

Eben swore softly when he realized he was already sweating beneath his black suit. He felt as nervous as a schoolboy preparing for his first dance. What had come over him?

"*Pa*," Amanda wailed.

"Coming," he said, giving his string tie one last adjustment before blowing out the lamp.

Amanda stood in the center of the room, her arms crossed, her foot tapping, her pretty face puckered into a pout. At the sight of her, Eben froze, stunned at how much she resembled Gisela. The same bright gold curls, the same sky-blue eyes, the same expression of discontent.

"What took you so long?" she demanded; then, with one of the mood swings that always left him baffled, her discontent vanished and she smiled beatifically. "How do I look?"

She spun around for his inspection.

"Is that a new dress?" he asked, feeling slightly confused by the change in her.

"No, silly, it's the same dress I wear every Sunday, but Miss Forester helped me make these bows." She fingered the pale blue satin lovingly. It matched her eyes. "Don't you think I look pretty?" she insisted.

He suddenly realized what had disturbed him. Breasts? When had Amanda grown breasts? And why hadn't he ever noticed? Good God, she was just a baby. Why did she need breasts? "Yeah, you look real pretty," he murmured, aghast.

Something flickered in her eyes, and her frown returned. "Let's go. We're already late," she snapped, and turned on her heel in a swish of skirts.

She was out the door before Eben could put out the lamp.

As she sat in front of Carrie Bartz's dressing table mirror, Isabel could hear the music from the dance wafting in the partially opened window. The fiddles weren't in tune, a situation that suited her own mood exactly.

"You look real pretty, Miss Forester," Carrie assured her. Carrie had worked on Isabel's hair for an hour, crimping it with the curling iron until it stood out around her face like a golden aureole. Even Isabel had to admit the effect was striking. If Isabel had only possessed the beauty to go with it, Carrie's labors might have been rewarded.

Unfortunately, the face staring back at her from the mirror was the same one she had been looking at for the past twenty-nine years, and no one in his right mind would find it beautiful. Still, she smiled gamely, knowing that the combination of her invisible-green gown and Carrie's handiwork made her look as pretty as she ever had. "Thank you, Carrie. You did a wonderful job on my hair."

"You're welcome, Miss Forester," Carrie said, blushing.

"Now you'd better do your own."

"My hair's done," Carrie said, her pleased smile vanishing.

"Oh, well, so it is," Isabel stammered, wishing she had the skill to transform homely Carrie the way Carrie had transformed her. "I've been so worried about mine, I never even noticed. You look lovely, and that dress is exactly the right shade of pink for you."

At least Isabel could give an honest compliment there. Both Carrie and Amanda had begun to wear only those colors Isabel deemed best for them, and Carrie had benefitted greatly.

"We'd better go," Carrie said. "The rest of the family is waiting for us downstairs."

"Yes, of course," Isabel said. How she dreaded the evening to come. She only hoped she would be allowed to slip out early so she wouldn't have to stay the entire night watching others enjoying themselves, while she sat there, ignored and alone.

At least she had the first dance to look forward to,

she thought as she collected her fan and handkerchief, then followed Carrie downstairs. She'd hardly
been able to believe it when Eben Walker had re-
quested the first dance of the evening.

Of course, she had no illusions that he'd asked her
for any other reason than kindness. Still, he would
save her the humiliation of having to sit out even the
very first dance. Her heart fluttered again, and this
time she knew it was from anticipation.

"Well worth the wait," Herald Bartz declared when
Isabel and Carrie had descended the stairs. He
glanced at his wife. "Maybe we ought to put a bag
over her head, my dear."

Bertha pulled herself up to her prodigious height
and glared down at her diminutive spouse. "Nothing
will help now that you have told every living soul
within a hundred miles what a good cook she is. I
only hope no one tries to carry her off tonight."

"Can we go now?" Herald Jr. demanded impatiently, ending all further discussion.

"Certainly," Bertha decreed, and the children
surged for the door, not waiting for the adults, who
followed more sedately.

Outside, the air was crisp and cool, and the scent
of wildflowers floated to them on the evening breeze.
The music was louder here, carried on that same
breeze from the schoolhouse, which had been transformed for the night into a social hall.

"Have you got all your dances promised?" Bertha
inquired as they crossed the street in the wake of the
children, who had already reached the schoolyard.

"Only the first one," Isabel said, then remembered
her strange encounter yesterday with Paul Young.
"Oh, and Mr. Young asked me to save him a waltz."

"I'm going to poleax that man," Bertha muttered.

"Shouldn't I dance with him?" Isabel asked, knowing she dared not give offense because of her position
in the community.

"You can dance with him if you want to, but don't

pay any attention to his nonsense. And when did you see him to promise him a dance?"

"Yesterday when I was walking home after choir practice. We met in the street."

"There she is!" someone in the schoolyard yelled, then everyone was pointing and shouting. At first Isabel assumed they were pointing at Bertha and Herald, although she couldn't imagine why anyone would be so rude, until Bertha took her arm and propelled her through the gathering crowd.

"Easy now, fellows," Bertha cautioned, "at least wait until she gets inside."

What? Isabel couldn't believe her ears. They were pointing at *her*, at plain old Isabel Forester, who had never attracted the slightest attention unless she happened to be singing too loudly. Was her petticoat showing? Had she committed some other social transgression? Then why . . . ?

"Save me a dance, Miss Forester."

"Me, too, miss."

"I want a waltz."

"I'll take a reel if I can't get anything else."

Before Isabel could begin to absorb the meaning of all this, she was inside the crowded hall. All the desks had been removed, and the benches had been moved to line the walls. Men and women mingled around the periphery of the room, while a few children shuffled about on the dance floor to the squawking cacophony of the out-of-tune fiddlers.

The instant Isabel entered, the music screeched to a halt. All the people in the hall turned their attention to her, and horror of horrors, they began to applaud!

Her face flaming, Isabel could only stare and try to keep her mouth from falling open. Then, from nowhere, Eben Walker appeared and offered his arm. Mechanically she took it, not knowing or caring where he might take her, just grateful to see a face she knew and trusted.

He led her to the center of the floor, the very last

place she wanted to be, and turned her in to his arms, the place she discovered she most wanted to be. His palm felt rough against hers, hard and masculine, just the way she remembered it. His shoulder felt solid and strong. Then the music started, hardly better than before but, for some reason, no longer discordant.

"I'm not very good at this," he said as he began to move her around the floor.

"I'm not either, I'm afraid. I used to partner the girls at the school where I taught in New York, so please forgive me if I try to lead."

"Forgive you?" he said with his glorious smile. "I'd be forever grateful."

His smile warmed her to her toes, and she forgot to worry about how her feet were moving. Had he always been so handsome? she wondered inanely, then chided herself for being foolish. She'd always thought him attractive. Until now she just hadn't had much opportunity to observe him so closely. How distinguished he looked in his suit and tie with the touch of gray at his temples and the fine lines fanning out from the corners of his eyes.

And his eyes were brown, not black as she had thought, although they were so dark she could hardly see the pupils. Although he'd shaved closely—if the cut on his chin was any indication—she could still see the hint of a beard on his sun-darkened jaw.

Eben glanced around and was pleased to see other couples had joined them on the floor. At least now it wouldn't be too obvious if he accidentally stepped on Miss Isabel's foot.

And it wouldn't be a wonder if he did. God, she felt so good in his arms, he could hardly keep his mind on the steps. Her hand in his was small and soft and delicate. He wished he could feel more of her with his other hand, but her corset barred him from any real contact with the curves beneath her gown. Still, to be this close to her was almost enough.

She smelled of lavender and the tantalizing scent of woman. Desire raced across his nerve endings.

"You . . . you look real nice," he blurted, knowing he had to say something before he got completely carried away.

"Thank you, but I can't take much credit. Carrie Bartz fixed my hair."

He wasn't even looking at her hair. He'd meant her eyes, which he saw now weren't blue as he had thought but purple, the color of the violets Amanda nursed so conscientiously on the kitchen windowsill.

"I see you aren't wearing your ring," he said to make her smile.

It worked. "You were right, it turned my finger black, but I put it in a very safe place."

He could just imagine.

"You look very nice tonight, too," she was saying.

"I even washed my hands," he said in an attempt at humor, releasing hers for a moment to show her his palm.

Remorse flickered in her eyes, and for an instant he was afraid he'd ruined the mood. Then her expression grew impish. "You did an excellent job, too, although you really should be much more careful when you shave."

Eben winced. "How do you know I wasn't just trying to cut my throat?"

"If you were, you missed by a mile. And, of course, I'd have to wonder why you were attempting suicide. Was the thought of dancing with me so onerous?"

Eben wasn't sure what onerous meant, but he got the idea. "Oh, no," he replied in kind. "I was just afraid of making a fool of myself out here. I haven't held a woman in so long, I might've forgot myself."

Her violet eyes widened. "Forgot yourself how?"

Eben couldn't possibly answer that honestly. "Why, I . . . I might've tromped you right down into a greasy spot or squeezed you so hard, you snapped in two."

She didn't seem to realize he was teasing. Her violet gaze measured the breadth of his shoulders speculatively. He felt the look like a caress, and his muscles tensed in reaction.

"I imagine you hardly know your own strength," she murmured.

"A smith knows when to be gentle, too," he assured her hoarsely. "When the metal is real hot—" like the way Eben felt right now—"it only needs the lightest touch."

He thought she shivered slightly, but perhaps it was only the tremor going through his own body. Instinctively he pulled her closer, and she did not resist. Her eyes were darker now, the pupils large. Her skin was flushed, and her breath came more quickly.

"You're not afraid of me, are you?" he whispered.

"I . . . No, of course not," she replied, her cheeks rosy now. Eben knew just how warm and silky her skin would feel if he pressed his face to hers, and how she would taste if he . . .

"The song's over, Eb. What're you trying to pull?" someone behind him said.

Eben was appalled to discover the song had, indeed, ended without their having noticed. He released her at once, and before he could so much as offer an apology, she was gone, swallowed up in the tide of would-be partners.

Isabel knew she must be dreaming. First Eben Walker had looked at her as if he could eat her; now she was surrounded by men clamoring for the next dance. It was too unreal. Recognizing Paul Young, she accepted his hand, murmuring to the others that she had promised him. Grinning broadly, he led her onto the floor as the fiddlers struck up a lively tune and the dancers formed squares.

Having had little experience with square dancing, Isabel made a few mistakes, but Paul Young only grinned tolerantly and guided her through the complicated steps.

"I can see you need more practice at this," he remarked as he spun her around. "Don't they have dances in New York?"

"Not like this," she replied breathlessly the next time they came together.

"I really wanted to waltz so we could talk," he said while he do-si-doed around her.

"I'm not much of a conversationalist," she said, trying not to trip as she walked backward around him.

"Looked like you were doing all right with Eben," he said, then grabbed her arm when she stumbled.

Isabel stared up at him in horror, wondering if everyone in the room had been able to read the longing on her face when she'd been in Eben Walker's arms. But Paul Young just smiled as he took her hand to circle left.

"You look mighty pretty when you blush," he told her while they skipped around the circle.

She opened her mouth to berate him for teasing her when she suddenly recognized the sincerity in his eyes. He wasn't teasing at all! Not only wasn't he teasing, but he was *flirting*, really flirting with her. The very idea was ludicrous, but she couldn't deny the facts staring her in the face. He'd been flirting with her since the first time they'd met!

And all these other men *wanted* to flirt with her, she realized when the dance ended and she was once again surrounded by a group of men entreating her for a dance. Overwhelmed, she selected a man who looked vaguely familiar and stood across from him in a reel. During the brief moments they came together in the dance, he tried to be charming, but Isabel was too stunned to respond.

What in heaven's name was happening?

After losing Isabel to the swarm of suitors, Eben wandered outside, determined he wouldn't stand and watch while man after man claimed her as a partner.

He found company in the men gathered around the whiskey barrel.

"She sure is a pretty little thing, ain't she?" one of the men was saying. "Almost makes me wish I was single again."

"I doubt you'd have much chance," Herald Bartz replied knowingly. "She'll have her pick, and since she can only pick one, there's going to be a lot of disappointed fellows."

"Is it true she's a good cook?" someone else asked.

"Makes the best cakes and pies I ever put in my mouth, and biscuits so light, you have to cover them with a weighted sheet."

The men chuckled, all except Eben, who couldn't quite see the humor in all this.

"I'm a meat-and-potatoes man," a third man protested.

"She made a stew the likes of which I've never tasted. Meat so tender I almost had to eat it with a spoon, and gravy . . ." Herald smacked his lips in appreciation.

"How old did you say she was?" the first man asked, and Eben could no longer restrain himself.

"What difference does it make?" Eben demanded in irritation. "Listen to yourselves. You're talking about her like she's a cowhand you're thinking of hiring on."

"Well, everybody knows how important it is for a man to have a good wife," Herald argued. "A single man has got twice the work, and half the time to do it in. A good woman can mean the difference between success and failure in this life."

"And a woman like Miss Forester would almost be a guarantee of success," Dave Weatherby said. Dave owned the town's saloon, Dave's Dream, and had provided the whiskey for the party.

Eben glared at him. "Somehow I can't see a preacher's daughter being much help to you in the saloon business."

"A refined lady is always an asset to a man with ambition, " Weatherby informed him. "I don't plan to run a saloon for the rest of my life."

"No, Dave expects to be governor someday, don't you?" someone scoffed.

"If I have to settle for that, yes," Dave replied over the ensuing laughter.

"Does Miss Forester know you plan to take her with you to Austin?" someone else inquired.

"Not yet, but then, I haven't had the privilege of meeting her yet, either."

The men howled at this, all except Eben, who was very much afraid Weatherby meant every word of it. Of course, Eben knew he didn't have to worry about Miss Isabel falling for Weatherby's dubious charms. No minister's daughter would hitch up with a saloonkeeper, unless she wanted to totally rebel against her upbringing. But Isabel didn't seem like that sort.

Or did she? Eben realized he knew precious little about her.

"If you'll excuse me, gents, I've got to get myself a bride," Weatherby said, tossing aside the cigar he had been smoking.

The taunts of the other men followed him into the schoolhouse. Then Eben noticed Paul standing on the edge of the crowd. He worked his way over to him.

"Didn't you hear? Weatherby's going after your Miss Isabel."

Paul made a disgusted face. "I'm not afraid of Weatherby. I wouldn't want a woman who could be taken in by him anyway."

"Changed your mind about her now that you've spent some time with her?" Eben asked hopefully.

"Not likely. I'm just a little confused is all. She don't act like other women."

"What do you mean?"

"I mean when I'm charming, she just looks at me like I'm crazy."

Eben didn't bother to hide his chuckle. "Maybe

that's why you've never had any success with women, partner. When you think you're being charming, they think you're crazy."

"It's not that," Paul said soberly, refusing to be baited. "It's almost like she doesn't believe I'm really serious, like I'm teasing her or something."

"Well, you said yourself she's an old maid. Maybe she's just not used to dealing with men."

Paul frowned thoughtfully. "Maybe you're right. Did you see her face when all those fellows closed in on her after the first dance?"

"No, I didn't," Eben said acerbically. "I was the one being closed out, remember?"

"Yeah, well, she looked almost scared, or overwhelmed, maybe. I don't know. Anyhow, she wasn't anywhere near as delighted as any normal woman would be to get all that attention."

"Miss Isabel is a proper lady. Maybe she doesn't think all that attention is . . . *proper*," Eben suggested, thinking his opinion of Isabel was rising by the moment.

Paul made a thoughtful noise. "Maybe you're right, but I think it'd be dangerous to try out that theory. While I'm courting her properly, some other joker might steal her out from under my nose."

"Sounds like you're caught between a rock and a hard place," Eben said without much sympathy.

"I just wish I could get her to look at me the way she looked at you when you were dancing."

"What do you mean?" Eben asked in surprise.

"You know what I mean, all doe-eyed."

"You really are crazy," Eben scoffed, fighting the hope that struggled to life within him.

"Maybe I am, but I'm not blind. Surely you noticed. Why, if you'd been a cupcake, I reckon she would've taken a bite right out of you."

Eben swore, certain now Paul was riding him. "Shouldn't you get back inside and keep an eye on your intended?" he asked in disgust.

Paul grinned. "No, because I figured you'd do it for me."

With another curse, Eben strode away, realizing too late he was heading right back toward the school-house.

Inside, the music stopped, and the head fiddler announced they would be taking a short break to "wet their whistles."

Isabel smiled at her latest partner and allowed him to lead her from the floor. He was a pleasant-looking fellow with a slight paunch and a full head of curly hair. From the tailor-made suit he wore, she guessed he must be a prosperous businessman. He'd made polite conversation as they danced, inquiring about her background. She only wished she could remember his name.

"Would you like some punch?"

"Yes, thank you," Isabel said, thinking she could probably drink the bowl dry. Her feet were screaming for relief, and she knew if she didn't sit down soon, she would fall down.

He led her over to the punch table and muscled his way into the press to claim two cups. Holding them high, he flashed her a triumphant grin and said, "Why don't we take these outside, where it's cooler."

Ordinarily Isabel wouldn't have considered leaving the dance alone with a perfect stranger, but she'd already noticed many couples leaving the building. "That sounds wonderful," she said, thinking how refreshing the evening breeze would feel on her over-heated skin.

She followed him out. The night air came as a blessed relief, and glancing up, she was struck once again by the glory of the Texas night sky. The stars sparkled like diamonds on a black velvet canopy that seemed to stretch endlessly.

Admiring the wonders of nature, Isabel didn't notice how far they had wandered from the school until her companion stopped and handed her a cup of punch. They were standing out beyond the corral, a little too far from the others for Isabel's taste, but she supposed they were still in plain sight, although only one other couple had wandered so far afield. They stood in the shadow of a nearby tree, and Isabel noted they seemed to be embracing. She hastily averted her eyes and drained her glass thirstily, savoring the cool sweetness.

"It's a lovely night, isn't it?" her companion asked.

"I'm starting to think you don't have any other kind in Texas," Isabel replied. "It hasn't even rained since I've been here."

"Better get used to it. We don't get much wet weather here at all, but when we do, most of the rain falls all at once, a real gully washer. Just hope you aren't caught outside when it starts."

Isabel only smiled, wondering if he was exaggerating to impress a naive Easterner.

"Do you like Texas, Miss Forester?"

"The part I've seen, yes, very much."

"So you're planning to make your permanent home here?"

"I hadn't really thought that far ahead," she said, surprised to realize it was true. What had happened to the sensible Isabel who always had everything so carefully planned?

"I certainly hope you will," he said, setting his empty punch cup on the corral post. "Texas could use a hundred women like you, and we certainly want to keep the one we've got."

"You're very kind," Isabel said, uneasy with the flattery. Unearned compliments always made her suspicious.

"Kindness doesn't have anything to do with it, Miss Forester. May I call you 'Isabel'?"

"No," she said firmly, but he didn't seem to notice.

"You're an exceptional woman, Miss Isabel, educated and refined, the kind of woman any man would be proud to have beside him."

"I . . . thank you," she said absently, having noticed a slight tussle going on between the couple beneath the tree. The girl pushed herself away, and when she emerged from the shadows, Isabel saw to her dismay it was Amanda!

"Yes, an exceptional woman," her companion was saying, "which is why I've decided you'd be the perfect wife for a man like me."

Distracted by the sight of Amanda, Isabel only half heard his preposterous statement. Before she could react, he grabbed her by the shoulders, pulled her up against him, and pressed his mouth to hers.

Isabel panicked, twisting and thrashing, pushing against him with all her strength, but to her total humiliation, she couldn't stop his assault. She had to endure his mouth pressing on hers in the most awful of intimacies until he willingly released her.

Stumbling backward, she encountered the rail of the corral as she wiped her mouth furiously with the back of her hand. "You . . . you *cad!*" she shrieked. "How dare you!"

Although no man had ever taken advantage of her before, Isabel knew exactly what to do. Instinctively she threw back her hand and swung, landing a resounding slap across his face.

Seething with fury, she could hardly get her breath, but she managed to gasp, "You should be horsewhipped," before whirling away in an attempt to escape, but she found her way blocked by a crowd of onlookers who were surging toward them in response to Isabel's screams.

"What's going on here?" someone demanded, but, of course, Isabel had no intention of revealing her shame.

"Let me pass, please," she said, trying to push her way through the crowd, but no one would give way.

"Miss Forester, is something wrong?" a woman asked.

"Please, I . . ."

"Isabel, what happened?" Bertha Bartz's voice commanded as she shoved her way to the front. She looked Isabel over quickly, then turned to her companion. "Dave Weatherby, what have you been up to?"

"Just doing a little courting, Miz Bartz," he replied with a smug smile.

Isabel wanted to slap him again. *"Courting?"* she echoed contemptously. "Where I'm from, men are *arrested* for the type of behavior you just exhibited."

"You're absolutely right, Miss Isabel," he said with just the slightest trace of remorse. "I'm truly sorry for my outrageous behavior, and I'm more than willing to make amends. My dear lady, will you marry me?"

Isabel couldn't have been any more shocked . . . until he actually went down on one knee in front of her and laid a hand beseechingly over his heart.

"Are you mad?" she cried, resisting an urge to push him over backward.

"Maybe," he conceded, "but I don't see you have much choice. I've compromised your reputation and—"

"What on earth did he do?" Bertha demanded, turning to Isabel.

"He . . . he *kissed* me," Isabel said, almost choking on the words. The crowd gasped their surprise, and Isabel felt the heat of humiliation burning in her face.

"So you see," Weatherby insisted, "she has no choice but to—"

"Shut up!" Bertha snapped. "And get up off the ground before somebody mistakes you for a cowpod and flips you over the fence!"

Weatherby scrambled to his feet as the crowd gaffawed. "I can't see this is any of your business, Miz Bartz," he protested.

"Seems like you've made it *everybody's* business," a deep voice said, and Isabel saw Eben Walker break through the crowd. "Was it your intention to embarrass Miss Forester? Because if it was," he added ominously, "there are still a few men in this town who know how to deal with manners like that."

Weatherby's confidence evaporated. "Now, Eben, you know I'd never—"

"I don't know anything of the kind. What I do know is you've frightened Miss Forester and given her a real bad notion of what men around these parts are like. Now, maybe you'd better apologize to her before some of us start to think you aren't properly remorseful."

Walker hadn't raised his voice, but Isabel could hear the ring of steel beneath his words. Others in the crowd murmured their agreement, and Weatherby swallowed audibly.

"I offered to marry her," he hedged.

Eben glanced at her as if seeking her opinion in the matter. Isabel shook her head furiously.

"Seems the lady has said no," Eben reported. "Now, about that apology . . ."

"Miss Isabel," Weatherby began, but when Isabel stiffened at the familiar form of address, he quickly corrected himself. "I mean, Miss Forester, I am truly sorry for having offended you, and I beg your forgiveness."

"And let this be a lesson to all of you," Bertha decreed. "Miss Forester didn't come here panting after a husband, like some people around here seem to think. She's not the least bit interested in tying herself up with some no-account man. She's only interested in teaching school." Bertha turned the full fury of her scorn on Weatherby. "Now, get out of her sight before she smacks your ugly face."

"She already did," Weatherby grumbled, straightening his coat and bending over to brush the dust off his pant leg. Then he strode into the crowd.

"Show's over, folks," Herald Bartz said, his voice shrill over the mutterings of the crowd. "We've got a lot more dancing to do tonight, so let's get started."

Slowly the crowd dispersed as Eben and Herald

herded them away. When she was alone with Bertha, Isabel shuddered. "What an odious man."

"Are you all right?" Bertha asked. "You're trembling."

"Just because I'm so angry. I never . . . I can't believe . . ."

"Didn't I warn you that you might receive a proposal of marriage tonight?" Bertha reminded her with a small smile.

Isabel looked at her incredulously. "Is this what you had in mind?"

"No," Bertha admitted. "Usually they're much more traditional."

"The men?"

"No, the proposals."

"You mean this happens *often*?"

"Only when we get a new single woman in town. Isabel, I thought I'd already explained the situation to you."

"You did, but . . . Bertha, they can't really want to marry *me*!"

"Why not? Maybe the men back East didn't want you, but they probably don't know the value of a good wife. Out here, things are different. A man needs everything he's got just to make a living, and not many of them have the energy to make a proper home for themselves on top of it. A man with a wife has a clean house and clothes to wear, hot food waiting when he gets home, and children to help with the work, not to mention another person to talk to when the sun goes down and the work is done. Life can be pretty lonely for a single man."

For a single woman, too, Isabel thought, remembering all the nights she'd spent in her tiny room at Miss Snodgrass's school when she'd longed for someone in whom to confide her innermost thoughts. She'd never even considered the possibility that men might suffer the same longings.

Of course, if a man was lonely, he had only to find

himself a woman and ask her to wed. Men certainly
had the advantage there, or so Isabel had always assumed. But then, she'd never before lived in a place
where single women were scarce.

"Then that man was serious about wanting to
marry me?" Isabel asked, still not able to believe it.

"You bet he was serious, although he's a lot bigger
fool than I ever gave him credit for being. Of all the
idiot things to do—"

"She all right?" Eben Walker inquired from behind
Isabel.

She turned to face him, absurdly pleased by his
concern, and managed what she hoped was a reas-
suring smile. "I'm fine, and I'd like to thank you for
. . . for what you did."

He frowned. "I'd've done a lot more if I'd seen him
lay hands on you."

"Well, no harm done," Bertha said briskly. "Have
you sent him on his way?"

"He's with the other men by the whiskey barrel. I
don't think he'll be bothering Miss Forester again,
tonight or ever."

"We greatly appreciate your help," Bertha said.
"Now, I'd better be off. There's no telling what mischief my children will have gotten into while I've been
busy here. You'll look after Isabel, won't you, Eben?"

Bertha left before either of them could protest.

"You feel like going back to the dance or do you
want to go home?" he asked softly.

"I'm not as fragile as all that," she said, wishing
she could think of an excuse to feel his arms around
her again. For some reason, she knew a great need
to be held. "I'm sure I can face everyone again without
fainting."

"I should hope so. Listen, don't let Weatherby upset you. He was doing a little bragging a few minutes
ago, and I guess the whiskey got the better of him."

"You mean he was drunk?" Isabel asked, newly
horrified. How could she not have noticed?

"Not drunk exactly, just feeling fine, like he could do whatever he wanted. A man who owns a saloon knows better than to get really drunk."

"He owns a saloon!" she cried in dismay. This was getting worse and worse. "Did he honestly think he could *force* me to marry him?"

"I don't know what he thought, and I don't reckon he does either. Just try to put the whole thing out of your mind. It won't happen again."

Isabel drew a deep breath in an effort to calm herself. After a moment she could even begin to see the irony of the situation. "Well, I suppose I did hope for a *little* adventure when I decided to come to Texas," she observed wryly.

"I reckon you were picturing wild Indians or something, though," he guessed. His finely chiseled lips curved up into a smile that threatened to undo her regained composure.

"Yes, or rattlesnakes or stampedes," she replied somewhat unsteadily. "An overzealous suitor never would have occurred to me." Or any suitor at all, she added silently, thinking she might have to rethink her whole outlook on life in view of these remarkable developments.

Eben's smile stretched into a grin, and suddenly she saw him in a whole new light. Was he as interested in finding a wife as the other men who had besieged her tonight? Might he, too, look upon her as a potential bride?

The possibility was delicious, and for the first time in her life Isabel began to sense her power as a woman. Would Eben respond if she tried to exercise it?

"I believe I'm ready to go back inside now," she said, trying a smile. "But I was wondering . . . that is, if you wouldn't mind . . ."

"What?" he urged.

"If you wouldn't mind going in with me. The thought of facing everyone alone—"

"Sure, I'd be proud to," he said, offering his arm with what Isabel thought was certainly enthusiasm.

Holding his arm was almost as good as being held by him. She could feel the tensile strength with which she'd seen him wield a hammer so large she couldn't even have considered lifting it. Eben Walker's woman need never fear man nor beast, she thought in a moment of romantic reverie, then chided herself for being fanciful. Modern men were rarely called upon to slay dragons for their ladies, although she couldn't help thinking Eben might just be up to the task.

Although Isabel had believed herself completely recovered, she was surprised to experience a strange reluctance to reenter the building when they finally reached it.

"You all right?" he asked as if sensing her hesitation.

She forced a smile. She couldn't let him think poorly of her. "Certainly." Drawing on her reserves of courage, she lifted her skirt and climbed the familiar steps, still holding fast to Eben's strong arm.

Inside, the fiddlers were just finishing a rousing reel, and Isabel watched the dancers stomping vigorously as they danced in time. At first no one noticed her arrival, and she took the moment to observe the scene as she had so often in her past life. The difference this time was that she knew she could rejoin the activities as a welcome participant whenever she desired. The knowledge brought with it a surge of elation such as she had never known.

She glanced up at Eben—and just when had she begun to think of him as 'Eben'? she wondered vaguely. He was watching her solicitously, as if he were afraid she might actually faint. In the intoxication of the moment, Isabel did what she never otherwise would have dared.

"Would you dance with me—for the first one?" she hastily amended.

Was his answering smile as delighted as she would have liked? She thought so. He even laid his hand over hers where it rested on his arm. The abrasion of his palm against her tender skin sent delicious shivers racing over her.

"If you aren't worried about the safety of your toes, I'll be happy to," he replied.

Isabel thought she just might die of happiness.

"I never saw a woman get so fired up over nothing," Dave Weatherby complained as someone pressed a glass of whiskey into his hand. He took a long swallow. "All I did was kiss her."

"You must've done a piss-poor job of it, then," one of his friends replied.

The other men laughed uproariously, but Weatherby only scowled. "You can laugh all you want, but I was this close to having that gal," he insisted, holding his forefinger and thumb an inch apart.

"You know, maybe Dave's got the right idea," Felix Underwood said. Felix was the town barber, so the other men were used to considering his opinions.

"You think attacking Miss Forester is the way to her heart?" someone asked skeptically.

"Of course not, but you heard what Miz Bartz said. She ain't interested in marrying *anybody*, which means we'll just be wasting our time trying to court her the usual way."

"Do you know of an *unusual* way to court?" Paul Young asked in amusement.

Felix sipped his whiskey thoughtfully. "You might say that. See, I've been considering the situation. Miss Forester don't want to get married, but we all do, and we know it'd be a sin to waste a perfectly good woman, don't we?"

The others muttered their agreement.

"Then it's really our duty to see she gets herself a man, willing or not."

"You better not be talking about taking her by force," Paul warned.

"Oh, no, nothing like that," Felix assured him. He had everyone's full attention now. The men had even stopped drinking. "All somebody has to do is compromise her."

"Dave already tried that," someone pointed out contemptuously.

"He only tried to kiss her," Felix scoffed. "Nobody cares about that anymore. Nowdays some women kiss three or four different men before they get married, and nobody thinks a thing about it. No, it's got to be something serious, something that'll make even Miss Forester think she's got to get married."

Paul Young looked over Felix's scrawny frame contemptuously. "You talking about getting her in a family way?"

"No," he insisted hastily, seeing the disapproving frowns around him. "A man wouldn't even need to lay a hand on her if he was smart. All he's got to do is ruin her reputation."

"She's a preacher's daughter," Paul reminded him. "She's been raised strict, and she won't stand for any nonsense. It won't be easy to trick her."

"Which is what makes this so fair," Felix reasoned. "Only a man clever enough to figure out a way to do it will be clever enough to deserve Miss Forester."

"What do you reckon a man ought to do if he wants to try it?" someone asked.

Felix shook his head and smiled smugly. "I've got my own interests to look after, fellows. I'm not going to give away any ideas."

"But you *are* going to try it, aren't you?" Paul said.

"Damn right. She could do a lot worse than me. I've got a good business and—"

"So do a lot of us," Paul reminded him.

"And some of us own our own land," a rancher said.

Unimpressed, Felix grinned. "Well, all I've got to say is, it's every man for himself."

"And all I've got to say is, you're crazy as a bedbug," Dave Weatherby growled. "I've got twenty dollars says Miss Forester shows you the door before you get within ten feet of her."

"It wouldn't be seemly to bet on such a matter," Felix said righteously, earning the scorn of the group.

"No, wait, Felix is right," Paul Young said. "Betting is damned undignified, and anyway, I'm sure Miss Isabel doesn't want her future husband gambling. What we ought to have is a lottery."

"A lottery?" the others echoed in amazement.

"Sure, a pot of money that goes to the man who manages to win Miss Isabel's hand."

Felix nodded his approval. "Sort of a wedding gift."

"Exactly," Paul said.

"But what if she don't marry anybody?" Weatherby challenged.

"She will," Paul assured him.

"Who contributes?" someone asked.

"Anybody who wants to marry her."

"Who holds the money?"

"Dave, of course," Paul replied. "He's the only one she's *sure* not to pick."

"Don't bet the ranch on it," Dave said sourly. "Some women like a man they can reform."

"Of course, you're welcome to try for her again," Paul said graciously, "but meanwhile you can keep the money in your safe."

"How much do we each contribute?"

"I think Dave set the rate: twenty dollars per man," Paul said. "I'll be the first." He reached into his pocket and pulled out a gold double eagle.

Within a matter of minutes, more than a dozen men had given Dave Weatherby their donations to the cause and the coffer had swelled to over two hundred dollars. With one accord, the men began to move to the schoolhouse, where they had seen Miss Isabel go.

"Maybe I'll just carry her off on the back of my horse," one fellow said in alcoholic rashness.

"Don't do anything to get yourself hanged," Paul warned as he followed him into the hall. "The money won't do you no good if you're six feet under, or the woman neither."

When Eben saw the group of men come in, he straightened from where he had been leaning against the wall observing the scene. Instinctively he tensed, ready to rush to Isabel's protection again, although why he thought he'd have to protect her, he couldn't imagine.

Things were well under control now, and after their dance, he had turned Isabel over to Herald Bartz for a reel. Eben had been enjoying the sight of her trim little figure swaying in time with the music, but now he sensed a new threat.

Paul Young's guileless grin didn't put his mind at ease, either.

"I see they've got you doing an important job," Paul remarked cheerfully.

"Yeah, this wall was just about to go down until I took over," Eben said, leaning back against it with feigned nonchalance. "Is Weatherby gone?"

"Lord, no, but he's drunk enough now so he won't bother anybody anymore. What a shocking thing. A decent woman's not safe anywhere nowdays."

Eben frowned, skeptical of Paul's outrage. He still looked far too cheerful. "What kind of trouble are you cooking up now?"

"None at all," he said as his gaze strayed toward the dance floor and locked on Isabel Forester. "Fine-looking woman, isn't she?"

Eben continued to observe Paul warily. His friend tucked his thumbs in his vest pockets and began to rock back and forth on his heels, a mysterious smile on his face.

"I get the feeling I'd better start watching for that lynch mob," Eben said, only half in jest.

"Don't get all grandmotherly on me, now," Paul chided. "Nobody's going to bother your precious Miss Isabel, at least not tonight."

"What do you mean, 'at least not tonight'?" Eben asked in alarm.

"I mean if you want her, you'd better get moving, because there's a lot of other men who want her, too."

"What makes you think I want her?" he asked uneasily.

Paul widened his eyes in mock astonishment. "Oh, yeah, I almost forgot you aren't interested in a wife. I'm mighty relieved to hear it, too, because I figure you're the only real competition I've got."

Before Eben could reply, Herald Bartz delivered Isabel back to him. His breath caught when he looked up and saw her flushed cheeks and shining eyes. Wisps of golden hair clung damply to her temples, and Eben had to close his hands into fists to keep from reaching out to brush them back. Did he want her? God, yes, and he sure as hell wasn't going to let Paul Young have her.

"Miss Forester," Paul was saying, "may I have the pleasure of the next dance?"

Her lovely smile faltered just a bit. She glanced at Eben, as if for approval, or perhaps she hoped he would make a counteroffer.

He would have, but Paul didn't give him a chance. "Eben doesn't mind, do you, sport? In fact, he just gave me his permission. Oh, what's this? A waltz. We'll finally get a chance to talk," he said in delight as he whisked her away.

"That sneaking son of a bitch," muttered someone to Eben's left, echoing his own thoughts. Glancing over, he was surprised to see an area rancher glaring at Paul Young with all the animosity he himself felt.

"He won't get nothing accomplished here tonight,"

Felix Underwood said to the rancher. To Eben's surprise, he too was glaring murderously at Paul.

Eben quickly surveyed the room and discovered at least ten men watching Paul lead Isabel around the floor. Every one of them looked ready to do murder.

What in the hell was going on?

Chapter 7

Since most of them hadn't been to bed the night before, the worshipers in Reverend Smiley's congregation were rather bleary-eyed the next morning. Isabel herself had a pounding headache and painfully swollen feet, but she had promised the children they could perform their first song that morning, so she sat erect if somewhat unsteadily at the organ and directed as they sang "Amazing Grace."

Amanda Walker's sweet voice rose above the others, strong and clear, and Isabel's heart swelled in response. She glanced over to where Eben sat in the congregation, expecting to see pride softening his rugged features. Instead he frowned, an expression of infinite misery on his handsome face. Why would he be distressed to hear his daughter singing so beautifully? Isabel wondered as her fingers found the organ keys automatically.

Then she recalled another verse of "The Village Blacksmith":

It sounds to him like her mother's voice
Singing in Paradise!

Isabel's heart sank. Of course! Hadn't Bertha
warned her Eben Walker might still be in love with
his lost wife? A man so kind and sensitive must feel
things deeply. Probably he had never recovered from
her death, and if he hadn't, then no woman could
ever take her place in his life.

But then she remembered how kind he'd been to
her last night, how solicitous of her well-being when
she'd been attacked. He'd acted as if he truly cared
about her, and if he did, was it possible his caring
could grow into something deeper? Was it possible
that after years of mourning, Eben Walker might finally be ready to love again?

Twenty-four hours ago, Isabel Forester would
never have imagined herself capable of winning the
regard of a man like Eben Walker, but after last night,
her whole perspective had changed. After all, this was
her brand-new life, and anything might be possible.
And she would have a whole week in his home during
which to make it possible.

Pushing away the thought for the time being, Isabel
signaled the children to begin filing back to their seats.
She patted their shoulders as they passed her, giving
each child a special word of encouragement. When
Amanda went by, she looked at Isabel with those
melting cornflower-blue eyes, the picture of innocence, and Isabel suddenly remembered seeing the
girl last night struggling out of the embrace of a young
man.

Isabel's own subsequent struggle had wiped the
memory from her mind, but now it came back with
a vengeance. The words of encouragement she had
been about to utter died on her lips, as she searched
Amanda's expression. The man most certainly had
been Johnny Dent, and what had Amanda been thinking to go off alone with him like that?

Amanda's lovely eyes clouded with confusion when Isabel didn't comment on how well she had sung, and the girl went to her seat frowning in disappointment. Isabel quickly turned to the next child and managed to say something appropriate even as her mind raced ahead to plan what she must do.

Thank heaven she would be spending the coming week at Amanda's house. The girl needed even more guidance than Isabel had suspected.

"Isabel?" Bertha called softly.

Isabel awoke slowly, disoriented and confused.

"I'm sorry to wake you, my dear, but you have a caller."

Isabel blinked and pushed up on one elbow, trying to get her bearings. Oh, yes, she remembered now. After Sunday dinner, everyone had lain down for a nap to recover from the sleepless night.

"A caller, did you say?" Isabel asked, fighting to make her brain function.

"Yes, Mr. Underwood. I believe you met him last night. He's our town barber."

The name meant nothing to her, lost as it was in the avalanche of names she had heard last night. Isabel tried to rub the sleep from her eyes. "What does he want?"

"I believe he wants to take you for a buggy ride."

Isabel blinked again. "You can't be serious."

"Oh, but I am," Bertha assured her. Isabel could now see she was smiling. "I believe Mr. Felix Underwood fancies himself a suitor."

Isabel groaned and collapsed wearily back onto the bed. Above her Bertha chuckled. "Don't worry, he's a perfectly respectable man. I doubt he even knows how to misbehave."

This was the least of Isabel's worries. "Why isn't he asleep, like any normal human being should be after last night?"

"Perhaps he couldn't sleep for remembering your

beauty," Bertha said, ignoring Isabel's skeptical glare. "You must see him, you know. It's only polite."

Although Isabel would much rather have lain down on the train tracks and waited for the sound of a whistle than go for a buggy ride with a man named Felix Underwood, she pushed herself back up again. "Tell him I'll be down in a few minutes," she said in resignation.

Felix was even worse than she had imagined. He stood a little over five and a half feet tall and looked for all the world as if he could use a good square meal. He'd slicked his brown hair back with a fistful of pomade, and his prodigious mustache stood out on either side of his nose in carefully waxed curls. The overwhelming scent of lilac water reminded Isabel that Bertha had said he was the town barber.

"Miss Isabel, you look lovely," he exclaimed, scrambling up from the Bartzes' settee.

Since Isabel knew perfectly well she looked as if she'd been dead a week, she didn't bother to acknowledge the compliment. "Mr. Underwood, how nice to see you again so soon," she said perfunctorily, hoping to remind him how recently she had been allowed to retire to her bed.

Her hopes were in vain. "I've taken the liberty of renting a buggy from Eben Walker's shop on the chance you might be willing to go for a ride with me this afternoon," he said, his pale blue eyes alight with anticipation.

"Some fresh air would be wonderful," she said, thinking how nicely it would dissipate the fumes from the lilac water.

"Did Felix tell you he's our town barber?" Herald asked as Isabel started for the front door.

"He's our undertaker, too," Bertha added.

Oh, perfect, Isabel thought, reaching for her bonnet beside the door.

* * *

Eben knew he was a fool. Only a fool would go on an errand like this. He tried to tell himself he was only concerned about his buggy. After all, it was getting dark, and Felix had said he'd only need it a few hours.

Of course, Eben had known instantly why Felix wanted the buggy. He might be a fool, but he wasn't stupid. He'd almost refused to rent it out, then realized there was no use in cheating himself of a fee, no matter how much it might gall him to help another man court Isabel.

It did gall him, too, regardless of how he tried to pretend the discomfort in his chest was something he'd eaten. The thought of another man spending time with Isabel made him want to grab a sledgehammer and put a hole in something.

Why he should feel so strongly about the matter puzzled him. After all, he barely even knew Isabel Forester, and he still wasn't sure he completely trusted her. She was, after all, a woman. The only thing he did know was that the thought of her with another man was driving him crazy.

And, of course, Amanda had started to fret, too, because Miss Isabel had promised to come to them right after supper. Surely she hadn't forgotten, and surely she wouldn't have missed supper at the Bartzes' as Carrie had reported when Amanda had gone over there to check on her. Something must have happened to delay her.

Maybe the buggy had thrown a wheel, Eben reasoned, although he would have bet his immortal soul against it. Eben maintained his wagons to perfection. A more likely possibility was that Felix had driven it into a ditch. If he'd hurt Isabel in any way, Eben would murder him with his bare hands.

Occupied with these thoughts, Eben at first did not realize what he was seeing as he rounded a stand of cottonwoods and saw his buggy in the distance. His initial relief gave way to confusion when he saw a figure in black walking down the road ahead of the horse. Was Felix leading the animal for some reason? Was . . . ?

But it wasn't Felix, it was *Isabel*. In another moment Eben could see Felix still rode in the buggy, although he appeared to be leaning out the side and addressing his companion.

Eben kicked his horse into a gallop. Now he could see Isabel was practically running, swinging her arms furiously as she strode along while Felix kept the horse at a walk so as not to overtake her.

"Miss Isabel, please, I said I was sorry," Felix was shouting, and suddenly Eben understood. That bastard had taken liberties with her, and she was so angry she wouldn't even ride in the buggy with him! Eben would ring his scrawny little neck, he decided as he sawed on the reins and brought his horse to a halt directly in front of Isabel.

She'd seen him coming, and she looked so happy, he was hard-pressed not to jump down and take her in his arms. Restraining himself with some difficulty, he turned his attention to Felix, who had stopped the buggy and scrambled out, ready to defend himself.

"What's going on here?" Eben demanded.

"Just a slight misunderstanding," Felix assured him, hurrying forward. "Miss Isabel took offense at something I said, and—"

"*Said!*" she cried, turning the full force of her fury on the little fellow. "You, sir, are beneath contempt."

Felix blanched under her wrath, actually retreating a step in the face of it, and suddenly Eben's own anger died. He wouldn't need to lay a finger on Felix, because when Isabel got through with him, there wouldn't be enough left to even get a grip on. Still, he wouldn't let Felix know he was off the hook. "Did you take liberties with Miss Forester?" he demanded.

"Eben, this isn't your concern," Felix protested.

"If you've insulted Miss Forester, I'm making it my concern."

"I'd never think of insulting her," the little man insisted. "I hold her in the highest esteem. I've even asked her to be my wife—"

"*Mr. Underwood*," Isabel replied in a tone so cold that Eben thought it could've frozen the gonads off a brass monkey, "I would prefer to be kidnapped by pirates and sold into slavery than to become your wife."

Felix winced. "I've never seen a woman so dead set against getting kissed," he complained, turning to Eben for support.

"*Kissed*? Mr. Underwood, you *assaulted* me, and I've a good mind to have you arrested the instant I get back to town!"

"Arrested!" Felix bleated as Eben vaulted from his saddle, his anger rekindled.

"Felix, just what did you do to Miss Forester?" Eben demanded between gritted teeth.

"Nothing, I swear to God!" Felix assured him, raising both hands defensively as he backed away.

"Using the Lord's name to support your lies only increases your guilt, Mr. Underwood," Isabel informed him haughtily.

"*Felix?*" Eben growled in warning.

"I tried to kiss her," Felix admitted, "but she hit me with her purse before I could get near her! She must have a brick in that thing, too," he added, rubbing his ear gingerly.

Eben noticed it was awfully red, and he glanced at Isabel, whose mutinous expression told him she was ready to clobber him again. The vision flickered momentarily in his mind, and he had to bite his lip to keep from smiling.

"Felix, were you going to let Miss Forester walk all the way back to town?"

"Let her?" he exclaimed. "I was begging her to get back in the buggy, but she wouldn't even answer me."

Eben glanced at Isabel again. Her cheeks were rosy,

and her eyes glinted with the light of battle. He had half a mind to leave her here with Felix just so the poor jackass would get the tongue-lashing he deserved, but Eben had other plans for Isabel's evening.

"I oughta take the buggy and let *you* walk home," Eben said, taking some small pleasure in Felix's look of panic. "But I'll leave you my horse so I can see Miss Forester back to town. Now, get out of my sight before I decide to make you real sorry you ever got the idea to take Miss Forester out in the first place."

Felix looked at Isabel, then back at Eben again. "I . . ." he began, then apparently thought better of finishing. "Thanks, Eben," he said, and mounted the horse with unseemly haste.

In another moment he was galloping down the road. Eben turned to Isabel. Her color was still high, but he thought the fury had left her eyes. "You all right?"

She nodded, and to Eben's surprise, she smiled. "Once again I owe you my gratitude for defending my honor."

"I'm always a little late, though," he admitted ruefully. Without warning, his anger rushed back on a hot tide, and this time it was directed at her. "What on earth were you thinking of to go off alone with Felix Underwood?" he wanted to know.

Her eyes widened in surprise. "There's no harm in allowing a gentleman to entertain me, is there? You can't expect me to sit at home twiddling my thumbs."

"Nobody said you had to," Eben said, feeling unaccountably annoyed by her attitude, "but can't you spend your time with *women* or something?"

"No *women* invited me out this afternoon," she replied, as cold and haughty as she'd been with Felix a minute ago. "Now, if you were serious about escorting me back to town, I'd like to go."

"Yeah, sure," he replied, nonplussed. How had he managed to get into a fight with her himself? he wondered as he followed her back to the buggy. Watching the sway of her hips, he noticed how dusty her black skirt was from walking in the road. How many miles had she covered before he came along?

When he tried to help her into the buggy, she shook off his hand and climbed up herself, obviously still irritated by his rebuke. Standing back to watch, Eben caught a tantalizing glimpse of well-turned ankle and even a bit of stockinged calf above her boot. His body quickened in response.

When she had settled herself in the buggy, he climbed up beside her. She was fiddling with her purse, which reminded him of what Felix had said. "Do you really have a brick in there?" he asked.

She looked up, startled, then slowly, almost reluctantly, her smile returned. "Not exactly." She lifted the drawstring bag from her lap and gave it a little shake. It rattled.

"What the . . . ?"

"Rocks," she explained, her violet eyes dancing mischievously. "A little trick I used to teach my students at Miss Snodgrass's school."

She'd clobbered Felix with a bagful of rocks! Although he tried to hold it in, a chuckle escaped him. Isabel chuckled too, a small, embarrassed sound. Then their eyes met, and in the next instant they were both laughing uproariously.

"You should . . . have seen . . . his face!" Isabel gasped, pulling a lacy handkerchief from her pocket and dabbing at her eyes.

She had the most wonderful laugh, like the tinkle of tiny bells. The sound warmed him in places where he had been cold for a long, long time.

"You're a piece of work, Miss Forester," Eben marveled when he had control of himself again.

"Is that a compliment?" she asked, a little suspicious.

"You bet," he replied, admiring the way the twilight shadows turned her eyes deep purple. The scent of lilacs engulfed him, and for a moment the urge to take her in his arms was almost overwhelming. But, of course, he knew how she felt about being mauled in a buggy, and he doubted that actually being hit with her bag of rocks would be as amusing as hearing about it. Using every last ounce of his restraint, he took up the reins, released the brake, and slapped the horse into motion.

"I'm awfully glad you came when you did," she said after a few minutes. "After all the dancing I did last night, I don't think I could walk much farther. How did you happen along, anyway?"

He glanced at her, wondering whether she suspected he'd come looking for her and, womanlike, was trying to get him to admit it. But he saw only ordinary curiosity in her violet eyes.

"I didn't exactly happen along," he admitted.

"You mean you were looking for me . . . us?" she corrected.

"Well, Amanda was getting worried," he hedged. "You said you'd come over after supper, and when you didn't, she went to the Bartzes' to fetch you. When she found out you hadn't returned yet . . ." He shrugged.

"So you only came to humor your daughter," she said. Did she sound disappointed? Eben didn't want her to be.

"Well, I was worried about my buggy, too," he allowed, checking her reaction from the corner of his eye. She still looked disappointed. Briefly Eben considered the wisdom of admitting his concern for her. It never paid to give a woman any sort of advantage, he knew from experience. She'd use it like a knife, to wound and hurt him when he was down. Still, her injured expression bothered him. "And I was afraid Felix might've turned the buggy over or something. You could've been hurt."

"How considerate of you," she said, somewhat mollified, and gave him a little smile.

Eben had to tighten his grip on the reins. This was

going to be a long trip. "Would you like to tell me what happened this afternoon?" he asked.

Isabel considered. She really did not want to discuss her encounter with Felix, but she also remembered that Eben had been outraged both times a man had offended her. Reinforcing those feelings couldn't hurt a bit.

"There really isn't much to tell," she said. "Mr. Underwood took me for a drive. He's quite garrulous, and we—"

"He's what?" Eben asked sharply.

"Garrulous. That means talkative."

"Oh," he said, and Isabel saw his broad shoulders relax.

Resisting the temptation to ask what he'd thought she meant, she continued. "He kept me entertained by describing the countryside to me. Then he . . . he said he should rest the horse for a few minutes."

She paused, prepared for him to chastise her for being so gullible, but he contented himself with a raised eyebrow and a small, knowing grin, which she ignored.

"While we were stopped, he . . ." Isabel found herself reluctant to admit the truth, even though he already knew what she was about to say.

"He made advances to you," he finished for her, and again she heard the ring of steel in his voice, almost as if his sledgehammer were striking the plate of his anvil.

Closing her eyes, Isabel relived the awful moment when she had realized Felix Underwood intended to embrace her. He'd been surprisingly strong for such a scrawny fellow, and her struggles had been in vain. She'd known one hysterical instant when she imagined having one of her eyes poked out by a corner of his stiffly waxed mustache before her common sense took over and she remembered her bag. Thank heaven she had taken the precaution, although even now she couldn't imagine why she'd ever thought she'd be attacked twice in two days by two different men. This was far more excitement than she had expected to encounter in her entire lifetime.

"Miss Forester?" Eben said, startling her back to the present.

When she opened her eyes, she found him watching her intently, his expression so tender it took her breath. "Please, call me Isabel," she heard herself saying. "I mean, after all we've been through and . . . and we are friends, after all," she amended lamely.

"Well, sure," he agreed, smiling a little. She wondered if he thought her forward, but before she could decide, he said, "You never did tell me how you came to be walking."

"Oh, yes," she said, instantly feeling the heat flooding her cheeks. "When Mr. Underwood would not stop his . . . his advances, I swung my purse and caught him on the ear. I'm afraid I hit him much harder than I'd intended. He seemed stunned for a moment, so I jumped out of the buggy and started walking."

"Weren't you afraid he'd chase you?" Eben asked with a frown.

"I didn't really consider the possibility. I only knew I couldn't . . ."

"You couldn't what?" he prompted when she hesitated.

"I couldn't stay in the buggy with him another moment."

"Because of what he did," he guessed.

"No, because . . ."

His expectant expression urged her to continue.

"Because his fragrance was making me ill."

"His *fragrance*?" Eben asked incredulously.

"Yes, he reeked of lilac water."

Eben lifted his chin and sniffed several times. His eyes widened in amazement. "Good God, I thought that was you! *Felix* had on that stuff?"

Once again, Isabel felt the urge to giggle, but she

suppressed it. "Yes," she confirmed as seriously as she could manage. "I suppose he wanted to make a good impression, and—"

"Lilac water? *Lilac water?*"

At first Isabel couldn't imagine why the buggy began to shake, then she realized *Eben* was the one who was shaking. His whole body quaked with silent laughter.

"Mr. Walker," she scolded, but her own lips quivered.

"I'm sorry, but did you see his *mustache*?" Eben asked brokenly.

Isabel's composure dissolved. She covered her mouth with both hands, but the laughter spilled out anyway. "I was afraid he'd put my eye out if he got too close!"

Eben howled, holding his side with one hand while the reins went slack in the other.

"And he used . . . so much pomade," she continued when she'd caught her breath, "it was melting down his temples."

This set Eben off again, and he pulled the buggy to a halt while laughter shook him. Isabel was enthralled. His huge shoulders trembled, and he threw back his head in abandon. The lines around his dark eyes squinched, and moisture formed on his thick, dark lashes.

She savored the few moments of pure, unadulterated joy while she waited for him to regain his composure. All too soon, he lifted a hand and rubbed his eyes with his thumb and forefinger. "Oh, God," he groaned, weak from the ordeal. He drew a deep breath and let it out in a long, ragged sigh. His dark gaze settled on her, and suddenly the confines of the buggy seemed much smaller even than they had when Felix Underwood had been forcing himself on her. "Miss Isabel, you are a piece—"

"—of work," she finished for him. "What on earth does that mean?"

"It means you're not like any other woman alive. Don't you know you should've fainted or something when he tried to attack you?"

"That would hardly be practical," she pointed out. "If I were unconscious, he could do whatever he wanted."

"You're right, but most women aren't very practical by nature."

"I beg your pardon, Mr. Walker, but I believe you are quite mistaken."

"Maybe, but all the women I've ever known didn't have the sense God gave a ripe gourd."

"*All* the women you've known?" she challenged in outrage. "Would you say Bertha Bartz doesn't have good sense?"

"But she's not a . . ."

His voice trailed off, and he looked rather chagrined. "Bertha isn't what?" she prompted.

"She's different, not like most women at all."

"Why? Because she runs her husband's business and has made a success of it?"

"Does she?" he asked, as if Isabel had just confirmed a long-held suspicion.

"Of course. Anyone with good sense could figure that out in an instant," she replied. "And what about your wife? Didn't she have good sense?"

Instantly his expression hardened, and he turned his attention back to the horse. "No," he said with finality, slapping the animal into motion again.

Oh, dear, Isabel thought in dismay. What had ever possessed her to mention his wife? The mere mention of her was enough to depress him.

"I'm sorry," she tried. "I didn't mean to offend."

"You didn't."

"Or stir up painful memories."

"*You didn't,*" he said impatiently. "Look, Miss Forester—I mean, Isabel—I didn't ride all the way out here to fight with you."

"Why did you ride out here then?"

"To make sure you got home safe and sound," he said in exasperation. "But you won't if I end up strangling you."

"Why would you want to strangle me?" she asked in alarm.

He glanced at her out of the corner of his eye, and she thought his lips twitched just a bit. "Well, I reckon it'd be safer than trying to kiss you."

Isabel gaped at him, uncertain whether to laugh or groan. Eben Walker was a . . . a *piece of work*. How dare he tease her about a thing like that? Of course, she realized with a start, if he did want to kiss her, he would be perfectly safe in doing so. The knowledge made her tingle. "Mr. Walker, I'm shocked," she said, trying for coyness and wondering how in the world a woman could let a man know she wanted to be kissed.

"Are you, Miss Isabel?" he inquired skeptically. "After what's happened to you in the past twenty-four hours, I wouldn't think anything could shock you."

"Perhaps you're right," she allowed, guiltily aware that even her own thoughts had grown shocking.

"And do you think you could call me 'Eben' just once?"

"I'm not sure," she replied, pretending to consider the matter. "Is it proper to address one's murderer by his given name?"

"It is in Texas," Eben assured her solemnly, making her laugh in spite of herself.

"Then I shall, by all means, *Eben*." The name felt good on her tongue, familiar, as if she'd always known it. "I've been looking forward to spending this week at your home."

"You have?" he asked. Was it politeness or skepticism that darkened his tone?

"Yes, I've developed a great affection for Amanda. She's a lovely girl."

"Unless she's throwing one of her fits, which is one

reason why I came looking for you today. I couldn't stand the thought of listening to her ranting and raving while we waited for you to show up."

"Why does she throw fits?"

"God only knows. She used to be such a sweet-tempered kid, but now everything sets her off. One second she'll be fine, the next she'll be crying like the world's coming to an end."

"Girls her age do tend to be high-strung," Isabel said cautiously, wondering if she should hint at her concerns about Amanda and the cowboy Johnny Dent. "They also quarrel with their parents quite a bit. It's all part of growing up. And, of course, they begin to develop an interest in young men."

"Thank God I don't have to worry about that."

"You don't? Why not?" Isabel asked in surprise.

"Because it'll be a long time before Amanda starts thinking about young men."

"What makes you so certain?"

He looked at her in amazement. "Amanda's only fourteen," he said, as if that explained everything.

"But she's quite grown-up for her age, probably as a result of her responsibilities at home. She may be thinking she'd much rather be keeping house for a husband than—"

"Amanda's just a baby herself," he insisted. "A husband is the last thing on her mind."

Isabel stared at him in despair. The problem was even worse than she had imagined, and the hardest job would be convincing Eben Walker he even *had* a problem.

"Amanda's just spoiled," he was saying. "She's run wild pretty much of the time with nobody to look after her, and now she's paying me back for neglecting her."

"Perhaps I could talk to her while I'm staying with you," Isabel said weakly, thinking this might be the best tactic after all. Certainly there was no reason to upset Eben with talk of Johnny Dent if she could

convince Amanda of her folly. She only prayed she'd
be able to do so.

When they reached town a few minutes later, they
saw Amanda standing on the front porch of the
Walker house. The instant she recognized the buggy,
she began to wave, vigorously. Her cries of welcome
drew the Bartz family from their house, and they came
hurrying down the street to where Eben stopped the
buggy in front of his home.

"What happened?" Amanda demanded the instant
the buggy halted. "Mr. Underwood wouldn't tell me
a thing except you were coming right along."

"Miss Forester and Mr. Underwood just had a little
misunderstanding," Eben explained as he climbed
from the buggy and reached in to help Isabel alight.

"What happened to your skirt?" Amanda asked
when she saw the dust-coated hem.

By then the Bartz family had arrived, and they, too,
began to clamor for an explanation. "Mr. Underwood
and I had a slight . . . disagreement," Isabel explained,
happy for Eben's suggestion. "I decided I'd rather
walk home than ride with him, but fortunately, Mr.
Walker came and escorted me home instead."

"What do you mean, you had a disagreement with
Felix?" Bertha asked suspiciously.

"Oh, you know . . ." Isabel hedged, but Amanda
had already figured it out.

"He tried to kiss you, didn't he?" she cried in delight.

"Did he, Miss Isabel?" Carrie exclaimed. "How terribly romantic!"

"Girls!" Bertha scolded, her bosom heaving with
indignation. "There's nothing romantic about being
taken advantage of by a cad!"

"Then he did try to take advantage of you!"
Amanda said, inordinately pleased.

"Girls, Mrs. Bartz is absolutely correct," Isabel insisted. "Your notions of romance are ridiculous!"

"But just think, Miss Forester," Amanda pointed

out, "two different men have tried to kiss you in two days!"

Isabel shook her head. How on earth could she begin to explain her revulsion to this poor deluded girl?

"Isabel, are you all right?" Bertha asked, silencing the girls' giggles with a stern look.

"Yes, I'm fine."

"But Felix isn't," Eben reported slyly. "She clobbered him with a bag of rocks."

"Rocks?" they all echoed in disbelief.

"Well, yes, I..." She held up her purse, which Bertha snatched from her hand and shook experimentally.

"It's filled with rocks," she reported to the rest. This information sent the children into hysterics, and to Isabel's chagrin, Bertha, Herald, and Eben laughed right along with them.

Finally Bertha noticed Isabel hadn't joined in the hilarity. She sobered at once. "I guess Isabel must be tired. She didn't get any sleep last night, and precious little today. Amanda, it's time for you to start playing hostess."

"Oh, yes," Amanda said, instantly assuming her role. "Won't you come in, Miss Forester?"

"I'll have the boys bring your things over," Bertha said as she herded her family away. "If you need anything, just holler."

Isabel waved her farewells, then turned to Eben, who said, "I'll put the buggy away, then come back to check on you."

He climbed into the wagon and drove off toward the barn behind his shop. Isabel felt a slight sense of loss as she watched him go.

"Miss Forester?" Amanda said anxiously.

"Coming." Isabel forced a smile and followed her into the Walker home.

Much smaller and plainer than the Bartzes' gingerbread monstrosity, the Walker house stood back from the street beneath two spreading cottonwood trees, which shaded the front veranda. Isabel noticed a few pots of bright flowers scattered across the porch, and strings stretching to the upper beams, where morning glories would climb in a few weeks. A well-used chair provided mute testimony to the fact that Eben Walker enjoyed smoking his pipe outside on pleasant evenings.

Inside, Isabel saw evidence that Amanda had tried to place her feminine touch on what would otherwise have been a barren bachelor's quarters. The main room served as parlor, kitchen, and dining room. A solid oak table in the center was surrounded by four equally solid chairs. A worn, brown settee took up one wall, a stone fireplace another, and an ornate sideboard a third.

Isabel supposed the settee and sideboard must be remnants of an earlier time, when Eben's wife had presided here. No crocheted doilies graced the arms of the settee or the surface of the sideboard, but Amanda had embroidered several samplers, which hung, neatly framed, around the room. The table had been scrubbed white, and a bowl of freshly cut wildflowers adorned it. The girl had even put a vase of flowers on the mantel next to the clock, which told Isabel it was far later than she had suspected.

"You must be starving," Amanda said. "I've got some stew left from supper. It's still warm because I knew you were coming. Sit down," Amanda urged, pointing to the table, and Isabel sank gratefully into a chair. In a moment Amanda set a bowl of stew in front of her and went to fetch a fork. "It's not as good as yours," Amanda was saying as she laid a fork beside Isabel's bowl. "I used your recipe and tried to do everything you told me, but it still isn't the same."

Isabel tasted and smiled. "Mmmm, it seems fine to me. I used a little more sage, which is probably why yours tastes different, but your meat is perfect, fork-tender. Did your father like it?"

To Isabel's surprise, Amanda frowned. "He said it was nice for a change, but I'd probably get tired of cooking so fancy all the time."

"Oh" was all Isabel could say. She would have to have a little talk with Eben about the importance of praising a woman's efforts.

"I hope you'll be comfortable here," Amanda hastened on. "Our house isn't anywhere near as nice as the Bartzes'. I've been telling Pa we should buy some new furniture, but he says what we've got is good enough." Amanda traced the grain of the tabletop with one long, slender finger. "When I'm married, I'm going to have a mahogany table like Mrs. Bartz."

"Has Mr. Dent proposed to you, then?" Isabel asked with feigned nonchalance.

"Oh, no!" she said, glancing guiltily over her shoulder to see if her father was near. "I mean, not yet. I was just saying 'when.'"

"I see. Well, I suppose cowboys are paid a substantial salary."

"What?"

"Cowboys. You said Mr. Dent works at one of the nearby ranches. He must be well paid if he'll be able to provide you with a mahogany table," Isabel explained innocently.

"Well, he won't always be a cowboy," Amanda said defensively. "He wants to get his own place someday."

Isabel glanced out the open front door. She could see no sign of Eben Walker. "I saw you last night," she said softly.

"Last night? What do you mean?" Amanda asked, stiffening.

"I saw you and Mr. Dent under the tree. It appeared that Mr. Dent was attempting the same thing with you that Mr. Weatherby was attempting with me."

Her cheeks turned rosy. "Johnny loves me. He . . . he can't help wanting to kiss me," she said, then instantly covered her mouth and glanced guiltily over

her shoulder again. So much for Amanda's insistence
that her father didn't care about what she did. Plainly
she was terrified he would learn of her escapade.

"If a young man truly loves you, he will respect
you, too, and restrain his impulses until after marriage," Isabel said, repeating a maxim she had often
quoted to her students back in New York.

Amanda jumped to her feet. "What do you know
about it?" she demanded.

Isabel didn't want to admit she knew nothing at
all. Certainly until last night, kissing had never been
a problem with which she had been forced to deal.
"Amanda, I'm only trying to . . ." She let her voice
trail off at the sound of footsteps outside. The two
oldest Bartz boys were carrying Isabel's trunk onto
the front porch. The youngest, Peter, lugged her port-
manteau in their wake.

"Bring them in here," Amanda called, hurrying to
direct them toward a door off the main room. The
boys quickly deposited their burdens and returned to
the parlor.

They paused to receive Isabel's thanks, then Herald
Jr. said, "Miss Forester, when are we supposed to be
finished with them sheep reports?"

"*Those* sheep reports," she corrected. "I felt sure
you would have them ready by tomorrow."

The boys exchanged a desperate look. "We don't
have no five hundred words yet, and we talked to
everybody in town! Hardly anybody knows anything
about sheep."

"Then perhaps you'd better look outside of town,"
she suggested. "To someone who actually raises
sheep."

"We can't go all the way out to see Mr. Plimpton,"
David protested, horrified.

"Then don't you know someone who shares his
enthusiasm for sheep?" she hinted. "Someone whom
you see every day?"

Isabel's heart wrenched at their pathetic expressions, but her smile never wavered as she waited for them to think of the idea themselves. It simply wouldn't work if she came right out and told them to do it, and she'd already given them as much direction as she could.

At last Herald's expression lightened. "Hey, I know! Barclay can tell us!"

"Who wants to talk to Barclay?" David asked in disgust.

"You do, numbskull, if you ever want to get this report finished," his brother told him contemptuously.

"Herald, that is hardly a proper way to address your brother," Isabel scolded, hiding her amusement.

He ignored the rebuke. "That's it; we can get him tomorrow at recess," he told the others.

"Then I can expect your reports on Tuesday?" Isabel said.

"Yes, ma'am," Herald called over his shoulder as he led his brothers from the house at a dead run.

She turned to Amanda, prepared to share her amusement with the girl, but she stood stiffly in the doorway to the bedroom, frowning. Her expression reminded Isabel they had been in the process of discussing a delicate subject when they'd been interrupted.

"Amanda, I'm sorry if I upset you—"

"You didn't upset me," she replied coldly. "If you're ready, I'll show you where you can sleep."

Oh, dear, Isabel thought as she finished the last bite of stew and rose to follow Amanda into the other room. She would have to mend her relationship with the girl quickly or this entire visit would be an ordeal for both of them.

Amanda went ahead and lit a lamp, so when Isabel stepped into the room, she could see everything plainly. She stopped dead in her tracks. "This . . . this is your father's room," she said uneasily.

The room displayed even more clearly the stark

simplicity of masculine taste. A faded quilt covered the plain iron bed in the center of the room. To one side stood a chifforobe, and beside it, clothes hung along the wall on pegs. Along the other wall, a washstand held a simple pitcher and basin, and a worn wing chair, which matched the settee in the front room, had been set near the window to catch the light.

Not one ornament softened the austerity of the furniture, nor were any personal items in evidence, but Isabel felt Eben Walker's presence in the room like a physical force.

"Pa took all his stuff down to the shop," Amanda explained, oblivious of Isabel's consternation. "He's got a room there with a cot in it. Sometimes he's got to sit up with a sick horse. People are always bringing him sick horses."

"Really?" Isabel said vaguely, still absorbing the fact that Amanda expected her to sleep in Eben Walker's bed.

"Yes," she continued, absently smoothing the quilt, "Pa's real good with sick horses. He can almost always figure out what's wrong with them."

Isabel realized Amanda was trying to keep the conversation on neutral ground. Unfortunately, Isabel found the subject of Eben Walker far from neutral. "I thought . . . that is, I assumed I'd be sharing a room with you."

"Oh, well, you could if you wanted, but that would be silly," Amanda reasoned. "Pa has to stay down at the shop anyways, so why let a perfectly good bed go to waste? I put clean sheets on it, if that's what—"

"I'm sure the sheets are fine," Isabel hastened to assure her, laying a hand over her quivering stomach. The thought of sleeping on bedclothes bearing Eben's scent was unnerving.

"Hello, the house," Eben's voice called from outside.

"We're in here," Amanda replied, moving back to

the front room. Isabel hurried after her, not wanting to be caught in his bedroom.

Eben came in, but he stood hesitantly just inside the front door with his hat in his hand, like a visitor uncertain of his welcome.

"I was just showing Miss Forester your room," Amanda said.

"Oh." He glanced at Isabel.

He seemed somehow larger inside the house than he did elsewhere, if that were possible. "You have a . . . a lovely home," she said, unable to summon anything more clever from her malfunctioning brain. The thought of sleeping in his bed had apparently unhinged her mind.

"Well, it's not much, but it's easier for us to take care of a small place," he said.

Isabel managed to give Amanda an approving smile. "Amanda is an excellent housekeeper, and a good cook, too, if tonight's supper is any indication."

"She said you taught her how to make it."

"I only supplied the recipe. She did the work."

He smiled slightly. "Yeah, she does a good job."

Amanda's blue eyes widened in surprise, and Isabel supposed his praise must be rare indeed to merit such a reaction. Pleased that she had succeeded in this small thing, Isabel relaxed a bit. "I feel guilty forcing you out of your own home."

"Don't worry about it. I sleep down at the shop a lot."

"Yes, Amanda was just telling me you take care of sick horses. Are you a veterinarian, too?"

He grinned, and Isabel realized she was coming to love that grin. "Not hardly, but a smith learns a lot about horses, working with them all the time. I know a few remedies."

"I suppose you know about sheep, too."

"Some," he allowed.

"How, Pa? When did you ever learn about sheep?" Amanda asked.

His grin vanished, and Isabel felt its loss. "I . . . I grew up in sheep country," he said shortly.

"Where?" she asked, taking a step toward him. "You never told me."

"East of here. It was a long time ago." He turned to Isabel, effectively cutting off Amanda. "If you need anything, just tell Amanda. She'll take good care of you. I'll be down at the shop."

"I . . . Thank you for everything," Isabel said, sorry to see him go so soon.

He shrugged. "Good night."

"Good night."

"Good night, Pa," Amanda said, fairly skipping across the room to see him out, but he barely spared her a glance.

"Night," he told her over his shoulder.

Amanda stood in the doorway, her slender shoulders slumped in dejection, and Isabel felt her pain. The poor child was desperate for her father's attention, but for some reason, he hardly noticed she was there. Something was terribly wrong between father and daughter.

Amanda closed the door and drew the bolt, then turned to face Isabel. Her eyes were suspiciously bright. "You won't tell him about me and Johnny, will you? Please, Miss Isabel, I promise I won't—"

"You don't need to promise anything," Isabel assured her. "I have no intention of telling your father, but I think you're wrong when you say he doesn't care what you do."

"Oh, he'd be mad, all right, if he found out about Johnny," Amanda allowed, walking over to the settee and slumping down on it. "He'd be mad because I embarrassed him, though, and not because he cared about *me*."

"Amanda, how can you even think such a thing?" Isabel cried, moving quickly to the settee and sitting down beside her.

"I can think it because it's true. You saw the way

he was just now. He never told me he knew anything about sheep or where he was from or even where I was born. Do you know I don't even have a photograph of my mother?"

"Perhaps she never had one made," Isabel suggested gently.

"No, she did, all right," Amanda said bitterly. "When I asked him about it once, he said he'd left all her pictures with her parents. *Her parents!* That means I've got grandparents someplace, but I don't know where they live or what their names are! And he won't tell me what my mother looked like. He won't talk about her at all!"

Isabel felt her heart twisting in her chest. Her worst fears were true. Hadn't she seen Eben's reaction this afternoon when she'd mentioned his dead wife? He'd claimed she hadn't had any sense, but Isabel had felt the pain behind his words. Even after all this time, he still couldn't bear to speak of her. What an idiot she'd been to think she could compete with a woman whom he'd held in his heart for so many years.

But as she well knew, the best cure for self-pity, was taking on someone else's problems. At the moment, Amanda's were far more serious than her own. "I'm sure your father loved your mother very much, so much that even speaking of her causes him anguish," she forced herself to say.

"Even to me?" Amanda challenged. "I'm her family, too!"

"Perhaps it's even more painful to talk to you about her simply because you are so close. And if you want to know what she looked like, you can probably look in a mirror to find out."

"What?" Amanda asked in surprise.

"Well, you certainly don't look anything like your father, so you must resemble your mother."

Amanda stared at Isabel in amazement. "I never thought . . . You mean like Carrie and Julie look like their mother?"

"Exactly. She surely must have had blond hair and blue eyes, and she must have been extremely pretty. She must also have been kind and good for your father to have loved her so much."

Amanda's face lighted with happiness. "Oh, Miss Forester, you're right, I know you are! Oh, thank you!"

She threw her arms around Isabel, and instinctively Isabel returned the embrace, glad for the comfort of another's arms to soothe the burning sense of loss she herself felt. In easing Amanda's hurts, she had only exacerbated her own.

She recalled the scriptural warning, "Pride goeth before a fall." Isabel had been proud, indeed, to imagine she could win a man like Eben Walker. Her fall had been swift and painful, but at least she had discovered her mistake before she made a complete fool of herself by throwing herself at Eben's head.

This one week in his home was all she would ever have of him. She would make the best of it.

Chapter 8

Isabel awoke slowly, groggy and disoriented. Then she heard the knock again and realized what had disturbed her.

"Miss Forester? Are you awake?" Amanda called through the door.

"Yes," she replied, her voice a hoarse croak. She cleared her throat and tried again. "Yes, I'll be out in a minute."

"I've got hot water so you can wash. Better hurry. Pa'll be in for breakfast soon."

Isabel sat bolt upright. Good heavens, no wonder she'd overslept this morning! She'd lain awake half the night trying to convince herself there was absolutely no reason for her to be disturbed about sleeping in Eben Walker's bed.

Everything about the room reminded her of its owner: The feather tick bore the unmistakable impression of his large body. Beneath its crisply ironed case, the pillow carried his distinctive scent, and every time she rolled over, she caught sight of his clothes hanging in a neat row beside the dresses she had placed on the pegs he'd left empty for her. The sight had seemed so intimate that it had triggered a painful attack of longing that kept Isabel tossing and turning for hours.

And now the object of her longing was coming to take his breakfast with her. Groaning, she threw off the bedclothes and swung her feet onto the floor. She would at least be washed and dressed when he arrived. She reached for her skirt, but paused when she saw the shirt hanging next to it. *His* shirt.

Glancing guiltily over her shoulder, she moved her hand sideways until her fingers closed around the fabric. Soft and faded from many washings, the shirt yielded to her grasp and lifted easily from its hook. Turning it, she saw the material was frayed at the neck and elbows from much wear. His powerful body had touched this, moved beneath it, strained against it. Soon it would need a patch or two, a patch she could sew on so deftly it wouldn't even be visible from a foot away. She would cut the patch from the tail, carefully press the raw edge under, then attach it lovingly, with stitches so tiny they would be almost invisible.

Touching the fabric to her cheek, Isabel inhaled the essence of Eben Walker, and her longing swelled into exquisite pain. She would do her mending in the evening, after supper, while they sat by the fire. He would move the lamp close to her so she wouldn't strain her eyes, and she would look up and smile. . . .

"Miss Forester? Are you ready for your hot water yet?" Amanda called.

Startled, Isabel dropped the shirt. "I . . . uh, yes, just a moment." Hastily she snatched up the shirt and threw it back over its peg. Dear heaven, what was happening to her?

Mercifully, Eben hadn't appeared by the time Isabel had washed and dressed. She even had time to sneak out to the outhouse, which she did after assuring herself he was nowhere in sight. Having accomplished her purpose and telling herself she now felt confident enough to face him at last, she left the small building, stepped out into the morning sunshine, and came face-to-face with him.

He grinned his wonderful grin, and Isabel's heart leaped into her throat. "Good morning," he said as casually as if they encountered each other outside the outhouse every morning.

"Good... morning," she replied weakly, completely mortified.

"Did you sleep well?"

"Uh, yes, fine," she lied. Heavens, he looked even better in the morning light than he did in the moonlight, even though he hadn't shaved yet. The dark growth of stubble lent him a rakish air, and Isabel realized with a start that this is how he would look if she happened to wake up beside him. The thought took her breath and turned her knees to jelly. For a second she felt just as she had the day she'd fainted into his arms.

"Are you all right?" he asked, frowning in concern. His dark eyes softened, and for a wicked instant Isabel considered feigning a faint just to feel his arms around her again.

"I... Of course, I'm fine," she managed breathlessly, forcing a smile, although her face still felt as hot as his forge. "I believe Amanda has breakfast almost ready."

"I was hoping you'd fix it," he said, his grin back. "I've been hearing a lot of stories about your cooking from Herald."

"I overslept." Although she'd managed to swallow her heart back down into its proper place, she couldn't seem to get her lungs to work properly. Perhaps she'd laced her corset too tightly.

"That bed's hard to leave, isn't it? It's got a real feather mattress."

Isabel knew she couldn't stand here outside the outhouse discussing the comforts of his bed and remain rational. "Shall I tell Amanda you'll be in soon?" she asked weakly.

"Yeah," he said, "as soon as I . . ." He gestured toward the outhouse.

"Oh! Of course," she squeaked, mortified again, and made her escape.

Eben lingered to watch her scurry away, admiring the provocative sway of her skirt and the way the sunlight glinted off her golden hair. He tried to feel at least a little guilty for teasing her, but failed. Of course, she'd been embarrassed to be caught coming out of the outhouse. He'd been a little embarrassed himself, but she looked so cute when she blushed, he just couldn't resist.

Besides, she deserved to be a little embarrassed after she'd kept him up half the night. The thought of her lying in his bed, her slim white body clad in only a thin nightdress tucked between his sheets, had about driven him crazy.

He'd have to make sure Amanda didn't strip the bed at the end of the week. The sheets would probably smell of Isabel Forester, all sweet with lavender and woman. . . .

Of course, he had also considered the possibility of keeping Isabel herself between those sheets so he wouldn't have to be satisfied with memories and imagination. For years now, Paul Young had been lamenting the bachelor's curse of sleeping alone, but until recently, Eben hadn't felt the lack. After all, he knew there were worse things, like sharing a bed with someone who turned away when you reached for her. Sometimes another body in the bed brought no warmth at all, and a man was the lonelier for having someone beside him.

Was Isabel like that? After all, she'd practically bashed poor Felix's brains out for trying to steal a kiss, and she'd put Dave Weatherby in his place, too.

But even as he considered the possibility, Eben knew it wasn't true. He remembered how she'd been in his arms the two times they'd danced, all soft and yielding. She wouldn't stand for any nonsense—she was a lady, through and through—but she wasn't cold, not by a long shot.

Eben's body quickened at the thought, and he cursed softly, glancing down at the telltale bulge in his pants. He couldn't go in the house like this. With a grin he decided he'd have to keep Amanda's breakfast waiting a few minutes longer until he was presentable again.

By the time Eben came in, Isabel had regained her composure. She'd helped Amanda set the table for breakfast and called herself a ninny for being so upset over their encounter outside. Why should Eben Walker's frankness have surprised her? She knew perfectly well how outrageous men were.

"Morning," Eben called cheerfully from the doorway as he wiped his feet on the mat.

Amanda looked up in surprise. "Good morning," she replied. Apparently her father rarely greeted her so enthusiastically.

"Good morning again," Isabel said, nervously smoothing her skirt and feeling as awkward as a schoolgirl. She forced herself to sit down.

He took his place at the head of the table, and Amanda set a plate of heaping flapjacks in front of him.

"Looks good," he said, spearing one with his fork and lifting it onto his plate.

Amanda's blue eyes widened at the compliment. She sank down in her chair, watching her father with a slightly dazed expression, as if she were uncertain of his sanity. "I . . . I hope I made enough," she stammered. "Mrs. Bartz sent over some honey, too."

"Good," Eben replied with a smile that made Isabel feel as if the sweet honey were flowing right through her body.

"Which of you usually asks the blessing?" Isabel made herself ask when Eben continued to fill his plate.

He dropped his fork instantly. "Uh, Amanda does, when we remember to do it at all," he said, looking endearingly sheepish.

Isabel instantly forgave him his heathen ways. She folded her hands and bowed her head, watching Eben do the same from the corner of her eye. He rested his elbows on the table and clasped his hands beneath his chin. The muscles of his arms strained the fabric of his shirt, and Isabel's stomach fluttered in response.

How could she have ever been repulsed by the sight of his work-stained hands? She remembered how he had stroked the horse that day in his shop, gentling and soothing it, and she imagined how those rough, strong fingers would feel against her naked flesh.

She shivered, and only when Amanda asked her if she wanted some flapjacks did she realize the prayer was over. "Yes, please," she said, offering her plate.

Although Isabel ate only three, and Amanda four, the mound of flapjacks soon disappeared, leaving Isabel to marvel at how much food one man could consume. Cooking for him would be a pure delight, she thought, then caught herself. She simply had to stop dwelling on such things. She was getting entirely too involved with this fantasy.

"Mmmm, this coffee is mighty good," Eben remarked as he poured himself a third cup. He glanced at Isabel, as if thinking she would take the credit.

"Thanks, Pa," Amanda said, surprising him. "I put in a dash of cinnamon. Miss Forester said it would give it more flavor."

"But, of course, I didn't have a thing to do with the rest of the breakfast, which was delicious," Isabel replied. "Amanda is quite an accomplished cook. You must be very proud of her."

"Grateful is more like it. I'd've starved to death long

ago if she hadn't took to the kitchen like she did."
Eben flashed the girl a smile. She pinkened prettily,
and Isabel's heart ached to see how much the simple
words meant to her.

"You . . . you never said you thought I was a good
cook before," she said in wonder.

Eben shrugged. "Didn't think I had to. I figured
you'd get the idea when you didn't have to throw
any food away."

"Oh, Pa!" she cried, jumping from her chair and
throwing her arms around his neck. She kissed his
cheek, and for an instant Isabel experienced the sour
taste of envy, knowing she would never feel Eben
Walker's skin beneath her lips. "Ouch!" Amanda
cried, drawing back with a laugh and rubbing her
mouth. "Kissing you is dangerous."

"Yeah, I reckon it is," he said, rubbing his prickly
jaw. To Isabel's surprise, his jovial mood had evaporated. He rose abruptly, his dark eyes clouded. "I
reckon I'd better get to work."

In another second he was gone, leaving Isabel and
Amanda staring after him.

"He . . . he must've been embarrassed about not
being shaved," Amanda supposed tentatively.

"Yes, I'm sure that's it," Isabel hastily assured her.
"Men are just as sensitive about their appearance as
women are."

"He doesn't ever shave until he's done work,"
Amanda explained, her earnest expression telling Isabel that she was really trying to justify his behavior
to herself. "He says the sweat makes his face burn if
he does it in the morning."

"Oh," Isabel mumbled uneasily, realizing she could
learn all sorts of intimate things about Eben Walker
if she were devious enough to pump his daughter for
information. She forced herself to consider Amanda's
feelings instead. "You see, your father really does
appreciate what you do for him," she said brightly.

"Men simply aren't as likely to express their gratitude as another woman would be."

Amanda's mood lightened again at once. "Yes, you're right. Pa hardly ever says anything at all, but he never says anything bad, so I guess he must like what I do."

"How could he not?" Isabel pointed out sensibly as she rose and began to clear the table. Still, while the newly cheered Amanda helped her do up the dishes, Isabel could not forget the sudden change in Eben when his daughter had impulsively embraced him. Why should her innocent kiss have disturbed him so? She could think of no logical explanation.

"I'm awful glad you came, Miss Forester," Amanda told her later as they were leaving the house for school. "I wish you could stay forever."

Isabel wouldn't have minded a bit.

Isabel had been sitting on the schoolhouse steps watching the children at play after lunch when she heard voices from the side of the school.

"Come on, Bark," Herald Bartz Jr. pleaded. "We need your help."

"Why should I be willing to help *you*?" Barclay Plimpton replied in his starchy British-Texas accent.

Isabel rose and casually strolled a few paces closer to the corner so she could hear the conversation more clearly.

"You ain't mad because we barked at you, are you?" Roger Stevens scoffed. "You know we was only funning."

"I saw no humor in it," Barclay informed him.

"Then you should be glad we're being punished," Roger replied.

"Yeah, and you should help us out 'cause it's your fault we got in trouble in the first place," David Bartz reasoned.

"Shut up," Herald snapped irritably, obviously re-alizing this was not a convincing argument. "Look,

Bark, we got to write five hundred words about sheep, but we can't unless you tell us what you know about them."

"Why should I?" Barclay asked.

Isabel held her breath. If he refused to cooperate, all her scheming would be for naught, and the other children would hate Barclay more than before.

The boys considered his question for a long minute. Finally Herald came up with a reason. "'Cause you're a kid just like us. We got to show Miss Forester she can't push us around. She prob'ly thinks we won't be able to get you to talk to us, and then she'll be able to tell our folks we didn't do our assignment and get us in even more trouble."

"Maybe you deserve to be in trouble," Barclay said, and Isabel's heart sank.

Roger made a disgusted noise. "Come on, he prob'ly don't know anything about sheep, anyways. If he did, he'd be bragging—"

"I know far more about sheep than any of you knows about *anything*," Barclay insisted.

"Then prove it!" Herald challenged.

Isabel held her breath again for what seemed a long time.

"All right, but you better write it down, because I won't tell you twice!"

The other boys shouted their pleasure and ran for their pencils and copybooks, almost knocking Isabel down in their haste. She hoped they wouldn't guess she had been eavesdropping, but they hardly seemed to notice how close she had been standing. Hazarding a peek around the corner, she saw Barclay standing alone, his hands in his jean pockets, his round face set in a determined scowl. Resisting the urge to beg him to be magnanimous, she withdrew and whispered a silent prayer.

By the end of the day, Isabel began to believe her plan was working. The instant she dismissed school, she saw Roger and the Bartz boys head straight for

Barclay, who waited patiently for them to catch up. They talked and argued all the way to the church, where they grudgingly separated for choir practice. As soon as she dismissed the practice, the boys gathered again, congregating beneath the shade of a live oak tree in the churchyard and pulling out their copybooks while Barclay held forth.

Isabel tried to hear what they were saying as she passed, but the girls walking with her were chattering too loudly. She allowed herself a small smile of satisfaction. At least something seemed to be working out.

"Mama's going to let me have a new dress," Carrie was saying. "Will you help me pick the pattern and the material, Miss Forester?"

"Certainly," Isabel replied absently as her gaze wandered toward the tree-shaded blacksmith shop where Eben worked. A wagon with a missing wheel sat in the yard. She felt drawn to the shop, although she admitted the real draw was Eben. Their time together was to be so brief, she yearned to savor every precious moment. Each of those moments would provide a memory that she could take out and examine again and again during the lonely years to come.

Oh, dear, she lamented, she really was getting dotty.

Then she saw a small, ragged figure appear in the doorway of the shop, wielding a broom twice his size. Larry Potts.

"Girls, will you excuse me a minute? I need to speak with Mr. Walker about something."

"But you promised to help me make something special for supper," Amanda reminded her.

"I won't be long. You can start getting the things together for piecrust. Sift the flour, and if I'm still not there yet, you may begin cutting the ham into chunks and peeling the potatoes."

"What are you going to talk to him about?" Amanda asked suspiciously.

"Larry Potts."

"*Larry Potts?*" the girls echoed in unison.

"Shhh, he'll hear you," Isabel cautioned. "He's working in the shop, and I've been hoping for a chance to encourage him to come to school."

"We don't want him in school," Carrie protested. "He smells."

Isabel briefly considered explaining the difference in meaning between the words "smell" and "stink," then thought better of it. "I'll be certain to have him bathe before he comes," she said with a smile as she strolled away.

From inside the shop she could hear the pounding of Eben's hammer on metal, *clang*, clink, *clang*, clink. The sound matched the pounding of her heart, which increased in rhythm with each step.

She paused in the doorway, allowing her eyes to grow accustomed to the dimness. Before she could make out more than Eben's shadow, he looked up and saw her.

"Miss Isabel? What brings you here?"

Did he seem pleased to see her? She took a few tentative steps inside. Although both the front and back doors stood open, little light penetrated the interior of the shop. "Doesn't it hurt your eyes to work with so little light?"

"I have to be able to judge the color of the metal."

"Oh," she said as he gradually came into focus. He looked just as he had the other times she'd seen him here, dirty and sweaty and supremely masculine. He'd rolled up his sleeves to reveal muscular forearms, and his shirt clung faithfully to his broad shoulders. Blue-black stubble shadowed his jaw, and his eyes seemed fathomless as they studied her. "I thought I saw Larry Potts in here working," she managed to say.

Eben glanced around, and Isabel did, too. They both saw the broom lying unattended where Larry had dropped it when he fled.

"Oh, dear, I seem to have scared him off again."

"Looks like," Eben remarked with a small smile. "Too bad all your students aren't so touchy. Your job would be a lot easier."

"I doubt the school board would retain a teacher who frightened the children away," she replied, answering his smile.

"No, I don't reckon we would."

She noticed he'd been working on a horseshoe, probably for the animal tied up in the corner of the shop. "I'm keeping you from your work," she said, feeling guilty for having interrupted him.

"I'm always glad for an excuse to stop, especially for a pretty woman."

Isabel started in surprise. *Pretty?* Was he teasing? Her cheeks went hot, and she hoped the light was too dim for him to see. Flustered, she decided to ignore the compliment. "Are you shoeing that horse?" she asked inanely.

"Yeah," he said, leaving her to scramble for another topic.

Sucking up her courage, she took a few steps closer to the anvil. "I thought you could buy horseshoes ready-made. Why do you make your own?"

"I don't. The ready-made shoes don't fit every horse, so I adjust them to each horse's foot."

"Oh," she said, again at a loss. She glanced down at the shoe lying on the anvil. "Why does that shoe have a bar across it?"

"Butch over there has sore heels. This bar will help throw his weight onto the frog of his foot instead of it all being on his heels."

"You mean you can do all that with just a piece of metal?" she asked in amazement.

"You can do a lot of things with a shoe. If a horse is knock-kneed or bowlegged, I can make special shoes to help straighten out his legs. On the other hand, if a smith isn't careful, he can *make* a horse lame by putting the wrong shoes on him."

"How interesting," she replied. "Amanda said you know a lot about horses, but I had no idea how important proper shoes could be."

"Yeah, a smith's job is important, all right," he said with a trace of pride.

"Are you fixing the wagon outside, too?"

"Just the wheel. The rim broke."

She glanced around the shop, searching for something else on which to comment. "Oh, dear, your horseshoe is upside down," she said, pointing to the shoe nailed above the entrance to the shop. "All your luck will run out."

"That's the idea," he told her with a grin. "A smith is the only one allowed to hang a horseshoe with the heels down so the luck will run out onto his anvil."

His grin took all the starch right out of her bones, and she could only manage a small "Oh" in response. They stared at each other for several heartbeats until Isabel realized she'd stopped breathing and forced herself to start again. "Well," she said, flustered, looking past him for a moment while she regained her composure. Then she noticed the flicker of shadow on the ground outside the back door.

Someone stood just out of sight, someone small. She pointed at the shadow so Eben would see it, too, and know someone was eavesdropping. "Well, if you happen to see Larry Potts again, will you tell him I'm looking for him?" she asked a little louder than necessary.

"Sure, but why do you want to see him?" Eben replied, playing along.

"I feel he should be in school with the other children. We have such a good time, and the children seem to enjoy singing in the choir, too. Perhaps he'd like to join us."

"I'll tell him if I see him again," Eben said, shaking his head to tell her he thought she was wasting her time.

"Well," she said, suddenly at a loss again. "I guess I'll see you in a little while, then."

"I'm looking forward to it." His smile seemed utterly sincere, and Isabel's heart quivered in response.

"So am I," she said boldly. "Well, I'd better let you get back to work." With a wave, she hurried away, hoping he hadn't noticed she was blushing again. What on earth did she think she was doing? Eben Walker had better things to do than suffer her feeble attempts at coquetry.

With a sigh, Eben watched her go, then laid down his hammer and tongs and walked to the door so he could continue to watch. The sight of her strolling up his walk and entering his house as if she belonged there touched something deep inside him.

He wanted her body, of course, wanted to feel her soft flesh beneath his, wanted to taste her passion and sink into her velvet depths. But he wanted more than that, too. He wanted to know she belonged to him. She would live in his house and eat at his table and sleep in his bed.

And she would love him.

The very thought filled him with despair. How could a woman like Isabel ever love Eben Walker? She deserved an educated man, an important man, not someone who could hardly read, and worked with his hands. And if she knew what he had done . . . No, the whole idea was nothing more than a futile dream.

The sound of sweeping drew his attention, and he turned to find Larry Potts diligently wielding his broom again. "Miss Forester was here looking for you."

"I know. You can tell her I ain't allowed to go to school, and I wouldn't even if I was."

"She's a nice lady. Maybe you oughta tell her yourself," Eben suggested.

Larry ignored him.

* * *

Isabel checked her appearance one last time in Eben's shaving mirror. From what little she could see, she looked presentable. Every hair was in place, and her face bore no visible smudges.

She'd found the dress in the bottom of her trunk, a peach-colored calico sprigged with clusters of tiny blue flowers. She had intended to wear it later, when her year of mourning was over, but here in the privacy of a home, she needn't observe strict mourning. Since no one was likely to see her tonight, she decided to bend the rules so she could appear before Eben in something other than unrelieved black.

" 'Vanity of vanities, all is vanity,' " she could hear her father quoting. She wondered if it was proper to ask for forgiveness *before* one committed a sin, but since she had no intention of changing her gown, she decided to wait until afterward.

"You look real nice, Miss Forester," Amanda said when Isabel entered the front room. The two of them had prepared a simple meal of ham, green beans, and potatoes boiled together, but her yeast biscuits and the apple pies cooling on the windowsill would make the fare more elegant.

Isabel laid a hand over her churning stomach and wondered why she was so nervous about sitting down at table with Eben Walker. They were just going to eat supper, for heaven's sake.

"All right if I come in?" Eben called from the porch, and Isabel's stomach did a complete flip.

"Sure," Amanda called back.

Isabel turned to face him, striving for nonchalance, but the sight of him stunned her all over again.

He'd bathed and shaved. He'd tamed his thick brown hair to lie flat against his head, although it still curled a bit on the back of his neck. His cheeks gleamed from the closeness of his shave, and the faint scent of bay rum wafted across the room to her. Most astonishing of all, he wore his Sunday suit, complete with boiled shirt and starched collar.

"Why're you so dressed up, Pa?" Amanda asked, as amazed as Isabel.

"Miss Isabel got dressed up," he pointed out. "Why shouldn't I?"

Amanda's expression said she was still mystified. "It's almost like a party, isn't it?"

"Yes, well, won't you come in and sit down, Mr. Walker?" Isabel said, growing more flustered by the minute.

To her amazement and Amanda's surprise, Eben hurried over to hold Isabel's chair for her. She sank down into it gratefully, certain her legs couldn't have held her up for another second.

Amanda and Eben were just about to sit down when someone knocked on the door.

"Who on earth?" Eben wondered aloud as he went to answer it.

"Evening, Eben," Paul Young greeted him jovially. "I just stopped by to return your hammer." He thrust a hammer into Eben's hands and entered the house without waiting for an invitation. For some inexplicable reason, he, too, wore his Sunday best. "Evening, ladies. I'm sorry to interrupt your supper. Mmmm, something smells mighty good." He waited expectantly.

Isabel could see from Eben's glare that he wasn't going to play polite host: it was up to her. Conscious of a pang of regret, she said, "Won't you stay to supper, Mr. Young? I'm sure Mr. Walker and Amanda won't mind."

Eben grunted. Paul smiled triumphantly. "There's nothing I'd like better, ma'am."

Everyone began to serve themselves. When Isabel saw how much Paul and Eben took, she wondered if they were having some sort of contest to see who could eat the most. She began to wish she had made another dozen rolls.

"Herald Bartz was right about your biscuits, Miss

Isabel," Paul remarked. "He said they were so light, you had to cover them with a weighted sheet."

"Good heavens," Isabel said with a self-conscious laugh. "I'll have to speak to him about telling such fibs."

"It's not a fib at all, is it, Eben?" But Eben's mouth was full, and Paul didn't wait for him to swallow. "Well, they're the best biscuits I ever tasted," he added, as if apologizing for Eben's lack of response.

"Thank you," Isabel said, somewhat gratified to see Eben scowling at his guest.

They ate in silence, as Isabel had learned was the custom in Texas, but Paul punctuated it with repeated praise for Isabel's cooking until at last she was compelled to say, "Amanda did a great deal of the work."

"But Paul didn't come here to see Amanda, did you, Paul?" Eben asked snidely.

"Why, no, I came to return your hammer, Eben," he replied innocently. Isabel quickly lifted her napkin to cover a smile, and Amanda pretended to choke so her father wouldn't know she was laughing. By the time they had served the pie and Paul had praised it lavishly, Isabel had begun to truly enjoy herself.

"Where did you learn to sing so well, Miss Isabel?" he asked.

"My mother taught me, at first. She had received training in her youth, and when she saw I had inherited her voice, she helped me to develop it. She also taught me to play the piano. Then, when I was older, I had a professional teacher."

"I know I speak for everybody in the county when I say I'm awful glad your mother recognized your talent. Isn't that right, Eben?"

Eben opened his mouth to agree, but Paul rambled on. "The only thing I can't understand is what made you decide to come all the way to Texas."

Isabel couldn't possibly explain about the dreariness of her life in New York or about the conversation she had overheard in the parlor of her father's rectory.

Instead she said, "I'm afraid it was a sudden whim. My father had just passed away, and I saw the advertisement. Since I had nothing to hold me in New York any longer . . ." She shrugged.

"New York's loss is our gain, right, Amanda?" he said.

"Oh, yes," Amanda began, but Paul didn't give her a chance to finish.

"I hear you're interested in sheep. Has Eben been educating you on the subject?"

She glanced at Eben and saw his scowl had turned murderous. "We haven't really had an opportunity to discuss it," she said sweetly. Yes, this really was an enjoyable experience.

"Well, old Eben never has been much for conversation. Sometimes goes for days at a time without saying a word, right, Amanda?"

"Not really—" the girl tried, but again he cut her off.

"I suppose you're used to a lot of conversation, aren't you, Miss Isabel?" Paul asked.

"Not really," she echoed, exchanging an amused look with Amanda. Eben's hands had curled into fists where they lay on either side of his empty pie plate.

But Paul was not to be deterred. "Living alone, a man gets starved for someone to talk to. When I think about how lucky Eben is to have you here all week, I get purely green with envy."

"I thought you looked a little peaked, Paul," Eben managed at last. "Maybe you ought to go on home."

Paul grinned expansively, ignoring the obvious warning in Eben's tone. "You're kind to be concerned about my health, Eb, but now that I'm with Miss Isabel, I feel perfectly fine."

Deciding enough was enough, Isabel rose and began clearing the table. "I suppose you gentlemen would like to go outside to smoke," she said by way of a suggestion.

Paul made no move until Eben rose and glared

ominously at him for a full minute. Then he, too, reluctantly stood.

"I hope you'll join us outside when you're finished, Miss Isabel," Paul said as he trailed Eben to the door.

"Of course," she replied, disappointed when Eben did not second the invitation. If Paul Young wanted to flirt with her, she would gladly let him, especially if he wanted to do it in front of Eben Walker.

"I think Mr. Young likes you," Amanda said when the men were gone.

"Do you?"

"Yes, I do. That business with the hammer was just a windy to get himself invited to supper."

"He probably only wanted a home-cooked meal," Isabel said.

"Maybe, but didn't you notice the way he kept looking at you? And he hardly talked to anybody else."

Her pleasure was somewhat tempered by the knowledge that Paul Young would never have looked at her twice if single women had not been so scarce here, but she had enjoyed his attention nevertheless. "He seems like a very nice man."

"Oh, he is," Amanda assured her. "Almost as nice as Pa."

Isabel looked up in surprise to find Amanda watching her intently.

"Don't you think my pa's nice?" she inquired too innocently.

"He . . . he seems to be," Isabel admitted warily.

"I thought you might like him when I saw how dressed up you got for supper," Amanda said ingenuously. "He was pretty dressed up, too. Did you notice?"

"I'm sure he was only being polite."

Amanda made a rude noise. "Pa never wears a suit unless he has to, and he sure doesn't have to in his own house. He was pretty mad when Mr. Young showed up, too. Mr. Young is his best friend, and usually he's real happy to see him, so I figure he was jealous."

"Jealous?" Isabel echoed hopefully.

"Jealous for sure," Amanda assured her. "He was so mad when Mr. Young kept talking to you, I almost expected to see smoke coming out of his ears."

"I . . . I'm sure you're mistaken," Isabel tried, although she had to admit Eben had certainly seemed angry.

"Then go outside with them and see for yourself. I can do the dishes by myself."

"I couldn't possibly," Isabel protested.

"Don't be a goose," Amanda said. "I don't mind at all. In fact, I'll be mad at you if you don't."

"At least let me help clear the table. It wouldn't do for me to go outside too soon: they'll think I'm too eager for their company."

"All right, but as soon as we're done, you go on outside."

After taking several deep breaths to calm her quivering nerves, Isabel found the two men sitting on the straight-backed chairs they had carried from inside. Paul had rolled a cigarette, and Eben puffed on his pipe. They both jumped to their feet the instant she appeared.

"Eben, be a good host and fetch Miss Isabel a chair," Paul said with a smile.

Isabel tried not to be deterred by Eben's frown. If he didn't want her out here, this could be a very awkward situation, but perhaps he was only annoyed by Paul's ordering him around. In any case, he disappeared into the house, and before he returned, Paul had directed her to the chair farthest from the door and taken the other himself.

Eben came back out with the third chair and saw exactly what Paul had tried to do. The son of a bitch was trying to put himself between Eben and Isabel, but he wasn't going to get away with it.

"Excuse me," Eben said, shooting Paul a murderous scowl as he crossed in front of them. He set his chair firmly down on the other side of Isabel's, putting her between them. As he took his seat, he hazarded a glance at her and was startled to see her smiling up at him. He pulled the pipe out of his mouth and smiled back. "Does the smoke bother you?"

"Not at all," she said. "I've always enjoyed the smell of a pipe."

Eben loved the soft, sweet sound of her voice and the way the fading sunlight turned her hair the color of warm honey. He tried to think of something to say, but Paul beat him to it.

"I notice you didn't say anything about cigarette smoke," he said, crushing the butt with the heel of his shoe. "I'm afraid I've got a lot of bad habits, Miss Isabel. A bachelor tends to develop them without a woman's influence."

"I can't believe you're so very bad, Mr. Young," she said, turning her lovely smile on Paul, who didn't deserve it in the least. Not very bad? Eben could tell her a thing or two about Paul Young. . . .

"Well, I do try to toe the mark, so to speak," Paul was saying, that disgustingly innocent smile still on his face. No woman in her right mind would believe that innocence for a minute. "You see, I have hopes that someday I might win the hand of a gentle lady such as yourself, and I wouldn't want her to find me *too* far past reformation."

Did he think he was being charming? Eben was just about to snort when he noticed Isabel's enraptured expression. "Most women like a little bit of a challenge," she said, to Eben's disgust.

"Are you saying you wouldn't mind the job of breaking me to harness?" Paul asked, entirely too confidently. Eben itched to wipe that smirk off his face.

Isabel laughed, a sound as musical as a thousand tinkling bells. She never laughed like that at the things Eben said. He wanted to break Paul's neck. "You read too much into my remark, Mr. Young," she scolded. Damn if she wasn't batting her eyes at him. "I only said *most* women wouldn't find the task too daunting."

"And are you like *most* women, Miss Isabel?" Paul teased, leaning closer—too close. He'd be lucky if she didn't rear back in disgust. But, of course, she didn't. In fact, she smiled again, just like she wanted him to keep flirting with her.

"If you aren't careful, I'll think you're just like Mr. Weatherby and Mr. Underwood," she said.

Paul widened his eyes as if he were shocked or something. "Miss Isabel," he said, affronted, "I certainly have my faults, but I hope I'm not as ill-mannered as those cads!"

"I hope so, too, although those other gentlemen also hinted of marriage before they . . ." She let her voice trail off, too ladylike to speak of the outrages she had suffered. Eben wanted to say something to make her feel better, but he'd never faced a situation like this one. The usual "I'm real sorry for your loss" hardly seemed appropriate. In any case, Paul didn't give him a chance to say anything at all.

"I'm not likely to try to take advantage of you while we have a chaperone," Paul pointed out, finally pushing Eben too far.

"I'm not a chaperone," he protested angrily.

"Now, Eben, you mustn't let Miss Isabel think you're trying to court her, too," Paul said, and continued before Eben could think of a reply to that outrageous statement. "Eben was just telling me the other day how he's sworn off marriage, so you don't have to worry about him. You're perfectly safe."

"Safe!" Eben exclaimed, wondering how on earth to refute Paul's assertions without sounding like an idiot. "Why wouldn't she be safe even if I *was* trying to court her?"

"Safe from unwanted advances," Paul explained with maddening calmness. "As Miss Isabel has learned, not all the men in Texas are as well mannered as I am. And since you're not the least bit interested in a wife . . ."

Eben looked at Isabel, hoping to gauge her reaction to this ridiculous statement.

"I'm . . . certainly relieved to hear it," she murmured, although she looked upset. Could she possibly be worried that he might try to attack her while she was under his roof? He couldn't blame her, of course, not after the treatment she'd received lately, and if she knew about the thoughts that had kept him awake last night . . .

"Paul, you oughta be horsewhipped for frightening Miss Isabel," Eben said, maintaining his temper with difficulty.

"I'm not frightened," she said, but her expression contradicted her words. She jumped to her feet. "If you'll excuse me, it's getting late, and I have some lessons to plan for tomorrow."

Both men rose, too, but she had already disappeared inside with a swish of skirts.

"Damn your soul," Eben hissed furiously.

"Me?" Paul asked innocently.

"What do you mean by telling her I'm not interested in a wife?"

"That's what you told me a few weeks ago. If you've changed your mind, you should've said something."

Eben closed his hands into fists and entertained a satisfying vision of smashing one of them into Paul Young's face. "I'm saying something now."

Paul shook his head in mock sympathy. "I'm afraid you're too late, partner."

"What do you mean?"

"I mean, if what I saw tonight is your idea of courting, you might as well save your energy for pounding iron. You hardly even spoke two words to the woman."

"I couldn't get one in edgewise!"

"Just as well. I don't cotton to the idea of other men conversing with my future wife."

"*Your* future wife?"

"Yep," Paul said with a satisfied smile. "Like I told you before, I figured you were about the only competition I had, and I can see now you're no competition at all. In a few days, Miss Isabel will be all mine."

With that pronouncement, he hopped off the porch in one lithe movement and strode jauntily away. He was halfway across the street before Eben got his tongue unhinged. "And don't think you can just show up here at suppertime every night and get a free meal!"

Paul turned. "You can keep the hammer," he offered with a small salute.

Eben wished he had it handy so he could fling it after him. He slumped back down onto his chair with a disgusted sigh. In another moment he heard light footsteps inside the house coming toward the door. He looked up hopefully, but it was only Amanda.

She glanced around. "Did Mr. Young go home already?"

"Yeah," Eben said sourly, thinking he hadn't left early enough.

She looked back into the house as if checking to see if Isabel could overhear them, then came a few steps closer to where Eben sat. "I think he's sweet on Miss Forester."

Eben eyed his daughter suspiciously. "What makes you think so?"

"The way he looked at her. Couldn't you tell? He hardly talked to you or me at all, either."

Eben grunted.

"It'd be nice if she married somebody close like that," Amanda continued. "I mean, we'd be neighbors."

Eben couldn't imagine anything less "nice." "Do you think she likes him?"

"I suppose she does, but she's not in love with him, if that's what you mean."

Eben guessed he *had* meant that, although the thought left a bitter taste in his mouth.

Amanda's expression turned cunning. "You like her, too, don't you?"

"What do you mean?" he asked in surprise.

"I mean it's pretty obvious Mr. Young is trying to court Miss Forester. Are you?"

"Amanda, this is none of your business," he informed her, irritated.

"It most certainly is my business," she replied. "If you're thinking about marrying Miss Forester, my life will be affected, too, and I think you'd be a fool if you *weren't* thinking about it."

"Amanda!" he exclaimed in outrage. Who did the little brat think she was, calling her own father a fool?

"Well, you would," she insisted, not the least bit intimidated. "Where else would you find a wife like her? And I'll tell you something else—I'm getting sick and tired of keeping house for you. Maybe you think I'll be around here forever to cook and clean for you, but you're wrong! If you're smart, you'll get yourself a wife while the getting is good."

"Amanda, go to your room!" he ordered furiously.

"No," she replied defiantly, "I'm going over to visit Carrie, and if you've got any sense at all, you'll use the time to speak to Miss Forester."

"Amanda, come back here!" he yelled, but she ignored him and skipped down the porch steps, into the street. Cursing under his breath, he watched her disappear into the Bartz house.

Having a fourteen-year-old girl telling him what he should do really rankled, but knowing she was right was even worse.

Where *would* he ever find a woman like Isabel again? If he let her go, he'd be every bit the fool Amanda had called him.

* * *

Isabel sat in Eben Walker's bedroom chair, staring blindly out the window and trying not to feel the pain. What had she expected, after all? She'd already known Eben still loved his first wife, but having someone else verify her suspicions made the knowledge agonizingly real.

It was all her own fault, too. She must be sinking into senility to have allowed herself to become infatuated with a man who could never love her in return. Even more ironic was the knowledge that the town abounded in perfectly eligible men who were practically desperate to claim her hand in marriage. Why couldn't she have fixed her affections on one of them?

As if from a distance, she heard Amanda's voice raised in anger and Eben's booming response. She winced. What on earth could they be arguing about? She listened for sounds of Amanda storming back into the house, but heard nothing. In the stillness, she reflected on her situation and wondered if she might somehow cut her stay with the Walkers short, in order to spare herself the pain of spending time with a man who would never want her.

"Miss Isabel?"

Eben's call startled her. He sounded angry. Perhaps he blamed her for Amanda's outburst. Perhaps he was going to order her from his home. Smiling at the irony of the thought, she rose from her chair, crossed the room, and opened the door into the parlor.

Eben stood in the center of the room, his arms rigid at his sides, his chin lifted belligerently.

"Yes?" she said, feeling a bit intimidated. He looked as if he really *might* order her from his home.

"Isabel, will you marry me?"

Chapter 9

Isabel stared at him in disbelief. "Will I *what?*"

"Will you marry me?" he repeated impatiently.

This couldn't be happening. In the first place, she had just learned that Eben wasn't interested in getting married again. In the second place, common sense and her own recent experience told her a man might use any one of several approaches to win the hand of his chosen lady, but she felt reasonably certain that belligerence wasn't one of them. She must have misunderstood his intention.

"Are you *proposing* to me?" she asked uncertainly.

Eben saw the puzzled expression on her face and knew he'd botched the thing. She looked so small and vulnerable and lovely, he just wanted to take her in his arms and hold her to his heart, but when he took a step closer, she stiffened in alarm. He had to remember she wouldn't stand for any nonsense, and if he so much as laid a finger on her, she'd turn him down for sure.

"Of course I'm proposing to you," he said, appalled to hear the exasperation in his voice. He wasn't doing himself any good at all since she would have no way of knowing he was exasperated with himself. Amanda was right, he *was* a fool. "I mean, I know this is kind of sudden," he corrected, softening his tone and attempting a placating smile. "We haven't known each other very long, but it doesn't take a lot of time for a man to come to appreciate you, Miss Isabel."

She blinked, still looking slightly stunned.

"I don't live real fancy," he continued doggedly, "but I make a good living, and I've got money put aside. If you want, I could even build you a house like Bertha's. You'd never lack for anything."

For a moment Isabel wondered if she might be dreaming. This was just what she'd wanted, wasn't it? Eben Walker was asking her to be his wife.

Except it wasn't *exactly* what she'd wanted. In her dreams, she'd imagined him confessing his boundless love for her, not hinting at "appreciation."

"Mr. Walk . . . Eben, you . . . you haven't said *why* you want to marry me," she hinted.

He looked a little startled but recovered quickly. "Well, because . . . because I think you'd make a good wife. You're an exceptional woman, Miss Isabel. Any man would feel lucky to have you."

Isabel's heart sank. "Because I'm a good cook?" she asked in dismay.

"Well, yeah," he said, warming to the subject. "And you're smart and educated. Amanda can't say enough nice things about you, and anybody can see how good you are with kids. . . . I mean, you'd be just what Amanda needs, and if we had any others . . ."

His voice trailed off in embarrassment. Isabel's heart constricted in agony at the thought. How she longed for children of her own, and the prospect of bearing Eben Walker's had been beyond her wildest dreams. She should have been elated, but instead she felt only despair.

She had envisioned an idyllic life with a man who adored her, but Eben didn't love her. He only wanted a housekeeper and a mother for his difficult daughter. If she accepted his proposal, she would be married to the man she'd chosen, but could she stand loving him and knowing he didn't care for her in return?

"Eben, I . . ." She clasped her hands together in front of her to stop their trembling and blinked at the moisture gathering in her eyes. "Do you care for me at all?"

He seemed surprised. "Well, sure, I mean, I told you I admire you. Any man would."

"Indeed, it seems *many* of them do," she replied bitterly. "Although even with all their faults, at least the others managed to convey a trifle more ardency then you've shown."

"What do you mean by 'ardency'?" he asked suspiciously.

Isabel felt the first flush of true anger. "I mean you haven't even bothered to *pretend* you want me for myself, as a woman."

"I don't have to *pretend*. I really do want you," he insisted.

Isabel raised her eyebrows at him. "Oh? Then you've shown remarkable restraint in keeping your true feelings hidden."

He gave her a puzzled frown. "What are you . . . ? Wait a minute, are you *mad* because I *haven't* tried to kiss you?"

Embarrassment scalded Isabel's cheeks. "Certainly not!"

"You almost bashed poor Felix's brains in when he tried it," Eben reminded her. "I didn't think you liked being manhandled."

"I don't!" she exclaimed, mortified.

"Oh, you don't like it, but you've come to expect it, is that it?"

"Eben, really—" she tried, but he was already coming for her. "*Don't!*"

He grabbed her arms anyway, and his mouth closed over hers, silencing her protest. He pulled her inexorably to him. Instinctively she put up her hands to ward him off, but she was no match for his strength, and her hands somehow slipped over his shoulders instead.

Instantly she realized this was what she'd been waiting for all her life. The man she loved was kissing her, holding her, crushing her, tasting her, wanting her. But she'd barely realized that fact before it was over. He lifted his mouth from hers and glared down at her.

His eyes glowed with some mysterious inner fire, and for some reason, she couldn't seem to get her breath. She tried to say his name, then his mouth took hers again.

Gently this time, his lips molded themselves over hers, pressing until her lips parted and she could taste him. The hands gripping her arms relaxed and slid around her back, caressing her through the fabric of her dress, molding her to him until her breasts flattened against the steel wall of his chest and all thoughts of resistance dissolved.

The blood roaring in her ears turned molten and seared through her body like liquid fire, melting her bones and igniting a need she couldn't even name.

Her fingers grazed his stiff collar, then found the silk of his hair where it curled on his neck. His tongue teased at the opening of her lips, touching the sensitive flesh inside her mouth, and sending icy-hot shivers racing over her. A sound escaped her, a muffled protest that became a sigh of surrender.

She reveled in his strength, the hardness of his shoulders, the power of his arms, all held in check in deference to her fragility. His heart thundered against her own, pounding out the evidence of his desire, while his hands cherished her tenderly, stroking her, discovering her.

He explored her back and shoulders, as if he would memorize every inch of her body, and she yielded to him, yearning to be explored. With one hand he caressed her waist, her side, up and up, until he grazed the curve of her breast. Her nipples hardened instantly, straining against her bodice, longing for his touch. She arched against him, aching, so that when he cupped her fullness, she felt relief and a whole new sunburst of desire.

His other hand found the curve of her hip, and the icy-hot shivers raced back again, coalescing in her belly into a hot core of need. He pulled her into the cradle of his thighs, hard against the swollen evidence of his own need, and the world began to spin. Isabel couldn't think, couldn't breathe, couldn't resist, and just when she thought the darkness of passion would finally claim her, Eben once again broke the kiss.

He lifted his head so he could look down at her, and at first she saw him as if through a haze. His breath came in labored gasps, as if he'd run a mile, and Isabel's own gasps answered his. His skin was flushed, his eyes bright, and a small, triumphant smile curved his lips.

"Was that ardent enough for you?" he asked.

Isabel stared at him in horror. He'd just been making a point! "You *scoundrel*!" she cried, wrenching out of his arms with a strength born of fury. "How dare you?"

"How dare I what?" he demanded. "You were the one who wanted to be kissed."

Isabel made an incoherent sound and threw back her hand to slap his impudent face, but he caught her wrist in an iron grasp. His smile disappeared.

"Don't try to pretend you didn't like it," he said. "We're good together, and if it's ardency you want, just wait. After we're married—"

"Stop it!" she shrieked, totally humiliated. He'd

used her love for him, taken advantage and perverted it into lust, but she wasn't stupid. Lust wasn't love, and Isabel would settle for nothing less. "Maybe you think that because I'm an old maid—"

"*Old maid?*" he protested, but she ignored him.

"Maybe you think I'm so desperate for a husband that I'll take any man who comes along, but you're wrong," she informed him, still breathless but emboldened by her outrage. "I have no intention of spending the rest of my life with a man who doesn't love me."

"Who said I don't love you?"

"You haven't said you do, and don't bother to try it now, because I won't believe you!" she added.

"Isabel, just give me a chance," he said, reaching for her with an urgency close to desperation. "Love'll come in time."

Isabel didn't need any more time. She already loved him with all her heart. "And how much time will it take for you to forget your wife?" she demanded, eluding his grasp.

"My wife?" he asked in apparent bewilderment.

"I can't compete with a ghost, Eben. As long as you're still in love with her, you'll never be able to love anyone else."

"Still in love...? Isabel, what are you talking about?"

"You know perfectly well what I'm talking about. I know why you haven't remarried before now, and I have no intention of trying to compete with your memories. I'd rather spend the rest of my life alone than live with a man who still loved another woman."

"Isabel, you've got this all wrong—"

"Eben, please," Isabel begged, feeling the hot sting of tears and knowing she wouldn't be able to hold them back much longer. "I don't wish to discuss this anymore. Would you please leave?"

"Leave? This is my house!" he reminded her curtly.

"Then *I'll* leave." She started for the door, but he caught her arm.

"Wait, we have to talk!"

Isabel drew on her last reserves of courage and pulled herself up to her full, if insignificant, height. "There's nothing more to discuss," she informed him coldly. "I won't marry you, Eben. I can't."

Slowly, reluctantly, he released her arm. Isabel felt the loss of his touch and wondered with a pang if she would ever know it again. Was she being an idiot to refuse him? She recalled an old saying about half a loaf being better than none. But wouldn't the pain of having only half of Eben's heart be worse than not having him at all? Wouldn't such a life be far worse than the one she'd left behind in New York?

"All right then," he said, stiffening. "I'm sorry I bothered you." Straightening his coat with an angry jerk, he turned and strode to the door and out into the twilit evening.

Only when he was gone did Isabel realize the consequences of what she had done. Men were proud creatures, and she had lacerated Eben's pride. He would never come to love her now, and he would never propose to her again, not as long as he lived.

Numbly she walked over to the sofa and sank down onto it. Tears blurred her vision, but she hardly noticed. She had lost Eben forever, and the agony of that loss seared her heart.

But even as she lamented, she knew she could not have acted differently. Eben Walker might be proud, but Isabel had her own self-respect. How could she have accepted such a cold proposal? How could she have given her hand and her heart to a man who didn't even bother to pretend he loved her? The thought of living as a glorified housekeeper with a man she worshiped in return appalled her. No, she couldn't have accepted Eben under those circumstances.

Still, she also couldn't forget the fire of his kiss and

the unfamiliar emotions she had felt while wrapped
in his arms. And he had promised her more, so much
more, if she would consent to be his wife. Would that
have made up for not being loved? Isabel didn't know,
and now she would never have an opportunity to
find out.

Huddled in the corner of Eben's sofa, she hugged
herself and let the tears flow freely down her cheeks
as the room grew dark around her.

Eben stomped into his shop and heaved the door
shut behind him. The resulting crash shook the building, but he scarcely noticed. Damn her to hell! What
had ever made him think she'd be a good influence
on Amanda? Isabel Forester was even more demented
than his daughter!

You know perfectly well what I'm talking about! she had
said when, of course, he hadn't the faintest notion.
And where in God's name had she gotten the idea
he was still in love with his wife? He could tell her a
thing or two about the dear departed Gisela that
would curl her hair, but unfortunately, such confi-
dences would do little to advance his case with Isabel.

And who did she think she was to tell him he wasn't
in love with her?

Of course, he hadn't given the matter a whole lot
of thought until she'd mentioned it, but he must be.
Why else would he be so obsessed with her? But just
because he hadn't said the right words, she'd turned
him down.

Eben strode angrily into the small room where he
kept his office, tearing off his tie and collar and cursing Isabel Forester's soul. He threw the tie and collar
onto the cot, stripped off his coat, and threw it down,
too.

He'd thought she was different. He'd thought she
was a woman you could talk sense to, a woman who'd
appreciate a man who wanted her for herself and who
didn't treat her like a two-bit whore. But she was just

like the rest after all, mad if a man did and even madder if he didn't. No wonder she was an old maid if this was the way she treated her suitors. Eben supposed he should count himself lucky: at least she hadn't slapped him, although he had only his own quick reflexes to thank for that.

What had ever possessed him to propose to her in the first place? He should have learned his lesson years ago. A man was better off without a woman. For one crazy minute he'd actually imagined Isabel might make his life happier. Instead he would have doubled his misery by bringing another impossible female into the house. He was actually lucky she'd turned him down. If she'd accepted, he would have been stuck with her for the rest of his life.

Yes, he was extremely lucky, he told himself as he sank onto the cot. Maybe if he repeated it a few thousand more times, he'd even begin to believe it.

When Isabel finally came to herself again, the room was pitch-dark. Wearily she searched her pocket for a handkerchief, wiped her face, and blew her nose. She really should wash up before Amanda came back and . . .

Amanda? Suddenly, Isabel realized the girl had been gone an inordinately long time. Where could she be?

Probably visiting the Bartzes, she told herself, rising stiffly from the sofa to glance outside and verify her theory. To her alarm, she saw the Bartz house was dark. In fact, the only building in town still lit was the saloon, and Amanda certainly wouldn't have gone there.

Isabel panicked for a moment, wondering what she should do. Fetching Eben seemed the most logical thing, but how could she face him so soon? In fact, how could she face him ever again? But she would worry about such things later, after she'd found Amanda.

Isabel hurried outside, hoping to find the girl loi-
tering in the yard. Squinting into the darkness, Isabel
saw no sign of her, so she picked up her skirts and
ran around to the back of the house. If Amanda wasn't
there, Isabel would have no choice but to tell Eben
she had not returned.

The darkness formed weird, deceiving shadows.
Isabel took a long moment to study them, hoping to
discern the shape of a young girl beneath the trees.
Lost in concentration she only half heard the sound
of laughter as it carried faintly to her across the evening breeze.

Amanda's laughter. What on earth . . . ? Isabel hastened toward the sound, which seemed to be coming
from the trees by the creek that gave the town of
Bittercreek its name. She opened her mouth to call,
but before she could, she heard an answering voice,
a *man's* voice.

"You're a tease, Mandy," he was saying. "Why'd
you meet me out here if you weren't going to kiss
me?"

"You said you wanted to talk to me, Johnny Dent,"
Amanda replied, but she didn't sound the least bit
angry, as she should have been.

It didn't matter. Isabel was angry enough for both
of them. She saw the two figures sitting on the grass
beside the creek. Johnny Dent was trying to put his
arms around Amanda, who was putting up only a
token struggle.

"What's going on here?" Isabel demanded.

Instantly the two figures broke apart and scrambled
to their feet.

Amanda gasped. "Miss Forester, what are you
doing out here?"

"I should be asking you that, young lady. Or you,
young man." Isabel turned her wrath on the taller
figure.

"Miss Forester, this is Johnny Dent. I . . . I've told
you about him," Amanda stammered.

"Pleased to meet—" he began, but Isabel cut him off.

"You didn't tell me he was a scoundrel."

"He's not!" Amanda cried.

"Wait a minute, Miss Forester, I didn't—"

"I heard what you were saying when I came up. Are you in the habit of luring young girls out after dark so you can take advantage of them, Mr. Dent?"

"I didn't—"

"He didn't—"

"Only because I came along," Isabel informed them angrily. "Amanda, I'm shocked at your behavior. Don't you realize you would be ruined if anyone found you out here with this man?"

"Then Johnny would marry me, wouldn't you, Johnny?" Amanda insisted.

"Well, uh . . ." Johnny stammered.

"Even if he would—and may I point out how reluctant he seems to commit himself," Isabel said coldly, "that is hardly any way to start a marriage."

"But Johnny and I love each other. Tell her, Johnny."

"Miss Forester, you've got the wrong idea," Johnny said instead. His smile made a white slash in the darkness, and Isabel suspected he'd spent most of his life charming his way out of trouble. "I'm real sweet on Amanda here, but I respect her, too. I'd never do anything to damage her reputation."

"Then why did you arrange to meet her here after dark?"

"Because she don't want me coming to the house," he replied glibly. "Her pa don't approve of me, so we have to sneak around to see each other."

"If you truly care for Amanda, and her father does not approve of you, you would do much better to spend your time trying to win Mr. Walker's confidence than in trying to seduce his daughter."

"Miss Forester!" Amanda cried in outrage.

"Miss Forester, I never . . . !" Johnny vowed.

"Are you going to pretend you weren't trying to kiss her when I came up?" Isabel challenged.

"Just one little kiss," Johnny insisted, but Isabel knew how dangerous "one little kiss" could be.

"Do you suppose Mr. Walker would be understanding if you made that excuse to him?"

"Well, no, ma'am, I reckon not, but—"

"Johnny, we don't need to make excuses. We haven't done anything wrong," Amanda said.

"Simply being here together is wrong," Isabel said impatiently. "Amanda, I think we'd better send Mr. Dent on his way before someone else comes to investigate. I assume you would not like your father to find you together."

Amanda sighed in the darkness. "Johnny, I suppose she's right."

"I'm sure she is," Johnny agreed. "And I want to thank you for showing me the error of my ways, ma'am. I sure wouldn't want to do anything to hurt Amanda."

"Please leave before I lose my patience with you," Isabel said, fighting the urge to shake him. Since he stood almost a foot taller than she, she suspected she would be foolish to attempt it.

"Real nice meeting you, Miss Forester," he said, apparently oblivious to her outrage. "I'll see you in church on Sunday, Mandy."

"Good-bye, Johnny," Amanda said wistfully, and Isabel supposed she was wishing she'd gotten the kiss Johnny had been trying to give her earlier.

"Come along, Amanda," Isabel said, starting back for the house.

The girl followed reluctantly, and by the time she reached the house, Isabel had already found a lamp and lighted it. "Amanda, what were you thinking?" she demanded the instant the girl came inside.

Amanda glared at her defiantly. "I was thinking I wanted to see Johnny, and when I got his note . . ." She shrugged.

"How was this note delivered?" Isabel asked suspiciously.

"Carrie Bartz gave it to me when I went over there after supper. A cowboy gave it to her this afternoon, one of Johnny's friends."

Isabel looked at her in dismay. "Amanda, I can't tell you how dangerous such behavior is! Don't you realize that if you lose your reputation, no decent man will ever want to marry you?"

"Johnny will marry me, I told you."

"If you remember, he did not verify your claim tonight. I suspect he's just seeing how far he can get with you before he casts you aside."

"You're wrong!" Amanda insisted, her cheeks scarlet. "He loves me."

"Which is another assertion he failed to confirm. Amanda, why are you taking such chances?"

"Why shouldn't I? Nobody cares what I do!"

"That isn't true. Your father cares."

"How would you know?" Amanda asked, flouncing onto the settee. "You don't know how he really is. When you aren't here, he never even talks to me."

"He's . . . he's not a very talkative person," Isabel said.

"And he hardly even looks at me, and when I try to kiss him, he . . . Well, you saw the way he jumped up and ran out of here this morning like a scalded cat. He hates me, Miss Forester. I'll bet he'd be glad if I ran off."

"Nonsense," Isabel said, hurrying to her side. Taking Amanda's hand in hers, Isabel wished she felt more confident on the subject of Eben Walker's true feelings. "I know your father cares very much what happens to you. He's spoken to me about you several times and asked my advice. He wouldn't have done that if he didn't love you."

Amanda's gaze lifted to Isabel's, and her clear, blue eyes narrowed. "I almost forgot he was going to talk to you this evening. Did he . . . did he say anything important?"

"Important? What do you mean?" Isabel asked, wishing she could stop the blush rising in her cheeks.

"He did, didn't he?" she exclaimed, brightening instantly. "I knew he was sweet on you when he came in wearing his suit tonight! Oh, Miss Forester, you have to forget all the bad things I said about him. I was just mad. He's really a good man. He works awful hard, and he always lets me have anything I want. And since you've been here, he's been so much nicer. If you two got married—"

"Amanda, we . . . we aren't getting married," Isabel said past the constriction in her throat.

"You aren't?" she asked, then brightened again. "Oh, I understand. You're going to make him court you a little first. That's only right."

"No, he . . . he won't be courting me, either," Isabel admitted reluctantly.

Amanda frowned in confusion. "But didn't he talk to you? I thought for sure he was going to."

"I really don't think we should be discussing this," Isabel said, unable to meet Amanda's probing gaze.

"Oh, no!" Amanda wailed in despair. "He ruined it, didn't he?"

"Amanda, please . . ."

"Did he offend you? Miss Forester, he didn't mean to, I'm sure he didn't. I know if you'll give him another chance—"

"Amanda, this is between your father and me. It isn't your concern."

"That's what he said, too, but you're wrong. You're both wrong. My whole life would be different if you'd marry him. If you were my mother, he wouldn't dare treat me like a child anymore, and he'd talk to me and listen to me. You'd make him, wouldn't you?"

Isabel wished she could assure Amanda that she would. "I'm sorry, dear, but I'm afraid your father and I just don't suit."

"Don't suit? What on earth does that mean?"

"It means I refused your father's proposal."

"But *why*?" Amanda moaned.

Isabel didn't think she wanted to explain her reasons to the fourteen-year-old daughter of the man she had rejected. "As I've been trying to tell you, marriage is a very serious step for a woman to take. She must be certain of the character of the man she chooses, and she must feel she loves him and that he loves her in return."

"Don't you love Pa? Is that it?" Amanda asked earnestly. "I can understand if you don't. He can be awful stubborn and cross sometimes, but I didn't think you'd ever seen that side of him."

"I've only known your father for a few days, hardly enough time to know if I even like him, much less to come to love him," she lied.

Amanda considered this for a moment, then she smiled beatifically. "Oh, I understand now. You just need more time. I know you'll like Pa a lot when you get to know him better. And I know I've been a lot of trouble, but I promise to be good from now on. I won't meet Johnny anymore when it isn't proper, and I'll try not to sass Pa anymore. But then, I guess I won't have to since you'll have charge of me after the two of you get married."

Isabel could have groaned aloud. "Amanda, I'm sorry if I gave you the wrong impression. I refused your father's marriage proposal, and I have no reason to think he will ever ask me again."

"*What*?" Amanda shrieked. "Oh, no! I can't believe it! He did something awful, didn't he? Oh, Miss Forester, I hate him, I just hate him!"

Before Isabel knew what was happening, Amanda was weeping on her shoulder. Her own eyes filled as she held the girl close. She could certainly understand Amanda's disappointment, although it was probably only one tenth as deep as her own.

After a few minutes, Amanda's tears subsided to

hiccups and sniffles, and she straightened, shame-faced, away from Isabel. "I'm sorry. You must think I'm an idiot."

"No, you have every right to be upset," Isabel assured her. "It must be difficult for you without a mother, but you mustn't be too hard on your father."

Amanda gave a skeptical sniff and used her sleeve to scrub the moisture from her cheeks. "I guess you'll marry Mr. Young then."

"Mr. Young?" Isabel said in surprise.

"Sure, he's nice, and he likes you."

"I have no plans to marry anyone at the moment," Isabel said acerbically, thinking she would need a lot of time to get over Eben Walker before she could even consider another man.

"Well, he's going to ask you. I heard him telling Pa."

"You shouldn't eavesdrop on other people's conversations," Isabel said uneasily. The thought of dealing with yet another marriage proposal unnerved her.

"I wasn't eavesdropping on purpose," Amanda replied. "I just heard it. Anyway, he said you'd be his in just a few days."

"He did, did he?" Isabel felt her hackles rise. Just who did these men think they were?

"Yes, which must be why Pa thought he had to get to you first, for all the good it did him." She sighed. "Men can be such fools."

Isabel decided to change the subject. "Amanda, please promise me that you'll be more careful of your reputation in the future. If I thought you ruined yourself because I wouldn't marry your father—"

"I wouldn't do a thing like that!" Amanda exclaimed. "I'm not stupid!"

In view of Amanda's recent behavior, Isabel could have argued the point, but instead she smiled. "I'm glad to hear it."

"Just wait until I get ahold of Pa, though," she threatened.

"Don't you dare say a word to him," Isabel said in alarm. "Men are extremely sensitive, and I'm sure your father would not take kindly to being reminded of his failure to win my hand."

"Humph," Amanda said noncommittally, causing Isabel some concern. Things would be awkward enough between her and Eben without Amanda making them even more difficult. If only she hadn't agreed to spend this week with the Walkers.

Suddenly Isabel realized she had a splitting headache, which was no wonder considering all she'd been through this evening. She sent Amanda to bed, then retired herself, with a wet cloth draped across her forehead. When she thought of facing Eben across the breakfast table in the morning, she whispered a silent prayer that morning would never come.

Breakfast was even worse than she had expected. Eben appeared looking like the wrath of God, glowering and unshaven, his eyes bloodshot, as if he'd slept even less than she had. He responded tersely to her tentative "Good morning," ate his breakfast without comment, then left quickly.

When Isabel and Amanda arrived at school, Roger Stevens and the three Bartz boys were waiting on the front steps.

"Can we give our reports today?" Roger asked, surprising Isabel with his enthusiasm.

"Certainly, if you're all finished."

"We're finished," Herald assured her. "Barclay gave us lots of good stuff. He's not so much of a stuffed shirt as we thought."

"I'm certainly glad to hear it," Isabel remarked, gratified to experience some little success to make up for all the recent disasters. "You may do your reports first thing this morning. Afterwards we'll allow the other students to ask questions."

"What if we can't answer them?" Herald asked in alarm.

"I'll appoint Barclay to moderate the discussion. Surely he will be able to handle any questions that stump you," Isabel said, anticipating Barclay's triumph. By the end of the day, he would no longer be a pariah.

Unfortunately, Barclay Plimpton did not appear. Isabel waited awhile, thinking he might have been delayed. When she realized he wasn't coming at all, she tried to put the other boys off, but in the face of their disappointment, she relented and allowed them to present their reports.

The discussion afterward was more than Isabel could have hoped.

"But my pa claims cattle won't graze after sheep because of the stink they leave on the grass," one boy insisted.

"Everybody knows how stupid sheep are," Roger replied importantly. "The sheep's feet leave the smell so if one gets lost, he can find the rest by following his nose, but the sun burns the smell off in a few hours."

"They ruin the grass. They pull it out by the roots when they eat," a girl protested.

"They eat it down more than cows do, but they don't pull up the roots," Herald explained, not willing for Roger to get all the glory. "What happens is, when the sheep are herded too close, their hooves cut up the ground and dig up the sod. If the herder is careful, that don't happen."

"But I thought . . ."

The arguments continued for most of the morning, and Isabel almost forgot her headache in the excitement. Her only regret was that Barclay wasn't there to witness it. When the children went outside for lunch, they were still debating the merits of sheepherding. Some remained unconvinced, but Isabel hadn't expected to make any converts, just to open a few young minds. They would carry the information back to their parents, and who knew what might result?

Isabel had just finished eating her sandwich when she saw Bertha Bartz approaching. Bertha's somber expression warned of trouble, and Isabel hurried to meet her.

"What's wrong?"

"Did the Plimpton boy come to school today?"

"No, what is it?"

"Herald just heard from a customer that gunny-sackers hit the Plimpton place last night."

"*Gunnysacks?*" Isabel echoed in confusion.

"No, Gunnysack*ers*," Bertha corrected her. "Night riders who wear gunnysacks over their heads so nobody can see their faces."

"What did they do?" she asked in alarm. "Was Barclay—?"

"No, the family wasn't hurt. They attacked one of the sheep camps. Beat a herder near to death and killed most of the sheep; knocked their brains out with wagon spokes."

"Good heavens! Will the man be all right?"

"Plimpton sent for a doctor, but I guess only time will tell."

"Is there anything we can do?"

"Eben went out to see. He said to tell you and Amanda he probably wouldn't be home tonight."

Isabel thought she should at least feel some relief at knowing she wouldn't have to face Eben tonight. Instead she experienced a strange sense of disappointment. Calling herself a ninny, she tried to concentrate on the problem at hand. "Shouldn't the women send out some food or something?"

"Spoken like a true minister's daughter," Bertha told her with a small smile. "Food is the universal balm for trouble, isn't it? I've already got a pot of beans on to simmer. Herald will carry it out later today and bring us back a report."

"I wish I could do something," Isabel lamented.

"Just pray for that poor man, and pray that Oliver Plimpton doesn't decide to pay somebody back in kind."

"He wouldn't take the law into his own hands, would he?"

"Since we don't have much law of any kind out here, he might be tempted, but I'm sure Eben will try to talk him into calling the Rangers instead."

"Oh, dear, I can see this could get very unpleasant."

"Neighbor against neighbor is never anything else," Bertha replied grimly. "Why don't you and Amanda come over for supper tonight. Herald should be back by then, and he can tell you what he's learned."

Isabel decided to inform the children of what had happened. She could not have planned a better object lesson on the results of ignorance, although had she done the planning, no one would have been injured and no helpless animals destroyed. The children expressed the proper degree of outrage, even those who still believed sheep were evil, and Isabel was able to guide the discussion to help the children decide on alternate ways to settle disputes other than by violence.

Amanda was the only one who didn't participate in the debate. Seeing her troubled expression, Isabel feared she might still be brooding over Isabel and Eben's problems. As soon as she and Isabel closed the door of the Walker house behind them that afternoon, however, Amanda disabused her of that notion.

"Miss Forester, I . . . I'm afraid Johnny was on the raid last night."

"What makes you think so?"

"When he arranged to meet me, he said he would be out because he had some business last night."

"Do you think his employer sent him or do you think he went on his own?"

"I don't know. He works for Vance Davis, who hates sheep more than anybody else around here, and that's saying something. Maybe Mr. Davis organized the raid, or maybe some of his men just took it on themselves. I don't know, and I don't want to know," Amanda said, her eyes full of despair.

"There now," Isabel soothed, "maybe you're wrong. Maybe Johnny had some other sort of business last night."

"Cowboys don't generally work in the dead of night, Miss Forester," Amanda scoffed. "What should I do?"

Isabel frowned. "Ordinarily I'd advise you to tell your father, but under the circumstances—"

"I couldn't do that!" Amanda cried. "He'd kill me if he found out I met Johnny."

"Exactly," Isabel said with a sigh. "Someone should know, however. Perhaps I could tell Mr. Bartz without explaining how I knew."

"I don't want to get Johnny in trouble!"

"If he really went on that raid, Johnny got himself in trouble," Isabel pointed out. "Civilized people simply cannot allow something like this to happen, nor can they allow the people who did it to escape punishment."

"I know Johnny didn't mean to hurt anybody."

"Nevertheless, someone *was* hurt, and someone must suffer the consequences."

"But not Johnny! Oh, please, Miss Forester, don't tell on him! I'm not even sure he went. You said yourself he could have had something else to do last night."

"And you said—"

"*Please!* You can't get him in trouble when we aren't even sure he went along!"

Isabel looked into Amanda's anguished eyes, and her heart went out to the girl. "All right, I won't mention Johnny by name, but I will have to tell Mr.

Bartz I have reason to believe some of Mr. Davis's men were involved."

"Oh, thank you, Miss Forester. I know Johnny didn't do anything wrong."

Isabel had her doubts, but she kept them to herself. When she and Amanda went over to the Bartz house, Herald told them much the same story Bertha had earlier, adding only a few details.

"The herder said there was about six of them. They all had gunnysacks over their heads, so he couldn't see their faces."

"Will he be all right, do you think?" Isabel asked.

"He's got some broke bones and a lot of bruises, but he seems all right otherwise. I expect we'll know more when the doctor gets here tomorrow. Seems like a waste of money bringing in a doctor for a Mexican herder, but Plimpton always was a queer duck," Herald remarked. Isabel waited for an opportunity to speak to Herald alone about the identity of the raiders, but none arose.

After supper, Bertha took Isabel aside. Isabel was thinking perhaps she should just tell Bertha her suspicions about Vance Davis when Bertha wiped all thoughts of sheep from her mind.

"I heard Eben proposed to you last night."

"Good heavens! How on earth . . . ?"

"Amanda told Carrie. The poor girl is quite put out with her father, and I can't say I blame her. Though I'd hate to lose you, you'd be a perfect wife for Eben and an equally perfect mother for Amanda. I am a little surprised that Eben had the sense to see it, though, what with his nonsense about his wife. Too bad he didn't also have the sense not to ruin things by asking too soon."

Isabel stared at her, speechless.

"Is something wrong?" Bertha asked innocently.

"I . . . I suppose I'm just having a difficult time getting used to the idea of everyone in town knowing my business," Isabel stammered.

"If you plan to stay around here, you'd better get used to it," Bertha advised. "I'm just hoping you haven't written Eben off completely. He really is a fine man. You could hardly do better, and if you're entertaining any fanciful notions about love, believe me, if a man is good and kind, you can learn to love him in no time."

"I'm sure," Isabel said faintly, wondering what Bertha would say if she knew Isabel's real reason for refusing Eben. Practical Bertha would probably scorn the "fanciful notion" that the man should love the woman in return, too.

And maybe she was right. Unfortunately, it was now too late to find out.

"You must feel awfully awkward around Eben now," Bertha was saying. "If you like, you can move back in here until it's time for you to go to the Stevenses' place. There's no use rubbing Eben's nose in it, now is there?"

"No use at all," Isabel agreed, grateful for such a simple solution to the problem. She would still be close enough to reassure Amanda—and to keep an eye on her, too—but she wouldn't have to face Eben morning and night. "I'll stay with Amanda until her father returns, then I'll move my things back over here."

Eben brought his hammer down with a satisfactory crash and lifted it again, ready to beat the living daylights out of the rosy horseshoe resting on his anvil. Thank God he'd had a lot of work to keep him busy today. Otherwise, he might have been tempted to release his frustrations by tearing the town apart board by board.

Yesterday had been bad enough. The sight of those pathetic sheep with their skulls crushed and the herder's broken body had filled him with impotent fury. He'd wanted to avenge Oliver Plimpton's loss even more than Oliver had, and in the end Oliver had calmed Eben down.

Not that Eben had any special love for sheep or for sheepherders either. It was just the idea that someone sought to impose his will on another by force. Of course, Oliver Plimpton wasn't exactly helpless. He could call in the Rangers, and he could certainly hire gunmen. Whether he would do either remained to be seen, but Eben had done his best to impress him with the need to do so.

Then, after he'd gotten up before dawn and ridden hard to arrive back home before Isabel and Amanda left for school this morning, he'd found Isabel had gone to Bertha's, and Amanda in one of her foaming tizzies because he'd driven Isabel out. Most women would have been flattered by a proposal of marriage, but trust Isabel Forester to take it as an insult and leave in a huff.

"Damn fool woman," he muttered as he slammed his sledge down onto the anvil again. The worst part was that Amanda seemed to think it was all his fault, that he'd done something to *make* her turn him down. He wondered what Isabel might have said to give his daughter that impression, and he took perverse pleasure in imagining trying to shake the information out of both of them.

As he lifted his hammer again, he glanced outside. From his position at the anvil, he commanded a view of most of the town through the open doors of the shop, but he usually found little of interest to distract him. Today, however, his gaze strayed more than once toward the schoolhouse door. Although it galled him to admit it, he felt compelled to at least see Isabel.

He'd watched her at lunchtime when she'd supervised the children at play, and he'd called himself a fool for the way his body still reacted to the sight of her slender, graceful figure.

Ever since the children had gone home this afternoon, he'd been vigilant, hoping to catch one more glimpse of her, if only to satisfy himself that she really wasn't anything special, certainly not worth losing any more sleep over. She hadn't appeared, though, and Eben was just beginning to wonder if he had missed her when she finally emerged from the school.

She wore her usual black skirt and jacket and carried an armload of books. A broad-brimmed hat shaded her eyes and concealed most of her face, but Eben didn't need to see her to know exactly how she looked. Her face had haunted his dreams for two nights now, her violet eyes laughing as he begged her to accept him. At least he'd never have to undergo that humiliation in real life again. It would be a cold day in hell before he had any more truck with Isabel Forester.

She moved down the street with the confident, gliding stride he had previously admired but which he now recognized as haughty. Unconsciously he laid his hammer and tongs on the anvil and took a few steps toward the door so he could observe her all the way to the Bartz house.

Skinny, dried-up old maid. She'd said so herself, hadn't she? What had he ever seen in her? Underneath all those petticoats, she was probably no more than a rack of bones. A man could get a splinter if he wasn't careful, he thought with a sneer.

"What the . . . ?" he muttered aloud when he saw she wasn't heading for the Bartz house after all. Instead of crossing the street as she always did—as all ladies did—she was heading right for the saloon!

Isabel couldn't be perfectly certain, but if she had not been morally opposed to gambling, she would have bet all her worldly goods that the man sweeping the sidewalk in front of the saloon was Larry Potts's father. He was about the right age, and his clothing had the same tattered look as Larry's.

" 'If the mountain won't come to Muhammad . . .' " she muttered to herself, smiling to think what her father would have said if he had known the sorts of things she'd read after she had escaped his influence.

When she was within speaking distance, she said, "Mr. Potts?"

The man looked up from his work. He hadn't shaved in several days, and his eyes were red and rheumy. "Yeah?"

Isabel could smell him from several feet away, and the odor was not pleasant. She schooled her face into a polite smile and tried to ignore the stink. "Mr. Potts, I'm Isabel Forester, the new schoolteacher. I understand you have a son who is school age and—"

"He ain't going to school," the man growled. "Somebody should've already told you."

"Larry himself told me, which made me think he was just like most boys, who, if left to themselves, would play hooky every day. Of course, as an adult, you understand the importance of education—"

"I do not," Potts replied sharply. "Book learning never got me nothing, and it'll never get Larry nothing either. Our people work with their hands. We always have and we always will, and no fancy woman from back East is going to change it."

"I'm not trying to change anything," Isabel argued, a little flustered by his rudeness. "I'm merely trying to suggest that Larry might do better in life if he could read and write and—"

"Do better than *me*, you mean," Potts snarled, throwing down his broom. "Well, let me tell you something, lady, we do all right. We eat regular and we got a roof over our heads. Larry's got it easier than a lot of kids, easier than I ever had it."

"I'm not criticizing the way you raise your son, Mr. Potts," Isabel said uneasily. "I only thought he might enjoy being in school with other children his own age."

"You mean so they can laugh at him to his face instead of just behind his back?" Potts took a step toward her, his eyes filled with fury and his hands curled into fists.

Fear wrenched a gasp from her throat, but before she could even back up a step, someone shouted.

"Potts!"

Potts whirled to face this new adversary, and Isabel saw Eben Walker running across the street toward them, his leather apron slapping against his powerful legs.

"Don't you know any better than to accost a lady in the street?" Eben demanded as he skidded to a halt beside them.

"She started it," Potts said, gesturing contemptuously at Isabel. "Larry told her he didn't want to go to school, but she's got to stick her nose in—"

"All right," Eben said, taking Isabel's arm in a none too gentle grip and jerking her off the sidewalk and into the street. "Just remember, next time you talk to a lady, you keep your hands to yourself."

"I never laid a finger on her," Potts snarled, glaring balefully at Isabel. He muttered something about a skinny little witch, but Eben was already dragging her away.

"Eben!" she cried when she stumbled, frantically juggling her books to keep from dropping them, but he only slowed his pace a little.

"Are you crazy?" he demanded when they were out of earshot of Will Potts.

"I shouldn't like to think so," Isabel replied tartly, trying in vain to wrench free of his grasp.

"Well, *I* think so," he said, glaring down at her. "Only a crazy woman would strike up a conversation with Will Potts."

"I am concerned about his son's future," Isabel informed him, digging in her heels.

Eben jerked to a halt, still gripping her arm fiercely. "You're just lucky he didn't take his broom to you, or maybe that's what you were hoping for. I forgot, you *like* being manhandled."

"I most certainly do not!" Isabel cried in outrage. "And I would appreciate it if *you* would stop man-handling me this instant!"

He released her as if she'd burned him. "Only too happy to oblige," he said with mock civility. "Please excuse me. I also forgot you can't stand being within ten feet of me."

Isabel gaped at him. "Where on earth did you get an idea like that?"

"Probably from the way you moved out of my house like it was on fire or something."

"I left because I thought you wouldn't want me there after . . . after what happened," Isabel said, her face scalding with humiliation at the memory.

"I'm touched by your concern for my sensibilities," he said sarcastically.

"I have sensibilities, too," Isabel informed him, "and they were thoroughly offended by the way you ignored me yesterday at breakfast."

"Maybe you expected me to be happy because you turned me down."

"No, I didn't, which is why I assumed you'd be glad not to have to see me every day."

He just continued to glare at her until Isabel felt like squirming. At last, overcome by regret and de-spair, she said, "Eben, I . . . I'm sorry."

His broad shoulders sagged as the anger drained out of his dark eyes. "Yeah, so am I," he murmured, then turned and walked away, leaving her standing alone in the street.

He looked so hurt, Isabel wanted to call after him and tell him she'd changed her mind. But, of course, he'd think her daft if she did such a thing, and be-sides, he really wasn't hurt, simply suffering from wounded pride. He would recover far more quickly than she, who would have to live forever with the knowledge that she had thrown away any chance she might have had with him.

Bearing the leaden weight of regret, she started

toward the Bartz house. She was halfway there before she realized Eben had come running to her rescue.

She stopped dead in her tracks and turned back, but he had already disappeared into his shop. If he was so angry with her, why had he come to her aid?

Eben glanced at the setting sun, noticing the rosy streaks painted across the sky more for their prediction of tomorrow's weather than for their beauty. In his present state of mind, he was immune to beauty.

He could see now he'd made a terrible mistake in not disciplining Amanda much earlier. The girl had a tongue that could cut a man to ribbons, and even when she wasn't screeching, she could raise blisters on a rock with those looks of hers.

She'd somehow gotten the idea he'd *made* Isabel turn him down by offending her, and nothing would convince her otherwise. Supper had been a disaster of clanking plates and bitter recriminations, and suspecting Amanda's accusations might be somewhat justified, Eben hadn't argued with her. Although he didn't often feel the need, this evening he intended to patronize Dave Weatherby's saloon, at least until he was sure his daughter had retired for the night.

Lost in thought, he didn't pay much attention to the empty hitching post in front of Dave's Dream until he got inside and found Dave and the bartender alone.

"Where is everybody?"

Dave sat at one of the tables scattered about the room. He looked up from the beer he'd been contemplating. "Why, they're courting the schoolteacher," Dave informed him sardonically.

"Courting? What do you mean?"

"When everybody heard why she'd moved out of your house and back to the Bartz place, they figured they better not waste any more time. They're calling on her over at Herald's house."

Eben whirled and went back to the doorway. Sure

enough, from here he could see half a dozen horses tied to the Bartzes' fence. He swore.

"Frank, Mr. Walker needs a drink," Dave said from where he still sat. "Whiskey?"

"Make it a double." Eben sighed, turning away from the door. He took the seat Dave silently offered and slumped down into it, breathing another curse.

"That woman is hell on wheels, isn't she?" Weatherby asked conversationally.

Eben waited until Frank, the bartender, had brought him his drink before he replied. Taking a long sip of the burning liquid, he savored the warmth and wished fervently it had the power to burn away all memories of Isabel Forester. "I reckon everybody's got the word by now. Paul ought to learn to keep his mouth shut."

"The word?" Weatherby asked.

"He told me he intended to propose to Miss Forester in a couple of days, and he's pretty confident she'll say yes," Eben explained bitterly.

"I hadn't heard. I just figured they were anxious to get the money."

"Money? What money?"

"The bet, you know."

"Bet? What are you talking about?"

"Well, I reckon it's really a lottery, or that's what Paul said, anyways. You remember, the night of the dance we all chipped in twenty dollars. The man who marries Miss Isabel is the winner."

"Good God!" Eben gaped at him in astonishment.

"You didn't know?" Weatherby asked. "I thought everybody'd heard about it by now. After what happened with me, and what the Bartz woman said, we all figured she wasn't going to marry anybody voluntarily. Somebody, I think it was Felix, said the only way to catch her would be to compromise her."

"Damn him to hell," Eben said in outrage.

"Indeed," Weatherby agreed, lifting his glass in silent salute. "Of course, as we learned, it will take a better man than Felix Underwood to compromise our Miss Isabel."

Just wait until Eben got his hands on Felix Underwood. Of all the rotten, low-down bastards . . .

"I don't know what they think they'll accomplish over at the Bartz house, though," Weatherby was saying. "There must be ten of them in there with her. She isn't likely to go off alone with any of them either, not after her run-in with Felix."

Eben remembered Paul's claim that Isabel would be his in just a few days, and wondered what he'd planned for her. If he laid one finger on her . . .

"We collected over two hundred dollars," Weatherby continued morosely. "Paul said it would take a real smart fellow to win it."

Yes, it would, Eben thought, but Paul Young wasn't going to be that fellow. If compromising her was the only way to win Isabel, then by damn, Eben Walker was the man to do it. Slowly, as he listened to Weatherby's ramblings with half an ear, he began to form a plan.

Chapter 10

Isabel simply couldn't believe this was happening to her. When Bertha had offered to let her move back in with the Bartz family, she had looked on the Bartz house as a refuge. The last few nights, however, the formerly quiet home seemed to have become a way station for every eligible bachelor within a hundred miles.

And every one of them wanted to court Isabel. She only wished the old biddies back at her father's church could see her now. They would certainly learn to use more care when classifying a woman as unmarriageable.

Unfortunately, Isabel could not enjoy her new-found popularity, not when she realized she would never love any of the men so intent on wooing her. Maybe if she'd been left to herself for a while so she could get over the disappointment of her first real infatuation, she could have turned her affections elsewhere, but the men of Bittercreek would not allow her that luxury. Afraid another would get to her first, they vied for preeminence so enthusiastically that Isabel had no opportunity to get to know *any* of them.

And, of course, she didn't really *want* to get to know any of them. What she really wanted was for Eben Walker to show up on her doorstep bearing flowers and candy, protesting his love for her and begging her to reconsider his proposal.

Lost in thought, Isabel was oblivious to the chatter of the Bartz children as they strolled to school with her on Friday morning. Only when one of the children in the schoolyard hollered to them did Isabel emerge from her fog.

"Look, Miss Forester! Somebody put it here overnight!"

"See, Miss Forester, the bell," Carrie said, pointing to where the triangular dinner bell had previously hung. In its place hung a similar instrument of an entirely different shape.

"It's a *heart*!" Herald cried in delight. "Somebody's sweet on you, Miss Forester!"

Isabel stared at the object in disbelief while the children laughed and shouted their amusement.

"Who could it be?" Carrie wondered slyly, following at Isabel's heels as she hurried to examine the bell more closely.

The bell was indeed in the shape of a heart, perfectly crafted by an expert hand. Only one person in town could have made such a thing.

"Was there a . . . a note or something?" Isabel asked, looking around anxiously.

"Nope," Roger Stevens informed her importantly. "I was the first one to see it. Wasn't no note or nothing."

Isabel was too distracted to even consider correcting his grammar. All she could think was that Eben wouldn't need to leave a note since anyone could easily guess who had made it. *Eben had sent her a heart!*

This was even better than flowers or candy. Joy sluiced through her, drowning her despair.

Isabel glanced around, hoping to find Amanda in the crowd of children, but she had not arrived yet. Had the girl put her father up to this? The gesture seemed foreign to Eben's nature, but then, what did she really know about his nature? Perhaps such gestures came as naturally as breathing to him. Perhaps if she had just given him a chance, he would have revealed this sweet, sensitive side of his character the night he had proposed to her.

Isabel put her hand over her mouth to hold back the joyous laugh trembling on her lips. *Eben cared for her!*

"What's the matter, Miss Forester?" one of the younger children asked in concern. "You ain't mad, are you?"

"Oh, no," Isabel replied, schooling her expression to solemnity. "It's quite well made, don't you think?"

Carrie giggled. "Mr. Walker's a good blacksmith."

"Yes, well . . ." Isabel looked around again, hoping for something to occupy the children before they guessed her true emotions. Mercifully, Barclay Plimpton rode up on his pinto pony just then. He hadn't been to school since the attack on his father's sheep, and the other children greeted him with shouts, running out to meet him.

Isabel followed, pushing thoughts of the bell from her mind. She'd have time enough later to think what she must do to acknowledge it.

Barclay's report on the events at his ranch thoroughly distracted the children from thinking about Isabel's gift. Feeling giddy with her secret knowledge about Eben, Isabel allowed the children to rehash the entire cattle/sheep argument for Barclay's benefit. This gave her time to compose herself so she could think coherently for the rest of the school day.

When Isabel had dismissed the children at the end of the day, she waited, watching to make sure all the boys who had stopped off at the blacksmith shop had gone home before leaving the schoolhouse herself. When she was certain Eben was alone, she gathered up her things, nervously smoothed her hair one last time, and made her way out of the school and down the street to his shop.

The sound of Eben's hammer clanking on steel echoed the apprehensive pounding of her heart as she slowed her step outside the shop door. She could see Eben silhouetted against the brightness from the opened back door and was reminded of a woodcut she had once seen depicting the god Vulcan at work at his forge.

The broad shoulders and powerful arms above a narrow waist and lean hips, the long legs spread wide for balance against the weight of his hammer. Eben raised the heavy sledge as if it had been a toy and brought it down with a crash. Sparks flew as the metal gave under the force of his godlike strength, and Isabel shivered.

Then, sensing her presence, he looked up. "Isabel?"

"Good afternoon," she said, trying for cheerfulness in spite of her nervousness. As casually as she could, she strolled into the shop. "I just had to come by and thank you."

He laid the hammer carefully down on the anvil and slipped his hand out of the tongs. "Thank me?"

"Yes, for your . . . uh, gift."

His expression betrayed no comprehension.

"The bell?" she tried.

Something that might have been surprise flickered in his dark eyes, but in the dim light she couldn't be sure. "Didn't you get the note?"

"What note?"

"I thought . . . Never mind." He smiled his wonderful smile, and Isabel's stomach quivered in response. "Did you like it?"

"Very much," she assured him, "although the children teased me about it."

"I figured they would, but..." He shrugged his broad shoulders, and Isabel bit back a sigh of admiration.

She shifted the books she carried and cast about for something else to say. He beat her to it.

"I was wondering... That is, I asked Herald, and he said it would be all right if I drove you out to the Stevenses' place."

"Why, yes, certainly," Isabel said, her heart pounding with excitement. She couldn't seem to get her breath, either.

"I know you were supposed to go tomorrow, but why don't I take you tonight? Maybe we could stop on the way and have a picnic supper or something."

"That sounds lovely," Isabel agreed, hardly able to believe her ears. Obviously he had forgiven her for refusing him. She had vastly underestimated him. "I'll fix us a supper and—"

"No, I'll get Amanda to do it." He smiled again. "She'll be happy to when I tell her what it's for. I'll come for you in about an hour."

"I'll be ready."

Isabel wondered if her feet even touched the ground as she left the shop.

Texas was beautiful, Isabel decided as she rode along, seated beside Eben in his buggy. The emerald grass rippled in the wind like an inland sea stretching as far as the eye could see. Above them the crystal-clear sky hung like an azure canopy. In the distance two birds—hawks, Eben had told her—swooped and soared playfully. Some might find the vastness of the land intimidating, but Isabel exulted in the sense of freedom it gave her, a sense she had never known within the strict confines of eastern society.

Yes, Texas was beautiful. In fact, the whole world was beautiful so long as Eben was beside her. She glanced at him for what must have been the hundredth time, still not quite able to believe she was really here with him. He'd bathed and changed since she'd seen him in the shop. He wore a crisp, blue plaid shirt, which looked suspiciously new, and well-worn jeans that hugged his thighs with wicked allure.

He'd combed his chestnut hair carefully, although he had only partially succeeded in taming the tendency to curl, and he wore a broad-brimmed hat like the ones the cowboys sported. All in all, he looked simply dashing.

She only hoped he found her equally appealing. Beneath her crocheted shawl, she wore her apricot sprigged calico, the same dress she'd worn the night he'd proposed to her. Although she didn't expect a repeat of the proposal tonight, she hoped at least to mend their relationship enough so he would feel confident in asking her again at some future time.

Giddy with excitement, Isabel paid little attention to the direction they took. When they'd been gone quite a while, she asked, "How far is it to the Stevenses' ranch?"

"Quite a ways. There's a place up ahead where we can stop to eat. It's an old line shack."

Did he seem ill at ease? Perhaps he was as nervous as she, and, indeed, he had far more reason to be. She, at least, could take comfort in the knowledge that he really did care for her. Didn't his gift and his determination to pursue her prove it? But poor Eben had no idea what Isabel felt for him. She would have to think of some way to let him know this evening.

"Is that where we're going?" Isabel asked, indicating a small building in the distance. Having no idea what a "line shack" was, she could only guess.

"Yeah, uh, that's it, all right," Eben replied with forced brightness. He glanced at her as if trying to judge her reaction, and Isabel was touched by his concern. The place didn't seem too prepossessing, but since they were only going to picnic there, not set up housekeeping, she saw no cause for complaint.

"It's a pretty setting," she remarked, trying to put him at ease. Although the shack itself was only a small, weather-beaten structure with shingles falling off the roof, the windmill behind it cranking relentlessly in the wind and the fledgling trees taking root in the overflow of the nearby stock tank gave the place a romantic air of man's struggle to subdue the wild land.

As usual, the setting sun was painting scarlet streaks across the sky and tinting the whole world pink. In this light even the shabby cabin took on an aura of fantasy, and Isabel couldn't help feeling something wonderful was about to happen.

Eben reined the horse to a halt beside the cabin, then hopped nimbly out and reached up to help her alight. Placing her hand in his, Isabel felt the pleasant abrasion of his callused palm against hers, and she shivered. When she hesitated at stepping down, he dropped her hand, reached up, and clasped her around the waist.

A startled "Oh!" escaped her as he effortlessly lifted her the short distance to the ground. She looked up into his eyes, and her breath caught at the expression there.

"You're no bigger than a minute," he said hoarsely, his hands lingering possessively at her waist. His eyes seemed even darker than usual, and a muscle twitched in his jaw. He bent toward her, and Isabel found herself unable to breathe.

Then he seemed to come to himself again, and he instantly released her, stepping quickly back. "I . . . uh, I'll unhitch the horse and unpack our supper. Why don't you look around?"

"All right," Isabel agreed, laying an unsteady hand over her clamoring heart. Taking a deep breath to make sure her lungs would still function, she obediently went to "look around." Not that there was much to see. The stock pond and the windmill took only a minute to observe. The shack promised few surprises, but for lack of anything better to do, she pushed the door open and stepped inside.

The cabin consisted of one large room lit by a window covered with some opaque material. On the far wall was a stone fireplace that had obviously seen the preparations of many meals. A fire had been laid on the hearth, although the rest of the place gave no evidence of recent habitation. Along the left-hand wall stood a bunk bed built right into the corner. Straw-filled mattresses lay on each bunk. To the right stood a homemade table with several three-legged stools. Boxes nailed to the walls served as cabinets and held a meager assortment of canned goods. Although the place had a forsaken air, Isabel noticed a peculiar lack of dust. Someone must keep the place up.

When Isabel went back outside, she saw Eben had unhitched the horse and turned him loose. She was about to protest such a foolish act when she noticed the animal had been hobbled so he couldn't run away.

"Do you want to eat inside or out?" Eben called.

"Outside, please," she replied. "It's such a glorious evening. Do you have something we can sit on?"

"Yeah, I think so." He lifted the tarp covering her luggage in the back of the buggy and began to rummage around.

Isabel hurried over to help. "Oh, you brought a blanket," she said when he had pushed her trunk out of the way to reveal the roll.

"I'll get it," he said sharply, but Isabel had already grabbed the rope tying it together and was lifting it out. She wondered at the size and weight of it. How many blankets had he thought they'd need for a picnic?

"Isabel, I'll do it," he insisted. He took hold of the roll and tried to wrest it from her, but she still held the rope, and the bundle pulled free. Instantly it came apart, spilling to the ground.

"Oh, dear," Isabel muttered, stooping to pick it up, but once again Eben tried to beat her to it, and in his haste, he jarred the bundle completely open. A pillow plopped out.

A pillow? What on earth . . . ?

Seeing her surprise, Eben was frantically trying to gather the bedding up again, but his clumsy efforts to hold the disintegrating bundle together caused a second pillow to plop out onto the grass.

"Eben?" Isabel asked, thoroughly confused. Surely he hadn't brought *pillows* on a picnic. "Is that a bedroll?"

"Well, yeah," he admitted, and Isabel noticed his neck had turned red. "I thought, that is, it'll be late when we get to . . . to where we're going and . . ."

"And you were going to ask Mrs. Stevens if you could spend the night at her place," Isabel guessed when he hesitated.

"Yeah, right, that's it," Eben agreed quickly.

Too quickly. Isabel had heard too many stories from too many students not to recognize a lie when she heard one. Besides, one small detail bothered her.

"Eben, why do you need *two* pillows?"

The red in his neck spread over his face. He scooped up the bedding and dumped it unceremoniously back into the rear compartment of the buggy.

"Eben?" Isabel said sharply, rising slowly to her feet.

He turned to face her, his expression guarded. "I don't suppose you're hungry?"

Apprehension prickled across her nerve endings. "Answer me, Eben."

He rubbed his hands on his pant legs. "I guess you might as well know. You've been kidnapped."

"*What?*"

"Kidnapped. Abducted. Whatever you want to call it."

"But *why?*"

"So you'll have to marry me."

Isabel could not have been more surprised if he had punched her in the face. "This doesn't make any sense," she said faintly.

"It makes perfect sense. If we're out together alone, overnight, you'll be ruined, and we'll have to get married."

Isabel stared at him in disbelief. "Did it ever occur to you to simply *ask* me?" she demanded indignantly.

"I *did* ask you," he reminded her, equally indignant. "For all the good it did me."

Isabel didn't know whether to laugh or cry. When had she lost control of her life? Since the moment she had fainted into Eben Walker's arms, nothing had made a lick of sense. "Eben, this is ridiculous. You can't kidnap a woman and expect her to want to marry you."

"I already know you don't want to marry me. You made that pretty clear the other night." Now his face was red from anger, and Isabel experienced another twinge of apprehension.

"If you thought I didn't want to marry you, then why . . . ?" She gestured helplessly at the buggy with its questionable contents.

"Because *I* still want to marry *you*, and I'm not going to sit by and watch you tie up with somebody else."

"I have no intention of 'tying up' with somebody else. I have no intention of getting married at all!"

"So we heard, which is why every man in the county has been trying to compromise your reputation. Whoever can do it first gets you, and it's going to be me."

If Isabel had thought she'd heard everything, Eben's explanation instantly disabused her of the notion. So *that's* why meek little Felix Underwood had suddenly turned into a masher, and that's why every man who called on her pressed her to take a buggy ride. Common sense had prevented her from accepting any of those other invitations, but when Eben Walker had offered to take her to the Stevenses' ranch, she'd accepted without a second thought. She was an absolute idiot.

Or was she?

As preposterous as it was, this kidnapping proved how desperately Eben wanted her. If only she'd known the other night when he'd proposed to her, how differently things might have turned out!

And the bedding he'd brought along tonight implied even more intriguing possibilities. Had he planned to *seduce* her, too, just to make sure of her acquiescence? The possibility should have outraged her, but when she remembered his kisses, she found herself trembling with anticipation. Of course, she wouldn't dream of actually surrendering to him, but she wasn't averse to letting him show her just exactly how *much* he wanted her either. But before she'd let him show her, he'd have to *tell* her.

"This seems like an awful lot of trouble to go to just to get a stepmother for Amanda," she ventured.

He studied her suspiciously for a long moment. "You're a good cook, too," he countered, "and I reckon you can keep house."

"I can also make all my own clothes. Is that why you want to marry me, Eben?" she asked, disappointment bitter in her mouth. "So you can have a housekeeper?"

"Hell, no!"

"Don't swear at me!"

"I'll swear if I have to! Dammit, Isabel, what does a man have to do?"

"That depends on what he's trying to accomplish!" she replied tartly.

"I'm trying to get you to *love* me!"

Stung, Isabel felt her face turn scarlet. "And what does a woman have to do to get *you* to love *her*?"

"Not much," Eben replied furiously. "She just has to faint dead away the first time she sets eyes on me and sing like an angel and come swishing into my shop every other day looking for lost kids—"

"I do not swish!"

"—and make my daughter act like a normal person, and get Barclay Plimpton to stop wearing a monkey suit to school and—"

"Eben, I've already done all those things!"

His glare told her he knew that perfectly well, and only then did the truth dawn on her. "Are you saying...?" She could hardly make herself speak the words aloud. "Are you saying you're already in love with me?"

"Why do you think I want to marry you?" he asked in exasperation.

"So you can have somebody to take care of your house and your daughter, and may I remind you those were the reasons you gave me when you proposed," she said when he would have protested. "If you loved me, why didn't you just say so?"

"You never gave me a chance!"

"As I recall, I asked you point-blank!"

"Yeah, and then you started insisting I couldn't possibly love you because I was still in love with my wife! Where'd you get a harebrained idea like that?"

Harebrained? "Eben, you don't have to spare my feelings. I know you must have loved her dearly, and from the way you look at Amanda sometimes... Well, she must resemble her mother and—"

"She does," Eben said through gritted teeth. "She looks exactly like her."

"I'm sure it must be difficult for you—"

"I didn't love her," he grated.

Startled, Isabel tried unsuccessfully to read his expression. "I told you, you don't have to spare my feelings. I'm not jealous of a dead woman, or not very much at least. I—"

"Isabel—" he tried, but she wanted to reassure him.

"Eben, you don't have to pretend for my sake—"

"I'm not pretending!"

"Of course, you'll always love her—"

"I do *not* love her! Dammit, I *killed* her!"

Isabel stared at him in horror. She couldn't have heard it. He couldn't have *said* it, and if he had, he couldn't have *meant* it. He couldn't have . . .

"Oh, God," he groaned, putting both hands over his face.

"Eben?" Her heart was in her throat. Tentatively she laid a hand on his arm.

Her touch seemed to galvanize him. He shook her hand off and whirled away. "I'll take you to the Stevenses' now," he said hoarsely, starting off to where their horse grazed contentedly.

"Eben, wait!" Isabel cried, grabbing his arm. "You can't just . . . What did you mean? You couldn't have . . ."

He stiffened and lifted his chin, looking up into the glorious evening sky as if for divine help. His face was ashen, his expression terrible.

"Eben?"

"I killed her, Isabel."

"But how? Why? It must have been an accident! You couldn't possibly have—"

"How do you know?" he challenged, turning his bleak gaze full upon her.

Chilled by the sight of his despair, she wondered how she *could* know. "Because you aren't that kind of man," she said with more certainty than she should have felt.

"You don't know anything about me," he reminded her bitterly.

"Then tell me, Eben. You *have* to tell me now."

He drew a deep breath and let it out in a long, weary sigh. "Yes, I suppose I do, don't I?"

She felt a tremor go through him and knew that this story would change her life. "Why don't we . . . sit down someplace," she suggested.

"Inside?"

"No," she said quickly, thinking of the dreary cabin with a shudder. "Out here." In the sunshine, she added silently.

Slipping her arm through his, she guided him back toward the buggy, where they picked up a blanket and spread it on the grass. Isabel sank gratefully onto her knees.

"Eben?" she said when he made no move to join her. Slowly, reluctantly, he lowered himself to the blanket, keeping as much space as possible between them. He sat with his knees spread wide and drawn up, his arms draped over them, his shoulders hunched defensively.

"Where should I start?" he murmured, more to himself than to her.

"At the beginning," she replied. "Tell me everything."

His hands clasped each other until the knuckles turned white. Just when Isabel thought he wouldn't tell her after all, he said, "I didn't have any family."

She inched forward, silently encouraging him.

"They all died of fever when I was about ten or eleven, my parents and my two brothers. I scrounged around after that, working for my keep, but nobody really wanted me: I was just uneducated trash to most folks; something that offended their clean, Christian tastes.

"Then I met Gunther. He ran the blacksmith shop, and I used to hang around there every chance I got. I was fascinated by the things he could do with iron. Finally he asked me if I wanted to learn to be a smith, and, of course, I said yes." He fell silent.

"Was Gunther German?" Isabel prodded.

Eben nodded solemnly. "There are a lot of Germans around Fredericksburg. They're the best ironworkers in the world, or so Gunther used to say. He taught me everything I know."

He turned to Isabel, and she almost gasped aloud at the pain reflected in his dark eyes. "He took me in, Isabel. *They* took me in, him and his wife. They treated me like a son, like I was one of them. They were a real family. Do you know how much that meant?"

"I can imagine," she said softly.

"They had a daughter, a cute little kid who used to hang around the shop and get underfoot. Gisela." His eyes clouded, and suddenly he wasn't looking at Isabel, or at least he wasn't seeing her. "Gisela," he said again.

"What a beautiful name."

He laughed, an ugly, mirthless sound that sent chills up her spine. "Beautiful. Yeah, she was beautiful, all right. When she grew up, I mean. Seemed like one day she was a kid and the next day she was a woman. The boys started flocking around, and she flirted with all of them. There'd be at least one fight a week over who got to take her out riding or who got to sit next to her in the porch swing, and she loved every minute of it.

"Everybody thought she was perfect, especially Gunther and his wife. In their eyes she could do no wrong, and they never refused her anything. They called her their angel, but she wasn't an angel, not by a long shot.

"Once she figured out she could get men to like her, she wanted *all* of them to like her. She'd always been like my kid sister, so at first I couldn't bring myself to flirt with her, even though I could see how desirable she'd become. That made her mad, so she set her cap for me. From what happened later, I figure she didn't really want me. I was too serious for her taste, but she couldn't stand it that I wasn't panting after her like all the rest. She started coming by the shop, teasing me and carrying on. When I still wouldn't fall for her, she started coming to my room at night."

"Oh!" Isabel cried, shocked to her core.

For the first time, Eben looked at her, his eyes bleak, his lips stretched into a bitter smile. "Yes, the little angel was really a harlot. She'd crawl into bed with me and . . ."

He looked away, his lips flat with disgust. "I threatened to tell her parents, but she only laughed. She said she'd only tell them I'd lured her there and tried to take advantage of her, and, of course, they'd believe her. They'd never believe their angel would go to a man's room.

"I resisted her as long as I could, but after a while it seemed stupid not to take what she was offering, especially when I wanted it so bad, so I . . ." He waved his hand in a helpless gesture.

Isabel held her breath as she waited for him to continue.

"She told me I'd have to marry her now, but she was only teasing. There were other men, and after a while she got bored with me and stopped coming to my room. By then I was in love with her, or thought I was, and I was angry and jealous. But when I saw how she treated the others, leading them on and then dropping them for someone new, I told myself I was lucky to be rid of her.

"I'd almost convinced myself when she told me she was going to have a baby, *my* baby. I think I was more scared than she was. All I could think about was how Gunther would hate me for betraying his trust and he'd throw me out. I'd lose my home and my family, all because of her." He sighed and shook his head at the memories.

"But, of course, just the opposite happened. Gisela told her parents we were in love and wanted to get married right away. They were surprised, but they had no reason to doubt her. The way she treated me after that, even *I* started to believe her. No man could have wanted a more devoted fiancée, and Gunther . . ."

His voice trailed off, and pain twisted his face. "Gunther shook my hand, tears running down his cheeks, and said now I'd *really* be his son."

Isabel reached for him, laying a hand on his arm, but he hardly seemed to notice. Lost in the past, he stared off into the distance, seeing things Isabel knew she could never share. "So you were married," she said gently.

"Yeah, just as quick as Gisela could arrange it. Her parents didn't know about the baby until later, and even when they found out, they never said a word. They must've known why we got married, but they loved us both too much to condemn us. I think they were just happy Gisela had settled down with a man they liked.

"For a wedding present they built us a house. They wanted us to live next to them, but Gisela insisted on a spot at the other end of town. I thought she just wanted to get away from her parents so she could feel like an adult, but I found out later she had other reasons.

"As soon as we were married, she stopped pretending she loved me. I'd always known she was spoiled, but nothing I did suited her. Her mother made excuses. She said women in a family way were usually short-tempered, and as soon as the baby came, Gisela would be her normal sweet self again."

Eben laughed bitterly. "After Amanda was born, things got worse. We fought all the time, and Gisela started sleeping in Amanda's room. I thought about taking her and the baby to San Antone or Austin. Gisela had always wanted to live in a big city, but when I thought about how much her parents would miss her, I couldn't do it.

"Then one day somebody came by the shop and suggested I should go home right away. I thought something might be wrong with Amanda, so I did."

This time when he turned to Isabel, she couldn't even name the emotion she saw on his face. Anguish and agony mingled into something terrible to behold. Isabel withdrew her hand from his arm and covered her mouth to hold back her own cry of despair.

"I found out why she wanted to live far away from her parents. She had a man with her, a no-good drummer who'd come to town selling dress goods. They were in bed together, in *my* bed." His voice trembled with fury and outrage. "I got my gun. I wanted to kill that bastard for taking what she wouldn't give me. She was screaming and he was yelling, begging me not to shoot him, both of them stark naked and him on his knees . . ."

"Eben," Isabel whispered, her throat clogged with tears. "You don't have to . . ."

He didn't seem to hear. "I was shaking so bad, I had to hold the pistol in both hands, and Gisela threw herself at me. She grabbed the gun and tried to take it from me, and somehow . . ."

His voice cracked, and he dug the heels of his hands into his eyes, fighting tears. Isabel's own cheeks were wet with them. "You didn't kill her on purpose," Isabel said, no longer able to resist the urge to comfort him. She wrapped her arms around his shoulders and drew him close. "It was an accident. I knew it was."

He shuddered and pulled away from her. His eyes were wet, but his expression was unrelenting. "Accident or not, I killed her."

"Surely no one blamed you!" she tried.

"No, but they might as well've hung me, because I lost everything that day. Accident or not, justified or not, I'd killed Gisela, and her parents could never forgive me. They turned their backs. I'd lost my home and my family. They never spoke to me again except to ask for Amanda."

"Amanda?"

"I couldn't work with Gunther anymore, and I couldn't stay in Fredericksburg, not after what happened. I had to go someplace and start over. I was all packed and ready to go when Gunther came to see me.

"He'd aged ten years in the weeks since Gisela's death. I could hardly look at him, and he couldn't look at me at all. After all those years together, we were like strangers. He asked me to leave Amanda with them to raise. He said I'd have a hard time of it, a man alone taking care of a baby and trying to earn a living, too.

"I could see how much it meant to him. It would be like having Gisela all over again, a second chance. But then I remembered how they'd spoiled Gisela, making her think she could have anything she wanted regardless of how it might hurt someone else. I didn't want Amanda to grow up like her mother, and besides . . ." He looked away, his jaw set grimly.

"Besides, you loved her," Isabel guessed.

"She was all I had left, the only family I'd ever have, so I told him no."

The despair in his voice tore at her heart. "No one could blame you for wanting your own daughter," she argued.

"Gunther died just a few months later," he replied bitterly. "They said it was his heart, but I know I killed him, just as sure as if I'd put a bullet in him, too."

"Eben, no!" Isabel cried. She threw her arms around him again, and this time she didn't let him resist. "Don't do this to yourself, my darling," she whispered, pressing her lips to his forehead.

His arms slid around her, pulling her close with a fierceness born of desperation. She clung to him, cradling his head against her breast.

"I thought if I told you, you'd hate me," he said.

"Hate you?" she replied, pulling away so she could see his face in the fading light. "Eben, I love you, and nothing you've said tonight changes that."

"You love me?" he asked in amazement.

She smiled at his surprise. "I can see I've succeeded admirably at keeping my feelings a secret."

"Since when?" he demanded, giving her a little shake.

Isabel shrugged. "Probably since the instant I fainted into your arms."

"Wait a minute," he said with a frown, maneuvering her so she lay across his lap. "Are you trying to tell me you were in love with me the other night when I proposed to you?"

She nodded sheepishly.

He swore.

"Eben, I hope I don't have to keep reminding you to watch your language," she said as primly as she could under the circumstances.

"If you were in love with me, why did you turn me down?"

"Because you weren't in love with me. After what you just told me about your own marriage, I know you'll understand my reluctance to live with a man who didn't care for me."

He swore again.

"Eben," she chided, but his arms closed around her and his lips found hers, and suddenly Isabel no longer cared about improving Eben's behavior.

His kiss was everything she remembered and more, sweet and exciting, giving and demanding. He pulled her close, until her breasts flattened against his chest and her heart pounded against his. His hands caressed her back, adoring her slender form and sending sensation streaking over her.

He slanted his mouth over hers, teasing with his tongue until she opened to him. He probed the delicate skin inside her lips, and Isabel gasped in response. He swallowed her gasp and took possession of her mouth.

Astonished at the invasion, Isabel tried to pull away, but he tangled his fingers in her hair and held her fast. At last his tongue found hers and stroked. Isabel shivered in response. She knew such an intimacy must be terribly wicked, so she tried to fight back, pushing his tongue with hers, but this only seemed to encourage him.

He groaned, pulling her more tightly against him, and his tongue tangled with hers in a playful duel that shattered all her resistance, and left her weak and trembling.

When they were both breathless, Eben lifted his head a fraction of an inch. "My God, who taught you to do that?"

"You did!" she gasped. "Is it . . . terribly wicked?"

"Oh, terribly," he groaned as he sank backward on the blanket, carrying her with him.

Isabel only had a moment to feel shocked at being on top of him before he slid her off so he could be on top of her. "Eben," she said by way of protest as he loomed over her, but the word sounded like a plea.

He silenced her with another kiss, and another, and another, until the world spun out of control and then ceased entirely to exist. Nothing mattered except her and Eben and what his body was doing to hers.

Isabel couldn't ever remember feeling so hot, as if a fire burned within her. Her blood roared, and all she could hear was the furious pounding of her own heart. Eben must have heard it, too, because he put his hand over it, cupping her breast as if to capture her very life force.

She knew she should protest such a liberty, but Eben was kissing her so she couldn't say a word, and after a while, she didn't want to. His palm seemed to burn right through the fabric of her dress, or perhaps her skin burned up to his hand. Whatever, her breast swelled beneath his touch, straining to fill his palm.

The next thing she knew, he was struggling with the buttons at her throat.

"Eben, what . . . ?" she began, then he pressed his mouth to the pulse throbbing at the base of her throat and she no longer wondered. She wanted him to kiss her, wanted him to find all the sensitive spots hidden beneath her clothes. She nudged his fingers aside, releasing all the buttons so he could spread open her bodice and worship the swell of her bosom above the lacy edge of her chemise.

Her nipples hardened, aching for his touch, and when he pushed aside the covering fabric, she moaned in mingled shock and pleasure. His callused fingers kneaded her tender flesh, lifting the pouting nipple to his hungry mouth. Isabel sustained a second shock when he suckled her. The vibrations echoed through her, curling her toes and fanning the fire within into an inferno.

"Eben!" she cried, although she could not have said what she wanted.

"You'll stop me, won't you?" he panted against the rosy peak of her breast.

"Stop you?" she asked stupidly.

"When I go too far."

How far was that? She had no idea, but she didn't want to stop him yet. "Yes," she murmured blissfully.

He bared her other breast and chafed it to aching awareness with the delicious abrasion of his fingers, then soothed it, too, in the moist haven of his mouth.

"You're so beautiful," he whispered, and for the first time in her life, Isabel actually felt beautiful.

She buried her fingers in the cinnamon silkiness of his hair and raised his face to hers. He kissed her slowly, thoroughly, exploring the depths of her mouth until she was panting with need. Her hands found the end of his shirttail where it had pulled loose, and she eagerly sought the warm skin beneath.

He groaned. Emboldened, she caressed his supple flesh, marveling at the satiny smoothness over rock-hard muscles honed by years of rugged labor. Reveling in the differences between man and woman, Isabel hardly noticed when he parted her legs with one of his own.

She froze when she felt his hand beneath her skirt. Surely this was the "too far" of which he had warned her, but the sensation of his hand against her thigh through the thin barrier of her cotton drawers wiped all thoughts of protest from her mind.

"Hmmm," he murmured against her ear, sending delicious shivers dancing over her. "You're not skinny at all, Miss Forester."

Although his hand caressing her hip distracted her, she managed to sound a little outraged. "Skinny?"

He nuzzled her neck, pressing a kiss into the sensitive hollow behind her ear. "I thought you might be. The way women dress, it's hard to tell."

"Do you think we should wear trousers like men do so you'd be able to tell?" she countered, gasping when his hand slid over her belly.

"No, I . . . I kind of like finding out this way," he said hoarsely, and Isabel gasped again as he found the opening between the legs of her pantalettes and slipped his hand inside.

"Eben!" she squeaked.

"Oh, God, Isabel, you're so hot. . . ."

And she was, burning in fact. He cupped her mound, the heel of his hand pressing into the curls while his fingers explored the part of her that wept for him. Instinctively she pressed herself to him, wanting something, wanting more.

"This is . . . wrong. . . ." she panted as his fingers did magical things to her.

"Do you . . . want me . . . to stop?" he panted back.

"Not . . . yet . . ." she managed, fighting the spiraling desire that threatened to overwhelm her.

"Touch me, Isabel," he said, but when she stroked his cheek, he shook his head. "No, here."

His fingers left her, and he grasped her wrist, guiding her hand down to his waist and below. "Oh, Eben!" she cried when he placed her palm over the hard bulge.

"See what you do to me?" he asked in a strangled voice.

She wondered if he knew what he did to her, and if her touch brought him the same pleasure his brought her, but before she could even think of asking, he touched her again and sensation exploded within her.

"I've never wanted a woman the way I want you, Isabel."

His voice seemed to come from far away, yet he was so close she could feel the vibrations of his pounding heart. She wanted him, too, wanted him in ways she couldn't even name. She wanted him close. She wanted to be part of him. She wanted...

Once more his fingers left her, and this time he worked loose the buttons of his pants.

"Eben, I..." Isabel began, but she didn't really want to stop him, even though she knew they had long since passed "wicked" and gone into territory she hadn't even known existed.

Isabel closed her eyes, unable to look at him. When he finished undoing the buttons, he took her hand again and gently closed her fingers around the hot, hard shaft. His hiss of indrawn breath told her she, too, wielded the power of desire, and although her cheeks burned with embarrassment and her eyes remained closed, she gloried in this newfound strength.

"You're making me crazy," he murmured against her scalding cheek, and when his fingers once more sought her center, she saw her own sanity slipping away. "I want you, Isabel. Please..."

His plea ended in a strangled sound as he pressed his mouth to hers. Before she could react, he rolled on top of her. The hard shaft replaced his fingers, pressing against the spot that burned so fiercely. His hips moved on hers, and she lifted in response, seeking the release only he could give.

"I... don't want to hurt you...." he groaned. Isabel knew he never would. Obeying his silent urging, she opened to him, offering what she had vowed to give only to the one man who had also won her heart.

He took her slowly, gently, so carefully she almost cried out in frustration until she felt his hardness straining against the barrier of her innocence. Clutching at his hips, she forced him on. The pain was sharp but fleeting, and he captured her surprised gasp with his kiss. Then he filled her, and she forgot the pain completely.

They lay completely still for a long moment while Isabel savored the bliss of ultimate union. At last she opened her eyes and found him staring down at her in wonder. "You didn't stop me," he breathed.

"I didn't want to. Oh, Eben, I didn't know it would be so wonderful."

He smiled the smile she loved so much. "There's more."

"More?"

She couldn't believe it, but then he started to withdraw.

"Not yet," she begged, not wanting to lose him so soon.

And he came back, sliding slowly into her again, and the flames within roared up again.

"Eben!"

"Oh, God, the look on your face," he marveled. Then he moved again, and Isabel had to shut her eyes against the brightness.

She wanted to tell him something or ask him something, but there was no time. The fire seared through her, melting away everything except the passion they shared. Soon she caught the rhythm of his strokes and rose to meet him. His answering moans told her he shared her response, and she exulted in the knowledge.

The fire blazed, brighter and hotter, until she could see it flickering against her eyelids. Flames danced, inside and out, scorching and searing, higher and higher, until she thought she might explode. And then she did, splintering into a shower of sparks so brilliant she dissolved within them, convulsing in white-hot incandescence as Eben filled her with liquid flame.

How long they lay together afterward, Isabel didn't know, but at last she began to feel the burden of his weight crushing her against the hard ground. When she stirred, he rose up onto his elbows, and she realized to her chagrin that their bodies were still joined down below. Without the fiery haze of passion to obscure her powers of observation, everything suddenly became vividly real. And terribly embarrassing.

"I . . ." she began, but no words came.

He frowned in concern and brushed a lock of hair away from her forehead. "Did I hurt you?"

Isabel tried to remember, but she could recall nothing of pain. She shook her head, feeling the color rising in her face.

"Are you blushing?" he asked in apparent delight.

"Certainly not!" she lied, even as her face burned more brightly.

"Oh, God, Isabel, why did it take so long for me to find you?"

Her embarrassment evaporated in the warmth of his smile. "Perhaps because I was living two thousand miles away."

He rewarded her with a kiss, which she returned with all the love overflowing her heart. When at last he lifted his head again, she felt him stirring within her again.

"Eben?" she asked in confusion.

"Yes?" he replied with amusement.

"Is it . . . is it over now or is there more?"

"More what . . . ? Oh," he said, grinning as understanding dawned. "For now, I suppose it better be over. Although I'd like nothing better than to enjoy your beautiful body all over again, I suppose you must be a little sore."

Isabel didn't think she was sore so much as exhausted, but she didn't argue. Still, when he lifted his weight from her, she experienced an acute sense of loss. Regret quickly gave way to embarrassment, however, as she realized she was scandalously ex-

posed. Frantically grasping the front of her dress together, she sat up and began to struggle with her skirt
and petticoats.

Beside her, Eben chuckled while he made his own
adjustments. "It's a little late for modesty, Miss Forester."

She supposed it was, but she couldn't help feeling
modest nonetheless. When her skirt was decently
covering her ankles again, she turned away and began
to fasten her bodice. Behind her, Eben rose up on his
knees and began to nuzzle the back of her neck. "Do
you know how delicious you are, Miss Isabel?" he
inquired.

His hot breath raised gooseflesh all over her and
made her hands clumsy on the buttons. "Am I?" she
inquired, wondering if such nonsense was a normal
part of lovemaking.

"Mmmm, yes, and after we're married, I'm going
to taste every inch of you."

She turned to face him, her half-buttoned bodice
forgotten. "We *are* getting married, aren't we?" she
asked as brand-new doubts assailed her.

He grinned at her concern. "What's this? Now
you're the one interested in getting married? I reckon
I handled this whole thing all wrong. I could've saved
a lot of time by seducing you first, and if I'd known
how much fun it would be—"

"Eben!" she cried in mortification. She'd surrendered to him outside of marriage, and even worse,
without so much as a *promise* of marriage. Had she
been a fool?

"Isabel!" he countered. "If you will remember, the
reason I brought you out here in the first place was
to force you to marry me."

"Or to seduce me," she replied, remembering the
bedding and the *two* pillows. "How do I know you
didn't just want to have your way with me to get
even—"

"Isabel, shut up!" he commanded, grabbing her by

the shoulders and pulling her to him. His mouth took
hers in a kiss that was part possession and part promise. When she was breathless, he released her. "And
if you think I was lying about wanting to marry you,
all you have to do is tell people I really did seduce
you. Half the men in the county will be only too happy
to arrange a shotgun wedding for us."

"I could never do that!" she protested, coloring
again at the very thought.

"Then it's a good thing you won't have to," he
replied with the grin that made her want to kiss him
again. "But if you try to back out, I swear I'll tell
everybody what just happened on this blanket—"

"Eben, you wouldn't!"

"Oh, yes, I would, so you'd better promise right
here and now that you'll marry me just as soon as
possible."

She studied his dark eyes and recognized the determination behind the teasing. He might be talking
nonsense, but he really did want her. Still.

"Well, all right," she said with feigned reluctance.

"*All right?*" he shouted in outrage. "The woman
has just been ruined and all she can say is 'all right'?"

"What would you have me say?" she countered
coyly.

She screamed with pleasure when he lunged for
her. He bore her back down onto the blanket and
kissed her senseless until she finally confessed how
very, very much she loved him and how very, very
happy she would be to become his wife.

He held her for a long time after that, until the sky
turned gray with approaching night. "I never thought
I'd ever be happy again," he murmured into the tum-
bled mass of her golden hair.

"I never thought I'd ever be happy at all," she
replied against his shoulder. "I can hardly believe I'm
going to be a wife and a mother in just a few days."

"You might not be so happy about the mother part

of it the first time Amanda throws one of her fits,"
Eben warned.

"You just don't know how to handle her," Isabel
said confidently. "I have far more experience with
young girls than you do." For the first time, Isabel
began to realize how fortunate she would be to gain
not just a handsome husband but a beautiful child as
well. "Oh, Eben, thank you for being willing to share
your daughter with me."

For some reason, her remark disturbed him. He slid
his arm from beneath her and sat up abruptly.

"Eben, what's wrong?"

"Nothing," he said, but once again Isabel recognized a lie.

She sat up beside him. "If you're worried about me
taking Amanda away from you, that could never happen. She'll always be your daughter . . ." Her voice
trailed off as Eben went rigid beside her. "Eben, what
is it?" she asked as she tried to figure out what she
had said to upset him. Surely he couldn't be offended
because she'd said Amanda was his daughter. . . .

Then she recalled the story of Amanda's mother,
and the truth hit her like a blow. "Eben, you can't
think Amanda isn't your child."

"Can't I?" he challenged grimly. "She doesn't look
anything like me, now does she? Gisela always
claimed I was the only man she'd been with, but after
she died, I found out different. Seems the drummer
wasn't the first man who'd visited her at our house,
and people had been talking for months. How do I
know there weren't others *before* we got married,
too?"

"Do you honestly believe Amanda isn't your
child?" she asked, horrified.

"*I don't know*," he said through gritted teeth.

Isabel thought back to what she knew about the
two of them and what she'd seen of their relationship.
Had Amanda sensed his doubts? Was this why she

seemed convinced Eben didn't care about her? "Is that why you don't love her?" Isabel ventured.

"Don't love her?" he exclaimed furiously. "Where'd you get a damn fool idea like that?"

Deciding to ignore his profanity this once, Isabel maintained her reasonable tone. "Well, you don't seem very close, and the other morning when she kissed you—"

Eben sprang to his feet, jammed his hands into his pockets, and strode away several steps before Isabel could scramble up, too.

"We have to talk about this," Isabel insisted, stopping him in his tracks.

He whirled to face her, his expression defiant. "What do you want to talk about?" he asked coldly.

"Eben, Amanda is just an innocent child. She has no idea why you treat her the way you do, and it isn't fair to her."

"*Not fair?* You want to talk about not fair, how about me? I've had her all her life. She's the only person who ever loved me. I always wondered, but it didn't matter until . . . until she started growing up."

"Then why does it matter now?"

"Because it's all right to hug and kiss a little child, but she's not a child anymore, and if she's not really my daughter . . ."

Pain twisted his face, and he spun away from her.

"Would it make any difference to you if she wasn't your daughter?" Isabel demanded.

He turned back cautiously. "What do you mean?"

"I mean if she wasn't your daughter, would you stop loving her or want her to leave your house or—"

"Of course not!"

"Then why should it matter that she's growing up? If you still love her, then she's still your daughter, and I'll tell you quite frankly, I've rarely seen two people more alike than you and Amanda. She may not resemble you, but she certainly has all your bad qualities."

"What do you mean, 'bad qualities'?" he asked, affronted.

"She's stubborn and willful and won't listen to reason."

"I'm not stubborn!"

Isabel feigned astonishment. "Oh, really? Then why am I here?"

He considered her point. "I'm only stubborn about important things," he insisted.

"And Amanda is just like you. Eben, she adores you, and she's terribly frightened because she thinks you don't love her anymore."

"Where'd she get an idea like that?"

"Probably from you," Isabel said wryly. "Children, especially girls, are quite sensitive. She must have felt your doubts even though she couldn't know what prompted them. Eben, she isn't responsible for her mother's behavior, and it isn't her fault she's growing up. She still needs her father's love, and no matter who sired her, you're her father, her *real* father."

He frowned, and when he didn't respond, Isabel sighed in disgust. "Oh, for heaven's sake, the Bartz children don't look anything like Herald, either. That doesn't mean a thing!"

To her relief, a reluctant smile tugged at his lips. "They don't, do they? Do you really think Amanda . . ."

"That Amanda is yours? Certainly, but she won't be for very much longer unless you let her know you still love her."

His smile spread into a full-fledged grin, and he reached for her. "Miss Forester, how did you get so damn smart?"

"Mr. Walker, I'll thank you to watch your language!" she replied with mock seriousness. "You are addressing a lady!"

He kissed her as no man should ever kiss a lady,

plundering her mouth with his tongue while he plundered her body with his hands until she couldn't even remember what she had complained about. When he was done, she pulled away in a huff, trying to feign outrage, but he only laughed and tried to reach for her again.

She dodged his embrace, suddenly realizing how dark it was getting. "Now, as enjoyable as our time here has been, I would greatly appreciate it if you would take me on to the Stevenses' ranch. You must agree, since I've already consented to marry you, you needn't compromise me any more than you already have, and I would greatly prefer getting married with my reputation intact."

To her surprise, he frowned again. "Uh, yeah, well," he stammered, shoving his hands in his pockets and looking away. "I reckon you oughta know. I wasn't exactly truthful about what I told you before."

"What do you mean?" Isabel asked, feeling a prickle of alarm.

"Even if we stay here all night, you won't be ruined at all."

Chapter 11

"**W**hy won't I be ruined?" Isabel asked in confusion.

"Well..." Eben refused to meet her eye, and his broad shoulders seemed to hunch, although the light was much too dim to be certain. "I arranged it so nobody'd know you were gone."

"What! How could you do that?"

"Didn't you tell the Stevenses you wouldn't be coming out until tomorrow?"

"Yes," Isabel said warily.

"And the only people who know you left town tonight are the Bartzes. They'd never know you didn't arrive until tomorrow."

This didn't quite make sense. "If no one knew we were together all night, then how were you going to compromise me?"

He shrugged, a little sheepishly, she thought. "*You'd* think you were compromised, and I'd get you to promise to marry me, or at least that's the way I planned it. Once you promised, I figured you'd be grateful to find out I'd really protected your reputation."

"Eben, that is the most ridiculous plan I've ever heard!"

"Aren't you grateful?"

"Well, yes, I suppose so," she admitted reluctantly.

"Then it worked," he replied triumphantly. "Now, do you want to go on to the Stevenses' or back to town?"

Just then Isabel's stomach growled, reminding her she hadn't eaten much all day. "Eben Walker, you are the most impossible man I have ever met, but I believe I will allow you to feed me before taking me back to Bertha's. She'll never forgive me if she hears about our engagement from someone else."

His grin was a white slash in the darkness. "Then let's see what Amanda packed us. I'll get the basket. Why don't you go on inside and see if you can find a lamp. There should be some matches, too."

Isabel turned to go, but Eben caught her arm and pulled her back for another quick kiss before releasing her again. She hummed happily as she strolled to the small cabin. Had she once thought it dreary? Why, it looked like a fairy palace.

Although the interior was now pitch-dark, she recalled seeing a lantern on the rough table. Feeling around, she found the tin of matches next to it. Soon a golden glow filled the small room. Impulsively she also touched a match to the tinder beneath the logs in the fireplace. The flame caught instantly, and within minutes a cheerful fire burned brightly. While she waited, Isabel made what repairs she could to her hair and clothing, hoping Eben wouldn't be too shocked at her appearance.

He didn't seem the least bit shocked. In fact, he greeted her with a smile that curled her toes.

"Well, hello, Miss Forester," he said, as if he were surprised to find her here.

"Hello, yourself, and what have you brought me?" she teased, reaching for the picnic basket, but he held it out of her reach and wouldn't relinquish it until she'd kissed him again. And again.

"We'll starve to death if you keep this up," she reminded him, but he didn't seem to care. A good five minutes passed before he finally allowed Isabel to open the hamper.

Inside, they found cold roast beef sandwiches and apple pie. They spread the food out on the table, and Eben pulled out her three-legged stool for her as if they had been dining in a fine restaurant.

Eben poured them each some cider from a jug he had carried in, and they ate in silence until they had devoured every last crumb of Amanda's picnic. Isabel kept glancing at Eben, almost afraid to look for fear he might have disappeared like the hero of some dream. But each time, he met her glance and smiled, reminding her of how much he loved and wanted her.

Isabel's most romantic fantasy had come true. Her love had been so desperate to win her hand that he had carried her off like some medieval conqueror and ravished her to stake his claim. The small cabin seemed so cozy now, with the lamplight puddling on the table, and the fire casting flickering shadows about the room, that Isabel began to wish they might stay there forever.

Or at least for a little longer.

"Eben?"

"Hmmm?"

"Are you sure no one knows we're together?"

"How could they? I even told Amanda I'd probably spend the night at the Stevenses', so she's staying with the Bartz girl. They all think I'm there, and the Stevenses' think you're coming tomorrow."

Isabel considered the situation. "If you ... if you hadn't convinced me so early on to marry you and you'd kept me here overnight, where ... ? That is ..."

"Are you wondering where we would have slept?" he asked, his dark eyes twinkling with mischief.

"Yes," she admitted reluctantly.

"I suppose I was hoping you'd let me share your bunk, but you'll notice there are two," he said, gesturing toward the beds in the far corner. "And if you'd been too outraged, I would've slept in the buggy."

"Would you really?" she asked in amazement.

"Well, only if I had to," he admitted with a grin. "I suppose I was hoping . . ."

"Hoping what?"

"Hoping you'd turn out to be a warm, passionate woman who wouldn't mind sharing her bed with me."

His eyes reminded her of exactly how passionate she'd been just a short while ago, and embers from the fire she'd thought Eben had extinguished began to flicker once again. She swallowed against a suddenly dry throat.

"We really should go back to town," she said, although even she could hear her lack of conviction.

"Why?" he countered.

"Well, Bertha—"

"Thinks you're safe and sound at the Stevenses' ranch," he reminded her.

Unable to resist the temptation, Isabel glanced at the bunks.

"If you're worried we'll be too crowded, don't be," he told her, his voice as soft and sweet as warm honey. He reached over and took her hand between his rough, callused palms. His skin felt hot against hers, and the heat spread inexorably up her arm and over the rest of her body. "I'd hold you in my arms all night. The two of us wouldn't take up much more space than one."

The thought of lying all night in Eben's strong arms turned Isabel's bones to jelly. "But we aren't married," she protested weakly.

"Out on the frontier, folks can't always find a

preacher when they need one, so the formalities sometimes have to wait."

"Reverend Smiley lives right in town," she reminded him.

"Town is pretty far from here," he pointed out.

"Yes, it is," she agreed inanely. She tried to remember all the arguments she'd used on her students at Miss Snodgrass's school, about how a man would take advantage of a girl if given the opportunity and then leave her.

Unfortunately, none of the arguments seemed to apply in this case.

"What are you thinking?" he asked.

"I'm thinking things a preacher's daughter has no business thinking," she replied briskly, rising from her chair. "We'd better get these things cleared away."

"It's pitch-dark outside now," he pointed out, helping her pack the remnants of their meal. "The horse might step in a chuckhole or something. Break a leg. We'd have to shoot the poor thing."

Isabel tried to glare at him to show him his argument hadn't impressed her, but he looked so innocent and hopeful, she couldn't hold her glare for long. "Eben, you can't expect me to spend the night with you!" she tried in exasperation.

"Maybe I can't expect it, but I sure can hope," he said, catching her around the waist and pulling her into his arms. "Think about it," he murmured, touching his lips to hers in a teasing kiss. "We'll take off all our clothes—"

"Oh!" she squeaked in alarm, but he kissed her a few more times until she went limp against him.

"And I'll hold you, with every inch of you touching every inch of me, and then I'll kiss you, starting with your sweet . . . sweet . . . mouth," he said, punctuating his words with illustrations. "Then I'll move down, a little at a time, lower and lower . . ."

One hand closed over her breast, kneading gently

until the nipple puckered obediently. His other hand cupped her bottom, pulling her into the cradle of his thighs. She could feel the evidence of his renewed desire even through the layers of petticoats, and her body quivered in response.

"Eben, you're a very dangerous man," she told him between kisses. The embers inside her had now burst into full-fledged flames, melting Isabel's resistance and consuming all her reason. What would be the harm? No one would ever know.

His tongue flicked out to taste her mouth. "If I go get the blankets, you won't change your mind on me, will you?"

Somehow she found the strength to shake her head. He released her slowly, as if afraid she might collapse without his support, and indeed, the possibility was very real. When he was gone, she leaned against the chair back, her body throbbing with renewed need. Surely they couldn't . . . not so soon, she thought, but then she remembered Eben's condition just seconds ago.

Desire pulsed in her, and she crossed her arms over her aching breasts. Was she some sort of wanton to want him like this? If so, she should get down on her knees and thank God he was determined to marry her. Otherwise, she would have been compelled to become his mistress.

When Eben returned, he spared her one glance, as if only to ascertain she had, indeed, not changed her mind. In a few moments he'd spread the blankets on the lower bunk and laid the two pillows provocatively side by side on the narrow mattress.

He turned to face her and began unbuttoning his shirt. She watched, fascinated, as he pulled the tails loose and peeled it off his bare shoulders. He was even more beautiful than she could have imagined. Dark hair swirled across his chest and down his flat belly. Isabel reveled in the sight of his rippled muscles beneath satiny flesh.

When he had pulled off his socks and boots, he rested his hands on his knees. "I'm getting ahead of you," he pointed out.

Isabel glanced down at her fully clothed body. He couldn't possibly expect her to take her clothes off right here in front of him! She knew he'd been teasing about taking off *all* their clothes. No one would do something so uncivilized!

"Do you want some help?" he asked with a grin, rising to his feet again.

"No!" she cried, trying to back away, but she bumped against the table. In an instant he was beside her.

"You haven't changed your mind, have you?" he asked softly, slipping his arms around her waist.

"I...no..." she murmured, feeling weak again. She loved the way he smelled, all musky and male. The scent was like an opiate, robbing her of strength and will, and when she touched the heated satin of his skin, she was lost. "Would you...get my... nightdress..."

"Nightdress?" he scoffed. "You won't need that, not tonight. If you get cold, I'll—"

"Eben!"

"—hold you closer and—"

"I can't!" she insisted, but he was already working on the buttons at her throat. His lips followed his fingers, filling the expanding opening with kisses, and by the time he slid the dress from her shoulders, she shrugged free without regret. He had a little trouble getting her petticoats untied, but soon they, too, lay puddled at her feet.

"You don't sleep in this thing, do you?" he asked, running his hands over her stiff corset.

"Not always," she replied, thinking how wonderful it would be to feel his hands on her, without the barrier of its stiffness. She had to help him with it, releasing the front hooks with fingers made clumsy by haste and desire.

He flung it away, leaving her in just her chemise and drawers, then he scooped her up into his arms and carried her to the bed. The straw mattress crackled beneath their weight as Eben lowered her to it, but Isabel's heart was pounding so loudly, she could hardly hear anything else.

"You're so soft and smooth," he marveled, running his hands over her bare arms and shoulders, and sending delicious shivers racing over her.

Isabel couldn't resist the urge to return his touch, and she stroked the solid muscles of his arms and chest in wonder, trailing her fingers through the hair on his chest until she found a flat nipple. It puckered at her touch, and her own responded as Eben's fingers pushed aside the flimsy barrier of her chemise.

Somehow it had come completely untied in front, and Eben was trying to slide it down over her arms. Torn between the need to cover her naked breasts and the necessity of stopping him, Isabel blurted, "At least put out the light!"

"But I want to see you," he argued, his breath like invisible fire across her bare flesh. "You're so beautiful, Isabel."

As if hypnotized, Isabel allowed him to peel the chemise from her shoulders. Before she could guess his intent, he'd stripped it down over her legs, too, lifting her hips with remarkable ease to free it. Too embarrassed to even wonder if the opening in her drawers was gaping or not, she squeezed her eyes shut and quickly crossed her arms over her chest while Eben made short work of removing her shoes and stockings.

He clicked his tongue in disapproval over her modesty as he rose from the bed. Thinking he was going to blow out the light after all, she opened her eyes to thank him, but the words of gratitude died in her throat. He was skinning out of his trousers, and he didn't have a stitch on under them!

She gasped in shock at the size of him. How had

he ever managed...? The very thought sent the blood rushing to her cheeks.

"Are you pleased, Miss Forester?" he asked impudently as he lowered himself to the bed again.

Pleased? Isabel didn't find the word exactly appropriate. Before she could think of one that was, he took her arms and gently uncrossed them.

"Don't hide from me, Isabel. You don't have to be ashamed."

Isabel didn't think she was ashamed so much as mortified. No one had seen her naked since she'd been a child, and in the face of Eben's splendid masculinity, Isabel felt her own lack of beauty even more.

"Eben, I'm not..." she began, but her words ended in a squeal of protest. "What are you doing?"

"Getting rid of these," he explained, brushing her hands aside as he slipped her underdrawers down over her hips. In spite of her feeble protests, she was soon naked beneath his heated gaze. When she would have covered herself again, he caught her hands and held them fast.

Her face flaming, Isabel closed her eyes again. "Do ...do other people...behave like this?" she asked in a choked whisper.

"They do if they have any sense," he replied. "I guess I was wrong about you, Miss Isabel."

Against her better judgment, she opened one eye to look at him. "Wrong about what?"

"I thought you were educated, but I can see you've got a lot to learn about *some* things."

His mocking smile annoyed her. "If you're unhappy with me—"

"Oh, I'm plenty happy," he assured her. "I'm half-crazy with happiness. Who would've thought there was such a gorgeous woman underneath those old-maid clothes? I might just burn all of them and make you go around like this all the time."

"Eben!" she choked, thoroughly shocked, but not as outraged as she should have been. For some reason the thought held a perverse appeal, especially when she imagined Eben looking at her all the time just as he was looking at her now.

"I'll at least burn your nightdresses," he insisted. "In our bed, I'll always want you just like God made you."

It was difficult to maintain one's indignant modesty in the face of such blatant admiration, and Isabel's began to evaporate. In its place grew a now familiar warmth.

"Are you going to . . ." she began, then faltered when she realized she had no idea how to phrase her question.

"Make love to you?" he replied with a wicked smile. "I'd guess you're a little too sore right now, but I do have some promises to keep."

"Promises?" she echoed stupidly.

"I said we'd take off our clothes, and we've done that. Then I said I'd kiss you all over . . ."

Her body throbbed in response, and a tiny, pleading cry escaped her. Instantly Eben was on top of her, holding her to him, crushing her lips with his. She wrapped her arms around him, clinging to his silken shoulders, and soon her legs tangled with his as she gloried in the sensation of his hair-roughened skin against her smoothness.

Keeping his promise as nearly as he could, he adored her body with hands and lips, kissing and caressing. When he had ravished her mouth and throat, he laved her breasts, tormenting her until her nipples stood in aching peaks. Once again his suckling stirred the flames of desire, and Isabel's loins ached from wanting him.

As if reading her thoughts, he moved on, sliding down her body to anoint the flat plane of her belly with his kiss. She squirmed beneath him, silently pleading, and when he spread her thighs, she thought he understood, but to her astonishment, he had something else in mind.

"Eben, you can't!" she cried, but he ignored her protest and pressed his mouth against her. She cried out again, this time in surprise, and when his tongue flicked the sensitive nub, the cry became a moan of ecstasy. Pleasure engulfed her like a tidal wave as he worked his magic. She called his name again and again, but only when she was incoherent with need did he come to her at last.

He took her gently, careful of her soreness, but she no longer cared, because pain was pleasure in this swirling vortex of desire. She filled herself with his strength, reveling in it, mindless with her need, and when he would have been tender, she raked him with her nails, urging him to the same wild frenzy until he drove into her with the force she demanded and brought them both to a shattering climax.

Afterward, she lay on his chest, limp in the afterglow of their loving, while Eben patiently pulled the remaining pins from her hair and combed it out with his fingers until it draped over them both like a golden curtain.

"In my wildest dreams, I never imagined it could be like this," he said as he tangled his fingers in the silken mass. Those were the last words she heard before she fell asleep.

Sometime near dawn, Isabel awoke. Momentarily disoriented, at first she could not quite figure out where she was or why she couldn't move. Then, in the first rays of morning sunlight, she recognized Eben's arm wrapped possessively about her and recalled the events of the previous evening. With a satisfied smile, she luxuriated in the pure sensuality of the moment, but only for a moment. Then she remembered she was still stark naked and morning would soon arrive.

Thinking she would greatly prefer to face Eben in the morning light at least partially clothed, she began to ease his arm from around her. Once free, she sat up carefully, casting about for the chemise Eben had so carelessly discarded last night.

She saw it lying nearby on the floor and was reaching for it when Eben said, "Now, that's a pretty sight for a man to see first thing in the morning."

Realizing he was looking directly at her bare bottom, Isabel yelped and scrambled back beneath the blanket, straight into Eben's eager arms. "Where were you going?" he inquired with a smirk.

"Nowhere," she replied, trying to pretend her face wasn't flaming and she didn't feel the swollen evidence of his renewed desire lying hard and heavy between them. "I was just going to get my chemise. It's almost morning and—"

"And almost time for us to leave. Do you want to leave, Isabel?" he asked, pressing his hips to hers and nudging her most sensitive spot.

"Not yet," she said breathlessly, then realized her mistake. "I mean, it's too early and—"

"Then we've got time for one more lesson before we go," he said against her mouth.

"Lesson?" she asked between kisses.

"Mmmm," he replied, his voice husky from sleep and desire. "To complete your education."

This time she didn't even bother to be shocked at the things Eben did to her. A riding lesson, he called it when he put her astride him, and once again he taught her things about her body she had never imagined. He was right, her education had been terribly incomplete, and she was more than eager to learn all she could, especially when the teacher was so inspiring.

When they woke again, the sun was high in the morning sky, and they teased each other about laziness as they rose and began to dress. This time Isabel only feigned modesty, and only so Eben would be forced to overcome it, tearing the blanket out of her hand so he could see her as she searched in the golden glow of morning for her scattered clothing.

In return, Isabel enjoyed Eben's complete lack of modesty, observing him as he dressed with mingled wonder and pride because he belonged to her. How long would they have to wait until they could actually be married? However long it was, every minute would be pure torture. Whatever guilt Isabel might have felt at spending last night in Eben's arms shrank to insignificance in the light of reality. The waiting would be easier because she would at least have the memory of this night.

Eben brought her icy water from the stock pond with which to bathe, and they shared a breakfast of canned peaches and jerked beef, which they found among the cabin's meager stores. When they judged the time to be around noon, they loaded up the buggy, hitched the horse, and started on their way to the Stevenses' ranch.

"Do you want me to build you a new house?" he asked before they had gone far.

"Not if it means we have to put off our wedding until it's finished," she replied without thinking.

He raised his eyebrows in feigned surprise. "Eager to enjoy your marriage bed, are you, Miss Forester?"

"Aren't you?" she countered tartly. "Eben," she said a little while later, having thought of one small cloud to darken their beautiful morning. "I . . . I might be too old to have children."

He frowned. "You're all I want, Isabel. If we have children, fine, but if we don't . . ." He shrugged. "Of course," he added with a small grin, "if *you* want them, I'll certainly do my best to give them to you."

She said primly, "That's very noble of you."

Eben felt compelled to stop the horse and kiss the impudence out of her, something he did more than once during their journey. By the time they arrived at the Stevenses' ranch, the afternoon shadows had started to lengthen.

Eben was the first to notice something was wrong.

"Wonder what's going on," he said when he saw the men gathered in the ranch yard. On Saturday afternoon, the ranch hands were usually in town, enjoying their day off. "Must be some kind of trouble."

As they got closer, Eben and Isabel could hear shouts, and the crowd surged forward to meet them. Isabel stared in horror at the familiar faces of her suitors, while beside her Eben swore eloquently.

"How long do you suppose they've been here?" Isabel asked in an alarmed whisper.

"Probably just since noon," Eben replied, his jaw tense.

Although they were still a ways from the house, Eben finally had to stop the horse because the crowd of men had moved in so closely. Isabel could see they were not pleased.

Paul Young shouldered his way through until he stood by Eben's side of the buggy. "I underestimated you, partner," he said, a grudging smile twisting his lips. "You outfoxed us all."

"I still say he oughta be horsewhipped," Felix Underwood piped up, his face crimson with outrage. "Keeping Miss Forester out all night and half the next day."

Isabel felt the blood rush from her head. *They knew!* They all knew!

"No sense in horsewhipping a man just 'cause he outsmarted you," Dave Weatherby insisted, shoving his way up beside Paul. "As soon as word got around that you'd taken Miss Forester off to the Stevenses' place last night, but that you never showed up here, I got this out of the safe and brought it over."

He plunked a sack down into Eben's lap. It clinked suspiciously like coins.

"What's this?" Eben asked in apparent surprise.

"Your winnings," Weatherby informed him triumphantly. "Remember I told you the man who compromised Miss Forester first would win it? Over two hundred dollars—"

"What!" Isabel shrieked.

Weatherby smiled with feigned sincerity. "Didn't he tell you about the reward? We set a high price on a lady's virtue around here—"

"Weatherby, shut your damned mouth while you still can," Eben snarled.

Isabel stared at Weatherby in horror. This couldn't be true. Eben would never . . .

But he refused to meet her eye. She glanced at Paul Young, hoping he would tell her Mr. Weatherby's ugly tale wasn't true. Instead he simply smiled benignly.

"May I offer my congratulations?" he asked with a remnant of his former charm. "When is the wedding to be?"

Isabel's stomach turned over, and once more she stared at Eben, hoping against hope he would tell her this was all some awful joke. But he just continued to glare at Weatherby, who seemed unconcerned by his wrath. And there sat the bag of coins, over two hundred dollars, the price of a lady's virtue in Texas.

For an instant the world spun, and Isabel feared she might faint for the second time in her life. How could Eben have done this? How could he have held her and kissed her and loved her so sweetly? How could he have taken her virtue and pretended remorse? How could he have made her think it was *her* idea to spend the night at the cabin when all the time . . . ?

"He at least oughta reimburse me for the school bell," Felix Underwood was saying. "He must've been planning this when he took my money for making it, so it's only right."

"You . . . *you* paid him to make the heart-shaped bell?" Isabel asked as she saw the last of her illusions crumbling.

Felix seemed surprised at her question. "Well, sure. Didn't you read the note? I tied it right on the—"

Isabel turned the full force of her fury on Eben.
"You even lied about *that!*" she shrieked.

"I didn't lie," he began, but she wasn't about to sit
here and listen to more untruths.

"Gentlemen, I hate to disappoint you," she said,
pleased to hear her voice hardly trembled, "but there
isn't going to be a wedding."

"No wedding?" someone echoed in amazement.

"What do you mean?" Paul Young asked with a
frown.

"I mean I'm not going to marry Mr. Walker."

"But you have to," Felix Underwood whined. "He
ruined you!"

"And what if I don't consider myself ruined?" she
replied with far more aplomb than she felt. "I believe
it is still customary for the lady in question to give
her consent, and I have absolutely no intention of
doing so. If you will excuse me, gentlemen."

In one hasty movement, she gathered up her skirts
and leaped from the buggy. The men pressing against
her side of the vehicle jumped back just in time.

"Isabel! Come back here and let me explain!" Eben
demanded, but she could already feel the hot sting
of tears, and she had no intention of letting these
bounders see them. She might be humiliated, but she
wouldn't be humbled, not for Eben Walker or any
other man.

"Isabel, I didn't know anything about this bet!"
Eben shouted after her.

"The hell you didn't!" Dave Weatherby replied just
as loudly. "I told you just the other night . . ."

Isabel broke into a run. How could he? she raged,
blinking furiously and praying the tears wouldn't fall
until she reached the privacy of the house. Melanie
Stevens, Roger's mother, stood in the doorway,
drying her hands on her apron and shaking her head
in disapproval.

"I tried to get them to leave," she informed Isabel

as she came flying into the house, "but nothing would do for them except to see you when you got here."

"Did you know? They had a *bet*!" Isabel gasped in outrage, scrubbing furiously at her tears.

"More like a lottery, the way they explained it," she said, her weathered face creased into a matter-of-fact frown. "They all chipped in, and the winner took the pot."

Isabel gaped at her. How could she take it so calmly?

"Better sit down," Melanie said, taking Isabel by the arm and leading her to the well-worn sofa. "You look like you've had a fright, which I expect you have. Nobody likes to be embarrassed in front of a crowd, and I reckon you were plenty embarrassed. No need to be," she added, settling Isabel more comfortably. "Nobody really thinks he . . . well, you know. We all know what a lady you are, and Eben Walker's not one to force a woman."

Isabel stared up at her, dumbfounded. "You don't think he . . . he seduced me?" she asked in a strangled whisper.

Melanie snorted in disgust. "Don't be a ninny. Course, that don't change a thing. You're ruined just the same."

"Ruined?" Isabel repeated stupidly.

"Well, sure, a man keeps a woman out all night alone, what else do you expect? Course, you two'll be married right soon, so none of it'll matter, which I suppose was Eben's idea in the first place. Who would've thought he'd have so much gumption?"

"I'm not going to marry him *now*!" Isabel exclaimed furiously, anxious to set the record straight. "How could I marry a man so despicable as to *wager* his future bride's good name?"

Melanie frowned and sat down beside Isabel on the sofa. "Maybe you don't understand," she said patiently. "Your reputation is ruined. If you don't marry Eben . . ." She gestured helplessly, unable to adequately express the consequences of such a foolish act.

Isabel drew a calming breath and let it out in a sigh. "I understand perfectly," she replied with equal patience. "Eben Walker betrayed me. He . . . he . . ."

"He prob'ly said he loved you," Melanie guessed. "Most men do whenever they want to get their own way, and sometimes they even mean it. I can't say for sure, but Eben prob'ly really does care about you. I mean, why else would he go to all this trouble to get you?"

"Because he needs a housekeeper and a daughter-keeper," Isabel informed her bitterly, wincing at the spasm of anguish the admission caused her. "He even told me so."

Melanie's eyes widened in surprise. "Didn't he even *try* to sweet-talk you?"

"Only when he saw he couldn't convince me any other way!" Isabel covered her face, mortified at her own stupidity. How could she have allowed herself to be deceived so thoroughly? How could she have been such a willing partner in her own seduction? Eben Walker must have thought her a simpleton, and she had proved him right.

But she wouldn't compound the error by marrying him. How awful it would be to live with a man you knew had tricked you. He would be laughing at her for the rest of their lives, and Isabel had no intention of being the butt of anyone's joke. Eben may have stolen her virtue, but she still had her pride. Though it offered but meager comfort, she intended to keep it.

Eben watched helplessly as Isabel disappeared into the crowd. Quickly he set the brake and tied off the reins, but when he tried to get out of the buggy, the other men blocked his way.

Dave Weatherby grinned triumphantly, and Eben

snatched up the bag of coins and flung them at him with far more force than necessary.

"Ooof!" Weatherby cried as he caught the bag against his chest. "There's no call to get violent."

"I'll get a lot *more* violent if you don't get out of my way," Eben informed him, shoving him aside as he forced his way from the buggy.

"No sense in getting mad," Paul soothed, although he was not quite able to contain his grin. "You didn't expect to keep the bet a secret, did you?"

"I didn't think about it at all," he said. "I never wanted the damn money! I just took her so none of the rest of you could have her."

"And you succeeded," Paul pointed out. "She has to marry you now, no matter how mad she is. Just give her a little time. She'll cool off and see reason."

Eben wished he could be sure. In his experience, Isabel had a nasty habit of only seeing what she wanted to see.

"Just tell us one thing," someone behind him said. "Is she worth all the trouble?"

Eben whirled blindly, drew back his fist, and hammered it into the leering face. The other men roared, and Eben turned on them, fists clenched and ready.

"Anybody else think Miss Forester didn't conduct herself like a lady last night?"

Paul instantly jumped into the breach. "Calm down, Eben," he urged, lifting his hands in a defensive gesture. "Bob here is a jackass. Nobody else thinks anything happened. How could it? Hell, you don't even have a black eye."

The other men chuckled nervously at the joke, and Eben felt some of the anger drain out of him. At least he wouldn't have to listen to a lot of suggestive remarks about Isabel and snide inquiries about how she performed between the sheets. He'd been an idiot to think he could protect Isabel's good name, although how anyone could have expected these men to pursue her all the way out here last night when they found out she wasn't at Bertha's, he was damned if he knew.

"I oughta stomp the lot of you," he growled. "Didn't anybody stop to think how embarrassed she'd be to have you all waiting here for her?"

"I don't reckon we did," Paul admitted.

"No, we was all more interested in seeing your face when you knew you'd won," Felix said sourly.

"And turning over your winnings," Weatherby added.

"Dave, if I hear one more thing about those 'winnings,' so help me God, I'll cram them down your throat piece by piece!"

"Eben," Paul interjected quickly, "maybe you oughta go see about Isabel. She was pretty upset."

"That's what I was trying to do," he muttered, shouldering his way past the other men and hurrying toward the house.

Once on the porch, he slowed his step when he heard what sounded like someone inside crying. God, if they'd made Isabel cry . . .

Melanie Stevens appeared in the doorway. Seeing Eben, she came out, pulling the door shut behind her. "Eben Walker, a man as foolish as you shouldn't be running around loose!"

"How is she?" he asked, unable to dispute her claim.

"Pretty upset, and who can blame her? Imagine being abducted and then having the whole world find out."

"I want to talk to her," he said, trying to push his way past her.

"Oh, no, you don't!" she said, blocking his way. "She doesn't want to see you just now, and I can't blame her a bit."

"But—" Eben tried to protest, but just then George Stevens came bounding onto the porch.

"What's the trouble?"

"Miss Forester doesn't want to see Eben, and he won't take no for an answer."

"Eben," George said when Eben would have insisted, "don't you think you've done enough to that poor woman? Give her a little time. She'll come around."

"George is right," Melanie said. "She's pretty mad right now, and she might say things she'll regret later. Give me until tomorrow to get her calmed down. We'll bring her to church, and by then she'll be reasonable again, so the two of you can work things out."

Eben looked at the Stevenses, then at the closed door, behind which he knew Isabel sat in abject misery, thinking he had betrayed her in some way. If only he could see her for a minute, talk to her . . . But what would he say? Gosh, I'm sorry I publicly humiliated you? Maybe Melanie was right. When she was a little calmer, he'd stand a better chance of convincing her he really did love her and that all the rest of it was just a terrible mistake.

"All right," he said reluctantly, taking a step back. "But you promise to bring her to church?"

"Cross my heart," Melanie said with a sly smile. "Don't look so hangdog. If she didn't like you, she wouldn't be so mad."

Eben hoped she was right.

"I'm not going to change my mind," Isabel insisted for what must have been the hundredth time that morning. After a nearly sleepless night during which she had tortured herself with memories of her and Eben's lovemaking and her own idiocy in believing he really loved her, Isabel had made the only logical decision. "I don't care what anybody says, I'm not going to marry him."

"Isabel, listen to me," Melanie argued. "Eben may have acted like a fool, but he's a good man and he'll make you a good husband. George says he's probably even rich, taking in money all the time at his shop and never spending a thing on himself in all these years."

Isabel sighed in despair. How could she hope to make Melanie understand that none of these things made any difference? Eben had betrayed her even more thoroughly than she had first thought. The truth had come to her sometime during the quiet hours before dawn: *Eben had never actually said he loved her.* For all his hints and all his passion, he'd never spoken the words, and now Isabel knew why. It had all been a ruse with which to seduce her so she wouldn't dare refuse to marry him, so he could use her just as people had been using her all her life! He didn't want Isabel the beautiful: oh no, he wanted Isabel the dutiful— a housekeeper, not a woman.

Setting her jaw stubbornly, Isabel said, "I'm sorry, Melanie, but I won't even consider it. The man is a liar and a . . ." She'd been about to call Eben a seducer but decided against it. If Melanie wanted to think him innocent of that sin, Isabel would foster the falsehood to save her own pride. ". . . a cad," she finished primly.

Melanie sighed in disgust and rose from where she had been sitting beside Isabel on the bed. "Then I wash my hands of you," she declared.

Suddenly remembering she was Melanie's guest, Isabel was instantly contrite. "I'm sorry to have been so much trouble, and I promise the rest of my visit will be—"

"Your visit's over, miss," Melanie snapped. "I can't keep a scarlet woman under my roof. What'll folks say?"

"Scarlet . . ." Isabel echoed faintly. "What are you talking about?"

"I'm talking about you spending the night with a man you weren't married to. If I let you stay here, folk'll think I approve of such behavior, and I most certainly do not!"

Isabel stared at Melanie in shock, trying in vain to

see some glimmer in her eye to indicate this was all some sort of joke. "But you said yourself you don't think anything improper happened," she reminded her companion.

"Don't change a thing. 'Avoid the appearance of evil' is what the Good Book says. You oughta know that, being a preacher's daughter and all. Even my kids know about what happened. What am I supposed to tell them? That it's usually wrong to stay out all night with a person you aren't married to, but it's all right for Miss Forester?" She snorted in disgust.

"But I was kidnapped! Abducted against my will! You can't *blame* me!"

"Not for that part of it, but I sure can blame you for the rest. Any woman in her right mind would be desperate to marry the man and set things right. Don't you have any pride at all?"

"Melanie, I can't! He'd be throwing it up to me the rest of my life about how he'd saved my good name and made an honest woman out of me. I don't need any man's charity!"

"Humph," Melanie grunted, stomping to the door. "Better get your things together. We'll be leaving you in town after church."

Again Isabel felt the sting of tears and wondered how she could have gotten herself into such a mess. At least she still had Bertha. Bertha Bartz wouldn't care what anyone thought. She was Isabel's friend, and she, above all others, would understand.

"Are you crazy?" Bertha demanded the instant they were alone in her bedroom.

"I shouldn't like to think so," Isabel replied stiffly. Up until this moment, Bertha had given her exactly the support she needed. When the Stevens family had dropped her off in the churchyard with her trunk, Bertha had rushed to her side, all clucking sympathy and encouragement.

When the other women gathered in groups, whispering behind their hands while the men gawked with ill-concealed curiosity, Bertha had ushered her inside and up to the front row, where Isabel wouldn't have to see people staring at her and wouldn't have to see Eben coming into the sanctuary. After the service, Bertha had ushered her past Eben, ignoring his attempt to talk to them, and taken her straight to her home and upstairs to the bedroom, closing the door behind them with a decisive click.

"If you're not crazy, then why won't you marry him? I couldn't believe it when I heard."

"Where did you hear it?" Isabel asked, wondering who was spreading rumors about her.

"From everyone! All the men who were there yesterday carried the story straight back to town, and when Eben came home without you, we knew it was true. Oh, I blame myself for this whole thing," she moaned, laying a hand on her expansive bosom and sinking into her boudoir chair.

"I fail to see how you could be responsible," Isabel replied sharply, too angry to sit down.

"When he asked if he could take you out to the Stevens place, I never for a minute thought . . . I mean, he's never done anything the least bit rash in all the years I've known him. Who would have imagined?"

"Not I, certainly," Isabel said acerbically.

"Well, what's done is done, and I can understand you're annoyed with Eben—"

"Annoyed?" Isabel shrieked. "Don't you understand? I *hate* him! He tricked me and made me a laughingstock and he . . . he . . ." Isabel held her breath, certain that Bertha, with her acute powers of observation, would sense the change in Isabel and know what else Eben Walker had done.

"But he wants to marry you!" Bertha shrieked back, apparently oblivious to the signs of Isabel's lost virtue. "You simply can't refuse!"

"I most certainly can, unless the people of this town

customarily force women to get married at the point of a shotgun."

"We've never had to before, since most women know what's best for them," Bertha informed her.

"I am the *only* one who knows what's best for me, and I will not marry a liar. Bertha, he made me believe he *loved* me, and all the time..." She covered her mouth to hold back the sob that threatened.

Unmoved by her distress, Bertha continued to glare at her. "Did he tell you he *didn't* love you?" she challenged.

Isabel drew an unsteady breath. "He didn't have to."

Bertha muttered something that sounded suspiciously like profanity and threw her hands up in despair. "It must be because you're from the East," she told the ceiling. "Living in cities makes people touched in the head."

"I am perfectly sane," Isabel insisted, growing angry again. Why would no one see her side?

"Leave it to a man to ruin everything," Bertha continued as if she hadn't spoken. "If he had a lick of sense, he would've seduced you so you wouldn't *dare* refuse to marry him!"

Isabel's jaw dropped. "You... you don't think he...?" she stammered.

Bertha fixed her with a contemptuous glare. "Certainly not. I know you too well, Isabel Forester. He'd have had to take you by force, and I don't believe there's a violent bone in Eben Walker's body."

"Bertha, I... I can't tell you how much I appreciate your confidence in me. As I suppose you know, I'm in need of a place to stay for the time being and—"

"You can't stay here!" Bertha exclaimed in surprise. "How could you even think such a thing?"

"But you said—"

"I said I didn't think anything happened, but that doesn't change the fact that your reputation is ruined.

What would my daughters think if I allowed you to stay in our home?"

"They would think you were showing Christian charity!" Isabel replied indignantly.

"No, they would think I condoned immoral behavior! They would think they could behave indecently and suffer no consequences."

"Why should I suffer consequences? I was the innocent victim!" Isabel demanded furiously.

"Because Eben has offered to marry you, but you have turned him down. Isabel, don't you understand? Only a loose woman would be so careless of her reputation."

Isabel stared at her friend in despair. "Then where am I supposed to go?"

"The only place you can go—Eben's house."

"Never! I'd rather die!" Isabel declared rashly. "I'll stay at the school until I can find another place."

"You won't find another place, Isabel," Bertha warned. "All the other women will feel exactly the way I do."

"Then I'll just live at the school."

Bertha shook her head slowly, her expression grave. "I'll let you go there tonight, but you can't stay there. You see, Isabel, as president of the school board, I have to fire you for immoral behavior."

Chapter 12

Isabel stared blindly out the schoolhouse window at the night sky. A million stars twinkled like diamonds against black velvet, but Isabel couldn't appreciate their beauty. All she could think about was the horrible predicament Eben Walker had put her in.

If she married Eben, knowing he didn't really love her and had lied and tricked her, her life would be a living nightmare. If she didn't marry Eben, she would starve to death or die of exposure.

Well, perhaps she was being melodramatic. The people of Bittercreek wouldn't let her starve, she thought, glancing over at the carefully wrapped packages of food several children had carried over for their parents the instant it was dark. And they would probably let her stay at the school for as long as she needed to, since the building wouldn't be used for anything else until they were able to hire another teacher.

But sooner or later, if she remained in this town,

she would be forced by the subtle pressure of ostracism and poverty straight into Eben Walker's arms.

With a sigh, Isabel turned away from the window, walked over to her desk, and slumped into her chair. Her only other alternative was to go home to New York or someplace equally far away. This was the most appealing of her choices, since the thought of staying around here and seeing Eben Walker every day for the rest of her life held little appeal. Unfortunately, it was also impossible because she had no money.

The town had paid her way here, and Isabel had squandered practically all of her sparse inheritance on her new wardrobe. She had only a few dollars to carry her over until she received the first installment of her salary. Now, of course, she doubted she would ever see a penny of salary, and even if they paid her for the two weeks she'd worked, she wouldn't have enough to get her to the next town.

What she needed was another job, but since under the circumstances the prospect of anyone in Bittercreek hiring her was virtually nil, she didn't see much hope of finding employment. She sighed again.

"Miss Forester?"

Isabel jumped. "Larry, what a surprise," she said, laying a hand over her pounding heart and managing to smile a greeting at the small, ragged figure standing hunched in the doorway.

"I heard they kicked you out," Larry Potts said.

Isabel started to contradict him, then stopped when she realized his assessment of the situation was painfully accurate. "You are very nice to come and see me."

"I thought you might be hungry," he said, venturing a few steps closer and reaching into his shirt for a small parcel crudely wrapped in yellowed newspaper.

"How thoughtful," Isabel said, touched by his kindness. She rose from her seat and went to where he stood in the middle of the room. "You're very sweet," she said as she took the package.

From the condition of the wrapping paper, she doubted the contents would be edible, but Isabel suspected he might have donated his own supper, so she could not possibly insult him by refusing his generosity.

"Ain't you going to eat it?" he asked when she made no move to unwrap it.

"I'm . . . I'm afraid I'm not hungry right now. When people get upset, they often lose their appetites," she explained. "I'll save it for later."

He nodded sagely, his clear blue eyes staring up at her from his grimy face. After a long moment he said, "Miss Forester, I'm sorry I never came to school."

"I'm sorry, too. I would have liked to know you better."

"I didn't tell you before, but there's a reason I don't come."

"Oh? What is it?"

"I . . . I can't read."

Isabel smiled. "You can't read because you don't come to school. If you did, I'd teach you in no time. . . ."

But he was shaking his head. "No, ma'am, you couldn't teach me 'cause I'm stupid."

"Larry, whoever told you such a thing?" Isabel cried in outrage.

"Lots of people," Larry told her with a shrug. "I didn't need nobody to tell me, though. I already knew. See, I tried to learn before, but I never could get it. We've had a lot of teachers before you, and I went to every one of them, but I just couldn't get the hang of it, no matter how hard I tried. Finally Pa got mad and wouldn't let me go no more, but I didn't care because by then I didn't want to, anyways."

Isabel nodded, wishing she'd had a chance with him. Perhaps things might have turned out differently.

"But I don't have to read to do what I want, anyway," he continued. "I want to be a blacksmith like Mr. Walker."

Isabel flinched inwardly at the sound of his name. "Really?" she said as casually as she could. "It's a good trade."

"Yeah, Pa says Mr. Walker's rich, and from the way he gives me a nickel every time I sweep up his shop, I figure he is, too."

The last thing she needed to hear right now was evidence of Eben's kindness. Isabel drew a breath to calm the quivering in her stomach. "Have you . . . have you discussed your plans with Mr. Walker?"

Larry frowned. "I couldn't tell *him*. He'd laugh."

"No, he wouldn't," Isabel promised, remembering what Eben had told her about his own youth. "I'm sure if you discussed it with him, he'd be able to help you."

"Help me? You mean teach me how to smith?"

"I don't know, but at least he'd be able to tell you how to get started," she said.

"Do you really think so?" he asked, his eyes shining.

"I'm sure of it."

Then he frowned again. "But . . . I mean, maybe you should talk to him first."

Isabel's stomach clenched painfully, but she managed a smile. "Mr. Walker and I aren't . . . we aren't on the best of terms at the moment," she explained. "I doubt he would be willing to do anything I suggested. You'll do fine. You have nothing to be afraid of."

Larry shrugged. "Maybe I'll talk to him tomorrow," he said noncommittally. "Well, I reckon I'd better get going. I'll see you," he promised, darting out before Isabel could thank him again for his offering.

She stood for a long time, staring at the empty doorway. As dirty and unkempt as he was, Larry was still a delightful child. If Isabel could have overlooked

Eben Walker's few flaws, she might have one day soon had a son of her own just as delightful.

She didn't even bother to wipe away the tear that trickled down her cheek.

The next morning Isabel awoke stiff and sore from having slept with only a blanket between herself and the hard wooden floor. Bertha had sent over enough bedding to keep her from freezing to death, but her generosity did not extend to comfort. If fact, Bertha would probably delight in making things as miserable as she could in order to drive Isabel to Eben.

After washing in the icy water from the pump, Isabel made herself presentable again in the hopes that at least a few children who had not heard the news would appear for school. Although she heard the sound of young voices at play nearby, none of them came for class. Isabel sat forlornly on the school steps, trying to absorb some of the warmth of the morning sunlight and wondering what on earth she was going to do now.

The noise of an approaching wagon didn't register until someone called, "Hallo! Miss Forester!"

Isabel looked up in surprise to see the three Plimptons crammed into their gaily painted dog cart. They all looked so cheerful and happy to see her, she knew they couldn't possibly have heard about her fall from grace. Her heart sank when she realized she would have to explain to them why Barclay could no longer attend school.

On leaden legs, she rose and walked out to meet them, her smile of greeting stiff on her lips.

"Came as soon as we heard," Oliver Plimpton informed her as he helped his plump wife down from the cart.

"Simply dreadful the way they've treated you," Rosemary Plimpton informed her, shaking her head so hard her cheeks quivered. "But then, what can you expect from a bunch of Colonials?"

"Ah, yes, Colonials, eh, what?" Oliver agreed, nodding his head as vigorously as his wife was shaking hers. "I daresay they've left you here to starve."

"Not exactly," Isabel said. "Some of the children brought me food and blankets last night. I'm fine, really."

"Fine?" Rosemary scoffed. "How can you be fine when you've been disgraced and sacked and cast out?"

An excellent question, Isabel thought, to which she had no answer.

"I think they're horrible, the lot of them," Barclay said. "It wasn't your fault Mr. Walker kidnapped you."

Isabel felt her face heat as she wondered if Barclay would be so eager to defend her if he knew the truth. "You're all very kind to visit me—"

"Isn't a visit," Oliver said. "We've come to offer you a position."

"A position?"

"Yes, we are in desperate need of a cook," Rosemary said with a small smile. "I'm hopeless in the kitchen, and it's so difficult for us to get good help."

"Ah, yes," Oliver agreed. "Sheep and all, you know. Terribly difficult."

"Say you'll come, please," Barclay urged.

"Well, I..." Isabel could hardly even comprehend the offer. A few moments ago she'd actually been considering death by exposure as one of her options, and now the Plimptons were offering to take her in and give her a job. "Mrs. Plimpton, I don't want to seem ungrateful, but... don't you realize the other women will ostracize you when they find out you've hired me?"

To her surprise, Rosemary threw back her head and laughed uproariously, while her husband guffawed, slapping his bulky thigh repeatedly. Isabel turned to Barclay for an explanation, but the boy was also howl-

ing with laughter. She waited in dismay until they
recovered themselves.

"Oh, my," Rosemary murmured, pulling out a
handkerchief to dab at her eyes. "My dear Miss Forester, we couldn't possibly be ostracized any more
than we already are because of our sheep. Hardly
anyone speaks to us, and I can't remember the last
time someone came to call."

"Right-o," Oliver agreed. "You're the one should
worry, joining up with a sheep camp. People won't
even deign to spit on you."

Isabel couldn't imagine sinking any lower in the
social strata than she already had. "I appreciate your
offer and I don't mean to sound ungrateful, but you're
being awfully generous to someone you hardly
know."

"Know you well enough," Oliver said.

"And we owe you a debt," Rosemary added, "for
what you did for Barclay."

"Barclay?"

"Jeans, you know," Oliver said. "Never would've
allowed it if you hadn't pointed out how odd the boy
looked compared to the others."

"And we heard all about the reports you assigned
to Roger Stevens and the Bartz boys," Rosemary
added. "Do you know Barclay is invited to Herald
Jr.'s birthday party next week?"

"No, I didn't," Isabel replied with a pleased smile.
Barclay blushed and looked away, but Isabel could
see his delight. "Of course, I didn't do anything except give the boys an opportunity to get acquainted
with Barclay. I was certain once they did, they would
like him."

"So you see, we have good reason to respect you,
Miss Forester," Rosemary said.

"And we've heard what a good cook you are,"
Barclay added. "Please, Miss Forester. Everything
Mama cooks tastes like shoe leather."

"Barclay!" Isabel scolded, but his parents only laughed.

"He's right, I'm afraid," Rosemary said.

"Ah, yes, shoe leather," Oliver agreed, nodding vigorously. "But only on her good days."

"Please come, Miss Forester," Rosemary said.

"We'll pay thirty a month and found," Oliver added. "I believe that's the expression you Colonials use."

"I'm not sure what I'm supposed to find," Isabel said wryly, "but thirty dollars a month is far too generous. I was only earning twenty-five a month as a teacher."

"You'll be working much harder for us," Rosemary reasoned. "Is it settled then?"

"I . . . I suppose so," Isabel agreed, thinking she should be kissing their feet instead of trying to convince them to reduce her salary.

"Do you have a trunk?" Oliver asked.

"Yes, inside," Isabel said. Before she could even point, he and Barclay were off to fetch it.

Rosemary linked her arm with Isabel's and led her toward the dog cart. "It will be so nice to have another woman in the house again. You can't imagine how bored I get with only men to converse with."

Isabel mused that since coming to Texas, she had practically forgotten the meaning of the word "bored."

"Mandy?"

Amanda straightened instantly from where she'd been sitting beneath the tree, and scrubbed the moisture from her eyes. "Over here," she called in a whisper.

Johnny Dent's tall figure emerged from the darker shadows as he picked his way through the night along the creek bank to her. She rose to meet him, stepping eagerly into his embrace.

"Hey, now, what's all this?" he asked when he felt her shuddering against him.

"It's Pa. Did you hear what he did?"

"You mean to Miss Forester? Yeah, a hell of a thing."

"She's gone, Johnny."

"Gone where?"

"She went to work out at the Plimpton place. They came and got her a couple days ago, and Pa won't do anything about it."

"What do you expect him to do?" Johnny asked.

"Go after her, of course! Mrs. Bartz fired her, and now nobody'll even speak to her, and it's all his fault! You should've seen the way they treated her on Sunday, like she had leprosy or something."

"What's leprosy?"

"It's a disease people used to have in the Bible. Johnny, what am I going to do?"

"I don't see as how *you* have to do anything," he said, pushing her a little away in an attempt to see her face better. "It ain't your problem."

"But I wanted them to get married!" Amanda wailed. "I just know Pa would be a lot easier to get along with if they did."

"Are you crazy? If Miss Forester was your ma, she'd never let us see each other again," Johnny reminded her.

"Not like this," Amanda admitted, "but she'd convince Pa he should let you call on me at the house. We wouldn't have to sneak around anymore."

He ran his hands over her back possessively. "I kinda like sneaking around."

"Well, I don't," Amanda informed him, pulling free of his embrace. "Sometimes I think Miss Forester is right about you."

"What does she say about me?" he asked warily.

"That you're only seeing how far you can get with me before you jilt me for some other girl."

"Oh, Mandy, you know that ain't true. I couldn't ever look at another girl."

"Do you love me, Johnny?"

"Sure I do, sweet girl. Haven't I said so?"

Amanda threw her arms around him again. "Not nearly often enough. Kiss me."

He did, pressing his mouth to hers fiercely until she pulled away, breathless.

"I love you, too, Johnny."

He tried to kiss her again, but she ducked away. "Johnny, if you really love me, you'd help me with my problem."

"Your problem?" he asked, then remembered. "I told you, it ain't your problem, and besides, if all you're worried about is Miss Forester working out at the Plimptons', you can stop worrying. She'll be back before you know it."

"She will? Why?"

"Because the Plimptons'll be out of business."

"Johnny, you aren't going to attack their sheep again, are you?" she asked, aghast.

"I told you before it wasn't me," Johnny insisted. "And *nobody's* going to attack anybody."

"Then how will they be out of business?"

"Somebody's taken steps. In a few days, the Plimptons' sheep'll start dying, and then we won't have to ever think about them stinky woollybacks again."

"You didn't poison their water, did you?" Amanda asked, horrified. This was an unforgivable crime, even when perpetrated against sheepherders.

"Naw, we just . . . Well, you might say we poisoned the sheep."

"How? What have you done? Oh, Johnny, if any harm comes to Miss Forester—"

"She'll be fine, except she'll be out of a job again right soon, which is what you wanted, ain't it?"

"Yes," Amanda said doubtfully, "but not if it means people are going to get hurt."

"I told you, just the sheep. Now let's quit talking

about Miss Forester. I came to see my girl, and we're wasting a lot of time."

Before Amanda could protest, he pulled her close for another kiss.

"Amanda?" Eben Walker called.

The lovers jerked apart instantly. "It's Pa!" Amanda whispered in alarm. "He'll kill you, Johnny! *Run!*" Amanda insisted, shoving him to start him on his way.

"Amanda, who's that with you?" They could hear Eben hurrying toward them now.

"Quick!" Amanda said, whirling and running toward her father. "Here I am, Pa," she called back, trying not to sound terrified.

He caught her by the shoulders when she reached him.

"Is something wrong?" she asked, her throat dry with panic.

"You're damn right there's something wrong. What're you doing out here this time of night?"

"Taking a walk. I like to look at the moon and—"

"Don't lie to me. Where'd he go? I heard a man's voice and—"

Just then they both heard the sound of horse's hooves running on the hard ground. Eben swore.

"I knew it. Who is he, Amanda?"

"I'll never tell," she replied, gathering her courage.

"You'll tell when I get through with you, and I'll take a strip off him a mile wide for messing with a child—"

"I'm not a child!" Amanda informed him, suddenly furious. "I'm a grown woman, which you'd know if you ever looked at me for more than two seconds at a time!"

"I've looked at you enough to know you've got a long way to go before you're a woman."

"Oh, yes, and you're such an expert on women!" she cried. "You know just exactly how to get one to hate you so much she'd rather die than marry you!"

"That's enough!" he said, giving her a shake.

"Is it?" she challenged, not the least bit intimidated. "Maybe you're going to hit me next. Is that how you treated her? No wonder she can't stand the sight of you!"

"Shut up!" he shouted.

"I will not! Somebody's got to tell you what an idiot you are!"

"But not you, little girl," he snarled, dragging her back toward the house.

"I told you, I'm not a little girl! And if you'd just asked me, I would've told you not to kidnap Miss Forester. Only a fool would think that was the way to win her!"

"Amanda, I'm warning you," he said through gritted teeth. "No matter how big you think you are, I can still turn you over my knee."

"And if *you* had a lick of sense, you'd go after her!" Amanda continued relentlessly. "She's probably praying you'll come! If you'd go out there and apologize to her, she'd marry you in a minute."

"Which just shows how little *you* know," he replied contemptuously.

"Don't you want her anymore?" she asked in astonishment.

"I . . . That's none of your business."

"Stop saying that! This is all my business! And what about the fact that you've made me a laughingstock in town?"

"You?" he scoffed.

"Yes, me! Everybody's mad at me because my father made Miss Forester so unhappy and made Mrs. Bartz fire her, so now we don't have school anymore, or choir practice, or anything."

They reached the house, and Eben dragged her into the parlor. He slammed the front door behind them. A lamp burned on the table, and for the first time Amanda saw the expression in his eyes. Her breath caught at the sight of such naked fury.

"I didn't make Mrs. Bartz fire her, and if I had anything to say about it, she'd be back teaching school in a minute."

"But you *do* have something to say about it! You can make her marry you if you try, but you just let her run off with the Plimptons like she doesn't mean anything at all to you."

"I didn't *let* her do anything. She's a grown woman, and she makes her own decisions. I can't help it that she decided not to marry me."

"So you're going to let her go after you ruined her good name and made her an outcast! I hate you! I wish I'd never been born!"

With a sob, Amanda ran into her bedroom and slammed the door shut.

"Amanda! Come back here!"

Eben hurried to the door, in time to hear the bolt slide home. "Amanda! Open this door!" He pounded on it, but she ignored him. He could hear her weeping, and he closed both his hands into fists in frustration.

"Amanda, I haven't forgotten you were out there meeting a boy," he shouted. "No daughter of mine is going to act like a harlot. Do you hear me?"

Her only response was a loud wail.

Eben swore as pain twisted his heart. She wasn't like her mother. He wouldn't let her be. "You aren't to leave the house again until you've proved I can trust you. Do you understand?"

"I'm ashamed to show my face in this town after what you did to Miss Forester, anyway!" she shouted back, and Eben slammed his fist into the door again.

For an instant he wanted to break the flimsy barrier with his bare hands and . . . Then he pulled himself up with a jerk. What was happening to him? He hadn't raised his hand in anger for thirteen years, and now he was actually thinking of doing violence to his own child.

Shaken, he staggered to the table and sank down

into one of the chairs. The hands he lifted to cover his face were trembling, and he cursed again. After Gisela's death, he'd sworn never to let his anger get out of control, and for more than a decade, he'd had no problem keeping his vow.

Until he'd met Isabel Forester. Damn her to hell, she'd turned his life upside down, and he had no idea how to set it right again. At this point, the only thing he knew for certain was that after spending the night in Isabel's arms, he couldn't bear the thought of living the rest of his life without her. The mere prospect filled him with horror and turned his heart to stone. He had half a notion to go out to the Plimptons' and drag her back by her hair. If he thought for one minute Reverend Smiley would marry them without Isabel's consent, he'd . . .

He groaned when he realized just how irrational he had become. Hadn't he learned anything from the disaster with Isabel? Stubborn as a mule, she couldn't be forced into anything.

But even a mule could be coaxed.

The plan came to him in a flash of inspiration. Of course; why hadn't he thought of it before? Maybe Amanda was right and he *was* a fool.

The hell with Melanie Stevens and Bertha Bartz, who'd insisted he should give her time to calm down and see reason. Isabel wouldn't see reason on the longest day she lived, but she might respond to a carrot, a sweet, juicy little temptation dangled in front of her to lure her back to him.

His gaze wandered to the locked bedroom door behind which Amanda pouted. Yes, Eben had just the right carrot to dangle, too. Isabel just couldn't resist helping a kid with a problem.

"Good gracious, will you look who's here?" Rosemary Plimpton called to Isabel, who was busy rolling out pie dough for supper.

Isabel's heart gave a little leap before she could stop

it. What made her think Eben Walker would be coming to see her, anyway? And in the middle of the day, too. "Who is it?" she asked with creditable nonchalance.

"Mrs. Bartz, and several other ladies," Rosemary exclaimed, bustling into the kitchen. She could not have been more flustered if the queen herself had appeared on her doorstep. "Do we have any of those cookies left from yesterday? And tea, we must make some tea. . . ."

"Go greet your guests," Isabel said, shooing her out. "I'll take care of the refreshments."

When Rosemary had gone, Isabel allowed herself a sigh of self-pity. She wasn't really disappointed because Eben hadn't come. After all, she hadn't really expected him. No, she was disturbed because she strongly suspected Bertha and the others hadn't come to see Rosemary at all, and she really didn't feel up to another lecture on where her duties lay.

Isabel could hear the visitors' voices when they entered Rosemary's tidy parlor. At least they would be impressed. Isabel and Rosemary had spent the better part of yesterday dusting and oiling the cherrywood furniture Rosemary had carried all the way from England. Not even Bertha Bartz had anything to compare with it.

Perversely, Isabel got out Rosemary's heirloom silver tea set and century-old china. After this visit they would have a lot more to talk about than Isabel Forester's fall from grace.

When she had finished preparing the tray, Isabel was a bit apprehensive about entering the room. Not only was she angry at the women she would be serving, she was also loath to face them in a menial capacity.

Not that the Plimptons treated her as a servant. On the contrary, they insisted she take her meals with them as if she were a member of the family, and Rosemary continued to help with the domestic duties, more as if they were colleagues than mistress and maid.

But Rosemary's kindness did not change the facts, and when Isabel carried the tray into the room, the others would see her for what she had become.

Or rather, what they had forced her to become. Isabel stiffened at the thought. Of course, why hadn't she seen it before? If Isabel was a servant, her abasement was their fault, not her own. She had nothing to be ashamed of. After all, "Honest labour bears a lovely face," she quoted to herself. If anyone had cause for shame, it was Bertha and her friends for having turned her out, and Isabel was going to let them know it. . . .

Assuming what she hoped was the "lovely face" of honest labor, Isabel picked up the heavy tray and made her way slowly into the parlor.

"Oh, thank you, Isabel," Rosemary said, jumping up to hold the door for her. "Everything looks simply lovely."

Isabel nodded to acknowledge the compliment, then carried the tray to the serving table.

"Isabel, it's so nice to see you again," Bertha said.

Isabel set the tray down and rearranged a few items on it before turning to face the visitors. "Is it?" she asked, thinking how her father would be turning in his grave at her rudeness.

"Of course it is," Mrs. Smiley assured her, jumping into the breach. Good heavens, Bertha had brought the minister's wife along, and Melanie Stevens, too. What did she hope to accomplish?

"Isabel, you mustn't think we're angry with you," Bertha tried.

"Why should you be? I'm the one who should be angry."

Bertha gaped at her in a most unladylike fashion, and this time Melanie tried to salvage the situation.

"You're absolutely right. We were pretty hard on

you, Isabel, but I hope you know we only had your
best interests at heart."

"I hope you never set out to hurt me on purpose,
then," Isabel retorted. "Were you going to starve me
into submission?"

"Isabel, you know perfectly well we wouldn't have
allowed you to go hungry," Bertha blustered, her
bosom quivering in indignation. "We were only
trying to—"

"What Bertha is trying to say," Mrs. Smiley interjected hastily, "is that we were trying to push you in
the right direction. Unfortunately, we failed to consider your delicate condition."

"What delicate condition?" Isabel asked in alarm.
Did they know what Eben had done? Did they think
she might be with child?

"The state of your emotions," Mrs. Smiley explained, her sweet, round face radiating innocence.
"We simply forgot how upset you must have been,
having been kidnapped and held against your will,
then returning to discover your reputation had been
destroyed, and all those men gloating."

"It was a terrible thing," Melanie agreed, "and we
weren't as sympathetic as we should have been." She
glanced at Bertha as if for approval before continuing.
"We've come to apologize."

Isabel blinked in surprise.

"Isabel, please join us, and I'll serve the tea," Rosemary gushed when Isabel did not respond. "Now,
don't be missish. Come, sit down," she urged, rising
and directing Isabel to the seat next to her on the gilt
settee.

At last Isabel found her voice. "Well, I'm glad
you've finally decided to see my side."

"We've always seen your side," Bertha insisted as
Rosemary began setting out the cups and pouring the
tea. "We never wanted you to be unhappy."

Somewhat gratified, Isabel sat back, prepared to

forgive them after they had groveled for a suitable length of time.

"Isn't this nice?" Rosemary remarked inanely, passing around the cups.

"After you went off with Mrs. Plimpton, we started to realize we'd pushed you into a corner," Melanie continued. "We know you understood the predicament you were in, but we were so mean to you, we didn't even give you a chance to do the right thing."

"Exactly," Bertha added. "We know you understand that you must marry Eben, but pride forbade you from accepting him immediately—"

"*Must marry Eben?*" Isabel interjected, anger welling in her again. They didn't really see her side at all! "And just exactly why must I marry him?"

The four women stared at her wide-eyed.

"Because you're ruined," Mrs. Smiley pointed out.

"And no decent man would have me now?" Isabel suggested scornfully. "I don't want a man, decent or otherwise, so what possible difference can it make to me if I'm ruined or not?"

Mrs. Smiley blanched at such scandalous talk, and Bertha's face mottled dangerously.

"Maybe it's just because you don't *feel* ruined," Melanie ventured. "I mean, we know Eben didn't . . . take advantage of the situation, and—"

"How do you know he didn't?" Isabel challenged in outrage. "How can you be so sure he didn't seduce and deflower me?"

"Because we know you, dear," Bertha said patiently. "And we know Eben would never—"

"Perhaps you don't know me at all," Isabel said, her anger getting the best of her. "Or Eben either. What if I told you he *did* seduce me?"

"Isabel!" Rosemary clucked in self-righteous dismay while the others shook their heads.

Isabel decided she was sick and tired of their condescension. If she was going to be ruined anyway, she might as well be a scandal, too!

"Well, he did," she informed them triumphantly.
"He kissed me and held me, and we slept all night
in each other's arms *without a stitch of clothes on*!"

The other women gasped in shock. Emboldened by
her success, Isabel determined to stun them senseless. "And he made love to me, not once, but *three
times*!"

She crossed her arms and glared at them, daring
them to show their contempt, but to her surprise,
they seemed more confused than shocked.

After a long moment of silence, Bertha said, "Did
you say *three* times?"

"Yes, three, and each time was more wonderful
than the last," Isabel declared, perversely pleased at
the prospect of being the most fallen woman they had
ever met.

The four other women exchanged glances, looking
from one to the other with a silent question in their
eyes. Isabel had no idea what the question was, but
each of them replied in the negative, shaking their
heads in quick, decisive jerks.

"What's wrong?" Isabel demanded uneasily.

Then, to her amazement, the other women began
to smile. Just tiny grins at first, but when they saw
they all shared the joke, the grins became smiles.

"Oh, my!" Mrs. Smiley said, covering her wrinkled
lips with her equally wrinkled fingers.

"Three times, can you imagine!" Melanie asked,
unable to suppress a chuckle.

"Yes, *three*," Rosemary giggled, her tea sloshing
over the side of her cup as her hand shook.

"And each time," Bertha said, choking on a laugh.
"Each time more *wonderful*!"

Isabel watched in horror as the four women dissolved into uncontrollable laughter. Bertha clasped
her hands to her bosom. Mrs. Smiley covered her face.
Rosemary cackled into her handkerchief, and Melanie
listed sideways in her chair, holding her stomach as
she howled.

"What is so funny?" Isabel demanded above the din, but they just laughed all the harder, and each time they seemed on the verge of regaining their self-control, one of them would mutter, "Three times!"

They laughed until the tears streamed down their faces and they were gasping for breath, while Isabel grew angrier with each passing second. How dare they ridicule her like this? How dare they find humor in what was the most moving experience of her life? How dare they . . . ?

"Oh, Isabel," Bertha managed at last, still panting from her exertion. "You've just proven . . . how innocent . . . you really are!"

"Innocent?" she echoed in confusion.

"Yes, you . . . you must have read . . . too many dime novels," Mrs. Smiley gasped, fanning herself with her handkerchief.

"If that's the kind of stuff that's in them, I'd like to read a few myself," croaked Melanie, holding her sides. *"Three times!"*

Isabel flushed crimson. "Don't you believe me?" she asked in amazement.

Rosemary reached over and patted her hand. "My dear, we all wish love were the way it's described in books, but . . ." She shook her head and smiled sadly.

"Isabel, if you really were, uh, experienced in such matters," Bertha explained kindly, "you would know what you have described is . . . is . . ."

"Impossible," Melanie supplied with authority.

"Definitely," Mrs. Smiley agreed.

"Unfortunately," Rosemary added.

"Especially for your first, uh, encounter," Bertha continued, her face purpling again, but this time with embarrassment. "Surely you must have been told the first time is, uh, usually a bit, uh, painful."

"A bit?" Melanie scoffed.

Bertha ignored the interruption. "Of course, subsequent, uh, subsequent times are not as, uh . . ."

"As uncomfortable, dear," Mrs. Smiley supplied

helpfully. "In fact, the marriage relationship can be quite enjoyable. We don't want you to think otherwise."

"Oh, no, certainly not," Rosemary exclaimed. "Unfortunately, reality is never quite as 'wonderful' as we might sometimes wish." The others chuckled knowingly and nodded their agreement.

Isabel didn't know whether to laugh or to cry. Which was worse, knowing they didn't believe her or knowing they were dead wrong? Suddenly Isabel began to entertain grave doubts about her decision not to marry Eben. Apparently what she and Eben had shared was not only a unique experience in her own life, but a unique experience for any woman. She and Eben had something special together. Hadn't he said so himself?

But was it enough?

Before she could decide, Bertha interrupted her thought processes. "Isabel, we just want you to be happy. Mrs. Plimpton was kind to give you a place here, but a woman like you should be taking care of her own house and cooking for her own family."

"She's right, you know," Rosemary said, still patting Isabel's hand. "As much as I love having you here, you deserve your own home."

Isabel couldn't argue with that. Unfortunately, she'd burned her bridges rather thoroughly. Unless Eben was willing to apologize to her and confess his undying devotion, Isabel didn't think she could bring herself to relent. She'd spent too many years already being useful and unappreciated. The prospect of marrying into the same sort of situation, committing herself to the emptiness of giving and loving without ever being loved in return, appalled her.

No, before she could marry Eben, she would have to know he loved her, not that he merely wanted her to make his life easier. She wondered if she could convince the good ladies to call in at the blacksmith's shop and explain Eben's part to him.

* * *

When she had finished washing the supper dishes, Isabel wandered out onto the Plimptons' back porch and sat on the steps to admire the glorious sunset. Streaks of gold mingled with indigo and violet, and the sky was so beautiful, it brought tears to her eyes.

Or at least that's what she blamed for the moisture brimming up and threatening to overflow. If she hadn't been so stubborn, she'd be watching this sunset with Eben from their own porch with Amanda beside them, and in a few more hours she and Eben would go into their bedroom and close the door. . . .

"Hello, Isabel."

Isabel jumped, not quite able to believe she had conjured him with her daydreams. "Eben?" she asked, scrambling up from the porch steps.

"Mrs. Plimpton said I might find you here. How are you?" he asked, coming closer.

"I . . . fine . . ." she said faintly, thinking he looked more handsome than ever. He wore a pair of stylish brown nankeen trousers and a matching jacket over a plaid shirt. The dust on his hand-tooled boots said he'd ridden here on horseback. "What brings you way out here?"

He pulled off his bowler hat to reveal recently trimmed chestnut hair. His chin and cheeks also bore the signs of fresh barbering, and she could smell the faint scent of bay rum. Isabel wondered absently if Felix Underwood had known why Eben sought his services this afternoon. "I came to see you," he admitted.

"Me? Whatever for?" she managed to ask, even though her throat had constricted dangerously and she found it nearly impossible to breathe. She couldn't look at his mouth, or she would remember what it felt like pressed against hers, but looking into his eyes was worse, because even now she could see the embers of passion glowing faintly, ready to flame up at the slightest provocation.

"I . . . I've been having some trouble with Amanda," he said, and the words were like a dash of cold water in her face.

"Amanda?" she repeated dully as her body went weak with disappointment.

"Yeah, she . . . she's been pretty upset about what happened, and she . . ." He pressed his lips together and looked away, as if he found the admission painful. "I found her with a boy last night."

"Oh, no!" she cried, instantly forgetting her own anguish. "What were they . . . Where were they?"

"Out by the creek behind the house. It was dark, so I didn't see what they were doing. I didn't even see who he was, and Amanda won't tell me."

"Oh, dear."

"I don't think it's too serious," he hastened to explain, taking a step closer until Isabel could smell his own musky scent beneath the bay rum. "I mean, this is the first time it's happened, but . . ." He looked away again, and pain flickered across his rugged face.

Isabel knew instantly what he feared. Was Amanda as much like her mother in character as she was in appearance? "Amanda's a good girl," Isabel insisted. "She'd never do anything so very wrong."

"What's to stop her?" he demanded bitterly, his dark eyes shadowed with memories. "She won't listen to me anymore. Ever since . . . since what happened with us, she doesn't respect me. She says I was mean to you, Isabel, and she's right, but I can't go back and change what's already happened."

Isabel's heart began to flutter again. "Do you *want* to change it?" she asked, hardly daring to hope.

"Of course I do," he said impatiently. "I never wanted you to be embarrassed. I thought nobody'd ever find out we were together."

"If no one found out we were together, how were you going to collect your bet?" she challenged.

"It wasn't *my* bet, and I didn't *want* to collect it,"

he said in annoyance. "Dammit, all I wanted was *you*!"

Isabel's heart jumped into her throat as he reached for her. She knew it was too soon, but her body didn't care. She melted into his arms and surrendered to his kiss with blissful abandon.

She buried her fingers in the dark silk of his hair, holding his mouth to hers while she parted her lips for his welcome invasion. His tongue tangled with hers, sending liquid fire racing through her veins and turning her knees to jelly. The kiss went on and on until such things as pride and principle ceased to exist. After what seemed an eternity, Eben lifted his mouth from hers.

"Isabel, Amanda needs you," he whispered passionately against her lips.

Amanda?

Before she could sort out her thoughts, she became aware of someone shouting.

"*Señor! Señor* Pleemton!"

"Who's that?" she asked stupidly as she fought to regain control over her body.

"It doesn't matter. Isabel—"

"*Señor* Pleemton, the sheep, they are dying!"

Chapter 13

Isabel and Eben joined the family group surrounding the Mexican sheepherder who had just come running in. Isabel tried to blame her breathlessness on the fast jaunt from the rear of the house, but she knew she'd been breathing rather poorly long before that. Eben's presence always seemed to affect her body's normal functions.

The sheepherder was in even worse shape than Isabel, having come on foot from heaven only knew how far away. Gasping for breath, he babbled brokenly in Spanish.

"Come now, man!" Oliver Plimpton insisted. "Can't understand a bloody word you're saying!"

"He's saying your sheep have caught the scab," Eben told him grimly.

"The hell you say? Is he sure?"

"*Sí, señor,*" the herder exclaimed, waving his arms excitedly. "They are scratching against the fence posts. Only a few, but the rest will start soon."

"Oh, no!" Rosemary cried.

"Bloody hell," Oliver muttered, then apologized profusely to the ladies.

"What is 'the scab'?" Isabel asked in concern.

"It's a disease the sheep get," Eben explained. "It's caused by a mite that digs in under the skin and itches like crazy. At first the sheep try to scratch their fleece off by rubbing up against anything that's handy, posts or rocks or trees. Then the mites get on those things, and any sheep that rubs against them later gets the scab, too."

"They can even get it from rubbing against each other," Barclay added solemnly, "which they do all the time when they're herded together."

"So before you know it, the whole flock is infected," Eben continued, "and in a week or two they'll all be dead of it unless they're treated. Plimpton, what've you got for dipping?"

"Laid in a supply of tobacco. Best thing for it."

Eben nodded. "Some swear arsenic's better, but I've seen too many sheep die from the treatment. Have you got a pit dug?"

"Not yet. Best send out riders to inform the other herders, too," Oliver replied. "If Manuel's flock has it, the others will also have to be dipped."

"How could this have happened?" Rosemary wailed. "Our sheep were perfectly healthy, and there isn't another flock within a hundred miles."

Manuel spoke rapidly in Spanish, and Eben's frown deepened. "He says he found a dead sheep this morning, dead from the scab, but it wasn't one of yours."

"Good God, man, do you know what you're saying?" Oliver demanded.

"Yes," Eben replied. "Someone purposely brought in a diseased sheep to ruin you."

Isabel gasped. Who would have done such a thing? A picture of Johnny Dent's guileless smile teased at her memory, but she pushed it aside. She couldn't believe him guilty of such a thing, no matter how sly he might be. But still, perhaps his employer was in some way responsible.

"It's too late to get started dipping tonight, but we can at least get the pit dug," Eben said. "Can your boy get the word around to the herders?"

"I sure can," Barclay called over his shoulder as he raced toward the corral.

"We'll put the pit over by the holding pens," Oliver said to Eben as they strode off.

The two women stared after them helplessly. "I suppose we should cook. We'll have a lot of mouths to feed tomorrow," Rosemary said with a sigh. "This couldn't have happened at a worse time, either."

"Why?" Isabel asked as she watched Eben moving away.

"Because we haven't sheared the sheep yet. They have their full winter fleeces, and when they're dipped and come out soaking wet..." She sighed again. "Do you have any idea how much water a full grown sheep's fleece can absorb? Or how heavy he is when soaking wet? The task of dipping an entire flock is horrendous."

"You mean they dip them in water? I thought Mr. Plimpton said something about tobacco."

"They mix the tobacco in water. It makes a rather potent solution that kills the mite without harming the sheep."

Isabel could hardly imagine trying to dip even one full-grown sheep, getting it into the bath against its will, then getting it out again when it was soaking wet and frightened senseless. A senseless sheep would be a wretched thing indeed. And a whole flock of them...

"How many sheep do you own?"

Rosemary sighed again. "Almost five thousand."

The next three days passed in a blur. When Barclay went into town to tell Amanda her father would not be home and to instruct her to stay with the Bartzes,

Herald Bartz and a few other men came out to help with the dipping. The extra hands made the work go more quickly, but the labor was still exhausting, and lasted from sunup to sundown.

Although Isabel saw Eben often, they never once had an opportunity to be alone or to continue the discussion they'd begun in the evening shadows of the Plimpton's back porch. Isabel told herself she was glad, because no matter how hard she tried to remember the kiss and the way Eben had made her feel, she also couldn't forget that when he'd had the perfect opportunity to confess his love or at least his need, he'd told her *Amanda* needed her instead.

As much as she wanted to believe differently, Eben was just like everyone else who had ever admired Isabel's accomplishments or appreciated her services or wanted her assistance. He saw her as a solution, not as a person. He would use her to solve his problems and warm his bed, and as much as her body might crave the second part, she simply couldn't let anyone else use her, especially not a man whose love she craved so desperately. Her brief period of independence had taught her that much, at least.

By Sunday evening, the last of the sheep had been dipped, and when Eben appeared for supper, he'd bathed and dressed again in the clothes he had been wearing when he'd first come to see her. They were a little the worse for having been worn during the digging of the pit, but not too bad, since Herald Bartz had brought him some work clothes the next day.

He kept watching Isabel expectantly as she served the meal, and Isabel knew the time had come to give him his answer. Indeed, when she finished the dishes and stepped outside, she found him waiting for her on the back porch.

Her heart began to pound, and she could manage only a tremulous smile. "Are you going back to town tonight?"

"I figure I'd better. I've left Amanda alone too long

already, and my customers'll be ready to lynch me for keeping the shop closed so long."

"Especially to help save sheep," she replied, finding it more difficult to breathe with each passing second, almost as if Eben's presence caused the air around her to evaporate.

"Isabel," he said, suddenly quite serious. "We got interrupted the other day. I never had a chance to say all the things I wanted to."

Isabel's heart leaped at the idea of what other things he might have wanted to say. "We have time now."

"Not as much as I'd like," he said grimly. "Or as much privacy either. Isabel . . ."

He reached for her, but this time she had the presence of mind to avoid his embrace, knowing that once he touched her, she would forget everything else. "You said you wanted to *talk* to me," she reminded him, even though every nerve in her body quivered with the desire to be held.

"Don't you want to kiss me?" he asked in surprise.

"Not until I've heard what you have to say," she told him sternly, although she did want to kiss him, quite desperately.

Apparently he'd been depending on his ability to romance her into compliance. He drew himself up and took a resolute breath. "Well, I guess you know how sorry I am for what happened. I mean, for everybody finding out what happened."

"Not nearly as sorry as I," she said stiffly.

"I never meant for you to be embarrassed. You've got to believe that."

"But you did mean to seduce me."

His eyes widened, and he glanced around, as if afraid someone would overhear. Satisfied they were still alone, he said, "Well, I can't say I'm sorry it happened. Although I can understand how you would be," he added quickly, seeing her frown. "I mean, when you thought I'd lied about trying to keep it a secret, and you thought I'd made a bet. But I didn't. You've got to believe me."

"I guess I do," she said reluctantly.

"I was a fool, Isabel. God knows, Amanda's told me enough times that I was, and she's right. I know I'll never meet another woman like you as long as I live, certainly not one Amanda likes so well. Isabel, you must know you're the only one who can talk to her."

He reached for her again, and this time she wasn't quick enough to avoid him. He clutched her upper arms, his dark eyes pleading.

"Please, Isabel," he whispered in the instant before his mouth took hers.

As always, Isabel went weak with surrender at the touch of his lips. His arms closed around her, and she sighed in submission, unable to resist his power. When he held her like this, she didn't regret what had happened, either. In fact, she wanted it to happen again and again. She wanted Eben to carry her inside to her room and lay her down on the bed and . . .

And tell her he loved her!

The thought jarred her instantly out of her sensual fog, and she broke the kiss. "Eben," she gasped before he could cover her mouth again.

"Mmmm?" he said, settling for the soft curve of her cheek.

"Eben, you . . . you haven't said . . ." Momentarily distracted by his tongue tracing the shell of her ear, Isabel lost her train of thought as delicious shivers danced over her.

"What haven't I said?" he wondered into her ear.

How could she come right out and demand he confess that he loved her? And what if he didn't love her? Would he lie?

"Eben, don't . . . don't *you* need me, too?" she tried.

"God, yes," he sighed against her flushed skin. "I need you so much. Can't you feel it?"

He pulled her hips to his, and the hard evidence

of his desire sent a spasm of answering desire pulsing through her. "Eben, I . . ."

But his mouth closed over hers again, sealing off any protest she might have made. No wonder ministers spoke so vehemently against lust, she thought wildly as her blood began to pound in her ears.

Eben pressed her to the wall of the house, holding her there with his strength, crushing her breasts to his chest and exploring her curves with eager hands.

"Oh, God, Isabel, every time I get into bed alone . . ." He groaned, deep in his chest, and Isabel sensed he was fighting for control even as she felt her own slipping away. He drew a shaky breath. "Amanda needs you, sweetheart. You can't just walk out on her now."

"*What?*" she demanded furiously, throwing her head back in surprise and banging it on the wall. "*Ouch!*"

"Are you all right?" he asked in concern, pulling her away from the wall.

"No, I'm not all right," she snapped, rubbing the back of her head as rage boiled up inside her. She shoved him away so she could get her breath. "What do you mean, coming here and trying to seduce me again just so you can get somebody to take care of Amanda?"

"What?" he asked in astonishment.

"You heard me! Did you think I was too stupid to figure it out? Or did you think you'd muddle my poor brain with your kisses?"

"I'm not trying to muddle your brain. I'm trying to get you to marry me!"

"Don't worry, you have made your intentions abundantly clear!" she replied, appalled to hear how loud and shrill her voice had become but unable to do anything about it. "You'd do better if you'd at least pretend you wanted me for myself, however."

"I *do* want you for yourself."

"Oh, yes, you want me in bed!" she screeched.

Eben hastily clapped one large, callused palm over her mouth. "Do you want everybody to hear?" he whispered furiously.

Grabbing his wrist with both hands, she jerked his hand away. "Everybody already knows!" she reminded him just as furiously.

"They don't know *that* part of it! What are you so mad about, anyway? I thought you liked it, too."

Humiliation scorched her face. "I gave you my heart and my soul, and what did you offer in return?" she challenged.

"I offered to marry you! Dammit, Isabel, most women would be *grateful*!"

"Then most women are stupid! I'm certainly not grateful to a man who makes me think he loves me just so he can seduce me and—"

"*Makes you think* I love you? Hellfire and damnation, I *do* love you!"

"Of course you say that *now*!" she replied in outrage. "And may I remind you I don't appreciate hearing your foul language—"

"To hell with my language," he shouted, giving her a shake. "What does a man have to do to get through to you?"

She sighed in despair. "I just want you to love me, Eben."

He groaned, pulling her into the warm circle of his arms and resting his forehead against hers. "Come home with me tonight, and I'll love you until you—"

"No! Not that!" she cried, even as her body began to melt in response. Struggling frantically, she broke free of his embrace. "I want *love*, not *lust*!"

"You might be surprised to know there isn't a whole lot of difference!" he informed her furiously.

"Maybe not to a man who's only interested in having a mistress for his bed and a keeper for his child!"

"I want more than that!"

"Oh, yes, I forgot! You want somebody to clean your house and cook your meals, too!"

"Isabel!" he protested, but she couldn't bear to listen to him anymore.

"Eben, I spent most of my life being humble and settling for second best and never thinking of my own needs. When I came to Texas I vowed I'd never do that again, and I won't. I love you, Eben, but I have too much respect for myself to marry you knowing you don't love me in return."

"But I *do*!" he insisted, and Isabel thought she might scream in frustration.

Tears started in her eyes, and she knew in another moment she'd lose control completely. "How dare you lie to me now!" she cried. "Get out of here, Eben Walker. I never want to see you again!"

"I can't believe it!" Amanda cried, throwing her hands in the air. "You were with her for *three whole days*. What were you doing all that time?"

"Dipping sheep," Eben told her through clenched teeth.

"Every minute?" Amanda challenged derisively. "Don't tell me you couldn't find five minutes to talk to her. I thought that's why you went out there in the first place!"

"Amanda, that's enough," Eben commanded. "Go to your room."

"That's your answer to everything, isn't it? To get me out of your sight! Well, you can lock me in my room from now till doomsday, but it won't change anything. Were you too proud to apologize to her, or did she have too much sense to forgive you?"

"I'm warning you, get out of my sight!" Eben snarled.

Something in his expression must have convinced her she'd gone too far. She turned and scurried toward her bedroom, then slammed the door and drove home the bolt.

Eben lifted a hand to his pounding head, staggered over to the settee, and sank down onto it, swearing under his breath.

What in God's name was he going to do with that girl? Especially now, knowing he wouldn't have Isabel to help him. He'd never have Isabel at all.

The realization was a lead weight on his heart, pressing down until sometimes he could hardly breathe. And all because she thought he didn't love her. The irony of it burned like gall. If she only knew how very much he did love her—so much he sometimes thought he'd go crazy from wanting her—she'd be camped on his doorstep, begging him to make an honest woman out of her.

Instead, she wouldn't have anything to do with him. His perfect plan to lure her back through Amanda had been a disaster. When would he ever learn that he simply couldn't predict how Isabel would react to anything?

With a sigh, he realized it didn't make any difference since he'd never have another chance with her now. Closing his eyes, he leaned his head back against the worn upholstery and devoutly wished he had a glass of whiskey to ease the throbbing behind his eyeballs and in various other parts of his anatomy. Unfortunately, he'd have to go to the saloon for that, and at the moment he didn't feel like facing any of Isabel's former suitors.

Or maybe he should, he thought bitterly. Maybe one of them would shoot him and put him out of his misery.

In the privacy of her room, Amanda lay on her bed, staring up at the ceiling and silently berating her father. Why couldn't he make things up with Miss Forester? If Amanda hadn't known better, she would have guessed he really didn't want to. After all, he'd done his level best to ruin things with her from the very beginning.

She'd been so happy when he'd told her he was riding out to the Plimptons', and when their sheep had taken sick—darn Johnny Dent; if he had anything to do with that, she'd murder him!—she'd been overjoyed at the prospect of her father spending several days with Miss Forester.

Unfortunately, things seemed worse than before. Although her father had told her nothing except that he and Miss Forester wouldn't be getting married, now or ever, Amanda could tell from his expression the choice had not been his. Somehow he'd managed to offend her once more, and so she'd turned him down again.

Amanda flopped over onto her stomach and punched her pillow in frustration. Maybe she should go out to the Plimptons' herself and talk to Miss Forester, try to convince her that Pa was really a nice man. But, of course, she'd already tried doing just that, without much success. No, if Pa and Miss Forester were ever going to get together, they'd have to work things out between themselves. But if she left it up to them, they'd probably never even speak to each other again.

If only there were some way to force them together, maybe a crisis of some sort over something they both cared about.

Something or *someone*. The idea came to Amanda slowly, like a golden, glorious sunrise that spread the light of understanding through her like a beacon. *Of course!* It would take careful planning, but she could do it, she knew she could. And when it was over and Pa and Miss Forester had made up, they wouldn't even be able to get mad at her!

Isabel's heart leaped when the cowboy brought her the note. Who could be sending it? she wondered. Although several perfectly logical answers occurred to her, she didn't want it to be any of them. She carried the missive into the small room off the kitchen where she slept and opened it with trembling fingers.

"Dear Miss Forester," it began in girlish script. Isabel's spirits sank, but as she read the rest, she quickly forgot her own frustrations.

> I know you'll be shocked and very disappointed in me, but I just can't stand it anymore. Ever since you refused to marry Pa, he's been as grouchy as a turpentined bear. He hasn't spoken a civil word to me in two days now, and he won't even let me out of the house because he caught me talking to Johnny the other night. I'm tired of being a prisoner, and I know that unless you give in and marry Pa, things will only get worse, so I'm running away.
>
> Johnny has promised to take me to Dallas. We can't get married before we go, but he said we will as soon as we get to the city. He's an honest man, so I know he'll do it. He loves me, no matter what you think, and he'll be good to me, a lot better than Pa. We're leaving as soon as Pa opens his shop, so we'll be well on our way when you get this.
>
> I just wish you and Pa could've worked things out, because I know if you were my mother, I wouldn't have to run away. Please pray for me.

> Your good friend,
> Amanda Walker

By the time she finished reading the note, Isabel could hardly breathe. How could Amanda have done something so crazy?

Now she'd run away!

If only she'd talked to Isabel first, surely Isabel could have convinced her not to do it. Now Amanda would be ruined, even more ruined than Isabel, because people would naturally assume the two young people had had illicit relations even if they hadn't. And, of course, the dastardly Johnny Dent would never marry her. His kind never did the right thing. No, he would take her away and use her for his pleasure, and when he was finished with her, he'd cast her aside. Heaven only knew what would become of her, a young girl with no money and no friends. She might even end up in a brothel!

"No!" Isabel cried aloud, startling herself. No, nothing like that would happen to Amanda if she could help it. Quickly she read through the note again. The silly girl had told her exactly where they were going and when they were leaving, almost as if she hadn't the slightest fear of being apprehended. Isabel checked the watch pinned to her bosom and realized Eben's shop had only been open for a little more than an hour.

"Rosemary!" Isabel called, running through the house until she found her.

"What on earth?" the Englishwoman asked when she saw Isabel's face.

"Amanda has eloped with a young man."

"What? You mean Eben Walker's daughter? But she's just a child, only a year older than Barclay!"

"Which is why we must stop her."

"Do you know where she's gone?"

"She says they're going to Dallas. Do you know which way that is?"

"Yes, they'd pass right by here, heading northeast. How much of a head start do they have?"

"Not more than a few minutes," Isabel said, remembering the ride to town took a little less than an hour from here. "We've got to catch them and get her back before her father finds out she's gone."

"But Oliver and Barclay aren't here," Rosemary wailed. "They're checking the flock to be sure the sheep haven't been tampered with again. I don't expect them back until suppertime."

"Then I'll go myself," Isabel decided.

"You can't go alone, not without a chaperone!" Rosemary protested.

Isabel gaped at her. "Rosemary, my reputation is already ruined. What more can happen to it?"

"But it isn't really ruined. I mean, not irrevocably," she explained.

Isabel brushed aside her protests with a wave of her hand. "Can you loan me a vehicle of some sort? Something fast that will catch up to them quickly?"

"I don't know," Rosemary said, frowning and shaking her head. "Oliver would never approve."

"Do you want them to get away? Do you want Amanda to ruin her life?" Isabel challenged.

"Well, no, certainly not, but—"

"Then help me!" Isabel cried impatiently. "I'd take a horse, but I don't know how to ride. Please, Rosemary!"

Within minutes the two women had hitched up the ridiculous dog cart. While Isabel fetched herself a bonnet and a shawl, Rosemary threw a few biscuits into a flour sack. "You really should take something more substantial," she warned as she handed it to Isabel.

"Hopefully, I'll be back with Amanda before I even have a chance to get hungry." After giving Rosemary a quick hug, she climbed up into the dog cart and slapped the horse into motion. Rosemary had selected a spirited beast that almost ran away with her before Isabel could get her bearings, but soon they were olling down the road toward Dallas at a brisk clip.

For the first time, Isabel allowed herself to feel anger. When she got hold of Amanda Walker, she was going to pin her ears back, good and proper. If luck was with them and Eben never found out, it would be her only punishment. And Isabel dearly wanted to keep Eben from finding out. The poor man had suffered enough without seeing his daughter ruined.

Although why she should trouble herself about Eben Walker's suffering, she didn't allow herself to wonder.

* * *

Eben sawed on the reins, and his running horse skidded to a halt in front of the Plimptons' house. Rosemary Plimpton appeared in the doorway, a puzzled frown creasing her pudgy face. She probably thought he was crazy, racing into her yard like this, but he didn't have time for social amenities. "Where's Isabel?"

"She isn't here," Mrs. Plimpton said, startled.

"She's not?" he replied in surprise. Where in the hell could she be? "I need to see her right away. Do you know—?"

"I said, she isn't here, and I can't begin to guess when she might return," Mrs. Plimpton insisted primly.

Damn all ladies and their manners. Isabel was probably just in the outhouse, but she didn't want to say. "I've got to see her. My daughter's run away and—"

"Oh, dear, you know about it then?" Mrs. Plimpton asked in dismay.

"Yeah, and I guess you do, too. Amanda left me a note where I'd find it when I came in to eat at noon. She said she was running away with some man and that she'd told Isabel where they were going."

"A cowboy brought Isabel a note from Amanda early this morning. It said they were heading for Dallas, and they hadn't been gone long, so Isabel thought she could catch them and bring Amanda back before you even found out about it."

"Did Isabel go after them alone?" he asked in astonishment.

Mrs. Plimpton nodded. "I tried to stop her, but she was quite concerned about Amanda, and my husband and son aren't here and—"

"Was she on *horseback*?"

"No, she took the dog cart."

Eben was beginning to hope this whole thing was a nightmare from which he would awaken momentarily. Indeed, the more he heard, the more unreal

the situation seemed. "How did she hope to catch
them in that thing?"

"It's quite swift, I assure you."

Eben bit back a sarcastic remark. "How long has
she been gone?"

"Since about nine o'clock this morning. I'm sure
she's caught them by now."

Eben doubted it, but he said, "Then I'll meet them
coming back," as he swung into his saddle again.

"If she hasn't caught them, you'll send Isabel
straight home, won't you?" Mrs. Plimpton called as
he turned his horse.

Eben didn't reply. Isabel had been gone over four
hours already. If he caught up with her at all, it
wouldn't be before dark. He only hoped she'd had
the sense to give up the chase and turn back so she
wouldn't be caught on the road after nightfall.

With the last of her strength, Isabel pulled the horse
to a stop, too tired to care she was blocking the road
and certainly too tired to do anything about it even
if she had cared.

She couldn't remember ever being so exhausted,
not even the day she'd first arrived in Bittercreek. Her
throbbing arms felt as if they had been pulled from
their sockets, and her hands were raw beneath her
torn gloves. Who would have supposed driving a
horse all day could be so strenuous? Certainly men
did it all the time, but then, she well knew how much
stronger men were than women. They were strong
enough to drive even a whole team of horses from
sunup to sundown, and they were strong enough to
ruin a woman's life, and a young girl's, too.

Because Amanda's life would be ruined. Isabel
glanced at the setting sun in despair and knew she
would never find them now. They would spend the
night together, and even if by some miracle Johnny
Dent did not actually deflower Amanda, his restraint
would make no difference at all. Once they had been

together, alone, overnight, people would assume the worst and shun her as they had shunned Isabel.

Exhaustion and despair brought tears to her eyes, and too fatigued even to lift a hand and wipe them away, she let them run unheeded down her cheeks. She had failed. Amanda was ruined, and Isabel had no one to blame but herself. If she'd had any sense at all, she would have sent for Eben and let him go after them. All day long, as she'd topped each rise with eager anticipation, she'd fully expected to see the fugitives just ahead of her on the road, but each time she had seen only barren emptiness.

She had finally realized, as any sensible person would have done long before, that Amanda and Johnny would be traveling swiftly, on horseback, mindful of pursuit and eager to outdistance it. Amanda might even have lied about their time of departure in order to throw them off the trail.

At least Isabel had the comfort of knowing she couldn't possibly be ahead of them. As many times as she had been forced to stop and rest, even someone traveling on foot would have eventually overtaken her. What had ever made her think she could catch them?

When she heard the clatter of hooves on the road behind her, she couldn't even work up any remorse for the inconvenience she would cause the rider. He could go around her much more easily than she could do anything at all, and he would have to, since she had no intention of moving a muscle. In fact, the prospect of simply sitting right where she was until she died of starvation or exposure held a remarkable appeal.

"Isabel?"

She started. What on earth?

"Isabel!"

It wasn't her imagination! She swiveled on the seat and saw Eben Walker riding toward her at breakneck speed.

"Oh!" she cried in surprise, covering her mouth as myriad emotions swept over her. Relief and joy at being found mingled with embarrassment and dismay at being found out. He would know she'd failed to intercept his daughter, but she also knew he'd take care of everything from here on, and Amanda would be saved after all. In the end, relief won over all the other emotions, and when his horse slid to a halt beside the dog cart, she gave him a tired smile of greeting.

"Just what in the hell do you think you're doing?" he demanded furiously.

"I . . . Don't you know?" she asked, somewhat taken aback.

"I know you must be a crazy woman!" he shouted, his face crimson with rage. "What were you planning to do if you did catch them, which, by the way, you never had a snowball's chance in hell of doing?"

"Eben Walker, how dare you speak to me in that manner!" she demanded in outrage.

"I'll speak to you any way I want! I've been chasing you half the day, not knowing if I'd find you in a ditch someplace with your neck broke, and all the time praying you'd have the sense to give it up and turn around before it was too late, but oh, no, here you are, in the middle of nowhere with the sun going down, and I'd bet my last dollar you don't even have a blanket with you."

"I don't need a blanket," she informed him haughtily. "I have no intention of spending the night beside the road."

"Then where *were* you intending to spend the night? At some wayside inn, perhaps?" he asked sarcastically.

He had her there, and for a moment she didn't know how to respond. Quite truthfully, she hadn't given a thought to where or how she would spend the night. She'd planned to find Amanda and Johnny and take them home, or at least chaperone them until morning. "I . . . I didn't realize how late it was," she tried lamely.

He sighed in exasperation. "I swear, Isabel, if they put your brains in a jaybird, he'd fly backwards!"

"I don't have to sit here and be insulted!" she cried.

"No, you can chuck that horse into motion and lumber on down the road for a hundred feet or so until you have to stop and rest again. I wouldn't've believed it, but that nag looks better-rested than you do!" Eben glared at her for a long minute, and she tried her best to glare right back, but he didn't seem able to maintain his anger any more than she could. Slowly his stiff shoulders sagged, and his dark eyes clouded with despair. He sighed and looked away, rubbing a hand wearily over his face. "Have you seen any sign of them at all?" he murmured.

Remembering why they were both here, she felt instant remorse. "No, I haven't."

"Do you know who she's with?"

"Johnny Dent. He's a cowboy, I believe—"

"*Johnny Dent?*" Eben repeated in astonishment. "He's a grown man!"

"Amanda thinks she's a grown woman, and she thinks he wants to marry her."

Eben swore eloquently, and Isabel didn't have the heart to reprimand him. His face twisted in anguish. "He won't marry her, you know. He just wants . . ."

His voice broke, and he stared fiercely down the road as if by the force of his will, he could make his daughter appear before him safe and sound.

Although Isabel held the same opinion about Johnny Dent's intentions, she couldn't bear to see Eben in such pain. "He seems like a nice young man, and he seems to care for her."

Eben's probing gaze swung around to her again. "You know him?"

"I met him once," she admitted reluctantly, knowing she had said exactly the wrong thing.

"You *knew* he was involved with Amanda?" he demanded incredulously.

"Well, yes, but—"

"*And you didn't tell me? You didn't do anything about it?*" he shouted.

"I was doing everything I could!" she insisted. "I warned her about ruining her reputation, and I told her he was probably only interested in . . . in . . ." She gestured vaguely.

"And you see how much good it did! Why in the hell didn't you tell me?"

"Well, we haven't been on the best of terms lately," she reminded him stiffly.

"Did you know about him when I came out to the Plimptons' the other day?"

Isabel winced. "Yes," she said in a near whisper.

He swore again. "Did you think you were protecting her?" he demanded.

"I certainly never thought she'd elope with him! If I had, I would have done everything in my power to stop them."

He gave Isabel and her dog cart a derisive perusal that told her exactly what he thought of her abilities in that area.

She shifted uncomfortably on her sore bottom and recalled with irony how she'd seen Eben as her rescuer. Now she only wanted him to leave again. "As enjoyable as this conversation is, shouldn't you be on your way? They'll have to stop for the night, and perhaps you can catch up with them then."

"I suppose you expect me to just leave you sitting here in the middle of the road."

"I'm perfectly capable of taking care of myself," she said huffily. Eben rolled his eyes and began to dismount. "What are you doing?"

He didn't reply. Instead, he led his horse to the rear of the dog cart, tied the reins to a piece of decorative molding, and proceeded to climb up onto the seat beside her. In spite of her irritation, part of her felt an immense relief.

"Do you think we can catch up to them?" she asked when she had surrendered the reins to him.

"No." He slapped the horse into motion.

"Then where are we going?"

"I'm going to look for a place to turn around and then . . . Wait a minute, what's that?"

He stopped the horse again, rose from the seat, then stepped up onto it for a better view.

"Do you see them?" Isabel asked, squinting into the distance but seeing nothing.

"Smoke," he said, pointing. "See it?"

At last Isabel saw the pale gray ribbon drifting off into the evening sky. "Perhaps it's a house."

"Nobody lives out this way."

"Could it be them? Do you think they would've stopped already?" she asked, her fatigue falling away as hope surged through her.

"We'll soon find out," Eben said, dropping down to the seat again. They lurched forward so abruptly, Isabel had to grab onto the sides to keep from toppling backward. "Even if it's not them, it might be somebody who's seen them. Did you pass anybody on the road today?"

"Yes, several riders," Isabel said.

"Did they tell you how far ahead they were?"

Isabel looked at him in amazement. "I didn't ask."

"What do you mean, you didn't ask?" he demanded with a frown.

"You can't think I would talk to strange men on a public road."

He glared at her. "Isabel, for a woman who's the scandal of the county, you've got some peculiar notions of what's proper!"

Resisting an impulse to push him off the seat, Isabel clenched her abused hands and glared right back at him. "May I remind you that the main reason I came on this excursion was to save your *daughter's* reputation, and I saw no reason to reveal what had happened to total strangers who might well carry the tale back to Bittercreek."

"Thanks," he said without the slightest trace of gratitude.

"Didn't *you* pass anyone?"

"Nobody'd seen them."

Isabel could think of no answer for that, so she concentrated on the smoke, which was becoming ever more visible. It appeared to be coming from a small stand of trees up ahead. The perfect spot for a campsite, Isabel told herself.

"What the hell?" Eben muttered as they rounded the trees to find a complete homestead. The house and barn had the raw look of new lumber, and a plow had recently turned the earth in neat furrows to form a field beside it. "Dryland farmers," he said in disgust. "Ruining the grass before they starve to death."

Isabel could hear the frustration beneath his contempt, a frustration she shared. The smoke they had been following curled from the homesteaders' chimney. "Perhaps they've seen Amanda," she said, unwilling to give up the last shred of hope. "They can at least tell us how far ahead of us they are."

"And I can leave you here while I go after them," he added with a measure of relief.

No sooner had their wagon appeared around the bend than two small children came running from the cabin, their bare feet churning up the dust as they raced toward them, screaming a greeting and waving furiously.

Touched by their enthusiasm, Isabel smiled and waved back as Eben skillfully avoided running them over.

"You younguns get back in here this minute!" a woman called from the doorway of the cabin. The children skidded to a halt, turned, and ran back just as quickly as they had run forward, their flour sack dresses billowing out behind them.

Eben pulled up close to the house and tipped his hat. "Afternoon, ma'am. We've got a little trouble, and we were wondering if you could help us."

"Why, sure, if I'm able," she said. Isabel judged her to be in her early twenties, although a hard-scrabble life had already aged her plain face beyond her years. Her faded calico dress hung loosely on her gaunt frame, but it was spotlessly clean. "My husband's just washing up. I'll fetch him. Daniel!" she called, ducking into the house for a moment.

When she returned, a man came behind her, wiping his hands on a flour sack towel. He was a tall man, as gaunt and weathered as his wife, and dressed in farmer's overalls.

"Howdy, folks," he said. "Ula says you've got some trouble."

"Yes, you see, my daughter's run away—"

"Eloped," Isabel corrected, thinking this sounded slightly more respectable.

Eben flashed her an annoyed look and continued as if she hadn't spoken. "We've been following them all day, but we haven't been able to catch up. I'd like to press on, but the lady here . . . Well, it's getting late and . . ."

"And you wondered if we could put her up for the night," the woman finished for him. "Nothing could be easier. We was just sitting down to supper, too, and we'd be proud if you'd join us."

Eben had already started climbing out of the dog cart. "I'm afraid I can't stay," he said, reaching up to help Isabel down. She needed every bit of his assistance, and when her feet hit the ground, she realized too late that her legs weren't about to support her.

"I can't—" she managed as she slumped, but Eben caught her before she fell, muttering a curse.

"Get her right inside," the woman commanded, and just as he had the very first time he'd seen her, Eben scooped her up into his arms and carried her.

"I'm sorry," she whispered, mortified but inexplicably glad to feel Eben's strong arms around her.

"I'll bet you didn't pack anything to eat when you set out this morning, either," he whispered back in annoyance.

"Did you?" she countered, knowing instinctively food would have been the last thing on his mind when he'd discovered Amanda was gone.

His only reply was a grunt as he set her in a straight-backed chair inside the sparsely furnished cabin.

"Seems kinda funny you'd bring your wife along on a trip like this," the farmer said, shaking his head in disapproval.

Isabel blanched, casting Eben a panicked look. Naturally they'd think she was his wife, and just as naturally, he would correct them.

Except he didn't. "Isabel found out what happened early this morning," he said without embarrassment. "She thought she could catch up to them before I got home at noon, so she set out on her own."

"You poor thing," the woman sympathized. "Let me pour you both some coffee, at least."

"That's quite a wagon you got there, ma'am," the farmer said, glancing back out the door at the Plimptons' garish vehicle.

"It's not ours," Eben explained, showing a little embarrassment at last. "Isabel borrowed it from a friend. I just caught up to her a little while ago. I was thinking I'd have to try to get her back to town when I saw your smoke. You folks must be new in these parts."

"Been here nigh on a month now," the man said. "Daniel Mason is my name."

"Eben Walker," Eben replied, shaking the man's hand. "I'd be much obliged if you didn't mention we'd been here. We'd like to keep this a secret if we can."

"Don't worry about a thing," Mason assured him. "And we'll look after your wife like she was family."

Isabel winced again, but Mrs. Mason pressed a steaming cup of coffee into her hands, and the delicious aroma compelled her to revive herself a bit before worrying about social niceties.

"I was wondering if you might've seen my daughter pass by. She was going to Dallas from Bittercreek. They left early this morning."

"A man and a girl, I reckon," Mason said thoughtfully, and shook his head. "I never saw hide nor hair of them, and I was plowing out there all day. Ula, did you see 'em?"

Ula shook her head, too. "No, and I can't help but know when every rider goes past. You saw the way my younguns run out to wave at you? They don't miss anybody. I've said more'n once, a garter snake couldn't cross the road without them noticing."

Isabel heard the sound of stifled giggling behind her. Turning in her chair, she saw the two towheaded children peeking out from what must have been their parents' bedroom.

"Kids," Mrs. Mason said, "did you see a man and a woman riding by today?"

"No, ma'am," they piped in unison, their blue eyes wide beneath the fringe of white bangs. Isabel judged them to be about three and four years old, and from the swell beneath Mrs. Mason's apron, they would soon have another sibling. Isabel wondered irrelevantly if Ula Mason knew what a fortunate woman she was. But then, she probably hadn't been lucky so much as sensible enough to accept the man she loved when he proposed to her, instead of acting like the crazy woman Eben always accused Isabel of being and refusing him.

"But they would've had to pass by here," Eben was saying, a puzzled frown creasing his handsome face.

"If they was going to Dallas like you said," Mason agreed. "Are you sure that's where they was heading?"

Eben gave Isabel a questioning look.

"I have her note right here," Isabel said, setting her coffee on the table so she could rummage in her pocket. Finding the wrinkled paper, she handed it to Eben.

He glanced over it quickly and made a disgusted noise.

"What is it?" Isabel asked in alarm.

"She lied," he said furiously, crumpling the note in disgust. "Didn't you think it was funny how she told you exactly when she was leaving and exactly where she was going?"

"I... I thought she was careless," Isabel said in dismay.

"She might be careless, but she's not stupid. The only reason she'd tell you all this is if she wanted to be caught—which we can assume she did not—or if she wanted to send us on a wild-goose chase."

"They might've gone by here without us seeing," Mason allowed. "Did you talk to anybody else along the way?"

"Nobody else saw them, either," Eben admitted reluctantly. "I should've known. I should've figured it out, but I was worried about Isabel and..." He gestured vaguely, and guilt swelled in her like a rancid tide. She had ruined everything!

"Oh, Eben, I'm so sorry!" Isabel exclaimed, jumping up to comfort him. "I should have told you when I got the note instead of going after them myself."

"It wouldn't have made any difference," he said dully. "We would've still thought they were going to Dallas."

"Not if I'd showed you the note," she insisted, taking his hands in hers. "You could've asked around, found out if anyone had seen them. Oh, Eben, it's all my fault!"

The tears she'd begun to shed earlier flowed down her cheeks, but before she could turn away, Eben's arms were around her, pulling her close against his comforting strength. They clung to each other for long moments, sharing their pain, and oblivious to those around them.

"Now, now," Mrs. Mason said at last, "no use crying over spilt milk, I always say."

"Ula's right," Mr. Mason agreed, as Eben and Isabel reluctantly parted. "You've done all you can."

When she looked up into Eben's face again, she silently begged him to forgive her, and the tender expression in his dark eyes told her he already had.

"And there's no sense in you going anyplace else tonight," Ula said. "Neither one of you's got as much starch as a bunny rabbit. You wouldn't last a mile."

"We can put you both up for the night, and tomorrow you can decide what you want to do," Mason suggested. "I'll go look after your horses."

"Problems always look worst when a body's tired out," Ula said when he had gone. "Now, both of you go wash up while I get supper on the table. Kids, come give me a hand."

Isabel meekly allowed Eben to take her arm and lead her to the rear of the cabin, where the Masons had set up a bench with a bucket of water, soap, and a towel. Eben's touch warmed her, and she resisted with difficulty the urge to lean against him and be taken in his arms again. Now was certainly neither the time nor the place for such things, and she knew better than to surrender to her body's desires where Eben was concerned in any case. If only she'd accepted his proposal when she'd had the chance . . .

"Eben," she suddenly remembered, "they think I'm your wife. Why didn't you tell them?"

He thrust a bar of lye soap into her hands and pushed her toward the bucket, but she resisted, determined to have an answer. He frowned at her, but he said, "I figured we'd caused enough scandal. What would they think if I told them we weren't married, we were just traveling together?"

He was right, of course, and she might have appreciated his thoughtfulness except for a few other considerations. "Have you thought about our . . . our sleeping arrangements?" she asked, her face burning.

"This isn't exactly a hotel," he pointed out impatiently. "They'll put you in the loft with the kids, and I'll sleep in the barn."

"Oh," she said, feeling foolish for even mentioning the subject. Now he would suspect she'd been thinking about spending another night in his arms, and although she had, she certainly didn't want him to know it. She stepped to the washbasin and started to peel off the remains of her gloves.

"Good God, what happened to your hands?" he demanded, grabbing her wrists and turning them over so he could see.

"I . . . I guess I should have worn sturdier gloves," she said, wincing at the sight of her broken blisters and the dried blood on her palms.

"Here, soak them for a minute," he said, placing them gently into the basin. His sudden concern touched her, and she fought back the sting of tears. He wet his own hands and lathered them, then took one of hers between both his own and began to gently bathe away the dirt and gore.

The soap stung, but she didn't mind, not when Eben was being so kind. When both her hands were clean, he took down the flour sack towel and carefully patted them dry. "Maybe they've got some salve you can put on them," he said.

She wanted to thank him, but the tears had clogged her throat, and she couldn't seem to swallow them down.

He studied her face, shook his head, and smiled sadly. "You look awful tired."

Isabel imagined she must look an absolute sight and devoutly wished she'd had the foresight to bring a change of clothing or at least a comb along on her adventure. But, of course, she hadn't intended to be gone more than a few hours, and she hadn't intended to encounter Eben at all. "I'm not used to driving a wagon all day," she managed to say.

"I don't reckon you're used to a lot of things you've done since you've been in Texas."

Isabel remembered the things she'd done with Eben, and the warmth in her heart spread inexorably over her entire body until she thought she might very well go up in flames. "Yes, well, they're waiting supper for us," she said lamely.

She started to turn away, but he caught her arm. "Isabel, I . . ." He hesitated, as if unsure of exactly what to say, and she waited, literally holding her breath while he considered, savoring the feel of his hand through the fabric of her sleeve and wishing she dared throw her arms around his neck, as she longed to do.

"I'm glad you're with me. When I think about Amanda . . ."

His face twisted, and Isabel instinctively placed her hand over his where it rested on her arm. His flesh felt so wonderfully familiar, she wanted to weep again. "We'll find her, Eben. We'll bring her back."

Although his eyes were still shadowed with doubt, he smiled. "Thanks."

"You two about ready?" Ula called from the doorway. "Supper's on the table."

Reluctantly they turned toward the house. Isabel noticed Eben retained possession of her arm, as if he needed the physical contact as much as she.

Ula stepped out of the way to let them pass, and Eben said, "We don't want to put you folks out. If you can make Isabel a pallet on the floor, I can sleep in the barn."

"Nonsense," Ula said. "I can see the way you two are hanging on to each other. You'll need comfort tonight, so Daniel and I'll sleep with the kids, and you can have our room."

Chapter 14

The instant the bedroom door slammed behind them an hour later, Isabel whirled on Eben. "Why didn't you tell them we aren't married?" she whispered furiously.

"Why didn't you?" he countered, sinking wearily onto the bed.

Deciding against answering his question, she said instead, "I know exactly why you did this. You think that if we spend the night here together, I'll have to marry you because I'll be too embarrassed to face these people again if I don't."

He stared at her incredulously. "Why in God's name would I think a thing like that?"

He was right, of course, she realized in chagrin. She'd already proven she wouldn't marry him just to satisfy the dictates of society. Still, she couldn't help wishing he'd insist upon it just once more. Really, this situation was much worse than the first one, since this time there were witnesses to say they had actually shared a room for the night. If Eben wanted her as much as he claimed to, this was his golden opportunity to insist she marry him and make it stick.

"And don't worry," he continued, "I have no intention of trying to force you to marry me again. I may be a little slow, but you don't have to hit me over the head with a sledge to make me understand you don't want me."

But I do want you! her heart cried. If only she could say so, but how could she when he'd just rejected her outright? "I hope you also have no intention of trying to share that bed with me," she said stiffly, trying to conceal her mortification.

"None whatsoever," he said, shocking her again. She'd expected at least an attempt at seduction. Even if Eben didn't actually love her, he had thoroughly enjoyed making love to her. Had she destroyed even that with her stubbornness? "I'm too tired to be a threat to anyone tonight, anyway," he added, rising slowly to his feet. "I'll go outside for a while and give you time to get into bed. Put a blanket and pillow on the floor for me, will you?"

"How will you get any rest on the floor?" she asked without thinking.

"I could probably fall asleep standing up, but if you're really worried about me, you can take the floor yourself," he said in disgust as he walked out and slammed the door behind him.

Resisting an impulse to call him back, Isabel walked over to the bed in question and sank down onto it. She, too, was weary beyond words, far too weary to be arguing with Eben. She wanted to cry—for Amanda and Eben and herself—but if she started, she'd never be able to stop, so she forced herself to get up again and prepare herself for bed.

Mrs. Mason had provided a bucket of hot water, and Isabel gratefully stripped down to her chemise and gave herself a quick sponge bath. Then she took down her hair and finger-combed the tangles as best she could. In the morning she would ask for the loan of a brush, but for tonight, this would have to do. When she was finished, she turned the lamp down as low as it would go and started to climb into the bed until she remembered Eben's instructions about making him a pallet on the floor.

Guilt told her she should let him have the bed. Sleeping on the floor was better than she deserved for being stupid enough to let Amanda and Johnny get away. What did it matter since she probably wouldn't be able to sleep anyway?

Quickly, before he returned, she pulled the top blanket from the bed and spread it on the floor in the corner. Taking one of the pillows, she carried it over and, hearing Eben's returning footsteps, hastily lay down on the pallet and pulled half the blanket over her.

Eben's figure loomed hugely in the dimly lit room as he paused in surprise. Glancing around, he quickly discovered her. "What do you think you're doing?" he demanded.

"I won't be able to sleep anyway, and you've got another long ride ahead of you tomorrow."

"Are you trying to make me feel like a skunk?"

"No, I'm trying to be sensible, and you know I'm right. Now, stop arguing and go to bed."

He sighed gustily, "Fine, suit yourself. I'm going to get undressed now, so don't look unless you want to be shocked."

Isabel closed her eyes, knowing she couldn't bear the sight of Eben's body. Although she tried not to listen, she couldn't help hearing the rustle of clothing and imagining each article as Eben removed it. In her mind's eye, she could picture his naked flesh gilded by the lamplight. The soft splash of water conjured pictures of the rough washrag gliding over his body, and Isabel clenched her hands against the longing to run them over those same places.

How could she have been such a fool? Maybe love

wasn't everything. What if Eben had been right? What if there was little difference between love and lust? Certainly in her case they seemed quite closely related, and perhaps the same was true for Eben. What if he did love her in his own way?

Tears stung her eyes, and she blinked against them, a serious mistake because the instant she opened her eyes, she saw him.

Clad only in his cotton drawers, he was bent over, his back to her, washing one of his legs. Her breath caught at the sight of his lean hips and strong thighs, and desire coiled in her, hot and compelling. What would he say if he knew what she was feeling?

And what would he do?

He straightened, revealing the broad expanse of his bare back, and tossed the washrag back into the bucket with a splash. Before she could think to close her eyes again, he turned to face her. "Isabel?"

Eben caught her staring, but she squeezed her eyes shut the instant he turned around. Her reaction irritated him. She'd seen him undressed before, and it hadn't bothered her then. But then, maybe the sight of him disgusted her now. He only wished he could find her disgusting, or at least unattractive.

"Isabel, you can't expect me to take the bed while you sleep on the floor," he said, letting his irritation show.

"I don't know why not," she replied in that haughty tone he was coming to hate. "Please put out the light," she added stiffly, probably because she didn't want to chance catching another glimpse of him.

With a sigh of resignation, he blew out the lamp Mrs. Mason had left for them.

When the room was dark, he tried again. "Isabel, be reasonable."

"I'm being perfectly reasonable," she insisted. "You may sleep on the floor if you wish, but I am not going to take the bed in any case, so you might as well have it. Please, Eben, I don't want to fight with you."

He didn't want to fight with her either, and short of picking her up and putting her in the bed himself, he couldn't think of any other way of getting her there. Not that picking her up didn't hold a certain appeal. God, how he wanted, no, needed, to hold her close. He hadn't felt so angry and frustrated and helpless and lost since the day Gisela had died. What he wouldn't give to feel Isabel's arms around him, her body pressed close to his. But, of course, she'd die before she'd hold him like that. She never wanted to see him again.

He sighed in disgust as he sank down into the blessed softness of the bed and stretched out. The bed seemed huge, just like his bed at home, empty without Isabel to share it. The difference, of course, was that at home Isabel wasn't lying just a few feet away. He moaned aloud at the thought.

Isabel heard him moan with relief at the softness of the bed, and she experienced a moment of envy as she shifted her bruised body in a vain attempt to find relief for herself. How much she longed to be there beside him, to curl up against his solid strength and find comfort in his arms.

But she deserved to suffer. Poor Amanda was ruined, Eben's heart was broken at losing his daughter, and it was all Isabel's fault. If she'd only sent for Eben this morning, if she'd only been firmer with Amanda, if she'd only told Eben about Johnny Dent the day he'd come to see her at the Plimptons', if she'd only accepted Eben's proposal, if, if, if . . .

The tears she'd managed to blink away before started again, stinging until she couldn't fight them anymore. She let them fall, and they rolled down the sides of her face into her hair. In the silence of the room, she didn't dare make a sound, so she held a corner of the blanket against her lips to muffle the sobs threatening to escape. How could she have been so stupid? How could she have made such a muddle of her life and everyone else's? How could she . . . ?

"Sweet Jesus," Eben exclaimed, and Isabel jumped. Before she could ask him what was wrong, his feet hit the floor and he was coming toward her.

"Eben," she protested, but the sound came out on a sob, and in the next second he was on the floor beside her, gathering her into his arms.

"For God's sake, don't cry," he begged, pulling her close until she could feel the pounding of his heart beneath her ear.

"I can't . . . help it. . . ." she gasped as she fought vainly to regain her composure. "I thought about . . . Amanda and . . ."

His embrace tightened reflexively. "I'm thinking about her too, and so help me God, when I get my hands on that bastard, I'll wring his neck!"

"Oh, Eben, she's just a child, and it's all my fault. If I'd only told you—"

"Don't, please, I don't want to hear any more about it," he said, pressing her head into his shoulder.

Somehow her arms had encircled him, and she clung gratefully to his strength. She remembered what Ula Mason had said about the both of them needing comfort tonight and wished Eben would kiss her and make all the unpleasantness go away.

Instinctively she pressed her lips to his skin, tasting his musky maleness, inhaling his intoxicating scent.

"Oh, God, Isabel," he murmured into her hair, and his own lips found the place where her heart throbbed in her temple. As if of their own volition, her palms slid up his back, tracing the corded muscles beneath the cool satin of his skin.

Hastily, clumsily, he stripped the blanket from her, and when his callused fingers found her flesh, all reason fled and instinct took control.

He said her name again just before his mouth took hers, and she opened at his urging, allowing him full access to her sweetness, meeting his tongue in a sensual duel. When they were both breathless, he pulled away a fraction of an inch. "Isabel, I . . . I know you don't . . . but I need you. I need you so much. Please . . ."

She needed him, too, if only for tonight. In answer, she pulled his mouth to hers again, and when he drew her to her feet, she did not resist, could not have resisted if she'd wanted to. Her body seemed to have passed completely out of her control.

He lifted her into his arms without even breaking the kiss, and when he laid her down on the bed, she refused to let him go, taking his weight with a grateful sigh. Cupping her breast in one hand, he slid the other under her, then rolled them both over until she lay on top of him. Her hair spilled over her shoulders, and Eben caught a handful of it and wrapped it around his fist.

"Do you know how many times I've dreamed about being with you again?" he asked against her mouth.

Joy bubbled up inside her, but she had no time to analyze anything. His free hand clutched at her buttock, pulling her hips to his, rocking her against the hard evidence of his desire, and all rational thought fled.

"I want to feel you up against me," he whispered, releasing her hair to fumble with the ribbons of her chemise, and Isabel helped, bracing herself against his racing heart while she pulled the fastenings loose. The instant she was finished, he jerked the garment from her shoulders, and she slid her arms free.

How many times had *she* dreamed about *this*? she wondered as she nestled her aching breasts against the furred warmth of his chest. She lifted her hips obediently as Eben pushed the chemise past them, and she swallowed his gasp of surprise when he found her naked beneath it.

He groaned as he rolled her over onto her back again. "I want to see you," he said, and Isabel cursed the darkness that hid him from her, too, but neither of them made a move for the light. Instead, he lowered his mouth to her breast and took one of her pebbled nipples between his lips.

She cried out in surprise when he nipped it lightly between his teeth, and he covered her mouth with his hand to stifle her moan when he soothed it with his tongue.

She buried her fingers in his silken hair, holding him to her while he continued the blissful torture. Meanwhile his hand had found her hip and begun to stroke, up and down, up and down, his rough palm gently abrading her skin with maddening precision, stoking the fires within until the heat parted her legs in silent invitation. Accepting her invitation, his fingers slid down her thigh and up again to graze the moist curls in a tantalizing sweep before moving on again.

"Eben," she begged, not knowing how to ask for what she needed so desperately.

"Shhh," he said. "I need you, too. Touch me, Isabel."

She'd *been* touching him, caressing every spot she could reach with eager, loving hands, but she knew what he meant, what he wanted. How could she refuse? The buttons on his drawers fell open easily beneath her trembling fingers, and she found him hot and ready for her.

She smiled in feminine triumph at his gasp of pleasure when her fingers closed around him. "Shhh," she warned even as she returned his tantalizing torture, determined to draw her name from his lips.

"My God, Isabel, you're a witch," he murmured brokenly against her ear, but before she could savor her victory, his fingers slipped inside of her, invading her most secret place and sending liquid fire racing through her veins.

She made a startled sound that became a moan as his fingers moved in imitation of the union she craved so desperately. As the flames rose, sparks scattered, dancing behind her eyelids, and she was done with begging.

With more boldness than she ever would have dreamed herself capable of, she guided him to her. He submitted willingly, yielding his power while at the same time overwhelming her with it, as he sank into her welcoming depths and took possession of her soul.

"Oh, Eben, I . . ." she gasped.

"Mine," he replied savagely. "You're mine, now, Isabel."

"Yes" was all she could say.

He moved within her, and more experienced now, she met him thrust for thrust until she could no longer tell where her body ended and his began. Indeed, such distinctions no longer mattered, either, since they were truly one, striving, straining, yearning together to that one shining, sacred goal.

She could see it, glowing like the gold of paradise, just out of reach but closer now than before, and even closer now, and closer still, the light white-hot and drawing her on. Not wanting it to end, she tried to fight, tried to hold back, clinging to him with arms and legs and lips. She called his name or thought she did in the instant before the end, and then she plunged into the flames and was no more.

Eben awoke in the pale light of dawn to find Isabel's body pressed into the curve of his own, her breast filling his hand, and her honey-colored hair spread out beneath his head. For one glorious second he savored his complete possession of her. "Mine," he whispered in the instant before reality intruded, bringing with it memories of what had brought them to this place.

Amanda, his baby girl. Dear God, where was she this morning, and what had happened to her in the night? Pain such as he had hoped never to know again twisted his heart and almost wrenched a cry from his lips.

He wanted to wake Isabel so he could feel her arms around him and know the blessed comfort only she could give him. But when he looked down into her face and saw the dark circles beneath her eyes and remembered what she had endured the day before, he knew it would be cruel to disturb her so early.

No, he'd taken enough from her already. He would have to bear the pain alone for now. Reluctantly and ever so carefully, so as not to disturb her, he moved away, tucking the blanket around her lovingly as he left the bed. Using the cold water from last night, he bathed quickly and silently, then dressed. Shaving could wait, he decided, running a hand experimentally over his chin. He had urgent business waiting.

As much as he hated to do so, he would leave Isabel behind and get an early start back to town, where he could, hopefully, pick up Amanda's trail before it got any colder. He could send Herald Bartz or maybe Paul Young back for Isabel.

And maybe he'd instruct them to deliver her straight to his house, he thought with a grin, because this time he wasn't going to take no for an answer. After last night, Isabel belonged to him, whether she liked it or not. All he'd have to do is point out that sooner or later the Mason family would come to town, and they would certainly ask after their friend "Mrs. Walker." Not even Isabel could withstand the ignominy of *this* scandal. The thought actually made him smile.

He found the Masons already up and Ula at work preparing breakfast. She and Daniel agreed with his decision to let Isabel sleep off her ordeal and wait there until Eben could send someone for her. Daniel went out with him while he saddled his horse, and by the time they were finished, Ula had breakfast on the table. Eben ate quickly, mindful of the two children who watched him in fascination.

When he was ready to leave, he called them aside, and they came reluctantly, shy but curious. "You two are pretty good scouts for your mother, letting her know whenever folks pass by the house, so I figure you deserve a reward, don't you?"

They nodded vigorously, and Eben bit back a smile. "Hold out your hands," he commanded, and they did so, showing him freshly scrubbed palms. He placed a silver dollar in each one.

"Mama, look!" the older one squealed, racing to show her prize, with the younger one on her heels.

"Hush, now, you'll wake Mrs. Walker," Ula scolded, and Eben felt a sense of pride to know that soon Isabel would bear his name in truth. "What's this now?" Ula said in surprise, examining the coins. "Mr. Walker, you shouldn't have!"

Eben shrugged off her complaint, glad to see she had not forbade the children to keep the money. Had he offered to pay for his and Isabel's bed and board, the Masons would most certainly have been insulted, but judging from Ula's willingness to accept his generosity, the money was appreciated nonetheless.

"I'm obliged to you for looking after Isabel. I'll send somebody out to fetch her as soon as I get back to town," he said, thinking this would be late in the afternoon. It would be at least two days before Isabel got home. He sighed to think how little she would like kicking her heels here without the slightest idea what was happening with him and Amanda. It would serve her right for her meddling, though, and maybe she'd learn a lesson from it and consult him next time, instead of going off half-cocked.

Yeah, and maybe rain would fall up someday real soon, too.

Eben was ready to go, but he hesitated, casting one last glance at the bedroom door behind which Isabel still slept.

"She'll be real put out if you don't at least say good-bye," Ula remarked, seeing the direction of his gaze.

"Don't worry about waking her. She can go back to sleep if she's still tired out."

His mind made up, he was halfway to the door when he heard a horse racing into the yard and an excited shout.

Daniel Mason was already in the yard, and Eben hurried out to see what the commotion was about.

"Hey, Mr. Walker, I figured you might be here when I saw the Plimptons' wagon in the yard!" Johnny Dent called, reining in and sliding to the ground in one fluid motion.

"You son of a bitch!" Eben roared, lunging at the boy.

Johnny threw his hands up instinctively, but his defensive gesture did no good. The force of Eben's charge carried them both to the ground in a heap, and Eben had already raised a fist to punch him when Mason reached them. He caught Eben's arm in midswing, and although he managed to deflect the blow, Eben's strength sent Mason plunging to the ground, too.

"Mr. Walker, wait!" Johnny yelled, holding his arms in front of his face and struggling frantically to be free. "We didn't elope! I swear it!"

Eben had shaken loose of Mason and was preparing to swing again when Johnny's words registered. "What did you say?"

Johnny peeked out warily from between his arms. "I said me and Amanda never eloped. She made the whole thing up."

"What?" Eben demanded, sitting back on his heels.

Johnny took the opportunity to scramble a safe distance away. "She made the whole thing up, Mr. Walker. She just wanted to get you and Miss Isabel together again."

"Miss Isabel?" Mason inquired in confusion.

Suddenly aware that Johnny's explanation might prove embarrassing to Isabel, Eben got to his feet. "Mason, do you mind if we talk in private?"

Obviously disappointed, Mason said, "Sure," and accepted Eben's hand up. "Maybe I should wake your wife and tell her what's happened."

"Yeah, good idea," Eben agreed.

"Wife?" Johnny inquired as Mason hurried away.

"We told them Isabel was my wife so they wouldn't wonder what we were doing out together," Eben said gruffly. "Now, what's all this about Amanda making the whole thing up?"

Johnny got slowly to his feet, cautiously watching Eben the whole time. "Like I said, Amanda got it into her head that if she caused some trouble, you and Miss Isabel would have to get together to work it out. I swear, Mr. Walker, I didn't know anything about it at all until last night. She sent me word and I . . ."

"Just tell me what happened, Dent," Eben snapped, more furious than he could ever remember being.

Johnny swallowed nervously. "Well, sir, she figured if she ran off, or at least if you thought she'd run off, you'd go to Miss Isabel for help. To make sure, she told Miss Isabel where she was supposed to be going and told you she knew, so you'd have to go to her. From what I hear, that's just what you did except she'd already set out on her own. When word got back to town last evening that she hadn't come home, Amanda started to get scared."

"Where was she all this time?" Eben said, holding his temper only with the utmost difficulty.

"Hiding at the Bartzes' house. Only Carrie knew she was there until Mr. Bartz told the family what had happened. Carrie told Amanda, and Amanda told Mr. and Mrs. Bartz what she'd done. They sent for me because they figured somebody oughta ride all night to catch up so you didn't get clear to Dallas before you figured out she wasn't going there."

"We'd figured it out already," Eben informed him murderously, "although we figured the two of you had just gone someplace else."

"But we didn't go anywheres, I swear. Honest, Mr. Walker, I'd never do a thing like that, not to Amanda—"

"Eben!" Isabel cried from the cabin door. "Johnny? What on earth . . . ?"

The two men watched as she ran across the yard toward them, her long, golden hair streaming out behind her. Obviously she'd simply thrown on her dress without benefit of underwear, and Eben felt an urge to cover her from Johnny Dent's gaze.

Johnny whipped off his hat as she reached them. "Morning, Miss Isabel," he said gravely.

"Where's Amanda?" she demanded, her blue eyes wide with alarm.

"Home in bed, probably," Eben informed her in disgust. "She made the whole thing up. Not only did Dent, here, not carry her off, he didn't even know about it."

"She was hiding at the Bartzes' house, miss, but she got scared when she found out how you'd gone after her all alone and hadn't come back. She sent me to fetch you home."

Isabel was still too groggy from sleep to make complete sense of it all. "She made it up?" she echoed uncertainly.

"She's safe, Isabel," Eben explained patiently. "Safe at home. She never left town at all, but she's going to wish she'd headed for Mexico when I get through with her."

"Eben, don't do anything until you've had a chance to calm down," she cautioned, laying a hand on his arm, and Eben wanted to kiss the worried frown off her face. Unfortunately, he didn't have time. If he was going to get to Amanda today, he had to leave right now.

"Dent, you see that Miss Isabel gets home, will you?"

"Sure thing, Mr. Walker," he replied, pitifully eager to placate Eben.

"Where are you going?" Isabel demanded in renewed alarm.

"Back to town," he said. "I've got a daughter to deal with. She's been alone long enough to have thought up a dozen more plots, and I'm going to make sure she forgets every one of them."

"Eben—" she protested, but Eben was too angry to listen to her arguments in favor of restraint. He'd been restrained with Amanda since the day she was born, and look what it had gotten him.

"Dent, these folks think Isabel is my wife, so you don't tell them any different, understand?"

"Uh, yes, sir," he replied amenably.

"And you call her 'Mrs. Walker,' you hear?"

"Yes, sir!"

"Eben, you can't just leave like this," Isabel insisted. "You haven't even thanked the Masons for their hospitality!"

"Yes, I have. I was leaving anyway, just as soon as I told you good-bye."

"Then let me go with you!"

"No, that damn contraption of Plimpton's'll slow me down too much, and after yesterday you're in no shape to travel fast anyway. Johnny'll bring you home when you're ready."

She looked ready to launch into another argument, so Eben grabbed her and kissed her, right on the mouth and right in front of Johnny Dent. "I'll see you, Isabel," he said, letting her go with profound regret. "And I'll deal with you later, Dent," he added in warning. He was on his horse before Isabel found her tongue.

He heard her calling his name, but he just waved and put the spurs to his mount.

Isabel watched him go in openmouthed fury. "Damn you, Eben Walker!" she shouted, knowing he couldn't hear her. How dare he leave her like that!

"Well, now," Johnny Dent remarked to no one in

particular. "Looks like Amanda's plan just might've worked after all."

Lacking a better target, Isabel turned the full force of her rage on him. "I'll thank you to keep a civil tongue in your head, young man!" she snapped.

"What'd I say?" he asked as she stalked back to the house.

"If you hadn't pursued Amanda in the first place, none of this would have happened," she informed him over her shoulder.

"You can't blame me for this," Johnny insisted, trotting to keep up with her. "If Mr. Walker would've let us see each other, we wouldn't've had to sneak around."

"If I recall correctly, no one ever gave him the opportunity to decide whether he would allow you to see her or not," Isabel replied, stomping into the house.

There she came face-to-face with the Mason family, all wide-eyed curiosity, and when she stopped dead in her tracks, Johnny almost collided with her back. Was that a headache starting behind her eyes? she wondered irrelevantly, or could she hope she was experiencing the onset of an apoplexy that would put a swift and merciful end to this whole ordeal?

Eben made good time on his return trip to town and reached the Bartz house in the early afternoon. The long ride had only served to increase his fury with his daughter. Leaving his lathered horse tied at the gate, he stormed up onto the porch and pounded on the front door.

A cautious, worried Bertha opened the door a crack and peered out at him.

"Where is she?" he demanded.

"Now, Eben, calm down. She's here, and she's perfectly safe. Did you find Isabel?"

"Yeah, she's 'perfectly safe,' too, no thanks to

Amanda. I left her resting at a farmhouse. Johnny Dent is going to see she gets home."

"Thank heaven," Bertha breathed, but she made no move to open the door farther and allow him inside.

"Bertha, I want to see my daughter."

"Of course you do, but you have to promise not to be too hard on her. She did a terrible thing, but nothing you do or say can make her feel any worse than she already does. She's been half out of her mind worrying about Isabel, and—"

"Pa?" Amanda's voice called from upstairs. "Is Pa here?"

He heard light footsteps running down the stairs, and at last Bertha stepped aside far enough to allow Eben to push his way inside.

"Amanda Jane Walker," he began furiously, but stopped when he saw her tear-ravaged face.

"Oh, Pa, is Miss Forester all right?" she asked tremulously, tears filling her eyes.

"Yes," he informed her gruffly, torn between his anger and the unexpected relief at seeing her as safe and innocent as when he'd left her last. "I found a farmhouse last night, and they put us up. Your Mr. Dent got there about dawn this morning to tell us what happened, and he'll be bringing her home."

"Thank heaven," she cried, running to him and throwing her arms around him. "I was so scared when I found out she went off alone and . . . and didn't come back," she sobbed against his chest. "Oh, Pa, I'm so sorry! I never meant to . . . to hurt Miss Forester. . . ."

Her voice dissolved in tears, and instinctively Eben put his arms around her, inexpressibly glad to be holding her once again. If anything had happened to her, how would he have borne it? As he patted her awkwardly, he blinked at moisture in his own eyes.

"Why don't the two of you go into the parlor so you can talk," Bertha suggested, blinking rather suspiciously herself. "I'll bring you some coffee, Eben. You look like you could do with a cup."

"Thanks," he muttered, turning Amanda in his arms and conducting her to the privacy of the parlor. Although his anger had abated considerably, he still had a few things to say to his headstrong child.

He closed the pocket doors behind them and led her over to the settee. When they were seated, Amanda peered warily up at him over her sodden handkerchief. "Pa, I'm awful sorry. I never meant—"

"Exactly what did you mean, then, young lady? First of all, you told a lie, but worse, you told a lie that hurt everybody who cares about you."

She sniffed, wiping determinedly at her nose, before replying. "I was mad at you, Pa. I knew you loved Miss Forester, or at least I thought you did." She paused, asking a silent question, which he refused to answer. "Anyway," she continued doggedly, "when you came back from the Plimptons', you said it was over between you and Miss Forester and you'd never be getting married now. Pa, I knew that wasn't right! I saw how miserable you were, and I figured she must be just as miserable. I thought maybe, just maybe, if the two of you could get together one more time, you could work things out, but I also knew you'd never do it on your own, so I . . . I figured if you were both worried about me . . ."

Crystal tears spilled from her red, swollen eyes and ran unheeded down her cheeks. Eben knew he should be furious at her, but he couldn't seem to work up any outrage since her ridiculous plan had worked exactly as she'd hoped, at least as far as Eben was concerned.

He wasn't about to let her know it, however. "Why did you tell Isabel where you were going if you didn't want her to go after you?" he asked sternly.

"So you'd have to go to her to find out. I never thought for a minute she'd come after me herself!

Please, you've got to believe me! I never would've
done anything to put her in danger."

Seeing her very genuine distress, he couldn't help
but believe her. "Do you know what could've happened to her?" he asked mercilessly, determined she
would at least understand the consequences of her
act. "She didn't take any food with her, not even a
blanket, and when I found her, she was out in the
middle of nowhere, too exhausted to drive another
foot."

Amanda's face crumbled in abject misery, and her
thin shoulders shook with silent sobs, but Eben
wasn't finished with her yet. "And what if some man
had come along and decided to kidnap her? We might
never have even found out what happened, and it
would have been all your fault."

She made an agonized sound, covered her face with
her handkerchief, and curled herself into a ball in the
corner of the sofa while her slender body shook with
broken sobs.

"I ought to beat the living daylights out of you,"
he said, knowing he couldn't possibly lay a finger on
her now.

She looked up at him with pathetically sad eyes
and nodded vigorously. "I deserve it, Pa. I deserve
that and anything else you can think of. Miss Forester
might've died and . . ." Her voice broke. "I'm wicked
and thoughtless, and I deserve to be punished."

Eben stared at her in astonishment, but he saw no
trace of deception in her swollen face.

"And then there's the matter of Johnny Dent," he
said relentlessly.

"I know I shouldn't've been seeing him," she
wailed in remorse. "Miss Forester tried to tell me, but
I wouldn't listen. I'm so sorry, Pa, and I know you'll
never be able to trust me again, but I promise I won't
see him anymore, him or any other boy, not for as
long as I live!"

If Eben had thought she stood a chance of keeping

such a promise, he might have been tempted to jump at this opportunity. Instead, he couldn't help hearing Isabel's warning not to do anything he would regret. What would she advise in this situation? he wondered with an inward smile. "You're too young to be seeing young men at all except maybe at church," he began, feeling his way.

She nodded again, perhaps a bit less vigorously.

"And no decent girl sneaks around to meet boys after dark."

"I'll never do it again, I swear!"

"But if you do find a young man you like, you bring him to the house so I can meet him."

She blinked in surprise. "But I won't ever—"

"Of course you will," he contradicted gruffly. "You're a pretty girl, and the boys'll be flocking around before you know it. I can't stop them, so it's up to you to keep them in line."

She blinked again. "Do you . . . do you really think I'm pretty?" she asked after a long moment.

He stared at her in astonishment. Was that the only thing she'd heard out of all he'd said? "Don't go getting vain, now," he warned.

"I'm not," she hastily assured him, "but you never said . . . I mean, do you really think . . . ?"

Suddenly Eben remembered what Isabel had said to him about the way he treated his daughter. He'd been holding back for so long, he hardly even knew how to show her his true feelings anymore. And Isabel was right; whether Gisela had been faithful to him or not, Amanda was his daughter in every way that mattered. "You're about the prettiest girl I ever saw," he told her gently.

Pure joy lighted her face, and she flung herself into his arms. "Oh, Pa, I love you!" she cried, and to his dismay, she started weeping again.

"Don't cry, now," he tried, patting her as he had before and feeling totally helpless. Although his

clumsy comfort seemed to accomplish little, soon her
sobs eased into whimpers.

For a long time, she lay limply against his chest,
and just when he began to think she might have fallen
asleep, she said, "Pa? I'm awful sorry things didn't
work out with you and Miss Forester. If you want,
I'll go out to the Plimptons' and talk to her. Maybe if
I—"

"You won't have to," he said, stroking her hair.

She pulled away with a jerk. "What do you mean?"

Eben somehow managed to hold back his triumphant grin. "I mean Isabel will be coming to live with
us, so if you want to talk to her, you won't have to
go anywhere at all."

It took a minute for the truth to dawn on her, and
when he saw the sly gleam in her eye, Eben instantly
regretting telling her so soon. "My plan worked after
all!" she exclaimed.

"No, it did not!" Eben insisted, but he knew he
was wasting his breath.

Amanda smiled radiantly. "Oh, Pa, no wonder you
weren't mad at me!"

A little while later, after Eben had drunk some of
Bertha's coffee and eaten the meal she pressed upon
him, Eben and Amanda returned to their own house.
He set his daughter to work cleaning in preparation
for her future stepmother's arrival, and he went over
to his shop to see what work had piled up while he'd
been gone.

As he was pulling open the door of his shop, he
heard Paul Young calling his name. Watching his
friend jogging across the street toward him, Eben bit
back a smile, thinking how sweet it would be to tell
Paul that Isabel was finally going to marry him. Of
course, she hadn't exactly agreed yet, but Eben knew
she would, just as soon as Johnny Dent brought her
home to him.

"Did you find Isabel?" Paul asked the instant he was within speaking distance.

"Safe and sound. Did you know there's some new folks in the area? Dryland farmers, name of Mason. Lucky thing we came upon their place when we did. They put us up for the night."

"Where's Isabel then?"

"Dent is bringing her in when she's had a chance to rest up a little. I guess you know he came after us."

Paul nodded. "I reckon the story's all over by now. That girl of yours sure is a pistol."

"Yeah, well, she won't be pulling any more pranks for quite a while, not if she wants to get any older."

Paul nodded again, but instead of smiling as Eben had expected, he frowned and glanced away, as if he were uncomfortable about something.

"Anything wrong?"

Paul put his hands on his hips and scuffed his boot in the dirt, still refusing to meet Eben's eye.

"Paul?" Eben prodded uneasily.

"Oh, hell," Paul said at last. "I thought maybe I shouldn't show this to you, especially not now, but . . . well, then I figured if I didn't show you and trouble came—"

"Show me what?" Eben demanded impatiently.

With great reluctance, Paul reached into his breast pocket, pulled out a folded piece of paper, and handed it to Eben. "I found it tacked on your shop door this morning when I came over to feed the animals like you asked me."

With sudden foreboding, Eben unfolded the paper. There he read a crudely scrawled warning, "Get out of town while you still can, sheep-lover."

"What do you suppose they plan to do if I don't leave?" Eben asked with studied calm, folding the paper back up carefully.

"People like that are cowards, Eb. They'd never face you."

"But they might do something behind my back," Eben suggested as he fought the cold fury rising within him. "I don't suppose you saw who did this."

Paul shook his head. "Like I said, it was here this morning. Listen, if there's something I can do—"

"You can look after the horses for me again to-morrow," Eben said grimly. "There's some people I need to see."

"Who?" Paul asked uneasily.

"Some cattlemen. It ain't hard to guess who might've sent this, and even if I get it wrong, I'll talk to enough folks so the message gets back to whoever's responsible."

"It ain't smart to stand up for sheepherders in this country," Paul warned.

"Or for farmers, neither, but I've got some to thank for maybe saving Isabel's life yesterday. I'm not going to turn my back on people because some jackass don't like the way they make their living."

"You're a businessman, Eben. If you get the cow-people mad at you, they can put you right out of business."

"If they do, then I *will* go someplace else, but not until then. Besides, I don't think everybody agrees with whoever wrote this," Eben said, holding up the wrinkled note. "Cattlemen'll never like sheep, but most of them are smart enough to know they can't stop sheepherders from moving in. Sheep and cattle live side by side in other places, and it's going to happen here, too, no matter how hard a few lard-heads try to fight it."

"Just be sure one of those lardheads don't put a bullet in you," Paul warned doubtfully.

"Like you said, they're probably cowards."

"Yeah, and cowards are the ones shoot people in the back."

"Then I'll try not to turn my back on any of them."

* * *

Suppertime came and went with no sign of Isabel. Eben had been reduced to pacing his front porch, and the setting sun was painting rosy streaks in the sky when Johnny Dent finally rode up to Eben's house.

Alone.

"Where in the hell is she?" he demanded before Johnny even got his horse stopped.

Somewhat taken aback, Johnny stared at him for a long moment. "You mean Miss Forester?"

"No, I mean the Queen of Sheba," Eben snapped. "Of course I mean Miss Forester. What have you done with her?"

"I left her at the Plimptons', just like you told me," Johnny said, watching him warily now.

"Just like I told you?" he repeated incredulously. "I told you to bring her here."

"You told me to take her home, so I did," Johnny contradicted.

Eben opened his mouth to argue, but realized it was fruitless. He couldn't blame the boy for misunderstanding, but why in God's name hadn't Isabel corrected him? Unless . . .

"Did she tell you where to take her?" Eben asked suspiciously.

"Well, sure. I mean, we had to take the wagon contraption back to the Plimptons' anyway, and that *is* where she lives. She never said a word about coming on to town with me, not even when I told her I was gonna stop to let you know we made it back."

"Didn't she give you a message for me?" Eben asked with growing unease.

"No, sir," Johnny admitted absently, suddenly looking past Eben at something behind him.

Eben turned to find Amanda standing tentatively in the doorway. His instinct told him to order her back inside, out of Johnny Dent's sight, but she looked so fragile, he didn't have the heart to be harsh with her.

"Amanda," he began gently, but she interrupted him.

"My pa says I can only see you at church from now on," she told Johnny, straightening her thin shoulders defensively.

Johnny whipped off his hat, just as he had done that morning when addressing Isabel. "I . . . I reckon that's only right."

Eben's glance darted between the two of them, noting their mutual distress, and he couldn't help sympathizing just a little. Not so much that he could forget Johnny Dent was almost twenty and Amanda was only fourteen, but enough so he couldn't exactly be angry.

"It'll be a while before I allow Amanda to have gentlemen callers," Eben said firmly.

"Yes, sir, I understand," Johnny said grimly. "But when you do, I'll be waiting."

Eben doubted it, but when he saw Amanda's radiant smile, he was glad Dent had been gallant enough to say it. She'd get over him soon enough, and in the meantime, she wouldn't be humiliated.

After a long, awkward silence, Dent said, "Well, I reckon I'll see you on Sunday, then."

"Yes," Amanda said happily. "And thank you for going after Pa and Miss Forester."

"I . . . You're welcome," Dent replied, a little embarrassed. "It was the least I could do. Well, goodbye for now."

" 'Bye," Amanda called, stepping to the edge of the porch to wave as Dent rode slowly back to the road, watching her over his shoulder until he was out of sight.

Eben ignored Amanda's dramatic sigh. She wouldn't change his mind about Johnny Dent even if she went into a decline.

"Isabel stayed at the Plimptons'," he announced in annoyance.

Amanda turned to face him, startled. "Why?"

"God only knows, and I've got some business to take care of tomorrow, so I won't be able to fetch her until Friday."

"Can I go with you?" she asked eagerly.

Eben considered the suggestion. Amanda's presence might make things easier, but not if Isabel was going to put up a fight. The fact that she hadn't come along to town, as Eben had made it perfectly clear he expected her to, made him suspect she was up on her high horse about something again. If she wanted a fight, Amanda's presence would only complicate matters. "We'll see," he said at last. "Now, you'd better get to bed. From the looks of you, you didn't get much sleep last night."

"You don't look like you did, either," she said ingenuously, and Eben blessed the gathering darkness that hid the heat he felt rising in his face.

"Yeah, well, I am kind of tired from riding for two days," he admitted, remembering some other, far more enjoyable "riding" he had done last night. "I'll be along in a minute."

"Good night, Pa," she said, and to his surprise, she kissed him on the cheek.

He couldn't reply because the lump in his throat blocked all sound.

"I wish you'd stop fussing over me, Rosemary," Isabel said in irritation, pulling away the pillow Rosemary Plimpton had just added to those supporting her in the bed. "I'm not an invalid."

"But such an ordeal." Rosemary clucked disapprovingly. "Driving that dog cart all day alone, then returning the very next day. You're completely exhausted. If you could only see yourself—"

"I *have* seen myself," Isabel reminded her, wincing at the memory of the drawn face, dangerously pale beneath a nasty sunburn, she had seen staring back at her from the mirror. "And I will be fine if I can just get a little rest."

"You must have spent a perfectly horrible night not knowing what had become of Amanda," Rosemary said, wringing her hands.

"Yes, uh, I was terribly worried about her," Isabel said, blushing.

"I hope her poor papa has punished her severely for her part in all this."

Isabel sighed, hoping just the opposite. The relationship between Eben and Amanda was already so strained that Isabel feared it couldn't survive if Eben vented his wrath on the poor girl.

"Rosemary, if you don't mind, I'd like to go to sleep now," Isabel said wearily.

"Oh, certainly, how stupid of me," Rosemary stammered, looking around to see if she might have forgotten to provide anything conducive to Isabel's comfort. "If you need anything—"

"I'll call," Isabel promised. "Good night, and thanks for everything."

"Good night," Rosemary said, giving the small room one last, anxious look, then blowing out the lamp before closing the door behind her.

Isabel sighed again and closed her eyes against the anguish roiling within her. How could Eben have just gone off and left her this morning? After last night, she'd been so certain . . .

But then she forced herself to recall what he'd said to her. He *needed* her, he'd said, needed her to comfort him and help him forget. And like a fool, she'd betrayed herself once again.

If Eben really loved her, he never would have kissed her like some trollop in the Masons' yard, told Johnny Dent to take her home, and ridden away with only a promise to "see her." What did he think, that any time he felt the urge, he could pay her a visit?

She savored her outrage, nursing it as a barrier to the pain lurking just beneath, because if she so much as allowed herself to consider how ready she was to give up her independence to wallow in Eben's arms, she would probably shatter into a million pieces.

But this time she wasn't going to wait around, hoping Eben would miraculously fall in love with her. No, this time she was going to get away while she still had at least a shred of self-respect left.

She would ask the Plimptons to pay her what she had earned, and demand Bertha give her the money the school board owed her. Between the two, she should have enough to get her to Dallas, where, with any luck at all, she would find some sort of respectable employment.

And where she would never have to face Eben Walker again.

Chapter 15

Eben started early the next morning, spurred by the righteous indignation he felt at being threatened anonymously. Choosing to stop at every ranch along his way, he simply informed each person he encountered about the note Paul had found stuck to his door. They all expressed outrage, even those whom Eben knew hated sheep with a passion, and all claimed to have no knowledge of who might have been cowardly enough to issue such a warning.

Still, Eben knew the word would soon spread, and when George Stevens took him aside for a private conversation, Eben decided the winds of change were already beginning to blow across the plains.

"Eben, I been meaning to ask, how'd Plimpton make out with his sheep?"

Concealing his surprise with difficulty, Eben managed to reply nonchalantly. "It was a hell of a job, dipping all those sheep with their winter fleeces, but I reckon we got them in time. Last I heard, the sheep seemed to be none the worse for it, and there haven't been any more cases of scab."

Stevens nodded solemnly. "I'm mighty glad to hear it. I reckon you know I got no love for sheep or sheep-herders or English dudes neither, but what they done to those sheep . . ." He shook his head in disgust.

Knowing Stevens's attitude, Eben had half suspected he knew who the culprit was or at least approved of the action. He didn't bother to hide his amazement. "I'm glad to know there's still some honest men in this county, George."

"Ain't so much honest as sensible. Hell, even my boy's arguing in favor of sheep now. He says they can run on the same grass as cows 'cause they eat the short stuff the cattle can't reach, and they make more money 'cause you get to shear the females and sell the wool while you're breeding 'em to sell the lambs."

Eben bit back a smile. "You got yourself a smart boy."

Stevens rubbed his chin and grinned, abashed. "I hope he takes after his old man. Hell, with cattle prices the way they are, it's just common sense to have something to fall back on in hard times."

"Well, if you decide to go into herding, I'll be glad to give you all the help I can, and I know Plimpton would be delighted to help, too."

"I reckon he would," Stevens said morosely, making Eben smile.

"But it works both ways," Eben added, sobering again. "If things get bad, I might have to call on you."

"You mean you really think somebody might attack your place?"

"Mine or Plimpton's," Eben said. "Would it make any difference?"

Stevens thought this over. "I reckon not. We can't have somebody taking the law into his own hands. Plimpton's got a right to run whatever stock he wants on his land, and if we don't protect that right, we're worse than those who're trying to run him off."

"Does anybody else feel the way you do?"

"A couple, three, maybe," Stevens allowed, and named some ranchers. "I'll talk to them."

"I'd be much obliged," Eben said, feeling suddenly far less outraged than he'd been when he began this job. Perhaps he should have had more faith in people. Hadn't some of the men from town come out to help dip Plimpton's sheep? He didn't really think anyone would attack Plimpton's land again, but it was good to know he'd have support if someone did.

However, Eben knew at least one man was still determined to drive the sheep from the area, no matter what the cost, and he had a pretty good idea who that man was.

By the time he reached Vance Davis's place, the supper bell had rung, and he and all his hands were eating the evening meal. Vance and several other men came out in response to Eben's "hello," but none of them seemed happy to see him.

"Walker!" Davis said in feigned surprise. A stiff smile twisted his jowled face, and he stuck his thumbs into the suspenders stretched across his sagging belly in an attitude of studied nonchalance. "I figured you'd still be off chasing after your girl. What brings you all the way out here?"

Eben knew that, as Johnny Dent's employer, Davis would have been among the first to learn of Eben's return, but he ignored the barb. "Somebody left a note on my door the other day calling me a sheep-lover and telling me to leave town," he said baldly, watching Davis carefully for his reaction.

"Did you stop to say 'good-bye'?" Davis asked sarcastically, confirming Eben's suspicions as the rest of his men crowded into the doorway to hear the conversation. Eben glimpsed Johnny Dent in the group.

"Not hardly. I don't know who sent me the warning, but I figure if I tell enough people my answer, the right person'll get the message."

"And what's your answer?"

"Not only 'no,' but 'hell, no,' " Eben replied coldly. "Only a yellowbellied coward would hide behind a piece of paper, and I'm not afraid of facing a man like that."

Davis's face grew crimson, but he tried to appear unconcerned. "Since I don't know who sent the note, I can't pass your message along."

"Just in case you find out, you can also tell him if he keeps on trying to run Plimpton off, he's gonna find himself fighting every other rancher around here."

"*Not hardly*," Davis mocked. "Every cattleman in these parts wants to see them sheep in perdition."

"I didn't say they liked sheep. Maybe they never will, but they're fed up with all this fighting and innocent people getting hurt. If you don't believe me, talk to some of your neighbors."

"Maybe I will," Davis grumbled.

His mission accomplished, Eben sat in silence for a few minutes, waiting for an invitation to supper, which western hospitality demanded Davis offer, no matter what his personal feelings for Eben might be. At last Eben said, "Sorry to have taken you from your meal."

Davis frowned. "You're welcome to join us," he said grudgingly.

"Much obliged," Eben drawled, climbing wearily down from his saddle.

"I'll tend to your horse, Mr. Walker," Johnny Dent offered, hurrying forward.

Eben wished the boy weren't so eager to please. It made it difficult for him to remember how much he disliked him. Davis's men slowly filed back into the cookhouse, while Davis lingered to follow his "guest" inside. Eben felt remarkably reluctant to turn his back on the rancher.

"Help yourself," Davis grunted when they were inside, dropping back into his own seat and resuming his meal without so much as another glance in Eben's direction.

Wishing he could ignore his growling stomach and ride straight off Davis's property, Eben reminded himself how far he was from town and heaped his plate high with beans and cornbread.

The rest of the men ignored him, too, as he took an empty seat away from the others and dug in to his meal. When Johnny returned a few minutes later, he picked up his plate and carried it over to where Eben sat, flashing him an apologetic grin and taking the chair across from him.

No one spoke a word for the rest of the meal. Although such silence was fairly ordinary when laboring men ate, Eben sensed an underlying tension in the air.

One by one the others finished eating, dumped their plates in the wreck pan, and left the building. Apparently feeling no obligation to entertain his guest, Davis left, too, and in a few minutes Johnny and Eben were alone.

Eben noticed Johnny had finished his meal, but he made no move to leave. Instead, he toyed nervously with his empty coffee cup for a few minutes, making Eben think he might be going to ask if he could court Amanda after all.

Steeled for such a request, he almost didn't comprehend when Johnny whispered, "We're gonna ride on the Plimpton place tonight."

When the words finally registered, Eben nearly choked on a mouthful of beans. Taking a gulp of scalding coffee to wash them down, he burned his tongue and cursed. He glanced around to make sure no one was near enough to overhear. "What do you mean, you're going to ride on their place?"

Johnny shrugged. "When Mr. Davis heard the sheep weren't gonna get sick, he said next time he'd take care of Plimpton good and proper. When we came in this afternoon, he told us we'd ride tonight."

"To attack the sheep?" Eben asked, feeling the first stirrings of apprehension when he thought of Isabel still waiting at the Plimptons'.

Johnny's glance darted nervously away. "He . . . he didn't say, but I don't think so, not this time."

"He wouldn't attack the house," Eben argued, as much to convince himself as to assure Johnny. "Not with women there."

"He didn't tell us for sure, but I'm afraid that's just what he's got in mind," Johnny said. "At first I figured I'd quit so I didn't have to go along, but then I thought about Miss Isabel being there and all and . . . well, I figured I'd go and make sure she didn't get hurt."

In spite of his own anxiety, Eben felt a reluctant admiration for the boy's courage even while cursing him for his foolishness. "Davis won't let you quit now," he said. "Better pretend you're going along, then drop out someplace along the trail. When you do, go straight to town and tell Herald Bartz what's going on."

"Yes, sir," Johnny said, sitting up straighter. "What'll you do?"

"I'll get some of the other ranchers together. We'll have a little welcoming party waiting when Davis arrives."

"Yes, sir," Johnny said, jumping to his feet. "I'll go get your horse."

"Don't be a damn fool!" Eben warned, grabbing the boy's arm. "If you keep kissing up to me, Davis is bound to get suspicious. He might even call off the raid." Eben considered the situation for a moment. "We'll have a fight," he decided.

"A fight?" Johnny said in alarm.

"We won't come to blows, if that's what you're worried about," Eben assured him, "but we'll get loud enough so everybody hears us."

"What'll we fight about?" Johnny asked in confusion.

"What do you think?" Eben replied, rising and carrying his plate to the wreck pan. When he turned back to face the boy, he couldn't help grinning at Johnny's worried frown. "Ready?" he asked mildly, then roared, *"You son of a bitch! I wouldn't let you within a hundred yards of my daughter!"*

Johnny blinked in surprise, but to Eben's relief, he caught on quickly. "But I only want to visit her, at your house—"

"You expect me to believe that?" Eben shouted, warming to the topic. In a minute, he'd stomp out in disgust, mount his horse, and ride away, leaving everyone with the impression he hated Johnny Dent's guts.

"You don't have to pack tonight," Rosemary said from the hallway just outside Isabel's room. She'd been watching and wringing her hands for several minutes as Isabel carefully laid her things into her small trunk.

"I want to be ready the instant the money arrives," Isabel said stiffly, praying she would not lose her tenuous composure and cry in front of Rosemary. All it would take was one tear, and poor Rosemary was quite likely to dissolve in sympathetic hysteria.

"But you only wrote to Mrs. Bartz this morning, and she can't make this decision on her own. She'll most certainly have to call a meeting of the school board, and when Mr. Walker hears of this, I just know he'll—"

"Rosemary, please," Isabel begged wearily. "We've been over this a dozen times. It makes no difference what Mr. Walker says or does. I want to live someplace where I'm not considered a fallen woman and where I'm not a laughingstock and where—"

"No one thinks those things of you," Rosemary

insisted, "not really, and certainly no one is laughing—"

"*Everyone* is laughing since they heard how I went after Amanda and had to be brought back like a child," Isabel contradicted.

Rosemary sighed in despair and would have launched into another argument had her husband not appeared at her elbow. "Rosie, haven't you given up yet, old girl?" he admonished. "If Miss Forester is set on being shed of us, we can't stop her, eh, what?"

"We should refuse to give her her wages," Rosemary announced. "She's certainly been an unfaithful servant, leaving us when she knows—"

"—when she knows you only gave her employment out of pity," Isabel finished for her.

"Not pity!" Oliver protested.

"Gratitude, then," Isabel corrected. "And you're right, I'm an ungrateful baggage who is unworthy of your generosity."

"Quite right," Oliver agreed wryly. "Look how you've upset poor Rosemary."

"Oliver, you aren't helping at all!" Rosemary wailed.

"Please try to understand," Isabel said impatiently. "I can't stay here and continue taking your money just because I feel guilty."

"Then take it because you do the cooking!" Barclay exclaimed, peering around from behind his father. "You can't go off and leave us to eat Mama's cooking again!"

At the sight of his stricken face, Isabel nearly regretted her decision, but only for a moment. The Plimptons could always find another cook, but Isabel had only a few remaining particles of self-respect. If she stayed here and allowed Eben Walker to seduce her one more time . . .

In despair, she covered her face with both hands, inspiring Rosemary to utter a cry of anguish, but when she would have rushed to Isabel's side, her husband restrained her. "Come, Rosie. I believe Miss Forester needs some time alone to finish her packing."

"But how can you just allow her to—"

The rest of her question was lost as someone slammed the door of Isabel's room, leaving her as alone as she'd wanted to be.

And as alone as she would always be for the rest of her life, she thought morosely. Of course, before coming to Texas, Isabel had never even considered any other possibility. The prospect of being a spinster hadn't even seemed too awful since she'd never known anything else and never so much as entertained the possibility of a different sort of life for herself. Eben Walker had ruined her in more ways than one, taking not only her virtue and her good name but also the peace she had managed to make with the world. Now she would never again be able to accept her fate with equanimity, knowing as she did the joys and passions she might have enjoyed if only . . .

If only what? she asked sternly, jerking herself out of the morass of self-pity. If only she'd been willing to let him take advantage of her love for him to get his own way?

" 'O, deliver me from the deceitful and unjust man,' " she quoted on a moan, sinking down onto her bed and wishing she might be rescued from this situation. Instead, she knew she had at least one more fight on her hands. Eben certainly wouldn't let her go willingly, not knowing how easily she would succumb to him.

Isabel dreaded the coming confrontation.

The Plimpton place materialized out of the darkness, and Eben breathed a sigh of relief to find it quiet. At least he'd beaten Davis and his crew, if they did indeed plan to attack the ranch house tonight.

He'd ridden ahead to sound the alarm to the Plimptons, but George Stevens, his crew, and as many of his neighbors as they'd been able to round up on short notice followed only a few minutes behind him. Johnny Dent would bring reinforcements from town, but with any luck, the fight would be over before they arrived.

And Eben would do his best to get Isabel and Rosemary away before the fight began, he thought with grim determination as he rode into the peaceful ranch yard and brought his horse to a sliding halt.

"Hello, the house!" he shouted, bounding onto the porch and pounding on the door. "Plimpton! It's Eben Walker!"

From inside he heard the sound of running feet, then someone struck a light in the front room. The door opened a crack.

"Good God, man, it's the middle of the night!" Plimpton huffed in outrage. "If you want to see Miss Forester—"

"Vance Davis and his crew are planning to raid your place tonight," Eben interrupted impatiently.

"*What?*"

Eben took advantage of Plimpton's shock to push his way inside. "I said . . . Oh, hello, Mrs. Plimpton. Sorry to frighten you like this but—"

"Mr. Walker, this is an outrage!" Rosemary informed him indignantly, pulling her wrapper snugly around her neck. "You can't possibly expect Miss Forester to see you at this time of night!"

Eben opened his mouth to explain, but before he could, Isabel stormed into the room, still tying her robe around her. "Eben Walker, I can't believe even *you* would be so brazen as to burst in here in the middle of the night!"

Eben gaped at her. At least he'd been right about one thing. She'd got a new bee in her bonnet about something. Unfortunately, he didn't have time right now to figure out what it was.

"Uh, he says someone's going to raid us," Plimpton stammered.

"Raid?" the women echoed in unison, and Eben was gratified to see Isabel's fury turn to chagrin.

"Yes, raid. When I got back home yesterday, I found out somebody'd left a note on my shop door calling me a sheep-lover and warning me to get out of town."

"How shocking!" Rosemary gasped.

"So today I rode around to all the ranchers, trying to find out who sent it. Nobody admitted it, of course, but when I got to Vance Davis's place, Johnny Dent told me Davis was planning to bring his men out here tonight to cause some trouble."

Rosemary uttered a faint cry of distress, and both Isabel and Oliver rushed to her and led her to a chair.

"I reckon we ought to get the women out of here," Eben advised.

"Do we have time?" Plimpton asked, looking up from chafing his wife's wrists.

"I think so. I stopped at George Stevens's place on the way here to round up some help. They're just a few minutes behind me."

"George Stevens?" Isabel asked in surprise. "Roger's father?"

"Yeah, he—"

"But he hates sheep!" Isabel insisted. "Why would he—?"

"Because he hates men like Vance Davis even more," Eben explained, feeling more frustrated with every passing minute. "You ladies better get dressed. Plimpton, you got a decent wagon around here we can put them in?"

"What's going on?" Barclay asked from the doorway, surveying the scene through bleary eyes.

"Trouble, son," Plimpton informed him briskly, dropping his wife's hands and rising to his feet. "Best get your pants on. We're about to be attacked."

"*Attacked?*" the boy asked with delight.

"Better send the boy with them," Eben advised. "You got a man who can drive them?"

"You can't expect me to leave my home, Mr. Walker," Rosemary said, with sudden spirit.

"There might be shooting, Mrs. Plimpton," Eben said patiently. "It'll be no place for ladies."

"I can shoot with the best of them," Rosemary informed him.

"She can, you know," Plimpton confirmed proudly. "Best hunter I ever rode with."

"But these targets'll be shooting back," Eben reminded them in exasperation.

"And you think we'll be safer on the road, alone in the dark?" Isabel asked, surprising him.

"At least no one'll be shooting at you, for God's sake!" Eben shouted, at the end of his rope. "Are you all crazy?"

No one bothered to answer him. Plimpton had gone to the gun cabinet and was pulling out the rifles and checking the loads. Rosemary rose with surprising vigor from her chair to help him. Barclay disappeared, presumably to get his pants, while Isabel just glared at him, arms akimbo.

He was torn between the urge to kiss her and to strangle her. Without having actually decided, he closed the distance between them in two long strides and grabbed her by the shoulders.

"If you'd gone to my place like I told you, you'd be safe now!" he informed her, shaking with helpless fury at the thought of her being in danger.

"*Your* place?" she echoed in apparent confusion. "You never told me to go to your place!"

"The hell I didn't, and don't bother to tell me to stop cussing, because what I really want to do is shake your teeth loose for being so damn stubborn!"

"I'm not stubborn!" she cried.

"I could argue with you on that, but we don't have time now. Will you please go get some clothes on, and take Mrs. Plimpton with you? This place'll be crawling with men in a few minutes and . . ." He gestured to her figure, barely concealed beneath her nightdress and robe.

She glanced down at her attire, and color blossomed in her cheeks. Eben felt an urge to kiss her again, the urge to strangle her long forgotten, but she was already pulling away.

"Rosemary, we must get dressed," she called, hurrying to draw the other woman away. "We can't fight bandits in our nightclothes!"

Eben opened his mouth to inform them they weren't going to fight anybody no matter what they were wearing, but they disappeared too quickly.

"I asked you about a wagon," Eben reminded Plimpton sharply.

"Got one, of course, but you won't get Rosie into it," Plimpton replied, still mechanically removing rifles from the racks and breaking them open to check the loads.

"Don't you have any control over her at all?" Eben demanded furiously.

"Wouldn't use it even if I did, old man. Can't feature sending two defenseless women out into the night when a force of men is on the way. Might decide just to kidnap them, eh, what?"

Much as Eben hated to admit it, he had a point. "So you'll let them stay here and maybe get shot?"

"Safer here than out on their own," Plimpton argued logically, and Eben had to agree.

"Here, I'll do that," Eben said, shouldering Plimpton out of the way. "You get your pants on. You got any men here?"

"My chief herder and a few riders. I'll send Barclay to wake them."

"Better tell them not to shoot at anybody until we know who it is. Stevens and his bunch'll be here in a few minutes, and we shouldn't give them the impression we don't want their help."

"Right-o, old man," Plimpton said with an enthusiastic grin as he hurried away.

Eben almost groaned aloud. The whole lot of them was crazy. He wondered if it came with running sheep.

When he had finished with the rifles, he began to prowl the room, pulling furniture away from windows and yanking loose the ties with which Mrs. Plimpton held back her velvet draperies so the windows would be covered and the people inside concealed.

While he was wrestling with the last one, Isabel demanded, "What are you doing?"

Startled, he almost pulled the thing loose from its moorings, and he turned in irritation, prepared to give her a rather large piece of his mind.

The sight of her stopped him. She'd thrown on her usual black skirt and white shirtwaist, but her long, golden hair hung loose around her shoulders. Even though her blue eyes were bright with fury, he couldn't help remembering how sweet and loving she'd been the other night when he'd been so worried about Amanda, how she'd held him and loved him and . . .

"I asked you what you're doing," she snapped. "You'll ruin Rosemary's draperies."

"I guess you'd prefer giving Davis and his men a good view so they'll have a better chance at hitting somebody inside," he said, jerking the drapery closed.

She pressed her lips together, the only sign she'd give that he'd got one up on her. How she could claim she wasn't stubborn, he'd never know.

"Plimpton says his wife won't leave, and he won't make her."

"I can't say I'm enthusiastic about setting out for town this time of night myself," she said tartly. "Especially knowing a large body of men is riding out here ready to do someone harm. Suppose we encountered them—"

"All right," Eben sighed in defeat. "I reckon the

two of you'll have to stay here, but you'll have to find a safe place to hide, out of range. Is there a root cellar or something?"

"Yes, but Rosemary won't go into it. She's determined to defend her home."

"I don't give a damn about Rosemary. If she wants to get herself killed, that's her lookout. All I care about is you."

She seemed startled, and suddenly all the anger vanished from her face, leaving her confused and strangely vulnerable. Eben realized he was wasting a perfect opportunity. Quickly, before she could think of something else to start harping about, he took her in his arms.

"Eben, you can't—"

He silenced her protest with his mouth. He felt her resistance—had expected it, in fact—but he didn't tolerate it. Using his superior strength, he held her to him, cupping her head with one hand and cradling her body with the other. She felt so wonderful in his arms, he almost didn't mind her lack of response.

Only when she refused to open her mouth to him did he finally give up. "What in God's name has got into you?" he demanded.

"Some common sense, I hope!" she replied, struggling vainly to be free. "If you think you can just walk in here and kiss me and . . . and . . ."

"And *what*?"

Her only answer was a furious glare, but from her scarlet cheeks he had a good idea she was talking about sex. As if he was going to take her straight to bed when he knew scores of riders would be arriving here for a gunfight any minute!

Unfortunately, Rosemary Plimpton and her son rushed into the room just then, so he couldn't point any of that out to Isabel. Reluctantly he let her go, and she turned away, crossing the room and plopping down on the sofa in a huff, her cheeks still blazing.

"Is . . . is everything all right?" Rosemary asked uncertainly.

"Oh, fine," Eben said sarcastically. "Or it will be if they don't burn the place down around our ears."

"Do you really think they'll try to burn us out?" Barclay exclaimed, his eyes bright with excitement. He raced over to the table where Eben had left the rifles and picked one up. "Don't worry, Mama, I won't let them near the place."

"Barclay, I was kind of depending on you to see the ladies got someplace safe and stayed there," Eben tried.

"You mean guard them?"

"Yeah," Eben said, but Rosemary interrupted him.

"I have no intention of hiding when my home is in danger, Mr. Walker, but this isn't Isabel's fight, and naturally she should—"

"I'm not going to hide either," Isabel informed them all.

"Don't be a goose," Plimpton said, coming in before Eben could get his temper sufficiently under control to respond. "Of course you'll hide. A man can't fight if he's worried about his woman."

Although Eben would have thought it impossible, Isabel's face turned even redder. "*I am not anyone's woman*," she declared coldly.

Plimpton cast Eben a sympathetic glance, but just then they heard riders approaching at a run. Ignoring Eben's shouted warning, everyone hurried to the windows to see who it was.

"Dammit, do you *want* to get killed?" he asked, grabbing Isabel and dragging her down to the floor. Shielding her with his body, he peered cautiously out through the draperies.

"Walker, it's George Stevens!" someone shouted.

Relief coursed through him, but before he got up, he gave Isabel a warning shake. "Don't stick your head up above the windowsill. Do you understand?"

"Yes," she snapped, but she didn't really look angry anymore. Unfortunately, Eben didn't have the time to find out for sure. He had to see how many men had come and help plan their strategy.

Isabel watched him go, her eyes narrowed speculatively while she massaged the arm he'd grabbed to pull her to the floor. She'd probably have a bruise there tomorrow, but she didn't think she'd mind. Instead, she would remember what he'd said about only caring what happened to her. If he didn't love her, he was doing an awfully good job of pretending.

"Good heavens," Rosemary murmured from the other end of the room. In defiance of Eben's orders, she was staring out the window. "Look how many men they've brought. Perhaps we should make some coffee."

"An excellent idea," Isabel agreed, scrambling to her feet, unspeakably grateful for the excuse to make herself useful.

They made gallons of coffee, and the men drank it while they assigned positions and built a barricade, behind which Rosemary and Barclay would hide while they worked at reloading guns, and another for Isabel to hide behind while she did absolutely nothing dangerous.

Then they waited. And waited. Apparently Vance Davis believed the small hours of the morning were the best time to pay someone a surprise visit. When the shouted warning of the attack finally came, Isabel had been crouched in her protective cave of furniture for what seemed like hours. Cramped and frightened, she crept out, unable to simply cower when, for all anyone knew, her help might be needed.

The drapes were still drawn, but the front door stood wide, and through it Isabel could see the ranch yard. At first everything was totally dark, and she began to think someone might have issued a false alarm. Then, at the edge of the yard, something burst into flame.

A torch! The fire illuminated the body of horsemen,

their faces covered by the requisite gunnysacks. The flaring torch ignited another torch, then another, and Isabel covered her mouth to hold back a cry. Eben had been right about the raiders wanting to burn them out. Dear heaven, what would they do?

But, of course, she knew exactly what they would do, and the instant the riders charged, screaming Comanche war cries and Rebel yells, the night exploded in gunfire from Plimpton's friends and neighbors who had been concealed in every possible hiding place.

A score of guns belched fire and smoke, catching the raiders in a deadly cross fire. The raiders' shouts became screams of panic from men and animals alike as bullets hit home. Isabel covered her ears, yet the noise still filled her head, the roar of guns, the shrill squeals of equine terror, the bellows of men in pain.

The scene grew fuzzy as powder smoke filled the room. Isabel's eyes stung, and she blinked frantically, trying to find Eben through the haze. He still knelt at an open window, rifle raised, firing and firing around the edge of the frame, pausing only to jack another shell into the chamber before firing again.

She wanted to grab him and drag him down the way he had done to her just a short time ago, down where he would be safe from the bullets Davis and his men would no doubt begin firing back in just a moment.

Then the drapery above Eben's head billowed out as glass shattered, and Isabel screamed his name.

He turned to her, his grim expression giving way to pure fury. "Get down!" he shouted, then another bullet crashed into the window, sending him diving for cover.

"*Eben!*" In an instant she was beside him. "You're hit! Oh, God, where—"

With surprising strength he pushed her face to the floor. "Dammit, woman, are you trying to get us both killed?"

Planting his knee firmly in the center of her back,

he held her down while he swiveled around to see what was happening outside.

"Are you hurt?" she managed, although the floorboard pressing on her lips made speech difficult.

"Not yet, no thanks to you," he replied ungratefully.

She tried to reply in kind, but he fired the rifle again, drowning her words in a roar.

Her ears ringing, blinded by gunsmoke, her face ground into the floor, she could no longer speak or even think. Somewhere in the room Rosemary and Barclay worked behind a barricade of furniture loading rifles and passing them to the men who manned the door and the windows of the house, but she no longer cared what happened to them.

On the floor beside her, something glittered, and she vaguely identified it as broken glass from the shattered window. Rosemary would be quite put out, she thought inanely. Then, without warning, the room filled with sunlight. Isabel saw the chunk of glass quite clearly now, and for a moment she couldn't think how dawn could have arrived without her noticing it.

Above her, Eben swore and lunged to his feet, nearly crushing her in the process. *"Water!"* he shouted, and Isabel realized the light came not from the sun but from *fire*. They'd somehow set the house afire!

Barclay came running, hauling a sloshing bucket. Fearing just this, Eben had made them fill every container in the place so they'd be ready. Isabel lifted her head in time to see Barclay hand the bucket to Eben.

"Get down!" he told the boy just as Isabel tried to push herself up and stop Eben from doing what she feared he intended to do, but his boot landed squarely in the center of her back, sending her face down onto the floor again.

If he didn't get himself killed tonight, she'd take

care of it the first chance she got, she thought wildly
as the brightness grew brighter still.

Eben had swept back the drape, and the blast of
heat told her the fire was right outside on the porch.
He'd be a perfect target in its light! A scream of protest
welled in her throat just as the splash of water told
her the deed was done.

Instantly the brightness faded, both from the
drenching of the flames and from Eben dropping the
drape back into place, and almost as instantly a hale
of bullets smashed into the window.

Her scream escaped but was muffled by Eben's
body falling on hers.

"Eben!" she cried in alarm, trying to struggle out
from under him so she could see where he was
wounded.

"Will you lay still, for God's sake?" he growled,
capturing her arms and clamping them to her sides.

"Are you hurt?"

"Yeah, I think I cut my hand on a piece of glass,
so will you lay still so it doesn't happen again?"

"You're not shot?" she gasped.

"In a hurry to get rid of me?"

Another hale of bullets smashing into the side of
the house made it impossible for her to answer, and
by the time someone outside shouted, "We got 'em
on the run, Plimpton!" she'd forgotten what she
wanted to say.

Eben's weight suddenly lifted, although he kept a
restraining hand on her shoulder. "You keep kissing
this floor, or so help me God, I'll shoot you myself!"
he said with a complete absence of logic, although
before she could point this out to him, he was running
for the door.

His name trembled on her lips as she watched his
booted feet disappear into the night. She whispered
a fervent prayer for his safety.

Only when he was gone did she notice the gunfire

had died away, to be replaced by men's shouts of triumph.

"More water here," someone called, and Isabel heard splashing outside the window as someone finished the job Eben had started.

"They got one on the barn roof," someone else yelled. "It's still smoldering."

Isabel lifted her head tentatively and looked around. She and Rosemary were the only ones left in the room. Rosemary sat slumped on the floor beside the overturned table behind which she had worked, loading rifles.

"Are you all right?" Isabel asked, scrambling over to her.

The other woman looked up at her with tired eyes and smiled benignly. "Quite chipper now, thanks," she replied. "I just hope no one was hurt."

"I'm sure some of the raiders were," Isabel said grimly. "I can't imagine they escaped unscathed."

"Do we dare go outside to see?"

Isabel considered Eben's warning and decided on discretion. "Perhaps we could peek out the window first."

"Mama!" Barclay hollered, bursting into the room and saving them the trouble. "Papa says to get some hot water and bandages. A few of the brigands are wounded."

"How about our men?" Rosemary asked, hauling herself to her feet.

"Not a scratch! Jolly fine show, eh, what?" Barclay crowed. Isabel blinked in surprise: apparently in the excitement, he'd forgotten to talk like a Texan.

Isabel tried to stand, too, surprised at how uncooperative her legs were being. Perhaps Eben's attempts to protect her had done permanent damage, she thought in annoyance, reaching around in an attempt to soothe her maltreated back. Rosemary lit a lamp, revealing the havoc the fight had created in the once immaculate parlor. Isabel was wondering how long it would take to set it to rights again when Eben appeared in the doorway.

He scanned the room, finding her instantly in the flickering light. "Are you all right?" he demanded, hurrying to her.

"Yes, no thanks to you," she informed him, rubbing her back gingerly.

He didn't look a bit relieved. "I swear, Isabel, for such a smart woman, you do some awful stupid things."

"I thought you were shot!" she replied indignantly.

Although his scowl was still murderous, his lips twitched suspiciously. "Were you going to tend my wounds?"

She wanted to deny it, until she saw the small flicker of hope in his dark eyes. "And what if I was?"

His scowl faded completely, leaving a ghost of a grin. "It would've almost been worth it to stop a bullet."

He lifted a hand to touch her face.

"Eben, you're bleeding!" she cried, catching his hand in both of hers and turning the palm up so she could see it better.

"It's just a scratch. I told you I cut myself on some glass."

"We have to get this cleaned right now," she told him, starting for the kitchen and pulling him along behind her. He followed with surprising meekness—although she didn't really notice this uncharacteristic behavior until she thought about it much later—and allowed her to swab out the cut with soap and water.

She tried to argue with him when he refused to let her bandage it, but he grabbed her and kissed her, pulling her into the haven of his arms, and suddenly she didn't want to argue anymore about anything. Clinging to him with all her strength, she opened to his insistent tongue and allowed him to plunder her mouth. A deliciously familiar lethargy claimed her, turning her bones to jelly and her will to mist that drifted away unnoticed. All she remembered was how much she loved him and how much she'd longed to be exactly where she was at that moment.

"Walker? Where are you . . . ? Oh, bloody sorry, old man," Oliver Plimpton sputtered from the kitchen doorway.

Eben and Isabel jerked apart, although Isabel noticed he kept a possessive arm around her waist. "Just getting my wounds tended," Eben explained with a grin, holding up his injured palm. "Ready to go?"

"Right-o. Don't want those chaps to get away, do we?"

"Where are you going?" Isabel demanded in renewed alarm.

"To catch Davis and let him know what we think of a man who tries to burn somebody out."

"What will you do to him?"

Eben shrugged, and Isabel's stomach roiled in apprehension.

"We'll decide that when we find him," Eben added, seeing her distress. "And in the meantime, I want you to go home!"

She blinked in surprise. "I am home," she reminded him.

"No, you aren't," he contradicted sternly.

"Uh, we'll be waiting for you outside," Plimpton said, withdrawing discreetly.

"Then where is my home?" she countered.

"At my house, and when I get back there, I want to find you waiting for me. Do you understand?"

"And if I'm not?" she taunted, trying to hide the quick rush of joy she felt.

"Then you'll wish you had been," he said, frowning ominously.

"I can't leave Rosemary here to clean up this mess all by herself," she protested.

"The hell you can't. Besides, there's a group of men coming from town any time. They can help. Johnny

Dent'll be with them. Tell him I said he was to see you safely home."

"Eben, just what gives you the right to order me around like this?" she demanded, feigning an outrage she no longer felt.

"Because I'm going to be your husband," he informed her, "whether you like it or not!"

Before she could reply to this outrageous statement, he pulled her back into his arms and kissed her ravenously. When she was breathless, he released her and headed for the door. Only after he was gone did she remember she hadn't told him she loved him.

But then, he hadn't said he loved her either.

Chapter 16

"Miss Forester!" Amanda cried when she opened the door to Isabel the next morning. "Are you all right? You look awful!"

Since she felt pretty awful, Isabel couldn't take offense, especially not when Amanda threw her arms around her in a welcoming hug. Isabel hugged back, loving her as much because she was Eben's daughter as she loved her for herself, and that was plenty.

Then she felt Amanda stiffen in her arms, and knew she had seen Isabel's escort.

"Johnny," she cried in surprise, pulling out of the embrace.

"Your pa said I was to bring Miss Forester home," he said, removing his hat.

They were both blushing furiously, and their rapt expressions spoke of emotions Isabel understood only too well. She couldn't help thinking she might have been wrong about Johnny's intentions. Maybe she'd discuss the matter with Eben soon, and see if something could be done.

That is, assuming she and Eben were able to work things out between themselves first.

"I believe Mr. Dent has earned at least a cup of coffee for all the trouble he put himself to last night and this morning," Isabel said, stepping past Amanda into the house as she untied her bonnet strings.

"I'll fetch your things first, Miss Forester," he said, grinning as happily as if she'd offered him the moon.

"Your things?" Amanda asked when he had hurried away.

"Yes, it seems . . . That is, your father insisted I come straight here." Isabel sank gratefully down onto the worn sofa.

"He did? I mean, why . . . ? Well, first off, tell me what happened last night, and where is Pa, anyways?"

As briefly as she could, Isabel told the story of the attack on the Plimptons' home. By then Johnny had returned with her trunk. Not quite certain exactly what her future here would be, she instructed him to leave it in the front room.

Amanda jumped up to start a pot of coffee, clumsy in her haste and because Johnny Dent watched every move she made with flattering intensity. When she'd put the pot on to boil, she said, "But I thought Johnny was supposed to be getting men to fight. At least, that's what Carrie said when she came over this morning to tell me he'd been to their house last night."

"I was," Johnny said with a grin. "We got there too late to fight, though. Your pa and the others had already run them off. We just took care of the wounded and helped Mrs. Plimpton get things back in order."

"Then where's Pa?"

"He . . . he and most of the original group went after the raiders who got away," Isabel said.

Amanda's eyes widened with understanding. "Oh."

"What will they do to them?" Isabel asked anxiously. "No one will tell me a thing." She gave Johnny an accusing look, which he ignored.

"Hang them, I suppose," Amanda replied ingenuously.

Isabel felt the blood rush from her head, and thanked heaven she was already sitting down. How could Eben do such a thing?

"They don't have much choice, miss," Johnny hastened to explain. "I mean, we don't have no law around here to speak of. What else are you going to do with a man who tries to kill a whole family and burn their house down?"

Isabel didn't know, but she felt sure in time she could think of something more civilized than hanging.

"Maybe you should go lay down for a while, Miss Forester," Amanda suggested. "You look kind of peaked."

Isabel would have liked nothing better, but she knew Eben would never approve of leaving his daughter alone with Johnny Dent. "I'll wait until Mr. Dent has had his coffee," she replied sweetly. "I wouldn't want him to think me rude."

"Oh, I wouldn't . . ." he started to protest until he saw the warning gleam in her eye. "Yeah, well, I'm always glad for your company, Miss Forester." He grinned, and Isabel thought poor Amanda had never stood a chance of resisting his charm.

The coffee revived Isabel somewhat, although she ached in every bone of her body. Amanda prepared a hot bath for her, and she soaked for a bit after Johnny had gone, trying not to think about where Eben might be or what he might be doing. Instead, she concentrated on what she would say to him when he returned.

Not that she had much choice in topics, of course.

After the way he'd behaved at the Plimptons', she knew he cared about her. Even if he didn't love her in the traditional, romantic sense, he held her very dear, dear enough to risk his life to protect hers. And regardless of how he'd treated her at the Masons' house, he'd fully intended that she come to him afterward. What woman would be foolish enough to turn a man like that away, especially when she loved him with all her heart?

Not Isabel Forester, certainly. She'd done some stupid things in her time, but she wasn't a total idiot. She and Eben could have a good life together, just so long as he didn't get the idea he could order her around as he had that morning. She'd obeyed his command to come to his house because she'd wanted to, but she couldn't let him think she would be so compliant in all things.

When she'd finished her bath, she dressed in the peach sprigged calico, the dress she'd worn the first time he proposed to her, and the first time he'd made love to her, too. Feeling jittery with anticipation, she joined Amanda in the front room to wait.

"You look real nice," Amanda told her with a warm smile. "You should probably try to get some rest, though."

"I will, later, but I won't be able to sleep until I've talked to your father."

Isabel sat down on the sofa, and Amanda joined her there. The girl's expressive face revealed troubled thoughts, although Isabel had no idea what could be worrying her now.

"Miss Forester, have you . . . have you and Pa . . . ? I mean, are you two going to get married now?"

"I hope so," Isabel told her honestly.

"Then you *do* want to marry him!" Amanda exclaimed.

"Well, yes, but . . ."

"But he still hasn't proposed, has he?" Amanda guessed in disgust.

"Not exactly," Isabel hedged, thinking the less Amanda knew of their unusual relationship, the better.

"Oh, but he will, Miss Forester! I know he will. He loves you so much!"

"He does?" Isabel asked in surprise.

"You mean he hasn't told you?" Amanda asked in equal surprise. "No wonder you two have so much trouble."

"Has he . . . has he actually said that he . . . he loves me?"

"He didn't have to," Amanda explained confidently. "I can tell by the way he's been acting, and when I accused him of it, he didn't deny it."

Hardly proof positive, but certainly encouraging, Isabel thought wryly.

"And I love you, too," Amanda continued. "I know I've misbehaved, but that was only so I could get you and Pa together again. If you two get married, I promise I'll never do another thing to worry you."

"Just the fact that you're so pretty worries me to death," Isabel informed her, "but I love you, too, Amanda, and I'd consider it an honor to worry about you for the rest of my life."

"Oh, Miss Forester!" she cried, throwing her arms around Isabel.

The hug only lasted a moment, however, because Amanda drew back suddenly to inquire whether she should address Isabel as "mother" after she married Eben.

This was planning Isabel did not feel prepared to do at the moment, at least not until she had finally settled everything with Eben. "We'll see what your father thinks," she decided, then considered the logistics of her coming meeting with Eben. If Amanda offered as much help as she obviously intended to, Isabel and Eben might never get together. "Amanda, would you mind terribly . . . I mean, when your father comes home, I'd like to speak with him alone. Could you possibly . . . ?"

"I'll go over to Carrie's," she offered, jumping right up to gather her things. "Do you want me to spend the night, too?"

"Oh, no!" Isabel exclaimed, scandalized that the girl would even think of such a thing. "I'm sure we won't need that much time."

Amanda flashed her a knowing grin that made Isabel wonder just how much the girl understood about her and Eben's relationship. She would have to have a talk with Amanda at the first opportunity and disabuse her of some of her dangerously romantic notions where love and sex were concerned.

When Amanda had gone, Isabel began to prowl the house restlessly and finally decided to prepare a meal since Eben would no doubt be hungry when he returned. In short order, she had put some stew meat on to simmer and had just begun to gather the ingredients to make a pie when she heard a horse outside.

Running to the window, she saw Eben riding past on his way to the barn. Her heart leaped into her throat at the sight of him. He was covered with dust, and his broad shoulders slumped wearily. After what he had been through yesterday and last night, she knew he wouldn't be in any condition to put up much of a fight. If she'd had any consideration at all, she would have taken mercy on him and told him to sleep for a few hours before they had their talk, but she couldn't help thinking how his exhaustion would work to her advantage. If she was ever going to get her way with Eben Walker, this would be the time.

Quickly removing the apron she'd borrowed, she hung it up and hurried into the bedroom for one last check on her appearance. Eben's shaving mirror revealed her hair was still in place. It also revealed the dark circles beneath her eyes, but her cheeks and eyes glowed in anticipation. Perhaps he wouldn't notice how haggard she looked.

When she heard his step on the porch, she drew a calming breath, laid a hand over her churning stomach, and walked slowly into the front room, arriving just as he came through the front door.

Her heart wrenched at the sight of his bloodshot eyes and drooping shoulders. He looked as if he'd been off fighting a war, and indeed, he had.

"Well," he said at the sight of her, apparently surprised. He surveyed her from head to foot, to head again, as if he couldn't quite believe she was actually here.

"Did you find Mr. Davis?" she asked, wondering if she really wanted to know.

He frowned, and she held her breath. "Yeah, we found him, all right. He'd bled to death before we got to him, though. Seems he caught a bullet in the fight. The rest of his men were long gone. I reckon they knew what would happen if we caught them, so they lit out."

Isabel sighed with relief. At least she wouldn't have to ever imagine Eben as an executioner.

Eben glanced around expectantly. "Where's Amanda?"

"I . . . She went to visit Carrie Bartz so we . . . I thought we should be alone."

"You did?" he said, the weariness suddenly vanishing from his face as he pulled off his hat with one hand and smoothed his dark hair back with the other. "What did you have in mind?"

Isabel instantly recognized the glitter in his eyes and put her hands up instinctively to ward him off. "Not what you apparently think," she assured him hastily. "Eben, we need to talk."

He hung his hat on a peg by the door, unbuckled his gun belt and hung it beside the hat, then grinned. "We always run into trouble when we talk, Isabel. I think maybe we should stop talking altogether."

His eyes spoke to her of remembered delights, and her body quickened in response, but she had no intention of giving in to her physical desires, at least not until they had a few things settled. Ignoring the way her heart had started to pound and her knees had started to quiver, she lifted her chin in defiance.

"Eben, I have not yet consented to become your wife," she reminded him.

"I haven't asked you," he shot back, taking a menacing step toward her. "I told you before, I'm done asking."

She stared at him in horror. Surely he couldn't expect her to become his mistress? To live with him in sin?

"No, Isabel, I'm not ever going to give you the chance to turn me down again," he continued, advancing toward her. "We're getting married, and that's that, even if I have to tie you up and stuff a sock in your mouth."

"Eben!" she cried in outrage, but he was already upon her and she'd forgotten to back away. He tried to take her in his arms.

"Eben, you're filthy!" she tried, stiffening her arms against his chest to hold him off.

He glanced down at his travel-stained clothes. He'd apparently tried to brush the worst of the dust off before coming inside, but with little success.

"And you haven't shaved since heaven only knows when. You can't expect me to . . . to . . ."

Heat rose in her face at his knowing grin. "What can't I expect you to do, Isabel?" he taunted.

"To *kiss* you," she snapped.

"I'll shave, then. I'll even take a bath. Have we got any hot water? I'll let you scrub my back, too, and then—"

"Eben!" she shouted.

"What!" he shouted right back, startling her.

How had this gotten so far out of hand? All she'd wanted to do was find out exactly how he felt about her. "You can't expect me to just . . . just jump in bed with you!"

He dropped his hands instantly, and his cocky grin disappeared. "Don't you want to?"

"I want to *talk* to you first! We . . . you . . . I don't even know how you really feel about me."

He gaped at her. "How I really feel about you?" he echoed incredulously. "What does it take to convince you, Isabel? I've made myself a laughingstock in this whole county chasing after you. I've proposed to you until I'm blue in the face, and all I've gotten for my trouble is more humiliation. A man would have to be crazy to put up with what I've put up with, so maybe you're right not to want to marry me, because I must be out of my mind!"

"But I *do* want to marry you!" she protested desperately. "I just . . ."

"You just what?" he demanded in exasperation.

"I just need to know you love me!"

"But I just told you!"

Isabel bit her lip, wondering if she wasn't being a total idiot yet again. "You've never told me right out. A woman needs to hear the words, Eben, so she can be sure."

She could see he was wrestling with his temper, trying to get control of it so he could understand what she was saying. "That's all you want?" he finally asked in amazement.

She nodded.

"That's why you've been turning me down all this time?"

She nodded again. "Mostly, anyway. You see, I couldn't be sure and—"

This time she wasn't fast enough to ward him off, and he crushed her to him, taking her mouth possessively and completely. His whiskers scraped her face, and the scent of horse and sweat engulfed her, but none of that seemed very important. When he had thoroughly staked his claim, he lifted his head and smiled down into her face.

"I love you, Isabel Forester. I love you from the top of your golden head to the bottoms of your pretty little feet, and I love a lot of other places in between."

Isabel felt a familiar warmth in her face, but he wasn't finished, and she didn't feel disposed to stop him.

"I love the way you think you have to solve everyone else's problems, and I love the way you stick to your guns, even when you're wrong and—"

"When was I ever wrong?" she challenged, but he ignored her.

"—and the way your eyes flash when you're mad, like right now, and the way they look when I'm inside you, loving you, and—"

"Oh, Eben, I love you, too!" she cried, pulling his mouth back to hers. Desire swirled in her, hot and sweet, melting her until the moisture dewed between her thighs. She wanted Eben more than she'd ever thought possible, and she didn't want to wait another minute.

Surely he would sense her need. Surely he would carry her off into the bedroom and claim her completely in just another minute. Except he didn't. He just kept kissing her and kissing her until she thought she would lose her mind.

Having no experience at seduction, Isabel had no idea how to convey her wishes. "Eben, I . . ." she tried while he trailed kisses down her throat. "Aren't you tired?"

"Not anymore," he replied hoarsely.

"I mean, don't you think you . . . you ought to . . . you ought to go to bed?"

His mouth stilled on her throat, and he lifted his head slowly, studying her face. "Anxious to get rid of me?"

"Oh, no!" she said too quickly. "I mean, I know you must be exhausted, and well, I am, too, and I thought..." She knew from the heat and from his grin that her face must be scarlet.

"Are you suggesting we go to bed *together*?" he asked, still grinning. She had absolutely no intention of answering such a question, and he must have known it, because he said, "And what do you propose we do once we get there?"

"Eben!" she cried, mortified.

"Did I mention I love the way you say my name?" he asked, unrepentantly. "Especially when you say it just that way, like you want to box my ears."

"*Eben!*"

"Or did I misunderstand you?" he continued blithely. "Maybe you don't really want to take your clothes off and let me kiss every inch of your beautiful body." As he spoke, his hands roved, caressing her breast and her buttocks, pulling her to him so she could feel his burgeoning desire. "And when I'm finished kissing you, I'll touch you here ... and here ... and *here* ..."

Isabel thought she might burst into flames if he didn't stop, but she remembered just in time that she, too, had power.

"And I'll touch you *here*," she whispered, slipping her hand down his belly. Rewarded with his gasp of surprise, she tormented him a bit as he had been tormenting her.

Then, confident of her success, she began to inch toward the bedroom. At first he tried to pull her back into his arms, but when she drew him forward a stumbling step, he quickly guessed her intent.

"Oh, no, you don't, you little witch," he said, taking her wrist in an iron grip and removing it from him.

"Don't you want to?" she asked in dismay, inadvertently echoing his earlier question.

He shook his head, but his grin and the smoldering expression in his dark eyes told a different story. "Oh,

I want to, all right, and I'm going to, but not right now."

"Why not?" she asked, hoping she didn't look as disappointed as she felt.

"Because every time I make love to you, you change your mind about wanting to marry me, and I'm not going to let it happen again. Come on."

He took her by the hand and started for the front door.

"Where are we going?" she asked in confusion.

"We're going to the Bartz house to pick up Amanda, and probably Herald and Bertha, too, because I know they won't want to miss this."

"Miss *what*?" she cried as he fairly dragged her out onto the porch.

"Our wedding, Miss Forester," he announced, pausing a second to savor her astonishment.

"You can't mean . . . *right now*?"

"Yes, *right now*, because I have every intention of making love to you all the rest of this day and into the night, or at least as long as I'm able to stay awake, and we've already created enough scandals around here, so we're going to be married this time."

Isabel stared up at him, unable to resist admiring his determination. Where would she be now if he'd been even a little less stubborn?

"You're not going to give me an argument, are you?" he asked when she didn't respond.

She considered it, because arguing with Eben could be quite enjoyable, but this time she decided to pass. "No, Eben," she said meekly.

He frowned, obviously not trusting her docility. "Not even an objection? I'm not exactly dressed for a wedding," he pointed out.

"Neither am I, but you're absolutely right, we've caused too much scandal already. We should be married as soon as possible."

His expression said he wasn't sure he'd heard her correctly, so she smiled sweetly to reassure him.

His frown deepened. "Isabel, you aren't going to stop fighting with me altogether, are you?"

His concern touched her. "Absolutely not, and I have several matters to discuss with you as soon as we're officially man and wife over which I am certain we will disagree," she assured him, thinking of Larry Potts's desire to learn blacksmithing and her decision that Amanda and Johnny should be allowed to see each other. "Until then, though, I'm taking no chances."

He grinned expansively. "Me neither," he said, pulling her back into his arms for one more kiss. When he lifted his mouth from hers, his eyes were laughing at her. "But can't you at least give me a hint so I'll be ready?"

Author's Note

I hope you had as much fun reading *Playing with Fire* as I had writing it. Eben Walker is very special to me because my maternal grandfather, Samuel Tucker, was the last practicing blacksmith in Jonesboro, Tennessee. He died when I was only two years old, so I have no memories of him. Doing the research for this book helped me feel that I came to know him just a little.

I'd like to offer special thanks to Mr. Jake Hause, the blacksmith at Old Bedford Village in Bedford, Pennsylvania. Mr. Hause answered a lot of questions for me about smithing and provided tremendous insight into the craft.

Since *Playing with Fire* is so different from the type of book I usually write, I'm anxious to find out how my fans like it. Please let me know, and send an SASE for a bookmark.

Victoria Thompson
c/o Cornerstone Communications
301 Union Avenue, Suite 372
Altoona, PA 16602

If You've Enjoyed This Avon Romance— Be Sure to Read. . .

THE MAGIC OF YOU
by Johanna Lindsey
75629-3/$5.99 US/$6.99 Can

SHANNA
by Kathleen Woodiwiss
38588-0/$5.99 US/$6.99 Can

UNTAMED
by Elizabeth Lowell
76953-0/$5.99 US/$6.99 Can

EACH TIME WE LOVE
by Shirlee Busbee
75212-3/$5.99 US/$6.99 Can

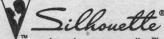